# SINFUL SACRIFICE

USA TODAY BESTSELLING AUTHOR
## CHARITY FERRELL

Copyright © 2024 by Charity Ferrell
All rights reserved.

Visit my website at https://charityferrell.com
Cover Designer: Lori Jackson
Editor: Jovana Shirley, Unforeseen Editing, www.unforeseenediting.com
Proofreader: Jenny Sims, Editing4Indies

No part of this book may be reproduced or transmitted in any form or by any means, electronic or mechanical, including photocopying, recording, or by any information storage and retrieval system without the written permission of the author, except for the use of brief quotations in a book review.

This book is a work of fiction. Names, characters, places, and incidents either are products of the author's imagination or are used fictitiously. Any resemblance to actual persons, living or dead, events, or locales is entirely coincidental.

# author's note

**Hi reader friend,**

*Sinful Sacrifice is a dark mafia romance. If you've read any of my other mafia books, Sinful Sacrifice is on the same level of darkness. My mafia men are true anti-heroes who have no limits and are not for the faint of heart. This story contains graphic violence and dark themes that may be triggering to some.*

**Sinful Sacrifice is a complete standalone.**

*xoxo,*
*Charity*

# PART I

# The debt

## PROLOGUE

# DAMIEN

EVEN AFTER ALL THIS TIME, I watch her.
  When I can't, one of my men do.
  I sit outside her apartment or dance studio at night.
  I know she sees me.
  Tonight, I need her to know something.
  I open my door and step out of my SUV.
  *She's still mine.*
  And I'm about to prove it to her.

# 1

# PIPPA

EVERYONE HAS that moment in their lives when they realize they've truly messed up. This is my moment.

My plan was simple—go into Lucky Kings Casino, pay my father's debt, and get the hell out of there.

The plan went straight to hell when a blackjack dealer dragged me off the casino floor and shoved me inside this room.

I hadn't wanted to come here, but my father begged me. What he'd failed to tell me until we got to the casino was that I was going in alone.

"If I go in, they'll kill me," he'd said, his body trembling.

Since we don't have all the money he owes, I believe him.

Everyone in New York knows the Lombardi mob family runs Lucky Kings. Those people also know they don't take it lightly when people owe them money and don't pay.

My attention whips to the door when it clicks. A pang forms in my chest, compliments of my racing heart, while I wait for whoever is behind it to reveal themselves.

*Pound.*

*Pound.*

*Pound-pound-pound.*

I clutch the poker chip in my sweaty hand.

The person behind that door will decide if my lack of funds means a lack of breaths in my lungs.

The door opens, a slight creak with it, inch by inch.

My pulse burns, and I suck in a breath, halfway on the exhale, when it happens.

The most gorgeous man I've seen fills the doorway. He's so tall that the top of his head nearly brushes the doorframe. He's dressed in all black—from his suit to the button-up beneath to his shoes. The black of his clothing matches his thick hair and the scruff that extends along the length of his jawline and cheeks.

His face is a host of devilish demeanor. His chartreuse eyes —a color I've never seen before—burn into me with accusation, as if he already knows I'm short on cash. I look away and study the chip, nervous my eyes will confirm he's correct.

He chuckles under his breath, a bully taunting their victim, and scrubs a hand over his stubbled, carved masterpiece of a jaw, determining my fate.

I've heard rumors, horror stories, of Vinny Lombardi, but never seen him in person.

People claim to suffer nightmares about him.

Say he's done inhumane things.

Prosecutors complain no one will testify against him.

And now, I might be his next victim.

He shuts the door, bringing with him the scent of menthol aftershave and amber cologne as he steps closer.

"Are you Vinny?" The words stumble from my mouth as I lay the poker chip on the table.

"No." His callous voice sends a chill through my body. It's deep, cautionary, and cold as ice. "What's your name?"

"Pippa." I immediately regret telling him this.

I should've lied.

But my gut tells me he'd know if I did.

He snaps his long fingers. "Last name?"

I hesitate.

"*Last name*," he stresses, raising his voice.

"Elsher." I nervously bite the inside of my cheek.

"Ah, you're Paul's daughter." He clicks his tongue against the roof of his mouth.

"I'm here to see Vinny." I slap my purse on the table, pull the cash from it, and smack the bills down. "My father instructed me to give him this."

Ignoring the cash, he casually slides his hands into his pockets. "Vinny isn't here, so you get me instead." He smirks.

"And *you* are?"

"Damien." He rests along the edge of the table, too close for comfort, but I'd be stupid to push him away.

He collects the money, flicks through the bills, and holds up the stack when he's finished. "Is there more money in that purse of yours, Pippa?"

I gulp, shifting in my chair and debating on offering him my purse, a lung, and the McDonald's Beanie Baby collection my mother passed down to me.

Not that he'd get much from my purse. Some loose change, tampons, and a wallet with zero-balance gift cards.

"My father will have the rest of your money by the end of the week," I lie, knowing damn well he won't.

He scowls, staring me down. "Why couldn't your father come here and deliver this pathetic amount of cash himself?"

"He didn't want you to kill …" I pause to select a better choice of words. Don't want to give the man any ideas. "Er … hurt him."

"He'd rather I kill … or, *er*, hurt you?"

I draw in a shaky breath.

Damien drops the cash on the table before sliding off the edge of it and standing in front of me. "What if I don't want the money?"

"That'd be"—I clear my throat—"very kind of you."

*But what does he want instead?*

Men like him don't just kindly forgive loans.

He catches my chin in his hand and tightens his grip when I attempt to jerk away. I shiver when he brushes his thumb over my cheek.

"Aren't you going to ask what I want instead, Pippa?"

"A high five?" My reply is ballsy. He could easily lower his hand to my neck and strangle me.

He raises my chin. "What if I said I want *you*?"

I breathe in through my nose when he plucks his thumb along my bottom lip.

"Too bad," I whisper against his thumb. "I'm not a means of currency to pay someone's debt." Tearing out of his grasp, I attempt to stand, but he cups my shoulders and pushes me back down on the chair.

His face hardens as he dips in closer. "You'd be surprised how many men would be perfectly okay with accepting you as currency." He works his jaw, as if surveying me like I'm an item for sale. "In fact, as much as you don't want to hear it, that's how your father saw you when he sent you in here."

My stomach tightens, and I stay quiet.

"Did that cross your mind?" He skims his fingers down my shoulder. "That whoever came in here would find a different way to make up for the missing money?" Each word is sneered and deliberate, driving the fact into my brain as deep as he can.

"My family's safety was the only thing on my mind."

"What about *yours*?"

I turn my head, hating the truth in his words.

He pulls back, standing tall. "Get up."

"What?"

"I said, get up." When I don't move fast enough, he stalks behind me and jerks my chair out from beneath the table as if I were weightless.

I struggle as he drags me up from the chair, forces me to my feet, and steps away to open the door. I snatch my purse at the same time he pushes me through the doorway.

He shoves the cash inside my bag. "You think of running, you won't get far." He stays behind me, a possessive shadow, while walking me outside.

The sun beats down on our bodies when we land in the parking lot.

"Where's your father parked?" he asks.

I scowl. "I drove myself."

"Fun fact about me, I fucking hate liars," he snarls. "I watched you on camera before I came into the room. Saw you exit his car. I was only curious if you'd be honest. You failed."

He leads me straight to my father's red Volvo. The window is rolled down, and my father drops the crossword he's holding when he sees us.

Damien doesn't give him a chance to react before he sticks his arm through the window, curls his massive hand around the back of my father's head, and slams his face into the steering wheel. The horn blares, drowning out my father crying out in pain.

"What the hell?" I yell, pulling at the back of Damien's blazer to stop him, but he doesn't budge.

He gives my father another steering-wheel face-plant, releases him, and steps back. My father pushes up his now-cracked glasses and scrambles for fast-food napkins to cover his bloody nose.

He grunts, dropping the napkins when Damien snatches him by the collar, tugging him closer.

"Don't you ever ask her to do this again," Damien yells. "Do you fucking hear me, Paul?"

My father violently nods.

"If I find out you do, your punishment from me will be worse than anything you can imagine."

My father holds up his hands in surrender. "Okay, okay. Never again."

Damien releases him. "Now, get the fuck out of here."

Tension in my body loosens, and my knees feel wobbly as I start walking around the Volvo toward the passenger door.

"I didn't say *you* could go." Damien captures my wrist and tugs me backward, my back connecting with his rock-hard chest.

"Damien ... Mr. Bellini—" my father sputters, blood dripping on his shirt.

*So, he knows this is Damien, not Vinny.*

"I won't hurt her," Damien sneers. "Not that you gave a shit about that earlier. Did you, Paul?" He says my father's name as if he'd just tasted expired milk.

My father stares at him, speechless.

When his attention turns to me, a flicker of apology flashes on his face.

Not enough for me to believe he's remorseful, though.

Damien keeps his hold on me, his fingers sinking into my skin. "You have until the end of the week to get us the rest of our money." He smacks the Volvo's hood with his free hand. "Don't come back until you have it all."

My father nods and slams his foot on the pedal. The Volvo bolts through the parking lot, a passenger short.

Damien whips me around to face him.

I glare at him. "I'm not going anywhere with you."

He smirks, licking his lips as if he can't wait to prove me wrong. I attempt to wrestle from his hold, but I'm not strong enough.

"Now, we can do this the easy or the hard way," he says, dragging me through the parking lot. "I'd hate to have to shoot your pretty little face."

People stare, but not one offers me help.

I talk shit as he hauls me toward the rear parking lot and

straight to a blacked-out Range Rover. I up my struggling game when he opens the passenger door.

"We're about to get to know each other so much better, Pippa." He shoves me inside the SUV and shuts the door before locking it.

Ready to flee, I hit the unlock button, but nothing happens.

*What did my father get me into?*

## 2

# DAMIEN

I TWIRL my key chain around my finger while circling the Range Rover, unsure of my plans for Pippa. I didn't have *take someone's hot-as-fuck daughter as collateral* on my agenda for today.

Pippa should consider herself lucky she got me and not Vinny. His psycho ass would've played games with her and not been so gentle. He and his brother, Antonio, usually deal with debt situations, but they're out today.

Well, Antonio is out.

No one knows where the fuck Vinny has been for the past week.

When they're unavailable, that responsibility falls in my lap.

Thank fuck it did today.

I unlock the SUV, slide behind the wheel, and inhale Pippa's sweet floral perfume.

"Do you live with your father?" I ask, starting the engine.

"No," she snaps.

"What's your address?"

"I'm not telling you. As a matter of fact, let me out of here." She presses the lock.

It doesn't make a sound or move.

I smirk at her next unlock attempt. She curses and smacks the door when the lock doesn't budge. After I purchased the Range Rover, I had the lock system modified. No one gets in or out without my permission.

While she fights with the lock, I snatch her purse and dump the contents in her lap. She stops as her phone, the cash, and other random, useless shit falls out. As soon as a wallet lands on her lap, I swipe it.

Her pouty lips pucker as I unzip the wallet and pluck out her ID. It takes only a few seconds for me to memorize her address. I toss the ID back to her and reverse from the spot.

"Um, excuse me?" she asks. "Where are we going?"

I turn out of the parking lot. "You'll figure it out the closer we get there."

"*Or* you could just tell me." She starts tossing her shit back into the bag. "God, what a way to spend my day off work. Kidnapped by a crazy my dad owes money to."

"If I were kidnapping you, you'd be gagged and tied up in my trunk."

She twists in her seat, scanning the back, as if expecting to find someone in that situation. It's comical she'd think I'd ever kidnap someone in my personal vehicle. You steal cars for that.

But I'm almost positive Pippa doesn't know who I am yet. Otherwise, she wouldn't give me this much lip. She'd be as terrified of me as she was while waiting for Vinny to enter the room earlier.

She slumps in the seat. "Is that supposed to make me feel better?"

"It should, considering you're not tied up."

Her cheeks warm, a stroke of pink on her sun-kissed skin. "Do you plan to tie me up?"

"Not unless you ask for it."

"Spoiler alert: I definitely won't."

"Bummer." I tsk.

"No, what's a bummer is you not letting me out of this car."

"Sweetheart, the biggest bummer of the day is your father sending you into the casino as his scapegoat."

"What was the alternative? You killing him?"

"Better him than you."

Paul knew the danger he was putting her in, yet he did it anyway. If Pippa wasn't with me, I'd have done more than break his nose. I'd have cut the fucking thing off. You don't use women, especially your daughter, to handle your debts. That's some cowardly shit.

Just as I told him, if he attempts to use her as leverage again, I won't make an exception, even if she's standing right next to me. The asshole racked up the debt. It's his responsibility to pay it.

The drive from the casino to her apartment is short, but New York City traffic is a fucking nightmare. When she grabs her phone, I veer to the left, causing her shoulder to smack into the door.

"Put it down," I snap.

She lowers her phone, glowering at me, but keeps it in her hand.

No spots are available in front of her building, so I parallel park across the street. I step out, straighten my blazer, and watch her glare at me through the windshield as I walk to her door. When I open it and extend my hand, she crosses her arms, refusing to take it like a goddamn child.

"I'm not above dragging your stubborn ass out," I warn, biting each word out and kneeling so we're eye level. When she doesn't move, I up the ante. "Fine, we'll drive around until I find your father. I'll make you wait in the car and watch me kill him. Does that sound like a better time for you, Pippa?"

She uncrosses her arms and reluctantly accepts my hand.

"You try to run or scream, you'll regret it." I draw her to her feet.

It's busy around us—people jogging, biking, jaywalking. I tighten my grip on hers, hoping she'll behave. It'd be a headache, bribing or killing someone she asks for help.

We walk toward an older building I'd bet my entire stock portfolio isn't up to code.

"Why are you doing this?" she asks, keying in the code to buzz us in. "Is this some kind of sick game you play before killing someone?"

"I don't plan to kill you." I crowd closer to see every number she hits. "I'm only curious."

"Be curious about someone else."

"Too bad. Blame yourself. You should've never come to the casino."

"If you think this is *my* fault, you need a trip to reality land."

"Considering what you did today, it seems you should join me."

The door buzzes, unlocking, and I hold it open, allowing her to enter first. As soon as we're inside, I nudge her toward the stairs. The entryway is tight and reeks of mothballs and BO. Chipped wall paint surrounds us, and locks are broken on a few doors. As we climb the cramped stairs, I can't stop myself from staring at her ass.

It's small yet plump.

Toned yet enough to fill my palms.

My hand tenses, urging me to smack it.

We pass two people on our way up. She doesn't ask either for help or show any signs of distress. But from the way they lower their gazes to the floor, I doubt they'd help her even if she asked.

We stop on the fifth floor and pass two doors before reaching hers. As soon as she unlocks the door, I follow her inside. Good thing she's the size of a bite-size Snickers. The place is as tight as a hamster cage.

Not that I expected anything lavish. Her father is a giant piece of shit and can't pay his debts.

While small, the apartment is clean and decently furnished. Pippa tosses her keys on the narrow kitchen counter as I shut and lock the door.

Leaning back on my heels, I look around. Tokens of her personality litter the place, giving away hints of who she is. A hideous purple couch, colorful pillows, mismatched kitchen stools, and so many family photos.

I pick up a framed photo from a small end table. It's a young girl, cheesing for the camera, front teeth missing, wearing a tutu.

I pick up another.

And another.

All while her gaze stays glued to me.

"You dance?" I ask.

She shyly bites into her lower lip. "Yes."

"Ballet?" I return the frame to its place.

"Since I was three."

I collapse on her stiff couch and drag my gaze down her petite body. Desire rushes through me like a drug.

I want to taste every inch of her skin.

I know it'd taste sweet.

Her pussy probably even better.

Pippa is beautiful. Her beauty is what caught my attention when I watched her on camera before entering the room.

She chews on the edge of her lip. They're light pink and delicate, like no one has ever kissed her passionate enough to rough them up.

That's exactly what I want to do.

Widening my legs, I prop my elbows on my knees. "I'll knock off half your father's debt if you dance for me, Pippa."

She freezes, gaping at me.

I check my watch. "You have ten seconds to say yes or no."

# 3

# PIPPA

DAMIEN STARES AT ME HUNGRILY, like a man who's been taken hostage and hasn't eaten in days.

I pinch myself, making sure I'm not in some freakish dream.

I grew up around men like him. They enjoy playing games with their victims, as if murder gives them a hard-on. And I'd stupidly become the easiest prey in history.

They'll mock me in true crime documentaries.

*She didn't scream, run, or even send a hand signal for help. Instead, she led him up the stairs, into her apartment, and stood before him, debating whether to dance for him. Oh, what a silly victim.*

Damien doesn't seem as cruel as others. If someone owed my uncle money and failed to pay, he wouldn't only slam their face into a steering wheel. He'd brutalize them, making the family watch, and then do the same to them.

But here I am, still breathing.

So is my father, to my knowledge.

I shake my head, trying to focus on my current problem—Damien's offer.

If he knocks off half my father's debt, we'd have enough to clear the balance.

I relax my shoulders, begging my tight body to do the same.

*It's just a dance, Pippa.*

I've danced for hundreds of people on stages.

This shouldn't be any different.

*So, why is my stomach flip-flopping with the worst case of stage fright ever?*

The people I've danced for didn't stare at me like this, is why.

His dark eyes probe mine, brimming with desire, a man ready to be rewarded.

There's so much on the line for this.

Yesterday, two loan sharks threatened to skin my mother and sister alive. A week before, someone burned down my mother's dance studio. I'm unsure of how many people my father owes money to, but they keep popping up like zits when I'm on my period.

Damien taps his watch face. "Ticktock, Pippa."

If dancing for him means helping my family, then I'll fucking dance for him.

I step forward, mind made up.

Damien's legs stay wide as he reclines on the couch. He stretches his arms along the back as if preparing for a lap dance at the strip club. He and his all-business-like demeanor look so out of place in my apartment. It's almost laughable as he sits on my hand-me-down couch, wearing a posh suit and polished loafers that I'm sure cost more than my rent.

He rolls up the sleeves of his blazer and shirt, his stormy eyes not leaving mine.

Everything about him screams intimidation.

Masculinity.

He's about to be thoroughly disappointed when I start the *Nutcracker* number I performed three Christmases ago.

I tap my foot, unsure how to start, and peer down my body. "I need to put on my pointe shoes."

He flicks his hand through the air. "Not necessary."

I gulp while kicking off my sandals.

"Five seconds," he warns.

His voice, sharp as a whip, startles me.

I perfect my posture, twirl on my toes, and nearly stagger into the wall. It's the worst spin in the history of spins. A toddler who hasn't even taken their first steps would've looked more graceful.

A thickness forms in my throat as I lift my gaze to his, inch by inch.

"Come closer." He crooks his finger.

I edge nearer but abruptly stop.

*Make this worth your while, Pippa.*

I cross my arms. "How much will you knock off my father's debt for that?"

He cocks his head to the side. "Are you selling yourself to me?"

"Hell no." I wince. "But if you're making me perform, I might as well ask."

"First off, I'm not *making* you do anything. I gave you the choice." He hooks his finger again, another demand to come closer.

I hesitate, shuffling my feet against the shag rug until I'm only inches from him.

Bending at the waist, he grabs me around the hips and yanks me onto his lap. I lose a breath as he gathers my face in his hands.

Hands so large that they could effortlessly crush my bones.

His eyes are stern and intrusive as he works his jaw. "I'd pay off every debt he owes for a night with you."

A sudden lightheadedness hits me.

"How do you know I'd be worth it?" I ask as he holds me in place.

He lazily sweeps his cold thumb along my chin. "I know it'd be worth it since I'd spend the rest of my night having fun with you, my sweet dancer."

Goose bumps pebble along my skin like a veil, and my lower lip tingles as he slides his mouth against it and sucks. It takes all my strength to turn my head away from him.

"One dance," I say, hating how my voice shakes. "That's our deal."

No way can I get pulled into Damien's magnetic field.

I have a feeling those who do are forever stuck there.

He chuckles connivingly, as if he doesn't believe me.

Edging closer, he brushes his lips along my ear. "Then, dance for me, Pippa."

Nerves flutter in my belly as I slightly flex my hips. He cups my waist, rolling me forward and then back. I gasp, my legs tightening when I feel his erection brush my core.

Damien might've told me to dance for him, but he's made himself the director of the show. He guides me slowly, wanting me to experience every inch of him.

I moan and hold his shoulders when he shifts his weight, providing me a better angle to slide against his cock.

A hiss escapes him when he moves me faster.

*Faster.*

*Faster.*

Showing me what he likes.

Showing me what *I* like.

I lose our rhythm when he releases me.

He splays his arms along the couch. "Now, you dance for me."

I rotate my hips forward, desperate to feel his length against my core until the end of days. My blood is on fire at the realization that this is no simple ballet dance.

A long moan escapes me, knocking me back into reality.

I stop. "We need music."

He prevents me from climbing off his lap. "Your moans will be our music."

"Someone sure is arrogant."

"It's not arrogant when you know it's true."

His hands find my waist again, and he resets our pace.

I desperately dry-hump him while he lifts his hips, meeting me thrust for thrust. I'm so in my zone that I don't stop him when he lowers my tank, exposing my bra.

And now, we've surpassed lap-dance level.

He yanks my tank off, unclasps my bra, and tosses it on the floor in one swift motion. I gasp when he cups his hands over my breasts.

Hands so big that they cover them completely.

Palms so cold that my nipples immediately harden beneath them.

My heart is on fire, and I keep our pace, my skin silently pleading for more of his touch.

He doesn't ask for permission before lowering his head and flicking my nipple with his tongue. Or when he takes it in his mouth, sucking it. I tip my head back as he swipes my hair off my shoulder to do the same with my other nipple.

His soft lips glide along my skin to the middle of my chest, where he sucks deep on the skin as if wanting to form a bruise. When he pulls back, I push his blazer off his shoulders, dragging it off his arms. It lands in a pile beside him.

"You're fucking beautiful, Pippa." His cock jerks as he smooths his thumb over my cheek.

He speaks like we've known each other forever.

Like he took an oath to always protect me.

His lips crash onto mine, and he cups the back of my head, tugging me closer to deepen our connection.

I've kissed plenty of men—okay, six—but none have ever given me such a rush or made me feel so desired.

I open my mouth, and he groans into it.

A warning he'll tear my life apart.

An unsteady breath catches in my throat when he hauls me to my feet and situates me so I'm standing, my heels sinking into the cushions.

My vagina is only inches from his face.

*I guess we're going for a* Nutcracker *remix.*

Even though it's the worst idea ever, I rest my palms on the couch as he holds me steady. My breathing is a ragged mess as he guides me to lift one foot, allowing him to peel my leggings down one leg.

Then, he does the same with the other.

I tremble as he rips my panties and flings them over his shoulder.

My knees shake, and without warning, he buries his entire face between my legs. He grips my ass cheek in one hand while the other holds my thigh in place.

His skilled tongue licks straight up my center.

I tense, aware letting this random man go down on me is a bad idea.

*But, God, it feels too good to stop him.*

I'm throbbing for him to do more.

Growing wetter and wetter with each flick of his skilled tongue.

"Your pussy is so wet for me," he groans against my leg, his voice raspy.

My legs tighten when he slips a thick finger inside me.

"It's been this wet since I put you in my car, hasn't it?"

I stifle a moan, resisting the urge to demand he stop asking questions and return to his pleasuring.

"Admit it," he presses. "You wanted me to come up here and

touch you. That's why you didn't scream. You'd rather I make you scream in other ways."

I grip the back of his head, shoving his face closer.

"Answer me," he clips yet also sounds desperate. "Tell me you wanted this as bad as I did."

"Yes," I cry out. "I wanted it bad."

As if satisfied with my answer, he shoves two ... maybe three ... fingers inside me. My knees weaken, and he tightens his grip on me.

I dig my nails into his hair, the other hand into the couch, struggling to handle the intensity of his mouth and fingers. Nothing has ever felt so right and perfect.

He hitches my leg higher, rubbing his scruffy cheek against my thigh. I love how abrasive and rough it feels against my skin.

Damien laps me up as if I'm something sacred he's never drunk before.

As if consuming me will grant him immunity from every sin he's ever committed.

"Ride my face until you come all over it." He pulls me back some so I can understand his words. "I want you to smother me with your sweet cum, my dancer."

He moans when I thrust my hips forward.

Forget smothering him with my cum. I'm riding his face so hard that I'm bound to crush his face with my thighs.

As a dancer, I've always felt in complete control of my body. But with Damien, it feels like he's hijacked all that control and taken over.

It's as if he wants to erase the innocence inside me and turn me into the devil he is so we become a better match.

He inches my legs farther apart. His mouth is wild between my legs, sucking on my clit, and his tongue laces through my slit while his fingers torture me.

I swear he doesn't take a single breath until I'm falling apart.

A tight string of ecstasy pulses through me—growing tighter and tighter and tighter—until it finally snaps. As I drop forward and cry out, he massages my pussy with his tongue, lapping up my release.

He clasps the back of my thighs as I catch my breath and collect myself. My panting continues as he lowers me to straddle him. I shudder, ready for more, when he skims his wet lips along my jawline.

"I wanted to loosen you up before your performance, baby," he comments with a slight humor in his tone, and he raises his lips to mine. "You were tight *everywhere*."

We've had a change of events.

A change of needs now.

No longer do I just want to dance off my father's loan.

I want *more*.

More of his mouth, his tongue, all of him.

And my orgasmed-out brain tells him this.

"Damien, please fuck me."

I've gone from fearing this man to wanting to fuck him.

He stares down at me, studying my face, and bares his teeth. "Ask me to fuck you again, Pippa."

I gulp in a breath. "Fuck me, Damien."

His hands claim my waist again, and he thrusts his tongue inside my mouth. My back arches when he sucks on the tip.

He doesn't stop me when I drag my hips back, providing enough room to unbuckle his belt. As I unzip his pants, he lowers his mouth to my throat, sucking on my sensitive skin. As soon as they're loose enough, I tug them down.

We freeze when his phone vibrates in his pocket.

"Ignore it." I drag his pants down farther.

"Unfortunately, I can't." He snatches my wrist to stop me and shifts to collect his phone with the other. He shuts his eyes and blows out a breath while checking the caller ID before silencing the call. "I have to go."

I peer away from him as he assists me off his lap and stands.

"You're leaving?" I fall back a step as embarrassment creeps through me.

"Consider the debt paid in full." He zips his pants and buckles his belt. "Keep the cash, and don't you dare give it back to your father."

My soul crushes when he presses a kiss to my forehead and walks out the door.

## 4

# DAMIEN

I'VE MURDERED plenty of people.

And right now, if my brother's call isn't important, he's joining that list of men. My sweet dancer was ready to give me anything I wanted from her.

Her mouth. Her pussy. Her everything.

As badly as I wanted to stay and worship every inch of her body, when duty calls, duty calls.

Duty doesn't care if you're on vacation.

Nursing a gunshot wound.

Or about to have the best fuck of your life.

My annoyance grows with every step I take out of Pippa's building. Once I'm back in the Range Rover, I return my brother, Julian's, call.

"Where the hell are you?" he shouts through the speaker.

"This'd better be important," I bark. "I swear to God, if it's you forgetting the Wi-Fi password again, I'm shooting you in the goddamn face."

"We have a Popov problem. According to my source, they have a plan in motion tonight. Meet us at the warehouse."

"On my way."

I hang up, start the SUV, and speed off.

I'm a capo for the Lombardi family, one of New York's most notorious Mafia organizations. My family has been involved with the Lombardis for decades. Antonio's father, Vincent, is don, and my father is his consigliere.

Julian nor I had other career options. When Julian was sixteen, he came home and told my father he wanted to be a doctor. My father laughed and told him he'd burn down any hospital that gave him a job if he turned his back on the family. We were born and taught to become masters of crime and manipulation and to always remain loyal to the Lombardi family.

The Lombardis opened Lucky Kings Casino decades ago to appear as law-abiding citizens. It's how we launder money yet look like we earn an honest living. In our defense, we do run the casino mostly as a legitimate business. Though, that always takes a back burner to everything else.

The warehouse is a short drive. Fifteen minutes later, I steer into the back alley that leads into it. I'm ready to get this shit over with and return to Pippa's. I lick my lips, almost certain her pussy is still dripping for me.

I'll fuck my sweet dancer, settle her father's debt to Lucky Kings, and make it clear no one loans Paul another penny.

As soon as I walked into her apartment, I knew it wouldn't be a onetime thing with her. The moment she allowed me to touch her, I knew she'd be mine, whether she liked it or not.

My footsteps echo through the warehouse when I enter it. My father, Julian, and Emilio are gathered in a huddle, talking. They all turn to me.

"Tell me what you know," I say, tucking my keys into my pocket.

"The Popovs started building on new ground," Julian explains, twirling a toothpick in his mouth. "One they stupidly believed we wouldn't find."

"Did we find it?" I raise a brow.

Emilio, another capo, cracks his neck. "Fuck yeah, we did."

"My source told me they're on a mission to find Vincent's address," my father adds. "They want to burn down his home in retaliation for us torching their properties."

The Popovs have become royal pains in my ass. They own a chain of casinos along the Jersey coast. We never considered them competition until they decided to expand their business into New York.

We warned them once.

Warned them twice.

We don't do third warnings.

Last year, they obtained permits to construct a casino too close to Lucky Kings. If we're being honest, within the same state is too close in my opinion. They started building, but all construction stopped when we burned it down. They found a second location and framed the structure, and we torched that as well.

You'd think after two sites were reduced to ashes, they'd stop construction and take their asses back to Jersey, where they belong. It seems they haven't.

I rub my hands together. "So, what's the plan?"

---

WE PARK a block away from the third casino building site. I exit the minivan I carjacked an hour ago and throw on a black hooded sweatshirt.

Julian and Emilio join my side, each of them holding gas cans.

My father appears behind them, removing two sets of matches from his shirt pocket. When he offers me one, I shake my head, holding up my own.

I'd never show up for an arson job without a healthy supply of matches.

A full moon floats above us as we stroll toward a poorly lit site. Their only security measure is two men sitting in a beat-up pickup truck. As we grow closer, I notice one is sleeping, and the other is focused on an iPad.

Emilio and my father creep to the truck while Julian follows me toward the newly framed building. He drenches it with gas. I strike a match, smiling at the glowing brightness around the flame. Just as I'm about to toss it, I notice the truck light up in flames from the corner of my eye. A man rolls out, his clothes on fire, and screams before collapsing.

I tsk and shake my head.

It didn't have to come down to this.

We tried to reason with the Popovs.

Even proposed a very generous amount of money for them to stay out of New York. But they played too many games—sending shoppers to Lucky Kings, trying to recruit our employees—and became a headache.

I don't mitigate headaches.

I fucking kill them.

A rush of energy courses through my veins as I toss the match, watching the fire consume the structure.

*Damn, being in power feels good.*

I swat mosquitoes away as we make our way back to where we parked. Julian pours the remainder of the gasoline on the minivan, and my father lights it on fire. Luis, one of our men, is stationed three streets over, waiting for us.

"You headed back to the casino?" I ask my father.

He shakes his head, running his fingers through his short black hair. "Your mother bribed me to come home by making her plum cake." He nudges me with his elbow. "Your grandparents and sister will be there. Stop by if you're free."

"If not tonight, I'll come by tomorrow."

He nods and slaps me on the back. "Love you, son."

Then, he does the same with Julian.

Luis drives us to the casino, and I beeline straight to my office. Antonio asked me to gather paperwork and then drop it off at the hospital for him. Amara, his daughter, is there, recovering from a tonsillectomy.

An hour later, I'm headed out the door.

First stop, hospital.

Second, Pippa's.

I stop when my phone rings, and Julian's name flashes on the screen.

He's screaming when I answer.

I listen to him, digest every word that's a knife to the heart.

My body loses all strength as I drop the phone and collapse to my knees.

## 5

# PIPPA

CLEANUP OF HUMILIATION in aisle five, please.

What's worse than begging a murderous stranger to fuck you?

Him rejecting you and walking out the door.

Correction: Him having sex with you *and then* leaving might've been worse. But I'm dramatic, thank you very much.

I wait two hours, just in case Damien returns, but he doesn't. To clear my head, I go to dinner with my mother and sister, Lanie. After that, we attend a local ballet recital. Neither helps me clear my head of him.

I don't tell my father about Damien not taking the money or how I danced half his debt off. My cheeks warm as I think about all the ways Damien touched me.

If my father found out I have the money, he'd demand it back.

*Including* what I loaned him.

Then, he'd gamble it away tonight.

It's after ten when I get home. I lock the dead bolt on the door and yawn, humming a tune from the ballet while strolling through my apartment. I stop in my tracks when my gaze hits

Damien's blazer draped over the couch. He forgot it on his rush out of here.

I glide my fingers along the expensive fabric and raise it to my nose before shamelessly drawing in a breath, inhaling his scent. My body relaxes as I shrug it on. It droops on me like a potato sack, the sleeves swallowing my arms.

*Take it off, Pippa.*

For all I know, there could be crime evidence on this.

A dead person's DNA.

*Here I am, dummy of the year, wearing exhibit A of a murder case.*

And now, *my* DNA is on it.

I pat the pocket, silently telling myself I'll only wear it for a moment.

Surely, DNA takes a few minutes to gather.

Like the five-second rule with dropped pizza rolls.

I keep the blazer on while kicking off my flats. My bare feet plod against the wood floor on my walk to the bathroom. Damien is on my mind as I shower, and I run my hands over my body, remembering how good his touch felt.

After showering, I slip on a bra and panties and tug the blazer back on. On my way to my bed, I snag my MacBook from the nightstand and climb underneath the blankets, making myself comfortable.

Then, I Google **Damien, Lucky Kings Casino**.

Nothing of relevance comes up.

I type **Damien, Lombardi, New York**.

That search brings up a few photos and news articles.

Nothing stalk-worthy.

I click on a blog post on the site, *New York Mafia Girlie*, that ranked men in the New York Cosa Nostra families by hotness, status, and viciousness.

Cristian Marchetti is number one.

No surprise there.

Also known as Monster Marchetti, Cristian is the cruelest mob boss in the city. Even though he's close to my father's age, Cristian is hot as hell. A total DILF. But his psychopathic tendencies are a bit of a turn-off for me.

Antonio and Vinny Lombardi are ranked fifth and seventh, respectively.

Damien Bellini is ranked twelfth.

Leaning in closer, I zoom in on the blurry photo of him. It's one someone took from afar, and he's standing in front of the city courthouse, shaking hands with the prosecutor.

I spend another twenty minutes scouring the internet for all Damien news before shutting my MacBook in defeat. It seems the only way to get to know this man is to either join a mob family or owe them a substantial amount of money.

Although the second might lead to my death.

Not that it matters.

Getting mixed up with a man like him is nothing but trouble.

A direct roadway to heartbreak—no U-turns, no reroutes. Straight off a cliff.

I set my laptop back on my nightstand and am on my third yawn as I drift off.

SANE PEOPLE DON'T bang on doors this late in New York.

I ignore it.

I've already dodged violence once today. *No, thank you* on putting myself in that situation again.

I fluff my pillow and lay my head back down.

But the knocking continues.

*Bang! Bang!*

*Pound! Pound!*

"Jesus," I shout, throwing off my comforter.

The last thing I need is my landlord evicting me for whoever is at my door, disturbing the peace.

"I'm coming," I yell, stomping through my apartment.

I peek through the door's peephole before swinging it open and stumbling back as Damien stands before me.

His shoulders are slumped as he stares at me gravely.

All his confidence from earlier is absent.

Gone is the pretentious suit, replaced with black sweats and a hoodie.

He opens his mouth, but no words come.

I retreat another inch when he silently invites himself inside, shutting the door with the heel of his sneaker.

"Damien—" I don't get the chance to complete my sentence.

He cups the back of my head and madly kisses me.

It's pleading.

*Hopeless.*

Breath-starved.

He guides me backward toward my bedroom, not loosening his hold.

The only light in my bedroom comes from the TV, but that's all he needs. He leads me to the edge of my bed, holding me in place, and I stumble when he frantically tears my panties down my legs.

His eyes leave mine as he trails kisses down my neck.

Every movement is rougher than he was earlier.

The dark side of him coming out at night.

"Damien," I croak out again, pushing at his chest to slow him down.

Stop him.

Get some sort of explanation.

He ignores me, digging his canines into my skin as if going for blood.

I nudge him again, harder this time.

He rears back, as if I suddenly tased him.

Pain fills his eyes.

Red, on the lines of reaching bloodshot.

He cups my face, gentler than he was seconds ago.

As if I were an heirloom, passed down through generations.

Those anguished eyes lower to mine.

A breath catches in my throat as I nervously hold his gaze.

"Pippa," he finally whispers, caressing his trembling thumb over my cheek. "My family was murdered tonight. Please let me stay here before I do something that'll haunt me for the rest of my life."

I open my mouth.

Ready to tell him I'm sorry.

Ask *how*.

*Why*.

He squeezes his thumb into my cheek, as if driving those questions away from my lips.

I nod—a silent understanding—and allow him to devour my mouth.

This man saved me from my father's problems earlier.

And tonight, it's my turn to save him.

## 6

# DAMIEN

I DON'T KNOW how I ended up at Pippa's.

Don't remember the car ride, buzzing myself in, or climbing the stairs.

Everything that happened after Julian's call is a blur.

My muscles spasm, my entire body shaking as I stare down at Pippa on her bed. I need her to keep me here, be my anchor in tonight's storm, and remind me there's still a sliver of humanity left inside this dark soul of mine.

When she answered the door, wearing my blazer, it heated my blood. I'd never set my eyes on something so perfect.

Like she's mine, *all mine*.

But my chaotic mind knew I could do better.

As sexy as she looked wearing my clothes, having her naked would be better.

No, her tight, naked body writhing underneath mine would triumph over everything.

I slide my hand from Pippa's face to her chest and press her flat against the mattress. The blankets are a wild mess. My other hand follows, both trailing down each side of her waist, slipping down her bare legs. Her smooth skin soothes my anger and rage like the earth's mantle holding a volcano's magma.

My precious dancer is too soft for me.

Too sinless.

Too fucking good.

But I want to desecrate that from her.

Destruct her soul, make it match with mine.

I drop to my knees, kneeling to her pussy, inhaling the sweet smell.

My mouth is salivating for her, counting down the seconds before I taste her sweet cum. My cock jerks in my pants.

The ceiling fan whirs above us as I lick my lips and trail the tip of my finger along her slit. Her juices are already drenching my finger.

I hold it there, allowing the liquid to soak into my skin.

My dancer is ready for me.

Dripping and waiting.

I'm so close to her pussy that I feel like I might die if I don't taste her again.

"Pippa," I say, continuing my teasing. "Tell me you want my mouth on your pussy, baby."

"Damien," she moans, holding herself on her elbows and staring at me.

"Say it," I demand, driving three fingers inside her. "Tell me you want me to taste your sweet pussy. That it's been waiting for me to come back."

Half her body slumps on the bed as she lowers one elbow to grip my hair.

"It's all I've thought about since you left," she confesses.

That's my green light.

I dive my entire face between her legs, soaking it, and ravish her pussy relentlessly.

I turn wild as I fuck her with my fingers.

Sucking and licking as if I'll never get enough of her.

I bite into her thigh, wanting to mark her so she knows who she belongs to.

I'm rough, harsh, my every touch brutal.

Her body squirms, and she moans above me.

Her fingers are no longer on my hair. Instead, both hands are digging into her sheets, giving her leverage to thrust her pussy against my face, grinding against it.

Feeding more of herself to me.

Wanting to be fucking devoured.

My blood hums, and I forget about everything, my every thought consumed with pleasing her.

*This woman, she's all mine. All fucking mine.*

And for a man who just lost everything, that means the entire world to me.

Right now, I feel like I've lost control of everything.

That I have no one.

But Pippa is here, giving herself to me, proving I'm not alone.

She moans my name, begs for more, pleads for me to slow down—which I fucking don't—and I can tell when she's close.

Her body trembles.

As I glance up, I find her head thrashing from side to side.

"Come on my face right now, baby," I demand, shoving four fingers inside her pussy. I lower one to her asshole and brush it against the rim. "Drown me with your cum."

Her body jerks forward, and seconds later, my baby falls apart above me.

I lick her up.

Savor her taste until I've devoured all her cum.

I stand, untie my sweats, and lower them. My cock springs free.

Hard and red and throbbing for her.

Then, I stare down at her, blinking away tears.

I'm remembering shit now.

It's all coming back.

A roller coaster suddenly rushing through my mind.

Pippa climbs onto her knees, and I wince as she holds my face in her hands, cradling it. "Use me, Damien." She emphasizes each word by tightening her hold on my face. "Fuck me. Release your pain on me, and I promise, I'll take all of it."

I don't move, and my muscles twitch beneath my skin.

"Use me, Damien," she repeats, climbing higher to skim her lips against mine. "*Please.*"

That *please* snaps me back to this moment.

To her. To us.

As I crawl over her, I open the blazer. It's like revealing a gift, and I lick down her stomach before positioning my cock at her opening.

Just as I grip the base, she stops me, digging her nails into my forearm. "Condom. Nightstand drawer."

My head spins, a surge of anger returning that I have to separate from her. But I remain calm while opening the drawer, snatching a rubber, and ripping it open with my teeth.

"Put it on me," I say, passing it to her.

I'm surprised at how stable her hands are as she rolls it over my throbbing dick.

As soon as it's on, I press her back down onto the mattress, and she moans my name as I slam inside her.

Her body jolts up the bed at the impact.

Shutting my eyes, I do it again.

And again.

And again.

I dig my fingers into her hips, holding her in place, and fuck her hard.

So hard that she moves up the bed again.

So hard that she cries out with each thrust.

My hands lower to her thighs, inching them open as I increase my speed.

"Shiiit," she says with a hiss of pain.

I still, knowing she'll have bruises in the morning.

*You should be gentler with her.*

I drop her limp legs on the bed and inch back.

She scrambles forward to stop me, holding my face in her hands. "Don't, Damien."

I blink away the wetness in my eyes.

The hurt making its way to the surface.

The volcano finally ready to erupt its pain.

"Fuck me," she says, raining kisses along my cheek, collecting the few tears beneath my eyes. "Use me. I'm right here."

Gripping my shoulders, she lowers us again.

I'm back between her legs, and she widens them, rotating her hips to brush along my cock.

I pause, meeting her eyes, and she smiles while offering me a simple nod.

Lacing our fingers together, I slam them on the bed on each side of her head.

I take all her permission and pound into her, following the pace of my speeding heart.

She moans along with it, in sync with me, like we're dancing to a favorite song we share. Her pussy is dripping, easily allowing me to slide in and out.

My balls smack against her pussy as I hike her hips up further. Sweat covers her chest. I lower her sports bra to lick it off and then suck on her nipple. In the same breath, I do the same with the other.

She pants above me.

My sweet dancer.

Loving my cock inside her.

"Come for me, Pippa," I say.

No, I fucking demand it. I'm so close to my release.

I need her to finish first.

Her pussy contracts on my dick before her entire body starts shaking.

My heart beats faster and faster, pounding against my chest like a caged monster begging for release. I clench my muscles to give myself more time, but it's impossible. Pippa feels too damn good.

My mind goes blank, all my troubles and problems erased, and my veins feel like they're burning as I come into the condom. I pull out of her, remove the condom, and release on the blazer.

I'm nearly energy-deprived as I scoop up her release with my finger and mix it with my cum on the blazer, swirling them together.

"Never wash this," I say. "I want it to always smell like us."

Then, I let the exhaustion take me. I collapse on her, no longer the ruthless man I'm expected to be. She accepts my weight, pulling in thick breaths. A few seconds pass before I fall on my back, cradling her to my body, as if she's all that'll keep my heart beating. My goddamn lifeline.

How the tables have turned.

I'm no longer her savior.

She's mine.

Neither of us says a word, and it doesn't take her long to fall asleep.

When a light snore leaves her, I carefully slip away, collect my clothes, and leave.

# 7

# PIPPA

THIS MORNING, I woke up to an empty bed with no signs of Damien.

No phone number scribbled on a napkin.

No *last night was great* note.

No breakfast.

A cliché one-night stand who left nothing but confusion, sore legs, and a dark hickey on my thigh.

At least he left the blazer as a reminder of him.

*The blazer he pretty much decorated with our cum.*

Now, it's three in the afternoon, and still no word from him. I never gave him my number, but given how resourceful he seems, he could easily find it.

"See you tomorrow, Jane!" I shout, waving goodbye to my boss.

The bell above the coffee shop door chimes as I leave. I've been a part-time barista at Brew Bliss since high school, but I've had to pick up more shifts after my mother's studio fire. Rent is due in two weeks, and my landlord doesn't take IOUs or lattes as payment.

I'm also sure as hell not offering up a lap dance for it.

## Sinful Sacrifice

Seventy-five-year-old Roy would have a heart attack.

After my two-hour dance practice, which only makes me sorer, I walk home.

*Fingers crossed Damien somehow broke into my apartment and is waiting for me.*

I frown when I find it empty, and spend the next three hours doing dishes, laundry, and anything else to get my mind off him.

"Screw it," I mutter, collecting my keys and driving to Lucky Kings.

Who knows if he'll be there? But it's my only way of getting in touch with him.

I need to make sure he's okay.

Comfort the criminal's heart.

That is, if he has one.

Patrons crowd the noisy casino. I walk across the patterned carpet, passing the roulette wheels and crap tables. The room smells like overpriced alcohol and desperation.

Before yesterday, I'd never stepped foot inside a casino.

As the daughter of a gambling addict, I've always hated them. There are too many memories of my father coming home drunk and broke after a casino night out. He and my mother would fight about him gambling away bills, rent, grocery money, everything. Not a dollar was safe from his greedy hands.

These places are the monsters that feed his selfishness.

Maneuvering around people, I beeline straight to the table my father directed me to yesterday. I'm *so close* to my destination when something stops me.

Or rather *someone*.

"Dad!" I charge over to the blackjack table. "What the hell?"

My father's spine stiffens at the sound of my voice, and he swivels on his stool to face me. "Oh, hi, Pippa."

All eyes swing to me. The dealer frowns at my interruption. My father's face mirrors his, as if he wouldn't stop the dealer from pushing me out the door so he can continue his game. He's wearing the same shirt and khakis from yesterday—the shirt now blessed with a ketchup stain to match the blood ones. He did manage to replace his glasses.

Two men seated on each side of him glare at me.

"Hit me and ignore her," one says, tapping the table. "I'm on a good roll here."

I ignore them and focus on my father. "You told me no more." Tears form in my eyes, and I blink them away.

"But didn't you settle my debt?" he replies so casually. "You gave Damien the money."

*Whoa.*

I flinch.

Did he get a concussion when Damien rammed his head into the steering wheel and forget he didn't have *all* the money?

Unless he assumes Damien got it out of me in another way. Disgust rises up my throat as a hard knot forms in my belly.

"You're unbelievable," I snarl.

I tug at my shirt as if the room suddenly grew fifty degrees warmer and glance around, searching for the nearest exit.

This is the sign I needed to stay away from here.

From Damien.

From places like this.

They're bad freaking omens.

I shake my head and turn to leave, but I don't make it far before running into a hard body.

A tall man in a sharp black suit holds me steady as I catch my balance. I rub my forehead. Jesus, it's like I ran into a brick wall.

"Pippa, Damien told me to escort you to his office," the man informs me before pinning his attention on my father. "And you need to leave, Paul. You're officially banned from the casino. Don't come back."

As if on autopilot, the bald dealer reaches forward and collects my father's chips.

Well, chip since he only had one.

"Good riddance," one of the players mutters.

"Says who?" my father huffs at the man.

"Damien."

"I want to speak to Damien, then." My father crosses his arms. "There's nothing wrong with my money."

The man scoffs. "Trust me, you don't want to speak with him."

My father stubbornly stays on his stool.

"Dad," I sigh. "Please, just leave."

When he doesn't listen, the man clutches my father's collar and yanks him to his feet. My father stumbles, but the man doesn't help him. He falls on his butt before slowly pulling himself up.

"Put in a good word for me, Pippa," he says when he's on his feet. "Get him to change his mind. You're a good girl."

God, it sounds like he's pimping me out to play a few rounds of blackjack.

The dealer, along with the other men, pause their game to look at my father in disgust. A bodyguard with the same muscle mass as Thor approaches us and escorts my father out.

"I'm Emilio," the man introduces before offering the dealer a head nod.

"Pippa." I swipe imaginary lint off my shirt. "But you, uh ... already knew that." I follow him without question.

We leave the main casino floor, pass a break room filled with employees eating and watching TV, and walk through a hallway with a line of offices. Some doors are open, some closed.

Damien's office is the third from the end.

When I step inside, it's like I'm entering the devil's playground.

If the devil had the world's biggest minimalistic interior designer.

The walls are dark green, there are no windows, and a small lamp on the desk provides the only light.

"Wait in here," Emilio orders and leaves, shutting the door behind him.

I stand there, taking in the boringness for a good ten minutes. Unlike my apartment, there's nothing personal here—not one sign of who works in this office.

No photos, no heirlooms, no personality.

All a mystery.

Like the man who works here.

Only a rich cherry-wood desk with the lamp, an iMac, and a keyboard. A black ergonomic chair sits behind it, and a deep-seated taupe couch is in the corner. I have a strong urge to snoop, but I don't.

He for sure has cameras in here, and I want him to trust me.

I plop down on the couch, make myself comfortable, and read a book on my phone while waiting for what feels like forever.

Or two hours, according to the time on my screen.

A little while later, the door opens, but it's not Damien, only Emilio bringing me a slice of pizza and water.

I eat and fall asleep, waiting for the man I shouldn't want.

---

THE FEEL of someone scooping up my sleeping body in their arms and carrying me out of the office wakes me. I pull back but relax seconds later at Damien's familiar scent. Burying my face in his shoulder, I allow him to take me outside. This time, I don't fight him when he places me in his SUV, clicks on my seat belt, and drives off.

The seat is warm, and I yawn, fighting to fully wake up.

I barely know Damien, but something in my gut tells me I can trust him.

That doesn't mean it's a good idea, though.

The car ride is quiet, and I perk up in my seat when we reach a guarded gate. The window squeaks when Damien rolls it down. He offers a two-finger wave to the guard, and the gate opens.

I sit up straighter, craning my neck to get a good look. "Is this your house?"

He shakes his head. "Antonio's."

"Why aren't we going to yours?"

"I don't know if it's safe for me to go home yet."

I slowly nod and stop with the questions.

After parking, he assists me out of the SUV. Once on the front porch, he blocks me from seeing the passcode he enters on the front door. An alarm fires off when we enter the house, and he quickly turns it off with another code.

The low light follows us into the house as he guides me toward a separate wing. He blocks me from seeing the door's passcode as he keys it in.

*Well, well.*

*He sure didn't have that same courtesy when it came to my building code.*

The lock beeps, and we enter a bedroom that smells like fresh laundry.

Like I'm in a live-action Tide commercial.

Damien flips on a lamp that emits the level of brightness you'd get from a lava lamp. "Make yourself comfortable. I'll be back."

He drops his keys on the dresser and walks through a dark doorway. He shuts the door, and seconds later, a light shines through the cracks.

I don't make myself comfortable. The king-sized bed's comforter is insane-asylum white. No way am I getting in it with these outdoor clothes. Just as I'm about to raid the dresser for pajamas to borrow, I hear commotion behind the door.

"Fuck," Damien hisses.

This time, I'm not above being nosy. I creep toward the door, to what I assume leads to a bathroom, and stop. Drawing in a deep breath, I slowly open it, surprised it's unlocked.

Damien stills, staring at me, unblinking.

I gasp, my hand covering my mouth as I sweep my gaze down his body.

He's bare-chested, his pants unfastened, his bloody shirt on the floor.

*Speaking of blood.*

Dried-up blood cakes his split, battered knuckles.

Bruises cover his chest, and there's a slash on his forehead.

He didn't give one sign of this earlier.

He walked fine, carried me through the parking lot with not one groan or limp, and drove without showing pain.

In the back of my mind, I hate that I know he's accustomed to pain.

I do a quick self-check for any transferred blood on me, but I'm clean. A gun sits on the vanity next to a pocketknife and brass knuckles. His vigilant eyes bore into mine as I move in closer. He draws in a long breath and curses beneath it.

"Pippa," he starts, hissing in torment while attempting to stop me.

"Shh." I press my finger to my mouth and sink to my knees on the tiled floor. Collecting his cold hands in mine, I softly kiss each knuckle.

His body tightens as if no one is supposed to touch him like this.

He stares down at me in shock as I lower his pants and briefs to his feet. His cock, growing harder by the second, springs free.

If I could see my reflection, I'm sure our expressions would match. I'm trying to appear more confident than I feel.

I've never been so impulsive before.

Reckless.

But right now, I don't care. All I want to do is help Damien.

He drops his hand to stop me. "You don't have to—"

*Sinful Sacrifice*

I *shh* him again and stare at his large cock while noticing a small scar on his right thigh. I slowly trace it with my thumb.

I've seen cocks before, obvi. His was inside me last night. But I didn't get a close-up.

He's the largest I've ever touched. The head has a purple hue, throbbing with need, and a bubble of pre-cum sits at the slit. It jerks when I wrap my hand around it. My fingers don't even fit around his width. As I stroke him, his body relaxes, vertebra by vertebra.

A low moan escapes his throat as I work his cock. I slide forward, gaining a better grip. My mouth waters at how close it is to my face. I open it slightly, contemplating with myself.

*Am I that daring?*

I'm not normally a first-move girlie, especially when it comes to blow jobs. But with Damien, it seems I am.

Pleasing him is like an adrenaline rush.

Damien reaches down to grip the base of his cock. "Do you want to suck my cock, Pippa?"

"Yes," I whisper.

"Look at me and say it."

"I want to suck your cock, Damien." I stare up at him with tired eyes, biting into my lip.

"Open up." He drags his cock along the seam of my lips. "Let me feed it to you." He tightens his hold and slips it inside my mouth, inch by inch.

When I've taken all of him in, he stills, waiting for me to do with him as I please.

He must know I'm at level one when it comes to experience from our other hookups. I've hit home runs, but I'm normally benched. Tonight, I want to show him I'm capable of more.

I slide my head forward, deep-throating him the best I can. Inhaling through my nose, I suck in my cheeks to create suction while bobbing my mouth along his cock.

I do this teasingly slow. My wish for this moment is to stay as intimate as it is. I wait until I can tell he's excited, near the edge of his peak, before speeding up. I cup his balls with my hand and stroke him with the other.

"God, baby," he groans, petting my hair and running his fingers through the strands. "Just like that. Suck it so good."

He praises me but doesn't force me to go faster or shove his cock farther.

My clit throbs as I suck him harder. I don't stop, even when spit drips down my chin.

I choke a few times.

Typical me.

But for the first time, I'm not embarrassed by this. He stops, allowing me time to relax my throat.

When I return to my normal pace, he grips the back of my head and grinds his hips against my face. My pulse speeds as I suck him as good as I can.

"I'm about to come," he warns. "Pull away if you don't want to swallow."

I drop his balls, still working him in my mouth, and give him a thumbs-up. Seconds later, he releases his cum in my mouth. He tightens his fingers in my hair, holding me in place, as if wanting me to swallow every drop of him.

My insides vibrate, and my clit aches. But tonight isn't about me. It's about him.

He catches his breath while I suck him dry, and when I start to stand, he helps me to my feet. His hand lingers at my waist as I turn on the shower, grab a rolled-up washcloth, and clean his knuckles while waiting for the water to warm.

I wait for him to tell me to stop.

To pull away.

But all he does is blow out a rough breath and allow me to take care of him.

"Strip," he demands when I'm finished.

"What?" I stutter, suddenly feeling shy.

"Take off your clothes. You're showering with me."

He helps me undress. His hand cups my ass when I lower my leggings, and when I unclasp my bra, he brushes his thumb along my hardening nipple.

"I'm sorry, Pippa," he says, noticing the hickey-slash-bruise on my thigh from last night. "I didn't mean—"

"It's okay," I interrupt, standing on my tiptoes. Even then, I'm not close enough to his face to kiss him. So, he lowers his head and presses his mouth to mine.

"You have nothing to worry about," I say. "I liked everything you did to me last night."

He nods, but I can tell he doesn't fully believe me.

He assists me in the shower and joins me.

It's so intimate as we wash each other's body.

I'm seeing a rare side of Damien. A side I'd guess not many see.

I carefully rub the washcloth along his bruised, scarred, and bloody skin, knowing there's a chance I'm washing away crime evidence.

The blood flows down the drain, taking my sanity along with it.

# 8

# DAMIEN

"Are you fucking nuts?" Antonio spits from behind the desk in his home office. He slams his fist on the desk, causing shit to rattle. "My daughter is here, Damien! My goddamn daughter."

His voice is harsh but low. He never yells when Amara is home.

"I fucked up," I reply, massaging my temples with my beat-up knuckles.

Knuckles that my precious Pippa treated so gently last night. Did it help heal them or reduce the pain?

Hell no.

But it felt nice to know someone gave a shit.

Not that I deserve her gentleness.

Her sweetness.

Us men in this world, we handle darkness and brutality. And even though we deny it, that shit haunts us.

Even kills us sometimes ... or the people we love.

I close my eyes, the memory of my family an endless loop in my head.

"Why did you bring her here?" Antonio asks, snapping me

from my thoughts. "That's out of character for you." He reclines in his chair, as if waiting to give me a therapy session.

I'm Antonio's right-hand man, and we grew up together. Our fathers were close friends. And although I'm three years older than him and closer in age to Vinny, I fucking hate his brother. Antonio and I are responsible and levelheaded. That's why we get along well. We keep to ourselves and don't create problems for the hell of it.

And while this life doesn't grant much privacy, we try our best to have ours.

Because of that, I don't bring anyone not affiliated with the family around. No friends. No women. No fucking one. There'd be too much guilt if they got caught in the crosshairs. It's too risky.

For reasons beyond me, I'm letting Pippa in. And it's not just the sex.

Hell, if she'd told me no, she wasn't ready, I'd still show up at her doorstep.

"The only reason I'm not threatening her life right now is because I know you're smart." Antonio harshly taps the side of his head. "I'm trusting you on this. Don't make me regret it, and don't you dare tell anyone else. She's a liability."

"You know I won't."

Vincent Lombardi would flip his shit if he knew I was getting close to the daughter of a gambling addict who's owed us money on many occasions. He runs the enterprise with an iron fist.

A knock on the door interrupts us.

"Yeah?" Antonio calls out, and the door opens.

Julian walks in, his face grim and his eyes bloodshot. His suit needs a goddamn iron—a condition he'd never have left the house in before. Knowing him, he hasn't slept either. Just like me, he's punishing himself.

We should've been there to protect them.

Should've waited to make a move on the Popovs.

And now, we're the only limbs hanging on what's left of our family tree.

"Antonio." He pays Antonio a respectful nod before tipping his chin toward me.

I return the gesture.

That's our version of a brotherly hug.

We've done well at holding in our composure. Since we're not ones to cry, we take our pain out in the form of violence.

"We killed two Popovs yesterday," he informs Antonio. "The CEO who'd paid for the hit and his son who'd arranged it."

Antonio nods in approval.

"We're tracking the locations of the CFO and his brother who knew about the plan," I add. So far, we're narrowing down their locations. They're out of the country, but they can't hide forever.

Antonio stands from his chair. "Make it happen and report back."

Julian scrubs his hand over his five-o'clock shadow while glancing at me. "Let me know if you hear anything else."

I nod. "You know I will."

As soon as he leaves, Antonio turns to me in agitation. "It's not only in your best interest to ditch her but also Pippa's."

He's right, and I need to consider that. She's in danger just being involved with me.

Rivals love to kill family members to prove points.

And right now, that hits closer to home than anything.

I dip my hands into the pockets of my slacks. "If she becomes a problem, I'll handle it."

"If she becomes a problem, *my father* will handle it."

His warning is clear. Vincent will easily kill anyone he can't trust. He doesn't like liabilities.

I need to make sure I can trust Pippa while also hiding who she is. Right after I kill some Popovs, of course.

We leave his office, and I head in the direction of the guest room—which is considered mine since I crash here so much and no one else is allowed in there. I hear laughter as I get closer to the kitchen.

That's not unusual since Amara and her grandmother from her mother's side, Clara, live here.

But it's not only their voices drifting down the hall. There's another. One I've become very familiar with the past few days.

Antonio spins on his heel and storms toward the kitchen while I follow.

"You've got to be fucking kidding me," he says as soon as he rounds the corner.

# 9

# PIPPA

I'M STANDING in a mob prince's kitchen as he glares at me.

This morning, when I woke up, I learned that falling asleep next to Damien is synonymous with waking up alone.

In need of water, I left the bedroom on a hunt for the kitchen. I found it, along with the cutest kid, Amara, and her grandmother. They stopped mid-conversation about magical ponies to stare at me in confusion.

Not that I blamed them. I am some rando, standing in the kitchen.

Unsure of what to do, I introduced myself as Damien's friend.

Which isn't a lie. I'm Damien's *something*.

Debt dance giver? Fuck friend?

We need to talk about that.

Establish something.

After I tell them that, Amara becomes completely at ease with me, even offering for me to babysit her pet goldfish. Clara is nice, but I don't miss the untrusting glances she makes with her every move around the kitchen. I'm waiting for her to shove a knife in her back pocket, just in case I get frisky.

But I must not give off too many crazy vibes. She didn't scream for Antonio.

"Daddy!" Amara squeals, dancing in her stool while sitting at the island.

Antonio and Damien stand in a massive doorway wide enough to fit both their bodies. They're dressed in black suits and both wearing humorless expressions as if it's part of their dress code.

Antonio hasn't formally introduced himself, but I recognize him from the blog post. His lean body is so tense that you'd think it's molded from stone, and his nostrils flare as he stares me down. All the tension in his face dissolves when his gaze slips from me to Amara.

As he stares at his daughter, I move my attention to Damien. His eyes are locked on me, and he pinches the bridge of his nose.

"Uncle Damien!" Amara slides off her stool, wearing pink dinosaur pajamas, and dashes over to him, hugging his legs. She's either not catching on to the serious mood change or just used to these men's stony demeanors. "I met your friend!" She turns to point at me and jumps up and down.

Damien squeezes her shoulders and half smiles down at her. "I see that."

*What's with the sudden coldness?*

Antonio kneels to face Amara and runs his hand along her cheek. "Time to get ready for school."

You can tell he keeps what little gentleness he can summon bottled up for his daughter.

"But my school is here." Amara frowns in confusion. "I never get ready for it."

"How about you get out of your pajamas and get dressed?" Antonio suggests, kissing the top of her hair. "Later, when I get home, we'll go out for ice cream, okay?"

Her face brightens. "Okay!"

57

"Oh, yes," Clara says, circling around the island and walking toward them. "Let's get you dressed, sweetheart."

Amara turns and waves at me. "Bye-bye, Pippa!"

I smile and return the wave.

Clara escorts her out of the kitchen, and as soon as they're out of earshot, Antonio glares at me.

"You need to leave my house," he snaps before shifting his glare to Damien. "Ten minutes, and I want her gone."

Damien nods before locking eyes with me and jerking his head toward the hallway. "Come on. Let's get you home."

Antonio retreats a few steps as if wanting to provide me with plenty of room to pass him. As soon as I'm at Damien's side, he turns and retreats down the hallway. The echo of his shoes hitting the marble flooring is the only sound around us.

"I take it that's Antonio?" I ask Damien.

He nods. "That's Antonio."

"The big, scary boss of the Lombardi family?"

"No, that'd be his father."

I cross my arms, now feeling brave that Antonio is out of sight. "Yeah, well, he acted like a complete"—I pause, leaning in closer and inhaling Damien's cologne, and lower my voice—"ass."

"He doesn't trust people around his daughter," Damien says simply. "Don't take it personal. He doesn't even allow his parents to visit Amara here."

I chew on the edge of my lip, grasping the weight of Damien's words. He brought me into Antonio's sacred place, the place he keeps his daughter safe. And if the rumors I've heard about their world are true, I understand his anger.

I don't know much about Damien's relationship with Antonio, but I have a list of questions I'm mentally adding in my brain.

That doesn't mean Damien will answer them all.

Or any, really.

He seems to be well-rehearsed in the need-to-know-basis language.

---

OUR DRIVE back to my apartment is quiet.

I had this man's cock in my mouth less than twelve hours ago, and now, I can't even ask important questions with said mouth. I mean, he does have a huge dick. Maybe it pushed down my ability to ask crucial questions.

Last night, I didn't ask questions either. Helping him get his hurt off his mind was my intention. I saw this broken man, battered and bruised, and wanted to make him feel better.

It wasn't the time to ask questions. But with the delicate situation, I'm unsure if there'll ever be a right time. I hardly know Damien. What makes me think he'll even confide in me?

I'm a stranger.

A girl with a shady father.

There must be some trust if he brought me to Antonio's. From the look they exchanged in the kitchen, it was clear Damien knew he was crossing a line. But it was also clear that Antonio wouldn't punish him for it.

I glance out the window, people-watching as we pass them. "Are you and Antonio close?"

"We've been close friends since childhood. He's my boss, and I'm also Amara's godfather."

"When you say *boss*, do you mean boss at the casino or boss in another line of work?"

He stares straight ahead, curling his hand tight around the steering wheel. "He's my boss."

*Alllll riiiighty.*

The silence reemerges for the rest of the ride.

"Do you want to come up?" I ask when he parks.

He grabs his key fob from the cupholder and exits the SUV. I open the door, but before I step out, he appears at my side and helps me.

As we walk toward my building, he runs his hand along my shoulders. It's a simple touch but lights my body on fire. We're quiet as we climb the stairs.

"Can I get you something to drink?" I ask when we're inside my apartment.

I've swallowed this man's cum, but I don't even know his drink preferences.

*Pippa the dancing slut over here.*

But Damien doesn't make me feel shame for that.

Somehow, someway, I feel comfortable with every line I've crossed with him.

"I'm good." He loosens his cuff links while I trail him into the living room.

"Let me change out of these clothes really quick." I go to my bedroom to swap my tank and shorts for a loose summer dress.

Damien is in the living room, taking in the space while I sit on the couch.

He slowly does the same.

*Has this man ever allowed anyone to get close to him?*

More-than-sex close?

I shift to face him and cross my legs. "I'm sorry about your family, Damien." My heart aches at what little information he told me. I can't imagine the pain sweeping through him.

His face is blank, and he doesn't say a word.

When I reach out to take his hand, he tenses, causing me to immediately jerk back. He winces as our eyes meet, a wild storm in his. My breathing catches when he grabs my hand and envelops it with his.

I scoot in closer. "What happened?"

His eyes don't meet mine, and his Adam's apple bobs as he

speaks. "A casino competitor blew up my parents' house, killing them, along with my sister and grandparents."

I gasp, covering my mouth with my free hand, and instantly regret my dramatic response. Damien doesn't need theatrics. He needs comfort.

When he came over two nights ago, it wasn't for sympathy. There was so much sadness and pain on his face that it was almost hard to look at. But it was nothing compared to the fury that started to take over his expression.

People grieve in many ways.

Some cry, displaying their sadness.

Others throw themselves in work, projects, anything to get their mind off their grief.

But men like Damien?

Violence is their coping mechanism.

I release my hold from his and crawl onto his lap. "Damien, I'm so sorry."

He opens his arms, allowing me to get comfortable, and grips my waist. My chest rises and falls as I slowly drop a kiss on his mouth. He rolls his tongue between his lips before sliding it along mine. I open for him, allowing it to slip into my mouth.

Our kiss doesn't last long until he rears his head back, cups the back of my head, and shoves his face into my neck. His breathing is heavy along my exposed neck before he starts raining slow kisses over my skin.

He flexes his hips upward, and I shut my eyes when he squeezes my waist before gliding me until I'm grinding against his growing erection.

As he sets a slow pace, I unbutton his shirt and slide it off his shoulders. He roams his fingers under my dress and up my thighs. I continue the pace he set for me.

But just like last time we were on this couch, I want more of him.

I lower my hands to his lap, cupping the outline of his dick, and unbuckle his belt. I freeze when he stops me.

Our eyes lock as he keeps us in place.

"I will kill those men," he flat-out tells me, no bullshit. "Before you ride my cock, I want you to know who I am, who you're getting involved with." He removes his hand from mine on his lap and uses it to cradle my face. "Tell me, my sweet dancer, are you okay with giving yourself to a demented soul like me?"

## 10

# PIPPA

*"Are you okay with giving yourself to a demented soul like me?"*

Those aren't the most romantic words a girl wants to hear before sleeping with a man.

But I have to give it to Damien for his honesty.

While his question teetered on the morbid side, I wish other men would do the same.

If only my exes had said:

*Are you okay with giving yourself to a man who sends nudes to his cousin?*

Or …

*Are you okay with me moving to college and sleeping with an entire sorority to win a bet with my frat brothers?*

While Damien might've asked if I was okay with giving myself to him, it feels like he's almost asking for my soul.

He's also giving me an out. The opportunity to deny him, not take his hand and follow him into his world of darkness.

Too bad that's exactly what I want to do.

*Get to know him.*

*See his world.*

*Show him mine.*

Our eye contact stays unbroken as he allows me all the time I need to respond. Not that I need much time. My body is ready to combust with need for him.

At this point, he could say he plans to chop off a limb after we have sex, and my vagina would ask, *Sure, but can you make me come first?*

I trace the shape of his lips with my finger before venturing them through his cheek scruff, remembering how rough it felt between my legs. In slow motion, I lower it to his hard erection and clench my thighs.

He tries to stifle a groan but can't fully restrain it. "Is that a yes?"

*Is it?*

I flash a playful smile. "Maybe."

"I need to hear you say it with one hundred percent certainty. Tell me that you're ready for me—all of me—and I'll fuck you so good that you'll never regret it."

## 11

# DAMIEN

I sit there, legs spread wide, my cock throbbing in anticipation. Pippa's dress falls over our laps, her panties brushing against my pants-covered erection. My cologne mixes with her perfume, creating the perfect aroma in the air.

It's important she understands who I am. I'll always keep secrets from her.

I'm not deceitful.

I just know it's dangerous for us both.

I've never warned a woman like this. There haven't been many to tell, honestly. I've fucked three women—all of them casual and forced to sign NDAs.

But Pippa is different.

She saw me at my most vulnerable.

At my moment of weakness.

I release a sharp hiss when she rolls her hips forward, her pussy gliding along my cock.

*Fuck, my sweet dancer.*

"Say it, baby." I clamp my hands on her waist, holding her still, and thrust my hips forward. "Say you're ready for all of me because I'm fucking desperate for all of you."

My words linger in the air for only a second before she says, "I want all of you, Damien. I crave your entirety."

Adrenaline dashes through me like I've taken an upper.

I'll fuck her until neither of us can walk for giving me this.

For saying yes and accepting me.

Cupping the back of her head, I tangle my fingers in her hair and tug her closer to devour her mouth.

"Damien," she moans as I pick her up, carrying her to the bedroom.

I flick on the light, and instead of laying her on the bed, I guide her to kneel at my feet.

"You want all of me?" I unbuckle my pants.

Her lust-filled eyes stare up at me in hunger. I'm sure mine are even more intense. Her throat moves as she swallows like she knows I'm about to abuse the fuck out of her throat.

I plunge my hand into her thick hair, my cock throbbing, and yank her face to my crotch. My roughness doesn't deter her. The way her pupils dilate shows more excitement than fear. Her movements are rushed as she shoves down my pants and briefs. My cock springs free, pre-cum already coating the tip.

I grip my length, brushing it along the seam of her plump lips. "Brace yourself for all of me, baby."

My cock twitches, and I gulp down a breath as her warm mouth sucks on the tip of my cock.

Throwing my head back, I groan, "Fuck, Pippa. That's my good girl."

This woman is completely taking me over.

She hasn't even deep-throated me yet, and I'm on the verge of shooting my cum down her throat.

"Take it all," I urge, ramming my hips forward.

Like the good girl she is, she obediently takes my cock deep in her mouth. It fills it perfectly, the tip hitting the back of her throat.

"Fuck yes," I grunt.

*Sinful Sacrifice*

She sucks me deep—*in and out, in and out,* and I get lost in the moment.

I feel possessive of her mouth.

I'm in love with it.

Goddamn addicted.

It doesn't take long until I'm ready to shoot my load down her throat.

But that can't happen yet.

No, I need more than that.

I retreat a step, stopping her, and my cock falls from her lips. "Get ready."

She blinks up at me. "For what?"

"I'm going to fuck your mouth *hard*." I edge closer, my blood thrumming with the need to come. I want to fuck her mouth until it's sore for a goddamn week. "Tap my thigh three times if it becomes too much."

She opens her mouth but doesn't make an argument. Her jaw relaxes, as if ready for whatever I'll unleash upon her. I love how a slight smile tugs at the corners of her mouth. Her eyes are shuttered as I grip my cock, crouch down to her face, and push it inside as deep as I can.

Surprised, she gasps for breaths.

I pause, my quads tensing as my cock fills her mouth. "Breathe in through your nose, baby," I say before pumping my hips. I shove my dick deeper and deeper down her throat.

She chokes, drool spilling down her chin and landing on the rug. But she doesn't complain.

Doesn't do a trio tap on my leg.

She fucking takes it.

Hell, she's moaning.

They're strangled around my cock, but they're moans.

Fuck, what I'd pay to compile a playlist made entirely of Pippa's moans. That shit would win a goddamn Grammy.

I stop her again. Coming down her throat this way will be too

67

much for her. I need her relaxed so she can suck every drop of my cum from my dick.

I step away, lie down on my back, and jerk off. "Now, come drink my cum."

Pippa crawling toward me with a shy smirk is the sexiest thing I've ever seen. She bows her head and gulps down my cock like she's craving my release more than I am.

I spill my cum down her throat. Keeping a tight hold on her head, I don't allow her to move it. My body shakes like an earthquake underneath her.

I rise, separating the distance between us, and haul her to her feet. Not giving a shit how expensive her dress is, I rip it off her body and toss it on the floor. Her panties are the next to go.

"Bed. Now," I demand. "Time for me to make you come on my tongue."

As soon as her body hits the bed, I drop to my knees.

Bow down to my sweet dancer like she bowed down to me.

We're so undeniably made for each other.

I swipe my tongue down her sweet pussy. Every time I taste her, it's better and better. I eat her out and finger-fuck her, sucking on her clit every few seconds until she's falling apart.

As she comes undone, I unbutton my shirt, remove my pants, and throw them aside. Right as I start to climb over her, she points at the nightstand.

"Condom," she says between pants.

It'd be heaven to fuck Pippa bare, but she gets the final say. It's Pippa's pussy, so it's Pippa's choice. Hopefully, she'll feel comfortable enough one day for me to fuck her with no barrier.

I quickly grab the condom and pass it to her. "Put it on me."

She rolls it over my cock, and I grab her ankles, tugging her to the edge of the bed. As I situate my cock at her opening, I appreciate the beauty beneath me. Curly brown hair a wild mess, forming a halo around her head. Her lip gloss smeared, compliments of my cock.

*Sinful Sacrifice*

I keep my grip on one ankle. I've never held something so fragile in my hands. Our eyes lock as I enter her. I don't move, giving her time to adjust to my size.

Even though her pussy is soaked like a fucking river, she's so tight that it still feels like a knot is tied around my cock.

I start out slow. That pace only lasts a few seconds. I lift her by the back of her thighs and pound into her. The sound of our bodies slapping together fills the room.

I let my anger, my frustration, out on her pussy, and she takes it all. She falls apart first, and her body is nearly limp as I lower her to her back and come. I switch out condoms and then fuck her slow and missionary.

By the time we come for the third time, our bodies are exhausted and sore.

I thought the best prescription for my grief was violence.

Turns out, it's Pippa's pussy.

Pippa's mouth around my cock.

And while temporary, it's a pleasant reprieve.

But that doesn't mean I won't kill men after.

WHEN I WAKE up the following morning, Pippa is peacefully sleeping.

I wore my girl out last night. Hell, I wore both of us out. Every muscle in my entire body aches.

I swipe her phone from the nightstand, punch in her passcode, and save my info in her Contacts. When I'm finished, I kneel next to her, brushing her hair from her angelic face.

"I have to go," I whisper. "I saved my number in your phone. Get some rest, baby."

She releases a sleepy yawn. "Can't you stay longer? You need rest too."

"As much as I'd love that, I can't."

She watches me as I stand and walk toward the doorway.

"Be safe, Damien," she says. "I'm here if there's anything I can help with."

I stop in my tracks. "There's actually something, but it's asking a lot."

She props herself up against the headboard. "Tell me."

## 12

# PIPPA

I've attended three funerals in my life—my great-aunt's, my grandfather's, and my sister's goldfish, Speckles.

Sitting in the front-row pew beside Damien, I run my hands over my arms. There's a mixture of sadness and comfort as I listen to Bishop Blake deliver the eulogy.

When I asked Damien if there was anything I could do, I didn't anticipate him saying, "Come to the funeral with me." Our first outing, date, whatever this is, is a funeral.

But I couldn't say no. Damien needs emotional support. His brother, Julian, is here, but he's just as cold as Damien, and he's hardly spoken a word. When Damien introduced us, he tipped his chin toward me—a silent hello—and walked away.

Jesus, these men need a goddamn group therapist.

They chose to have a collective funeral for the family. I eye the framed photos placed atop the caskets.

All of them, gone way too early.

It's heart-wrenching and tragic.

It should also be a warning sign to keep my distance from him.

But right now, I'm too dumb to listen to it.

The air is heavy with grief and quiet sobs from the people packed in the pews around us. Damien's body is a bundle of tension. As the bishop speaks, he rolls his shoulders. I grab his hand and give it a tight, comforting squeeze.

Julian whispers something to Antonio next to him, and he casts a glance at Damien and nods.

When Antonio saw me arrive with Damien, the shock and disapproval were clear on his face. I don't think the man likes anyone other than his daughter.

Once the service ends, a line forms as people approach Damien and Julian, offering their condolences. He introduces me to every single one.

Just as Pippa, nothing more.

I could be the funeral director for all they know.

Everyone's bodies immediately straighten when a short, stocky man with a cane approaches us.

"Pippa, this is Vincent Lombardi," Damien introduces.

*Ah, the notorious crime boss.*

He doesn't look nearly as intimidating as I envisioned in my mind.

Vincent leans forward and shakes my hand. "Thank you for coming, Pippa."

Just as he drops my hand, a man steps out from behind him. "And *who* might this be?"

Vinny Lombardi.

I recognize him from the blog post when I was stalking Damien. The photo matches him to a T. Dark black hair and handsome face. Total Ted Bundy vibes, if you ask me. His good looks serve as a cover for his madness.

Damien tightens his strong jaw, pressing me so close to him that our shoulders collide.

"Vinny Lombardi." He extends his arm while ignoring Damien.

*Sinful Sacrifice*

His arrogance makes sense.

He's next in line to the Lombardi throne.

The man I was initially supposed to meet.

And thank Jesus he was out that day. From the way he rolls his tongue over his lips, I know he wouldn't have shown me the same kindness Damien did.

Not wanting to appear rude, I take his hand. "Pippa."

Just like everyone else, Vinny is only getting my first name.

"Pippa. It's so lovely to meet you." When Vinny lifts my hand to his mouth, Damien inserts himself between us, removing my hand from Vinny's hold.

"That's enough, Vinny," Damien barks.

I stand on my tiptoes to catch Vinny's reaction.

He snarls at Damien, balling up his fist.

"Vinny, son"—Vincent clasps Vinny's shoulder—"I just saw Severino Cavallaro. We need to have a word with him."

Vinny glares at Damien and shakes his head before walking away with his father.

"Damien, you can't punch the Lombardi heir at a funeral," Julian admonishes.

"Why?" Damien snaps. His touch lingers on my shoulder as he steps to my side. "I can blame the violence on my grieving."

Julian points at him. "Valid point."

"My brother, always the fucking asshole." Antonio steps next to Damien and slips his gaze to me. "My apologies, Pippa."

*Wow.*

*All I needed was for Antonio's prick brother to go all creep mode on me to make him nice?*

"Are you okay?" Damien asks, his gaze searching mine.

I smile. "I'm okay."

"Let's get you home."

I nod and offer my condolences to Julian once more.

Holding my hand, Damien leads me through the cathedral.

A knot forms in my stomach, and I freeze when a familiar voice calls my name.

The voice of the person I desperately prayed wouldn't be here.

## 13

# DAMIEN

Pippa's hand clenches in mine when she suddenly stops. As we turn, I spot Cernach Koglin casually strolling toward us. He wobbles with every step in our direction. Two men shadow him like obedient dogs. A pinned Celtic knot is on his lapel. It's rare to see him without Irish symbolism.

I have to commend the man.

He has a deep appreciation for his ancestry.

"Uncle Cernach," Pippa says, curling her lip when he reaches us.

*Uncle?*

*Cernach is her fucking uncle?*

"My sweet Pippa."

When he reaches out to hug her, she backs away. He's unfazed by her reaction.

His hardened eyes center on her for a moment before traveling to me. "You two know each other?"

"Uh …" Pippa stammers.

"Yes," I answer, my tone laced with a touch of impatience as I state the obvious.

I hold back my curiosity about this newly learned connection with Boston's infamous crime lord. I'm pissed at myself for not doing better research and missing that. But I act casual, concealing that this is new news.

"Interesting." He taps his chubby finger along the edge of his mouth.

One of his men steps behind him. I recognize his face but can't put a name to it. We rarely engage in business dealings with the Irish.

"Excuse us," I tell them. "We have somewhere to be."

When I place my touch on Pippa's lower back, the stiffness in her body eases. Nodding at both men, I quickly guide her away. I'll question her about this in private.

And I have plenty of goddamn questions.

I MIGHT WORK for the Lombardi family, but my trust in them isn't unconditional. When it comes to complete trust, only Julian and Antonio make the cut. So did my father before his death.

Trust is sacred to me.

It must be earned.

Proven over time.

I take Pippa home after the funeral before attending the repast. As soon as we reach her apartment building, she unbuckles her seat belt and rushes inside. I want to chase her, but I have to be at the reception. Julian needs me. Saying goodbye to our family is tearing pieces of our hearts out.

Pippa being with me at the funeral made a difference. When she's around, some of my loneliness fades away. She brings me a sense of calm. She's the person I didn't realize I needed during moments of grief.

IT'S past midnight when I silently drive back to her apartment. I park my SUV, buzz myself in, and take the stairs two at a time. As I gently rap on the door, I can't help but think about the inconvenience of not having a key. If she won't provide me with one, I'll pay her landlord to make me a copy.

After the third knock, she answers, as if expecting me. She's dressed in black pajamas with small coffee cups printed on them. Her hair is thrown back in a messy bun, strands flying in every direction, and her eyes look tired.

"You never told me your relation to Cernach," I say, walking inside.

She scrambles back a few steps so we don't run into each other, and I catch a whiff of her sweet body wash as I pass.

She shuts the door behind us. "I didn't know it was necessary."

I turn to face her. "He's the head of the Boston Irish mob."

"Who I have no relationship with."

"I assume the relation is on your mother's side?"

No fucking way is Paul affiliated with Cernach. He'd kill him before allowing a family member to bring shame with unpaid debt and gambling addictions.

She nods. "He's my mother's brother."

*Ah.* I've heard stories of Cernach's sister. Cernach ousted her for running off to Vegas and marrying some loser. The loser being Paul. He already had her contracted to marry another man, and she broke that agreement. Cernach cut her off from the family and all allowances. If one family takes arranged marriage seriously, it's the Koglins.

"Today is the first time I've seen him in years." She crosses her arms.

I detest her relation to him. I'm not stupid. I recognized the familiar look in Cernach's eyes when he saw us together to know what's coming. He might've kicked her mother to the curb for disobedience, but he now sees Pippa as a bargaining chip. It's how men like him think.

Years ago, I swore I'd never drag a woman into this world. I saw what it did to my mother. And even though she handled it well—the woman was a goddamn saint—I saw the burdens she endured.

But Pippa is changing my mind.

I want to drag her into my purgatory.

Make her shine some light in my darkness.

Antonio advised me to end it with her after learning about Cernach. He isn't a Koglin fan, so that doesn't surprise me. But even though I know her bloodline will create a trifecta of issues, I can't bring myself to let her go.

## 14

# PIPPA

I DROP my dance bag on the floor with a thud and collapse on the couch in exhaustion. It's been more than a week since I last saw Damien, but he's stayed in touch through texts and calls.

He calls every night before I go to sleep.

And every morning, like clockwork, he texts.

In this short time, he's become a staple in my life.

He's also a different man than the one who dragged me out of the casino. While he's doing a decent job of hiding his pain, I notice it beneath the surface and hear the sorrow in his voice.

Losing his family broke him, but with his upbringing, he won't allow himself to expose it. Mafia men aren't allowed to be broken.

They're only allowed to do the breaking.

I'm also pissed the fuck off at everyone in the Lombardi family for not forcing Damien to take time off to mourn his family. Instead, he's been busy nonstop. Coldhearted Mafia bastards.

I stand and head toward the kitchen for a glass of water. A knock on the door interrupts me. Making a detour, I peek through the peephole.

*Oh, hell to the no.*

"How the hell does he know where I live?" I grumble.

Cernach has never visited my apartment.

He's here for a reason.

I have a strong suspicion it has something to do with my new Mafia friend.

*Sorry, Uncle Demon, not today.*

*Or tomorrow, or the next, or the next.*

I tiptoe away from my door, trying my hardest to stay quiet, but my creaky floorboards become traitors. God, how I wish he'd remove me from the family tree and toss me aside like a rotten apple.

"I know you're in there, Pippa." He pounds his fist against the door. "Open the door, or I'll break it down."

Knowing my uncle, that's not an empty threat.

He'd kick it down *and* get me evicted.

"Asshole," I mutter as I yank open the door.

There he stands.

Certified asshole uncle of the century, wearing a posh navy-blue suit, alligator shoes, and his Celtic knot pin. My mom told me a story once about him mercilessly plunging the pin into a man's eyeball until it became a pulpy mess.

"I'll overlook your disrespect of ignoring my knock." His heavy-boned body barges past me and inside my apartment.

A man wearing a fedora follows him. I narrow my eyes as I spot the dirt trail from his shoes.

I slam my door shut. "Is there something I can help you with, Uncle?"

"Lose the attitude, you little bitch," he snarls, advancing closer to jab his pudgy finger in my face. "Remember who you're speaking to."

I slam my mouth shut. While I can't lose my attitude, I'll misplace it for now. All I want is for him to say what he wants and leave.

He steps back and checks out my place like a real estate agent ready to make an offer. "You're going to marry Damien."

I burst out in laughter.

While I was prepared for something like this, I didn't expect it to sound so cliché. The mob boss ordering a marriage.

*Give me a break.*

He tried to pull the same crap with my mother, but it didn't work. He should know disobedience runs in my blood. I'll lose that blood before I ever give in to him.

"I'm not laughing," he snaps.

"Are you insane? We barely know each other."

I want the whole nine yards before I marry someone.

The pursuit. The special dates. The flirting. The drops to one knee and proposes. No way am I settling for less.

"Yes, and what's your point?" Cernach touches a photo of my mother and me at my first dance recital. "He seems to be infatuated with you, though I'm not sure why."

*Okay, rude.*

Another reason I hate him. For some reason, he thinks of me as trash floating around New York streets.

"You're basing that assumption on just a one-minute-long conversation with us?"

"I read people like a book, Pippa."

"What's in it for you if I marry him?"

"The Lombardis have good connections and would make a solid ally."

"No, thank you." I grimace. "Find another pawn to use for connections." My stomach twists. "What did you tell my mother years ago? We're dead to you and the entire Koglin family? Please continue that frame of thinking. I'd appreciate it."

As he puts the frame back, his blond-red brows furrow. "It won't be long before your mother needs my help."

"We'll be fine without you," I sneer. "We have been for years."

Fedora Man shakes his head like a disappointed father.

"I'd barely call this," Cernach says, slowly taking in my living space, "living." He puckers his lips as if I live in filth. "You'll be coming to me for help soon enough. And when you do, it'll be with the understanding that you marry Damien."

Cernach walks toward the door. Just before he reaches it, he swings out his arm and sends a row of photos crashing to the ground. They all shatter.

Stepping over the glass, he motions his head toward it. "That won't be the only mess I'll create if you play with me, girl." He menacingly smirks.

As soon as they leave, I rush to the door, frantically bolting the lock behind them. I rest against it while catching my breath. After counting to ten, I retreat to my living room to clean up the glass mess.

Ten minutes later, there's another knock on my door.

*God, what does he want now?*

*A fucking kidney?*

Probably wants to bludgeon it with his stupid pin.

I swing the door open. "I said no, Cernach—" I retreat a step at the realization it's not Cernach, thank God.

Two women stand in front of me. One with messy brown curls and the other with bright maroon hair. Darcy and Genesis. I recognize them from the funeral.

"Hi, Pippa." Darcy adjusts her Chanel bag on her shoulder.

My gaze bounces between them as I search for answers. "Hi."

Genesis's smile puts me at ease. "Damien sent us to help get you ready for your date."

"I'm sorry ..." I blink at them. "Date?"

Darcy nods.

Since I don't know what to do and definitely don't want Cernach overhearing us, I wave them inside. As soon as Genesis shuts the door behind her, I speed-walk to the couch for my phone to call Damien.

"Darcy and Genesis are here to help me with a date I have no clue about," I say as soon as he picks up.

"They're taking you out for the day. Spoil yourself, and I'll pick you up at eight." He hangs up.

I drop my phone on the couch. "I guess I'm going on a date tonight."

Genesis squeals.

Darcy grins.

---

TWO YEARS.

That's how long it's been since I've gone on a date.

I still have date PTSD from that one.

A girl from my barre class set me up with her brother. He was an hour late, took me to a steak house despite knowing I was a vegetarian, and conveniently "forgot" his wallet. I ended up paying for both my side salad and his one-hundred-dollar porterhouse. After that, I blocked his number.

I decided I'd find a man the traditional way.

No, not by arranged marriages or offering up a dowry.

*Through fate.*

Eventually, I'm destined to come across a hot guy in a coffee shop or on a train.

Or have a wild incident where a handsome man threatens me in a casino.

Not that dating has been a priority for me. My life revolves around dance and my family. Your family's survival becomes a priority when your father squanders every penny gambling.

That's the reason I moved out.

Not a piggy bank is safe in the Elsher household.

Genesis and Darcy practically pull me out of my apartment. I don't put up much of a fight, though. They just lost their best friend. They could ask to move in with me, and I'd say yes.

We pile into Darcy's white BMW. I take the back seat, my mind buzzing with questions, but stay quiet during the drive.

"Here we are," Genesis says, parking in front of Serenebelle, an upscale spa nestled between New York skyscrapers.

Not that I've ever stepped foot inside.

The local news recently showcased it as the city's premier spa destination. Celebrities come here. I also stumbled upon a blog post titled, "Places in New York None of Us Peasants Can Afford." Serenebelle was listed as number three.

I follow them into the spa, and a gentle breeze carries the scent of essential oils through the air. The desk clerk beams, circles the counter, and greets Genesis and Darcy by name.

"This is our friend Pippa," Darcy introduces.

"Susie!" calls out the clerk, whose name tag reads Vera.

A frazzled blonde—Susie, I assume—scrambles toward us, carrying a tray of champagne glasses. Only minus the champagne. There isn't a trace of fizziness in them.

"Care for a spagarita?" Susie asks, already handing me one.

I smile, taking it from her. Taking a sip, I taste a lavender-infused water and refreshing tang of lemon.

It's also giving *no liquor*.

"We'll do facials first, then massages, then hair and nails," Vera says, motioning us forward.

The spa is a peaceful oasis, a vacation within the chaos of the city. Soothing music plays in the background, combined with the gentle sound of a waterfall flowing along the path to the changing rooms. Vera leads me into a room where a robe that smells like the spagarita hangs on a hook.

If you don't count the five-dollar face masks I buy, this is my first true facial and spa experience.

I undress, slip on the robe, and check my phone.

*Sinful Sacrifice*

No calls or texts from Damien.

Frowning, I gather my hair into a lopsided ponytail and join Genesis and Darcy in the facial room. They're sitting next to each other in massage chairs. I smile at each of them before taking the chair beside Darcy. As I settle and turn on my massage settings, the estheticians enter the room, starting our facials.

"Thank you for attending the funeral with Damien." Darcy slips her gaze to me. "He probably won't admit it, but it relaxed him. I could tell."

"Agreed." Genesis nods and sips her spagarita.

My face softens at the compliment. "You and Melissa were best friends?" I ask, referring to Damien's sister.

"Since we were babies." Genesis gestures toward Darcy. "Our parents called us the Trouble Trio."

"Her death has been hard," Darcy adds. "When Damien called and asked us to bring you here, it kind of brightened our day. It's nice, getting out of the house."

"Serenebelle was Mel's favorite," Genesis says. "We always came here for her birthday. Damien's treat." Her face mask gets smudged when she wipes a tear off her cheek.

The esthetician leans in and fixes it for her.

Darcy grabs Genesis's hand, giving it a comforting squeeze. "She'll always be here with us."

Genesis sniffles and nods.

Darcy gives Genesis's hand another squeeze before flitting her gaze to me. "Melissa would've liked you. You're good for Damien."

I shift in my chair. "Has he done this for any other woman?"

"No," Genesis replies with total certainty. "And we'd know since he would've asked Mel to do it."

I smile to myself at her response.

*Only me.*

By the end of our spa day, I'm swinging my arms through the air as we walk toward Darcy's car. Tia, my massage therapist, had hands of a god. Turns out, my shoulders were as tense as a rod, and my neck was a mess of knots. My dance coaches always suggested massages, but I never had the extra money.

No one has ever spoiled me like this.

We listen to Darcy's Hot Girl Playlist on the ride home, the three of us singing loudly to the songs. When we're back at my building, Darcy pops the trunk and pulls out three garment bags.

"What are those?" I ask.

"Oh, just a surprise for you," Darcy sings out, handing me one of the bags.

I take it, and Genesis holds the door open for us.

"That massage made my legs feel like rubber," Genesis groans as we walk up the stairs. "They're turning into Jell-O more with each step."

We enter my apartment, and I hang the bags over the couch.

"For you, from Damien." Darcy pulls a black jewelry box from her purse and holds it out toward me.

My face brightens, my body feeling all bubbly as I take it from her. They crowd around me while I carefully open it.

A handwritten note lies on top.

> MY SWEET DANCER, WEAR THIS ON OUR DATE. TONIGHT, I'LL SPOIL YOU LIKE YOU DESERVE. MAYBE WE CAN END THE NIGHT WITH YOU DANCING FOR ME.
> —DAMIEN

I run my finger over his name.

His handwriting is smooth and simple.

Easy to read with no swirls or dashes.

"Can we read it?" Genesis peeks over my shoulder but still gives me space in case I say no.

"Let's let the girl keep her romantic note to herself," Darcy tells her.

I smile, a small laugh slipping from my lips.

I like them. Maybe I'll ask for their numbers and see if we can hang out again sometime.

I remove the note, and we gasp in awe, nearly in sync, at the gold necklace underneath it.

I've never seen such a unique piece of jewelry.

It's stunning and definitely one of a kind.

The rope features a pattern of rubies and diamonds. Two charms hang in the center—a ballet slipper and a deck of cards, each embellished with more diamonds.

"Holy shit," Darcy says. "That is gorgeous."

I stare at the necklace, nearly bug-eyed, too nervous to take it out.

Terrified I'll drop it.

"Want me to help you put it on?" Genesis offers.

My eyes meet her brown ones as I carefully take out the necklace and pass it to her.

With the same caution as I had, she grips it tight. "Let's go to the mirror so you can see yourself."

They follow me to the full-length mirror in my bedroom. Genesis stands behind me. Since she's nearly four inches taller than me, she easily sees my reflection.

Darcy stands by my side as Genesis clasps the necklace around my neck. My heart is on fire as I rest my hand on the necklace. I press it into my skin as if wanting to fuse it there. We take a moment of silence to appreciate the beauty of the necklace.

"It's gorgeous, Pippa," Genesis says, brushing her fingers along my shoulder.

"You are gorgeous," Darcy adds. "Have a great time tonight, babe. You'll find dress options in the garment bags on the couch."

I nod, dancing my fingers over the charms.

*The dancer.*

*The deck of cards for his life at the casino.*

My heart flutters.

Ten minutes later, I hug them goodbye. "Thank you so much for today."

I'm on top of the world, still wearing the necklace, and unzip the garment bags to find three stunning dresses.

The price tags are missing, but the labels reveal each one is more expensive than anything I'd ever be able to afford.

"Two hours," I mutter to myself, checking the time. "Two hours until he's here."

# 15

# PIPPA

Damien knocks on my door at 7:58.

Nervously tugging at my sleeves, I walk to the door. I spent an hour deciding which dress to wear, trying on each one three times before choosing a linen-silk corset dress with long, wispy sleeves.

A chill runs up my spine when I answer to find him standing in front of me.

"Baby." He swipes his thumb along the edge of his mouth. His dark eyes roam down my figure before returning to mine. He runs his tongue across his lips. "You look gorgeous."

If any other man gave me that kind of stare down, I'd call him a disrespectful ass. But with Damien, it feels romantic and makes me feel beautiful.

I have no shame in doing the same with him. Even though he's shaved, his familiar five-o'clock shadow is still etched on his jawline and cheeks. Fallen strands of hair brush his thick eyebrows. I appreciate his black suit and crisp navy button-up that hug his body just right.

"Thank you," I say softly.

"You ready to go?" He offers me his hand. "The car is waiting."

He clasps mine tightly, escorting me downstairs. The sun casts a graceful orange hue across the sky when we walk outside.

"New wheels?" I ask when he stops us at a black Escalade and opens the door.

"We have a driver tonight." He assists me in the back seat, and I settle against the leather.

An older man in the driver's seat peers over his shoulder at me and smiles. "Hi, Pippa. I'm Augusto."

I return the smile and wave. "Hey, Augusto."

Damien ducks into the back seat with me, sliding over until our thighs are pressed together. Our closeness steals my breath, and I rest my hand on my leg to calm myself. He always gets a reaction out of me.

"L'ultima Cena," he instructs Augusto.

Augusto salutes him. "You got it."

Damien reaches forward and pushes a button. A black panel rises, creating a privacy barrier between us and Augusto.

"Is it weird for me to say I've missed you even though we don't know each other that well?" I ask.

"Not weird at all since I missed you like fucking crazy." He turns to face me, and I close my eyes as he runs his hand over my face. "You're like my goddamn Xanax when I'm having a stressful day."

"Hmm, I think it's time I refill that script for you."

If there's a scale for cheesy lines, that might proclaim the top spot.

He runs his fingers along the necklace, sliding beneath it, and traces my collarbone. "Do you like it?"

A rush of tingles cascades through my veins.

I slip my hand under the necklace, pressing it against his and intertwining our fingers. "I love it and how it represents us both, making us come as one together."

He spreads his fingers open, running them along my chest. "I love when we come as one together."

My breathing quickens, and I'm rubbing my thighs together when he leans in and whispers, "Your pussy is wet, isn't it?" His hand slowly travels under my dress, brushing my thigh. "It wants my mouth on it, doesn't it, baby?"

*Oh my freaking Godddd.*

*This man and his mouth.*

He's really driving that mouth point hard.

It's a struggle to hide my smile as I nod.

He leans in close, his mouth only inches from mine. "We'll have a nice dinner, and then I'll have you for dessert."

My throat tightens as I gulp, and I nod again.

It's the only reaction I can manage at the moment.

Otherwise, we won't make it to dinner. I'm tempted to straddle him right now.

*Who is this woman?*

I've never been so desperate for a man's touch.

Never thought about riding his cock in a back seat.

"I can tell Augusto to take a trip around the block," Damien says, flicking his tongue along the seam of my lips, reading my mind. "I'll finger-fuck you until you come on my hand, and then we'll enjoy a nice dinner." He turns my head and sucks on my neck.

I shudder, blowing out a series of breaths.

*I do want that.*

Gripping his shoulders, I crawl onto his lap. Just as I settle myself, the Escalade stops. I peer out the tinted window, seeing we've arrived at L'ultima Cena. A large body of people is crowded around the door.

Damien caresses my cheek with his knuckle. "I can tell him to keep going."

"No, it's fine." I tip my head forward. "We're here, and people are staring."

"They can't see in."

He pushes my panties to the side and plunges his fingers inside me. I rise some on my knees, allowing him a better angle, and shove my face into his neck to cover my moans.

I pull back when the door opens, and Damien yanks it back closed with his free hand. After locking it, he cracks the window.

"Give us a minute," he snaps.

"But, sir—" a man starts.

Damien raises his voice. "Give us a minute, or you'll lose your job."

"Apologies, sir," the man stutters.

I hear voices coming from the other side of the door, but no one is speaking to us any longer.

"We shouldn't do this," I whisper.

Instead of answering, Damien returns to thrusting his fingers inside me. I've never felt so inside out. His fingers feel so good, and I tell him that around a moan.

As I grow closer, I ride his hand, throwing my head back and pushing myself against his lap. I can feel his cock growing harder underneath me.

"Yes, baby," Damien groans. "Come for me."

And that's exactly what I do.

I'm catching my breath, and as I lean back, he gently pulls his fingers from my pussy. With his other hand, he fixes my hair and wipes away my smudged makeup.

"Do you want to clean your fingers?" I ask him.

He raises a brow. "Fuck no. I want this shit to soak into my skin like a goddamn moisturizer." He sucks on them, making a slurping sound.

I shyly look away and cast a glance at the door.

"Take all the time you need," he says.

"People are behind us, waiting."

"And? They're of no importance to me. You're my only concern."

When I'm finished fixing myself the best I can, he smiles up at me. "The way your cheeks blush after you orgasm is gorgeous. If I could find that shade of pink, I'd ink it onto my skin."

He smacks a kiss on my lips and helps me off his lap.

When he finally opens the door, we step out. Augusto is waiting, as if he was standing guard.

We're the center of attention as Damien leads me from the SUV to the entrance. I avoid making eye contact with people. I'm nervous they're furious we held up the line. No one says anything when he cuts in line to the hostess stand.

"Mr. Bellini," the hostess greets. "Welcome! We're so happy you could join us. I'll show you to your table."

L'ultima Cena is far from your typical Italian restaurant. To get reservations, you either have to be someone important or have Mafia connections. There's always been speculation about its close ties to mob families and how they dine in the private rooms in the back. They turn a blind eye to crimes committed here. The translation of the name even means *last supper.*

We follow the hostess to the table as the scent of fresh garlic and pasta lingers in the air. A white cloth is draped over our table in the corner of the room. Damien blocks the hostess from pulling out my chair, doing it himself. He lightly touches my shoulder and plants a kiss on my hair as I sit.

"I wasn't sure if we'd go into a back room," I comment before immediately regretting it. It's what I do when I'm nervous —say things I shouldn't.

*Those are only rumors, right?*

Probably not, but I don't want to give him any ideas to take me to the private rooms where people are supposedly murdered while others eat lasagna.

Damien, unfazed by my comment, unrolls his silverware. "I thought I'd go gentle on our first date."

*Gentle.*

Finger-fucking me in the car sure as heck wasn't *gentle.*

Blame it on my environment and how he can't go gentle or rough with me at the moment, I grow a little ballsy.

"What if I don't want gentle?" I ask, that ballsy-ness turning a little shyer.

He raises a brow. "I'll gladly arrange that ... *after* we leave here. As much as I'd love to fuck you on this table, I can't have other men seeing your beautiful body. I'd have to slit their throats with my steak knife."

So romantic. So violent. So dreamy.

So *something is ridiculously wrong with my head.*

"Welcome to L'ultima Cena."

I jump at the server's masculine voice.

He's a tall, middle-aged man wearing a white button-down shirt with L'ultima Cena stitched into the left corner of his chest.

"Hello, I'm Tony, your server for tonight." He smiles, his teeth an overbleached bright white. "Have you dined with us before?"

Damien nods.

I shake my head. "First-timer."

"Welcome." Tony bows his head in my direction. "May I interest you in our wine selection?" He hands the booklet to Damien without waiting for a response.

Damien takes it from him and passes it to me. "We'll have a bottle of whatever she orders."

My eyes widen at being put on the spot. I nervously flip through the wine list, pretending to know what I'm looking for.

I have no freaking idea.

I don't drink fancy wines.

I drink stuff I can buy in the grocery aisle or in small bars during girls' nights.

Tony taps his pen against his notepad.

Swear to God, I'm so close to just blurting out I'll take a bottle of Capri-Sun when I think to ask, "What are your recommendations?"

He pauses his tapping. "I recommend our Petrus 2018 or Dom Pérignon Magnum."

Dom Pérignon.

I've heard about that in enough songs and episodes of *Cribs*.

But I don't want to order it and sound cliché either.

"We'll take the Petrus 2018." I hand him the wine list, feeling more self-assured.

Tony's gaze whips to Damien, his mustache furrowing. "Is that okay, sir? It's one of our highest-priced bottles on the menu."

My stomach sinks.

Of course. Leave it to me to choose the highest-priced bottle on the menu. I should've ordered a damn Capri-Sun at this point.

I gulp, crossing my legs and then uncrossing them.

"Why are you asking me?" Damien snarls at Tony, but his tone is relaxed. "I told you, we'll have what she orders. That's what she ordered, so that's what we'll have." He leans back in his chair while fixing his harsh stare on Tony. "For the rest of the evening, if she orders it, you bring it. I don't give a fuck if she asks for the entire menu. Understood?"

My eyes widen.

Just like with everything Damien-related, this behavior shouldn't turn me on. But it does.

"Certainly, sir," Tony says with a slight stutter before scurrying away from the table.

"You didn't have to do that," I tell Damien before taking a sip of water, hoping to wash down the excitement between my legs.

"Yes, I did." Damien levels his stare at me as if he's giving me life-changing advice. "Always demand respect, Pippa."

"I didn't mean to order the most expensive wine. I'm sorry."

"I don't care how much anything is you order." He skims his finger along the rim of his glass. "I wanted to know your drink of choice."

"Honestly, that isn't it. I just didn't know what else to say. I'm more of a cheap-wine girl."

"You could be a chocolate-milk girl for all I care. I want to make sure my home is stocked with the things you like. I think it's time we have some sleepovers at my place."

My heart thuds. For a man considered so dangerous, Damien makes me feel safe, adored, special.

Tony returns with the wine and presents the bottle to me as if he were a game-show host revealing a prize. "Would you like a sampling first?"

I peer at Damien, but he only provides me with a *you're the boss* expression.

"No, you can go ahead and pour."

Tony fills my glass first, then Damien's, and we order.

Once Tony is gone, Damien dips his fingers into his wine—the same digits that were inside me in the SUV—and swirls them in the glass. I watch the liquid swish around the rim and swallow his fingers.

He drags his fingers from the glass, sticks them in his mouth, sucks hard, and groans. "Now, this might be my favorite drink of all time. Pippa's cum mixed with alcohol. A fucking delicacy."

Blushing, I rub my thighs together, trying to alleviate the tingling between my legs. "Your dirty mouth ..."

"Loves doing dirty things to your pussy," he finishes for me before reaching forward and dragging those same fingers over my lips. "Open."

I do as he said, too modest to look anywhere else but him. Everyone's eyes could be on us, and I wouldn't know. He slides his fingers into my mouth for only a brief second before pulling back.

He straightens himself in his chair, as if completing his goal of making me hornier for him. "How was your spa day?"

"Amazing," I say, swallowing our taste and relaxing my shoulders.

"Schedule yourself for one monthly, then. Tell them to bill me."

My mouth drops open. "Are you serious?"

"Unless there's another spa you'd like to go to? I can arrange that as well."

"No, I mean, like, *are you serious* to paying for that again? That place is crazy expensive."

He grabs his wineglass. "And?"

"And it's *crazy expensive*." I stress the last two words as if he's not understanding.

"Did it make you feel spoiled?"

"Well, yes."

"Then, I don't care how *crazy expensive* it is. Schedule yourself a day. If you don't, I'll have Genesis and Darcy kidnap you again." He takes a long swig of wine. "Besides the spa, did you do anything else?"

My body tightens.

*Does he know about Cernach coming to my apartment?*

There was no missing the disdain on Damien's face when he found out our relation at the funeral.

I play with my napkin in my lap. "Work, dance, then home before the girls came and we went to the spa." I smile and raise my fingers to the necklace, playing with it. "Another thank-you for making my day so special."

"When can I watch you dance?"

A flush runs down my neck. "I think you already have."

He cracks a smile, as if reliving the memory. "While I *love* that dancing, when can I watch you perform for an audience that isn't only me? I want to see you in your natural environment."

"I get too nervous when people I'm close with watch me."

"Just act like I'm not there."

"If I have any upcoming shows, I'll let you know."

"How did you start dancing?" He laces his fingers together

and leans closer, resting his elbows on the table, giving me his full attention.

I'm thankful for the conversation change. "My mom was a dancer, and for as long as I can remember, I knew I wanted to follow in her footsteps."

"Why are you working at the coffee shop instead of something dance-related?"

"Stalking me?" I tease.

"Doing my research."

I sigh, a pang of sadness hitting me. "My mom had a studio I used to teach at. I loved working there, especially with the younger kids." My shoulders slump. "She doesn't have the studio anymore, hence why I'm at the coffee shop."

"What happened to her studio?"

"Someone burned it down." I squeeze my eyes shut at the memory of the day we found out. The studio was reduced to nothing but ashes.

"Do you think your father had something to do with it?"

"He either did it for the insurance money or someone he'd pissed off did it."

"Can you not work at another studio?"

"If I worked for a studio that wasn't hers, she'd see me as a traitor. Even though she broke her *loyalty* to her family when she married my father, she still believes it should be held in other circumstances. She wants me to wait until she's able to open another studio. Until that happens, I'll stay at Brew Bliss."

My mother grew up in a Mafia-ran home, and while she doesn't follow everything to their code, loyalty is important to her.

You don't work for another family's business.

You tough it out with yours, no exceptions.

Sacrifices are always made in life. You must think about the good of your family before personal happiness. That's why I sacrificed my dream of finishing school to support hers of running a successful dance studio.

He nods in understanding. "I get that. Family over everything. It's been my way of life as well."

"What about you?" I ask. "What have you been up to?"

He cradles his glass in his hand, gently tapping his fingers against it. "Working."

"Working?" I repeat slowly.

He holds his glass with two fingers. "Yes, working."

"In the city?"

"Here and there."

"Are you finished working *here and there*?"

"As much as I can. I prefer to work here. New York is and always will be my home."

I nod, sipping my wine. It's decent-tasting. Not the-most-expensive-wine-on-the-list quality—in my opinion—but still decent.

"Your uncle Cernach got in contact with me," he says, straight-faced.

I recoil at the subject change.

I'd rather speak about anyone or anything. At this point, I'd have no problem going in detail about when I started my period at school. I was nicknamed Shark Week for the entire year.

"Samesies." I frown. "He came to my apartment today."

"According to him, you'd like me to propose to you?"

I spit my wine back into my glass. Sure, Cernach mentioned it to me, but I didn't expect for it to go further after I said no.

"Excuse me?" I say after composing myself.

"I take it you don't want me to propose, then?" He stares at me, skeptical, like maybe my goal was to reel him in for some business deal.

"Uh, negative," I say.

Doubt is still on his face.

"If you were to get down on one knee and propose to me right now, no offense, but I would say no."

"Should I test that theory?" He sets his glass on the table and starts to stand, gaining the attention of diners.

I dart my hand across the table to stop him. "Oh my God, no!"

He sits back down.

"You don't trust me," I mutter.

"I don't know you enough to trust you."

"Yet I'm supposed to trust you?"

"Yes."

"Pot, meet kettle."

We're interrupted by Tony and the food runner delivering our main course. I pick up my fork, waiting for Damien to do the same, but he doesn't. My heart races at how intense his stare is.

Damien clears his throat when they're gone. "If we're being honest, I'd have no problem marrying you, Pippa."

I blow out a breath, shocked I don't fall out of my chair.

My heart pulsates in my chest at his declaration.

As good as it feels, all it means is one thing: If I ever marry Damien, there will always be the thought that Cernach is getting what he wants.

"That wasn't to scare you," he says. "I see that you're clearly uncomfortable with the idea."

I'll always be uncomfortable with it. My mother has told me too many horror stories of arranged marriages for me to even think of agreeing to one. The family chooses your spouse, divorces aren't allowed, and if the husband hurts you in any way, it's your fault, not theirs.

My mother's older sister's husband was a monster, and eventually, she took her own life, seeing it as the only escape from him. When you enter an arranged marriage as a woman, you sign your freedom away.

It'll be a cold day in hell before I let that happen.

I also refuse to give Cernach anything he wants. If he wants a marriage with Damien, I'll never give that to him.

"Can we talk about something else?" I whisper.

"Yes, *after* I tell you this," Damien replies. "We might not have a contract that puts a ring on your finger and marries us, but you're mine."

*You're mine.*

Two simple words, but they make my heart swoon.

### Three Hours Later

I MOAN when Damien slams my body against the wall, his hand up my dress. He slips my panties off, shoving his fingers inside with no warning.

My heart is racing.

My pulse wild.

My clit throbs for him.

It's like my body has become completely dependent on this man's touch.

This time, as if he came prepared, he pulls a condom from his wallet and rolls it on his hard cock. He shoves my dress aside, squats, and pushes inside me. My head bangs against the wall every time he thrusts inside me.

This man makes me feel good all the time, every time.

I went into this thinking it was a fling.

My time with the bad boy.

But this organ inside my chest is beginning to open up to him.

And I'm worried he'll rip it apart.

## 16

# PIPPA

"I'D LIKE TO OFFER A SUGGESTION," Damien says, barging into my apartment.

Last night was amazing. After he fucked me against the wall, he fucked me in my bed, then fucked me again in the shower. Nothing has ever felt so perfect before.

And this time, when I woke up, the other side of my bed wasn't empty. Damien was propped up against the headboard, shirtless, with his phone in his hand.

Twenty minutes ago, he left for a coffee run while I contemplated life before rolling my lethargic ass out of bed. Somehow, I have no problem pulling hours-long dance practices, yet I'm exhausted after a night of being fucked by Damien.

He's freshly showered and clean for the day while I'm dressed in a tank and sweat shorts, my hair swept back in a slick bun. I have the day off from Brew Bliss and no dance practice.

"What's that?" I ask as he hands me the coffee. I walk into the living room and settle on the couch, stretching out my legs.

"You move somewhere without a thousand fucking steps." He sets down his coffee to collect my feet in his hands. He positions my legs to create room for him to drop onto the couch and settles my sock-covered feet on his lap.

"The rent is fair, and it's all I can afford." I shrug and sip my coffee.

"You could move in with me."

I gulp to stop myself from spitting out my coffee.

A heads-up that he's offering batshit crazy ideas would've been nice.

The urge to laugh hits me, but I don't because when his eyes meet mine, there's no humor in them. He's serious.

I raise my cup in a *hold it, mister* gesture. "We've had one *official* date. If we're counting in terms of steps, we need about fifty more of"—I pause to gesture back and forth between us—"*this* before even thinking about living together."

I worked my ass off to move into this apartment, and it wasn't easy to find. I won't give it up for a short-term relationship.

"I'm not a fan of steps." He leans forward, his six-pack pressing against my feet, and snatches his cup.

"Steps give you exercise." I smirk as he makes himself comfortable again. "Cardio. A *great ass.*"

"Use me as your exercise." He takes a sip of coffee, staring at me in question over the rim.

"You're a busy man."

"Never too busy for you."

While I try to turn the conversation playful, he's still serious.

Like he's laying out the perfect business deal in a board meeting.

"Your building also has shitty security," he continues. "You're not protected here."

I frown. "I don't need security. I've lived here for over a year without one problem."

"You absolutely need security."

"Why?"

"Because of your relation to your uncle." He drums his fingers against the Styrofoam cup before settling it on the table. He tips his head back and cracks his neck.

The mention of Cernach gives me a sudden chill, and I wrap my arms around myself. "My uncle doesn't exist in my life."

"Maybe he didn't before, but he sure does now." He massages my feet, causing me to squirm, and lowers his voice. "We could have him draft a contract, see what he wants."

The mood of the morning has shifted. We woke up and had morning sex, and he showered before leaving for coffee. All was good in the Damien and Pippa world, but now, he wants to talk Cernach and contracts?

"What sort of contract?" I hate that I already know the answer.

"An arranged marriage contract." He shrugs as if his suggestion wouldn't be completely life-changing.

My head spins as I furiously shake it. "Arranged marriages aren't for me."

"What is for you then, Pippa?" His eyes stay pinned on me as he kneads his knuckle into my heel.

"I'd need a year of dating *minimum* before I ever considered accepting a marriage proposal."

And that marriage proposal had better not be anything Cernach-involved. Otherwise, I wouldn't care if it'd been a decade. It'd be an automatic no.

He opens his mouth, but I continue speaking. "I'd also need a hundred-word essay on what kind of husband he'd be."

Marrying me won't be easy.

Unlike my mother, I won't elope in Vegas.

I want it to be perfect.

And that includes not allowing someone to select my husband.

He runs his free hand up my leg. "I believe those are referred to as vows."

"No, *vows* are what's said during the ceremony. I need a prologue to the vows, a proclamation of why I should even accept a proposal and why he'd want me as a wife before that. Not for the sake of a business deal."

My heart will never be for sale.

"You're looking for a true happily ever after," he states matter-of-factly with a hint of disappointment in his tone.

I slowly nod. "I deserve nothing less."

He cocks his head to the side. "What happens if that's impossible to find?"

"I guess I'll have to search until I find it. But I won't settle."

"Who's to say a happily ever after can't come from a contract?"

"My happily ever after will never come with terms and conditions." I quickly stop myself. "Other than the typical vows, of course. Monogamy, respect, in sickness and in health. All that stuff."

A brief silence happens, as if he's digesting what I said and considering his options. Since he mentioned allowing Cernach to draw up a contract, it seems he doesn't see it as terrible as I do. I blow out a breath and chug my now-lukewarm coffee. One of my feet slips off his lap when he shifts to collect his phone from his pocket.

He unlocks it and makes a show of displaying the screen. The Calendar app is open.

"It seems I have eleven months to go, then." He hits the plus button to add an event and types, *Pippa is mine*, onto the date a year from now.

"I said a year *minimum*," I correct.

I don't expect this to last a year. Damien will grow bored of me and shatter my heart. He'll become only a memory, my hot fling with the bad boy.

"You wouldn't make an exception for me?"

"I wouldn't make an exception for the Pope." I lower my eyes, feeling like I'm letting him down.

"Your mother went against Cernach's wishes and married for true love. That didn't turn out that well."

"My father sold my mother a fairy tale he couldn't deliver."

"I'm surprised Cernach didn't kill him for it."

"Cernach knew my mother would eventually pay for it."

And she did. I squeeze my eyes shut, remembering the stories of how badly they treated my mother.

"And the man she was contracted to marry?"

"Cernach paid him off. Rumor is that the price wasn't cheap either." I straighten my back. "Her family treats her like discarded trash now—no longer useful to them. Which is why I'll never allow Cernach to draft a marriage contract with my name on it, not even to find out what he wants out of it. I like my life the way it is. Hard pass on being the Mafia niece."

"You'd be more than a Mafia niece. You'd be *my wife*."

I'm shocked we're even talking about marriage. The only reason I can come up with for this conversation is that Damien is grieving his family. Other than his brother, who's as closed off as my feelings when my ex told me dance wasn't a real sport, he has no one. Damien most likely believes a wife would fill that void.

*Or* he's had ulterior motives with me from the start.

Maybe the Lombardis need something from my uncle, and I'm the meal ticket.

"Twelve months," I state. "No marriage contract. Those will always be my terms."

He works his jaw, unsatisfied with my answer. "Men like your uncle always get what they want."

Behind his words, he's holding back another detail.

He's just as much mob-affiliated as my mother's family.

That means he also gets whatever he wants. He made that

clear when he forced me out of the casino and into my apartment.

The coffee churns in my stomach. I no longer want to have this conversation. I want *contract* and *Cernach* to leave any part of my vocabulary for the rest of my life.

"Did you ban my father from the casino?" I ask, changing the subject. As much as I want to pull my legs to my chest, tucking myself together, I don't want him to think something is off.

"I did," he confirms as if it's no big deal.

"Why?"

"To prevent him from accumulating more debt with us. I settled his loan this time, but I won't do it again. Vincent won't be as nice to him next time, and it was my way of preventing him from using you again."

"What if he goes to another casino?"

"That's beyond my control." He watches me closely, studying me, as if worried I'll make the mistake of helping my father again. "Don't you dare do it again, or I'll raise goddamn hell."

"Why do you care, Damien?" I whisper, my throat tight.

"If something happened to you, I wouldn't be able to handle it. I can't lose anyone else."

My voice remains a whisper. "We hardly know each other."

His jaw twitches, and he doesn't blink once as he says, "I don't need a certain timeframe to know what I want. It took me less than an hour to know I wanted you—and not just to fuck. When I said you were mine, I didn't mean that in a temporary way. Marriage or no marriage, there's no getting rid of me. You are mine, and I'm yours."

## 17

# DAMIEN

I'M NOT in the mood for coffee.

But I am in the mood to see Pippa.

Before today, I've never stepped foot inside Brew Bliss. I'm not a fan of coffee shops or fancy drinks. I find them too small, too hipster, too evasive. The tables are too close together, providing no privacy.

Further proving my point, the place is packed when I walk in. Within seconds, I overhear two conversations. One about the weather and another from two Wall Street bros, arguing over who spent more on coke this year.

I stand in line like the Good Samaritan I am not. While I'm usually not one for patience for standing in lines, I'm okay with this one. It gives me an excuse to watch Pippa work as I wait.

Jazz music plays around us as she moves behind the counter with ease, like the graceful dancer she is. Two other employees are with her, not counting the girl taking orders, but Pippa seems to be in charge.

When it's my turn, I step to the register.

The cashier, whose name tag reads Sasha, flashes me a red-lipped smile. "What can I get for you today?"

I peer up at the menu board—something I should've done long before, but I'd refused to look away from Pippa. I'm surprised someone didn't call the cops on my ass for looking like a crazed stalker.

I point at Pippa. "What's her favorite coffee?"

When I grabbed coffee for us before, she requested coffee and creamer, nothing special. But I also went to the closest place that had coffee options matching that of a gas station.

Sasha blinks at me. "Huh?"

I point at Pippa again. "That barista. What's her favorite coffee?"

Sasha whips around to see who I'm referring to. "Pippa?"

At the sound of her name, Pippa turns to us. Her gaze catches mine, and she sets down the cup in her hand before scurrying over to us.

"Damien," she says in a long breath, wiping her hands down her apron. "What are you doing here?"

"Ordering coffee," I say simply.

Sasha looks past me to the long line and flicks her gaze to Pippa. "He asked what your favorite coffee is."

Pippa's face scrunches in confusion. "Why?"

I smirk, straightening my cuff links. "I want to make sure it's always stocked in my kitchen."

"Oh my God." Sasha bumps Pippa's hip with hers. "I think he's hitting on you."

Pippa shakes her head. "No, we know each other." Her cheeks redden.

"There's my favorite shade again," I mutter, and she breaks out in a grin. Leaning in closer, I rest my elbows on the counter, ignoring the disgruntled customers behind us. "I don't think I got her favorite the other morning. I can't have that happening again."

Sasha practically squeals in elation.

Pippa mirrors my movement so only I can hear her response. "You can't say things like that here, Damien."

I dip my head so low that my mouth brushes her ear. "Quit being so cute, my little dancer, or I'll drag you out of this coffee shop and into the back seat of my car, and we'll have a repeat of what we did the other night."

Her blush deepens, and her breathing quickens as she quickly pulls away.

"Iced blonde vanilla latte." She's frazzled as she punches numbers on the order screen.

I tip my head forward. "That's what my order is."

"Pippa!" one of the women she's working with calls from behind her. "Did you finish that cold brew?"

"Shit," Pippa says, turning around, snatching the cup she had earlier, and returning to work.

Sasha tells me the total, and after I pay, I slip a hundred into the tip jar. I move out of line, watching Pippa finish the drink she's working on and then move on to mine.

"Damien," she calls out, handing it to me, not meeting my eyes.

I grab it and take a seat at a table in the corner. I have a free hour, and I'm spending every second of it watching her.

Pippa-watching is one of my favorite pastimes.

Taking out my phone, I text her.

> Me: When do you get a break?

When she checks her phone, she hurriedly replies before slipping it back into her pocket.

> Pippa: 30 min.

> Me: I'll be right here.

"How's the coffee?" Pippa asks thirty minutes later, taking the chair across from me.

I don't pay the drink a glance. "Not nearly as good as you." I took one drink of that sugary shit and put it right the fuck down.

"Hey." She dramatically frowns. "I made yours."

I lean back in my chair, crossing my ankles. "I never said it wasn't good. I said it wasn't nearly as good as you." I check my watch. "How long is your break?"

"Fifteen minutes."

I'm tempted to go bribe her boss for extra time. Hell, to give her the day off. I'd happily match Pippa's pay and throw the owner a couple hundred for doing me the favor.

I stretch my neck. "What are your plans for tonight?"

She glances around the room, suddenly failing to meet my eyes. "Uh, nothing really."

I shift in my chair, uncrossing my ankles. "I'll come over then."

"I have plans with my mom and sister," she rushes out, her face reddening. "Maybe after, though? I'll call you when I'm home."

"Yeah." I slowly nod. "You call me."

I told Pippa I don't like liars.

Yet, she just lied straight to my face.

I'll punish her for that tonight.

## 18

# DAMIEN

"Get rid of the piece of shit," I tell Emilio, removing my leather gloves and cleaning blood off my shoes.

"Got it." He salutes me before spitting on the bleeding-out body at his feet.

As I leave the warehouse, I wipe sweat off my forehead and walk to my SUV. Before heading to the theater, I swing by the market to buy fresh flowers. Over the past few weeks, I've immersed myself in endless research on Pippa. Hell, I could have a PhD in the arts of her life.

She's twenty-six, born in Boston but raised in New York. After a year at Juilliard, she dropped out to help her mother run a dance studio that's no longer in business.

When I enter the dark theater, I make my way to the back row, blending in with the audience. I place the roses at my feet, settle into my seat, and silence my phone. Pippa can't know I'm here yet. I don't want her to see me and get nervous.

The show starts, and I'm captivated by her. As she dances, she radiates perfection, her beauty undeniable. She takes over all my thoughts, causing me to forget all my life troubles.

The hurt from losing my family.

The casino.

All of it dissolves.

I'm fully present, entranced by her.

Happiness was never in my life plan.

I never saw myself as being a man happily married or obsessed with a woman like I've become with her. Pippa already feels like family, like home, and I never want to let that go.

This is my first ballet, so I wasn't sure what to expect. Pippa gracefully dances across the stage with other dancers and performs a solo near the end. I don't know how much time passes, and I don't care. I could sit here all night and watch her.

When the show ends, the dancers take their final bow. The audience breaks out in applause, giving them a standing ovation. I clap as the man next to me whistles.

There's a moment where I don't think she'll notice me. But as she rises from her bow, she locks eyes with me and freezes.

*Hello, my sweet dancer.*

## 19

# PIPPA

Holy shit.

Damien is here.

I break our eye contact as I scurry offstage with the other dancers and into the dressing room. Everyone is riding the show high, hugging and telling each other congrats. We busted our asses in practices for this. It's my first show in a while since I spend so much time helping my mother.

After removing my makeup, I change into sweats and a sweatshirt before heading toward the exit. I wasn't lying when I told Damien I don't like people coming to my shows. With my mother and Lanie as the exception, I've never had a man I was dating attend one.

I told my mom and Lanie they didn't need to come tonight, and my father hasn't attended one of my shows in over a decade. Not that I'd invite him. I'm always scared he'll embarrass me. Probably ask people for spare change.

Alex, my dance partner, stops me for a high five. "We killed it tonight!"

"We did!" I hug him. "I couldn't have done it without you."

He brushes his hand through his curly brown locks. "Have a good night."

This was my first ballet with Alex, and so far, we're getting along well.

When I leave the dressing room, Damien is standing in the lobby, a bouquet in his hand.

He walks over to me, holding the flowers over my head, and presses his lips to mine. "You're perfection."

"How'd you know?" I ask, grinning as he hands me the bouquet of red roses.

"Something to learn about me: I always know *everything*."

Call it cliché, but no one has ever brought me flowers after a performance. It's nice to feel like someone cares.

Damien makes me feel special.

This is the fate I wished for.

But deep in my gut, I'm scared it won't work out. He's dangerous. His line of work could get me killed. It did his family. The odds of us having a real relationship aren't in our favor. Right now, us seeing each other like this, is doing more harm than good to my poor heart.

He leads me to his car and praises my performance on the entire drive to my apartment.

"You were breathtaking."

"I've never seen someone dance so beautiful."

"I had to stop myself from grabbing you off that stage and dragging you into the dressing room to worship your body, baby."

When we're back in my apartment, he locks the door, his demeanor changing. Annoyance lines his features.

"Now, I know you were the star of tonight's show, but you need to atone."

I drop my bag on the floor and gape at him. "Atone?"

"For lying to me." He strolls through my apartment and falls on the couch. Every movement reminds me of the first time he was here. He spreads his legs wide, resting his elbows on them. "You're going to suck my cock for that, and then, after I come in your mouth, you're going to dance on my dick until you come." His tone turns stern. "I told you I don't like liars."

He doesn't wait for me to reply as he starts unbuckling his belt.

"The longer you take, the harder I'm going to fuck that gorgeous face of yours," he warns.

Even though my body is sore from tonight, I strut toward him and fall to my knees between his spread legs.

"That's my good little dancer," he says, raising his hips to lower his pants farther. As I make myself comfortable, he grabs a handful of my hair and pulls me closer to his crotch.

I take his entire cock in my mouth.

Deep-throat him. Gulp down his cock.

Damien is bossier tonight than usual.

"Go slower, baby. I want this to last longer."

"Less teeth, more suction."

"Mmm ... my good girl takes directions well."

He doesn't only come in my mouth. He stops me, making me tip my head back, and comes on my face. Then, he helps me to my feet, stands, and throws me over his shoulder, carrying me to the bedroom.

He undresses me and bends me over his knee.

My next punishment.

I've never been spanked before. In fact, I've stated on several occasions if a man ever attempted to *spank me*, I'd drop-kick him.

But I like it with Damien.

I moan, telling him harder.

Asking him for more.

He spanks me until tears are in my eyes and I apologize.

He makes me promise I'll never lie to him again.

Then, he kisses each cheek before bending me over the bed. I moan as he fucks me mercilessly. With each stroke, he slaps my ass again.

And then, after I come, he falls on his back.

"Ride me," he says. "Dance on this cock like I said."

I crawl across the bed to him, and he guides me to straddle him.

It's my turn to take over.

*To dance for him.*

I grind our bodies together.

I move up and down.

I ride him so damn hard that I know his hips will be bruised.

I fuck him hard because I'm falling for him hard.

And I love every second of it.

## Two Weeks Later

I WALK OUT of Brew Bliss and am checking my phone when a man dressed in a black tee, jeans, and blue-mirrored Ray-Bans stops me.

"Pippa?" he asks, blocking me from seeing inside the coffee shop.

I stare at him uneasily, seeing my reflection in his glasses. "Who wants to know?"

He shoves his hand into his pocket and pulls out a police badge. "I'm Detective Kinney. Can we talk?"

I cross my arms. "What's this about?"

He waves toward the outdoor seating area. "Let's chat."

"Am I under arrest or something?"

"Of course not." His demeanor is so indifferent, hard to read. He strolls toward a table, sits, and pats the chair next to him.

Not knowing what else to do, I follow.

"Alllll riiiighty," I say dramatically before sitting.

Not in the chair he patted.

The one across from him.

There's only one man who's allowed to boss me around, and it sure isn't this one.

"How do you know Damien Bellini?" he asks.

My body stiffens in my chair, and I wish it hadn't. "Why?"

"You don't have to answer that. We've watched him with you." He runs his hand over his trimmed facial hair. If he wasn't playing Twenty-One Questions, I'd probably take the time to appreciate his attractiveness. "I'm sure I don't need to tell you that he is extremely dangerous, along with the Lombardi family he works for."

I cross my arms and immediately uncross them, not wanting to appear defensive. "I have no idea what you mean, Detective."

He lowers his voice as two men take the table across from us. "They're a crime family."

"Damien and I have had dinner together a few times." I shrug. "That's it."

He scoffs. "I don't think *that's it*."

I shrug again. "I don't have anything else to tell you, Detective Kinney."

"You talk, and we'll reward you greatly. All we need is for you to wear a wire—"

I immediately stand, hefting my bag over my shoulder.

"Wait," he says, jumping to his feet and gesturing for me to sit back down. "Give me five minutes."

"You have two." I hold up two fingers but don't sit back down.

"You help us put them behind bars, we'll pay off your father's gambling debts."

"Don't try to use my father against me just to get me to lie," I snap.

"Lie?" For a moment, he sounds out of patience with me

*Sinful Sacrifice*

until he corrects himself. "You know they're dangerous. They commit crimes. *Kill people.* I'm not asking you to lie. All I want is to put these criminals behind bars. We'll provide protection for you, your mother, and sister. We'll give you a better life away from here."

I hold up my hand to stop him from talking. "I have nothing to tell you. Now, if you'll excuse me."

"You think of anything, you let me know." He hands me his card.

I take one look at it and crumple it before tossing it onto the table.

He scoffs. "Stay safe, Pippa. You'll need it."

I glare at him. "Damien keeps me plenty protected."

"He will until you cross him." He raises his brows. "Once he doesn't need you anymore, he'll dispose of you."

I storm away from him, the urge to flip him off heavy. But I don't. He is a man of the law and could easily find a reason to arrest me. I survey the scene around me, as if feeling people's eyes on me.

Damien and I don't discuss his *job*, but I'm not stupid. Before I even googled him, I knew he was involved with the Lombardi crime operation. I'm also convinced he's high up in the ranks, though I'd never ask him. From what I read on the blog, his family has been involved with the Lombardis for decades.

"Asshole," I mutter, kicking a rock on my way home.

I feel like people are coming at me from everywhere.

My father, asking for money, favors, and access back into Lucky Kings.

My mother, wanting to rant about my father and help me figure out a way to open a new studio.

Cernach, who wants me to become a Mafia-ordered bride.

I won't be the one who pushes Damien and me apart. It'll be the forces around us.

Damien has slept over every night since our dinner date, though he pleads with me for us to crash at his place. But sometimes he's back late at night, and other times, it's early morning. His schedule is chaotic.

He attended another one of my shows, this time with my knowledge. It didn't make me nervous. It actually did the opposite, making me feel a sense of pride. Although now, I have Alex asking me hundreds of questions about our relationship.

When I make it back to my apartment, two men are standing in front of my door. One has a serious case of bad odor, and the other's eyes are so bloodshot that I'm surprised he can see.

As soon as I see them, I attempt to turn around and flee.

"Oh, no, you don't," red-eyed guy says, grabbing me by my braid.

He jerks me back, and I fall on my ass.

I try to fight the man off my hair, but he only tightens his hold on me and slaps me in the face with his free hand. He's holding my braid so tight that it hurts my scalp.

"You Paul Elsher's daughter?" the other guy asks.

"Nope." I'm not in the mood for this shit.

He retrieves a gun from his pocket and points it at me. My breathing becomes shallow as I continue to struggle with the man.

"The bitch is lying," the man holding me snarls. "I saw pictures of her in his wallet."

BO guy stoops to my level. "Where's your father, cunt?"

"I have no idea what you're talking about," I say, grimacing at the pain.

The man finally loosens his grip on my hair, and I manage to break out of his grasp. He doesn't attempt to grab me again, but he does block me from running down the stairs.

"Go away, or I'm calling the cops," I warn, raising my voice in hopes that someone will hear us.

BO guy chews on a toothpick and laughs. "Word is, you pay

your dad's debts for him. Since we can't reach your father, we're here to collect the payment from you." He motions toward my door. "You can either give us the cash he owes or I'm sure we can come up with other ways you can pay it off."

The other laughs, and they exchange creepy smiles.

I take this moment to ram my knee into his balls. He screams, falling to his knees, and I jump over him. Red-Eyes grabs the strap of my bag, attempting to drag me back, but I shrug my purse off. As bad as I don't want them to have my shit, I don't want to be around them more.

I run outside and stop the first person I see on the sidewalk. The man removes his headphones from his ears and raises a brow.

"Can I"—I struggle to catch my breath and bend at the waist. Maybe Damien had a point with all these stairs—"use your phone?"

The guy laughs. "Good one. I've already had that trick pulled on me and got robbed."

"I'm serious," I say, tears gathering in my eyes.

"Sorry, find someone else." The guy plugs his headphones back in and mutters something as he walks away.

I turn at a car door slamming. The man who escorted me to Damien's office, Emilio, comes charging in my direction.

"What happened?" he asks.

"Two guys ..." I inhale breaths. "They're in my apartment."

"Stay here," he orders, storming past me into my building.

I scurry behind him. He flies up the stairs, taking two at a time, and I'm about ten behind him as I follow. When I reach my apartment, the door is open. I peek inside to find Emilio punching BO guy in the face. Red-Eyes attempts to charge toward him, and Emilio stabs him in the stomach. The man doubles over, wrapping his arms around his torso, and falls to his knees.

*Oh my God.*

Emilio snatches BO guy around the throat, rams him into the wall, and stabs him next.

Jesus, I am definitely not getting my deposit back.

Once both men are on the ground, bleeding and not moving, Emilio spins around to face me. "Damien is on his way. Stay in the hallway."

## 20

# DAMIEN

For the past few weeks, I've had Julian or Emilio watch Pippa's every move when I'm unavailable. Her day-to-day life is mundane, and they've complained about being bored as fuck, but I always want eyes on her. Pippa might believe she's safe, but she's wrong. Cernach and her piece-of-shit father make her a target.

My point was proven when Emilio called fifteen minutes ago and told me Pippa fled her building like a goddamn serial killer was chasing her.

I swerve into the no-parking zone in front of Pippa's building and sprint up the stairs. When I reach her floor, she's standing by the door, back to the wall, body trembling. She runs into my arms the second she sees me.

I hate that she's in danger, but love that it drags her to me.

That she knows I'm her security blanket.

That she needs me.

"Baby." I clutch her tightly, running my hand down her back.

Her breaths are ragged as she shoves her face against my chest.

"Let's get you out of here." I press a soft kiss to the top of her head and inch away from her. Running my hands down her sides, I make sure she's good to walk before guiding her toward the stairway and collecting her purse from the floor before handing it to her.

"What about my apartment?" she asks, stopping me. "Emilio is in there with the men."

"Emilio will make sure your apartment is cleaned." He'll do a lot more, but I don't tell her that. Mainly because I'll join him in that activity. For now, I'll take her to my office so she's safe.

She chews on her lip. "Should I pack a bag?"

"Wait here." I hate that I have to separate from her.

I rap my knuckles against her apartment door twice, and Emilio steps into the doorway. He nods, and I enter. Both men are alive. Bleeding yet alive.

"What should I do with them?" Emilio asks.

I immediately recognize the Razzo brothers. "They're useless bookies."

I kneel so I'm at Fred, the eldest's, level. "You come near Pippa again, and you'll deal with me." I stand and shove the heel of my loafer into his stab wound.

"Sorry," Fred sputters. "I didn't know she was yours. We just wanted our money."

"Now, you do." I lift my foot to shove it into his face.

He cries out, cowering in pain, while his brother whimpers beside him. They're bleeding all over Pippa's floor. I'll pay her landlord to fix it as well as approve her to break her lease. She's not sleeping another night in this dangerous shithole.

I leave the apartment, capture Pippa's hand, and lead her out of the building. Later, I'll have her write out a list of belongings to grab from her apartment and pack them for her. I help her into the Range Rover before joining her.

Pippa's phone rings, and she shuffles through her new purse for it.

"It's my mom." She accepts the call and surprisingly puts it on speaker. "Mom, now's not really a good ti—"

"That son of a bitch left!" she screams through the phone, interrupting Pippa. Her sobs creep out from the phone's speaker.

"Who?" Pippa asks, and it's that moment I see the red mark across her face. I hold in my anger, waiting until she's off the phone.

"Your father! He's gone!" Her voice heightens. "Two men came to the house yesterday, threatening all of us. I came home today to find him and all his things gone. He finally answered my hundredth call and told me he had to flee New York and is never coming back."

Pippa rubs her cheek. "You know how Dad is. He'll leave for a few days and return when he's out of money."

"He's never packed his bags like this before. He always leaves his shit. This time, it's for real."

"Mom," Pippa says around a sigh.

"Please come over. I need you here. Lanie needs you."

Pippa's shoulders slump. "Okay, I'm on my way." She ends the call and peers over at me. "Can you give me a ride to my mom's?"

"Did one of them put their hands on you?" I cup her chin in my hand and clench my jaw. My blood boils. I scoot in closer to examine her face, and she winces as I caress her cheek.

"I'm okay." She clasps her hand over mine. "Can we leave? She's probably on the verge of a breakdown right now."

I nod, start the ignition, and head toward her mom's. There's no need for the address. I have it memorized.

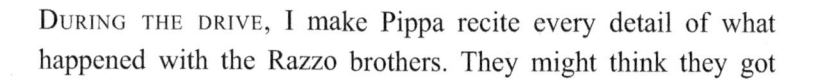

During the drive, I make Pippa recite every detail of what happened with the Razzo brothers. They might think they got away with their behavior now, and I planned to be semi-lenient with them, but now knowing they put their hands on Pippa, I won't have any mercy on them.

I want to shield Pippa from my dark side for as long as I can. I warned her I had one, but she hasn't seen it to its maximum level yet. The longer I can hide it, the better.

Her mother's split-level home is in the suburbs, twenty minutes from the city. Most of the landscaping is dead, but it does have a fresh coat of paint. I park in the driveway behind a bright red VW Beetle and follow Pippa into the house.

Lanie is comforting their mother, Enya, on the couch. Enya's face is red, tearstained, and her shoulders are slouched forward. The woman looks like she hasn't slept in weeks. Pippa dashes to Enya, hugging and telling her everything will be okay.

I crack my knuckles, unsure why Pippa is lying to her.

Nothing will be right in Enya's life for a long-ass time. Her husband left her in a mess. Paul might've skipped town, but that debt didn't leave with him. People will continue to show up at their doorstep, wanting their money.

As Pippa sits next to her, Enya's gaze flicks to me. "Who are you?"

"Damien," I say simply. I'm never one to elaborate on that question.

"Are you her boyfriend?" Her gaze slips from me to Pippa. "I didn't know you were dating."

"He's my friend," Pippa explains.

That sure as hell stings.

*Boyfriend* sounds so fucking juvenile anyway.

I'm just hers. Her protector. Her lover. The one who'll do anything for her.

While Pippa works on consoling Enya, I fish my phone from my pocket and start making calls.

"Two of my men are coming here to change your locks and

install an alarm system and video surveillance," I tell Enya thirty minutes later. "They'll also walk you through how to work everything."

Enya holds up her hand. "Who's supposed to pay for that? I can't afford it. I can barely make ends meet as it is."

"I'll help," Pippa says, stroking Enya's arm.

"You won't be billed," I assure her.

Enya's green eyes widen, and she thrusts her chin forward. "*You're* paying for it?"

"Yes." I shove the phone into my pocket.

"What happens if you break up?" Enya motions between Pippa and me. "Will you have *your men* come here and rip it off my wall?"

Pippa sighs. "No, Mom. Don't be dramatic. Damien is doing something nice." She glances at me and mouths, "*Thank you.*"

I wait for Julian to arrive before leaving. Pippa stays behind, and I instruct Julian to escort them anywhere they go.

"I'll be back," I tell Pippa, kissing the top of her head.

Enya and Lanie stare at us in curiosity. I don't blame Pippa for not telling them about us. It's complicated, and her mother grew up similar to my life. Different organizations but same dynamics.

I return to Pippa's apartment, where Emilio is watching TV while the Razzos are tied up with tape over their mouths. I sent him a text, telling him not to help them.

I screw a silencer on the end of my Glock. Freddy attempts to scoot away when I approach him.

"You touch things that are mine, you die," I say before pressing the barrel against his temple.

His body jolts when I pull the trigger.

I don't kill his brother yet.

I want him to sit there and have to stare at his dead twin for a few hours.

Think about his stupid actions.

Then, either Emilio or I will put a bullet through his idiotic brain.

## 21

# PIPPA

WHAT A DUMMY I was for always insisting we sleep at my apartment instead of Damien's brownstone.

His bed is ten times comfier.

The sheets softer.

There's central freaking air.

No one is stomping upstairs or vacuuming their apartment.

The spot next to me is empty and cold, but Damien's masculine scent lingers on the sheets, relaxing me.

I didn't argue when he told me I was sleeping at his place. I no longer feel safe at my apartment right now. It sucks since I adore my place. It isn't much, but it's still a home I worked hard for.

Groaning, I throw an arm over my eyes to block the sunlight streaming through the curtains covering a wall of windows. Yesterday's events swallow my thoughts, a bitter reminder of the chaos.

The loan sharks.

My father fleeing New York.

My mom losing her shit.

The detective.

*Shit!*

I forgot about the detective requesting I become his personal rat.

*Should I tell Damien or keep it to myself?*

The anxiety of that conversation causes a dull ache to throb inside my head as I roll out of bed and plod through the bedroom to the en suite bath that belongs in a spa.

A duffel bag, filled with my clothes and personal items, sits on the island in the closet. Per Damien's demand, I texted him a list of stuff to grab from my apartment. His packing me a bag felt weird at first, but I'm growing more comfortable with him. I don't see him as some creep who'll sniff my panties.

Okay, not like in a creepy way.

More in a sexy way because I'm pretty sure he's pocketed a pair of my worn panties before. Damien moves so quickly that it's hard to keep up with what he does.

He moves like a predator.

Swift and intentional.

Sometimes, you don't even know you've fallen victim to him before it's too late.

I brush my teeth, my hair, and change into fresh clothes. It took Damien's men three hours to install everything in my mom's home yesterday. They spent another hour walking us through how to work them.

Damien isn't only spoiling me, protecting me, but he's also extending that courtesy to my family. I have nothing to give him in return, and he doesn't care.

I leave the bedroom and run my hand along the brass staircase rail while moving down the steps.

*Not a fan of steps, huh?*

Damien's brownstone is timeless. He preserved its beautiful history while also renovating the space, making it contemporary. He—or whoever designed the space—gave it the perfect balance. It's a piece of art tucked between walls. The open-floor plan and large windows provide plenty of natural light.

When my feet hit the bottom step, the front door opens.

Damien walks in, carrying a box of doughnuts. A short woman with silver hair follows him, holding a grocery tote and peering around the chef's kitchen.

"Pippa," Damien says, setting the box on the black marble island in the kitchen. "This is Monique. She's one of the best vegetarian chefs in the city."

*Oh, I recognize her.*

I follow her on Instagram and have tried—and unfortunately failed—to recreate her recipes.

I smile, sending her a tiny wave. "Hi, Monique."

She returns the smile. "It's very nice to meet you, Pippa. I'm excited to work with you."

"Monique will be your chef from now on," Damien says simply, slipping off his blazer and draping it over the island chair.

"I started a menu this morning," Monique adds before glancing at Damien. "Do you mind if I familiarize myself with your kitchen and make a list of items I'll need?"

"It's all yours," Damien answers. He swipes the doughnut box from the island and hands it to me. "Until she gets started, I brought today's breakfast."

"Thank you." I open the box, finding the most elaborate doughnuts I've ever seen. My mouth waters.

"Can't have my baby going hungry." He kisses the tip of my nose and clasps my hand.

I follow his lead upstairs, our footsteps echoing through the space, mixing with the sound of Monique moving around the kitchen. When we're back in the bedroom, Damien softly shuts the door behind us.

"How did you sleep?"

"Good actually." For once, I didn't wake up with achy muscles.

A cocky smirk spreads across his face. "Told you my place was better."

"You have stairs."

"Stairs that aren't the size of a toenail or made of rotting wood."

"Stairs are stairs." I shrug. "Your bed is also surprisingly comfortable."

"Surprisingly?" He raises a dark brow. "Where did you think I slept? On the concrete in some dungeon or a prison mattress?"

"No, it's just that most men don't have comfortable mattresses."

Damien glares at me. "I'd suggest you never refer to you and another man's mattress again, Pippa."

"Why? Do you plan to kill every man and mattress I've ever sat on?"

"If I'm having a shitty day, possibly." He motions to the box of doughnuts. "Eat. You didn't have dinner last night."

"Neither did you." I'm not one hundred percent positive of that since we weren't together most of the evening.

"I had coffee this morning." He stalks around me to sit in the chair in the room's corner.

He moves his head from one side to the other, and I hear his neck pop. He pops his knuckles next.

*His bruised knuckles.*

My broken man—always bruised and cut on both the inside and out.

His eyes level on me as I sashay toward him.

"I have to keep my protector strong." I remove a doughnut and drop the box on the floor before straddling him.

"Sugar isn't what keeps me strong." He smirks, brushing his knuckle over my cheek, and I shiver.

"Then, what does?"

"Getting what I want." His hand descends my neck, between my breasts, and stops at the waistband of my leggings. "And what I want right now is to taste this sweet pussy." He slightly pulls the waistband back and snaps it back into place.

My blood warms, and my legs tremble against his hard thighs. I tilt my hips forward, feeling his growing erection beneath me. His fingers trail along my waistband while I decide to have some fun.

I dip my finger through the doughnut frosting and spread it across my lips.

He smirks again, his gaze cruising to my mouth, enticing me further.

I spread the frosting down my neck.

Monique is downstairs, and any other time, I'd be mortified at the possibility of someone hearing me during an intimate moment. But with Damien, *here*, I feel comfortable in my body and sexuality.

He dips his head closer and skims his tongue along the seam of my lips, collecting the frosting. His eyes hold me hostage. Someone could barge into the bedroom, and I wouldn't be able to look away.

When he flicks his tongue against my lips, I part them, allowing him entry.

My body is on fucking fire.

Burning with need for him.

His mouth leaves mine to trail kisses down my cheek and neck, capturing the frosting there. His soft tongue easily glides across my skin.

My clit throbs, and he hasn't even slipped his hand into my panties yet.

He snaps my waistband again before gripping my hips and hoisting me to my feet. I lose a breath, excitement rushing through my veins, when he takes the doughnut and drops it on the table beside the chair. He rises, towering over my body like a threat.

I gulp, peering up at him.

We're not speaking, but so many emotions burn between us.

Desire. Darkness. Like nothing other than this moment matters.

He holds me in place, one hand back at my waistband and the other at my waist, digging into my skin through my shirt. "From now on, when you're here, you wear fucking dresses," he grits out. "Taking these off is a pain in the ass."

He peels my leggings off my body, kneeling to pull them off my feet, and I kick out of them. My panties are the next to go. But they don't join my leggings on the floor. He slips them into his pants pocket.

"My gorgeous dancer, always so soaked for me," he mutters, as if speaking to himself more than me. "God, I love touching this pussy." He uses his knee to separate my legs, jerking them apart, and slips a finger inside me. "Love that you give it to me, knowing all the good and bad things I'll do to it."

He slides his finger out and smacks my pussy with his palm.

Then, I get a little brave.

I decide that maybe, for once, I'll try to run the show.

There's a sense of satisfaction as I push his shoulders back.

That satisfaction fizzles right out when he hardly moves.

The man has, like, fifty pounds on me and has probably never been pushed around. All I've ever pushed are my parents' nerves and the balance on my credit card when I see a candle sale.

He focuses on me, a smile building on his face. "Does my dancer want to take control?"

*Why do I suddenly feel shy?*

He retreats a few steps and collapses on the chair again.

His carnal eyes watch me as he unfastens his cuff links, setting them to the side, and rolls up his sleeves.

*Sinful Sacrifice*

I gulp, watching his Adam's apple move.

He rests his elbows on the chair's arms. "Come take control, baby. I want to see you do it."

I scrape my teeth against my bottom lip.

Here I am, having stage fright with him again.

"Don't get shy on me now, Pippa." He tsks me. "Either come ride my dick or spend the rest of the day craving it because in five seconds, I'll leave this room and deprive your sweet pussy of my cock." He relaxes in the chair while unbuckling his pants.

For some disturbed reason, his words calm me.

They also give me a push in his direction.

"Five," he clips out.

I inch closer.

"Four."

*Closer.*

"Three."

I take the final step, where I'm standing above him. My chest heaves, my breathing fluttering like a butterfly.

"Two."

He shoves them, along with his briefs, down to his ankles. My heart thrashes in my chest as I take the last step and his cock springs free.

It's hard, throbbing, pre-cum already on the tip.

He spits in his hand and slowly starts stroking himself. I peer down at him, watching his gaze sweep down and land on my bare pussy. He licks his lips and slumps down in the chair, as if wanting a better look.

"Quit playing games and ride this cock," he grunts.

I sink my toes into the rug before palming his shoulders and pushing them backward. His gaze returns to mine as his body flattens against the chair. Silence surrounds us as I slowly straddle him. He hisses under his breath as I grind my hips forward a few times, rubbing my pussy against his cock. I stare, fascinated at our connection and how my juices are coating him.

He curls his fingers into my waist, lifts me until I'm above his cock, and slams me down on it. "You move too slow, baby. I need to fuck this pussy quick because I can't stay long."

I gasp, my back arching, as he fills me. His cock expands inside me.

Damien doesn't give me time to adjust to his size.

I grip his shoulders and dig my nails into them as he holds me in place, pumping in and out of me. He turns his waist, making me feel him from every angle.

My teeth chatter. He's holding me so tight and fucking me.

I get closer and closer and closer.

My orgasm building.

My body warming from the inside out.

I slump forward, shoving my face into his neck, and nearly feel like a rag doll as he fucks me. His thumb finds my clit, and he bites into my shoulder before coming inside me.

That's when reality hits me.

My eyes flick to his.

Wide and stunned.

Seconds later, he lowers his gaze to our connection.

When he winces, I know he's realized the same.

*We didn't use a condom.*

"Shit, sorry, Pippa." He bows his head forward and curses under his breath.

"It's okay." I pat his shoulder while trying to control my breathing. "I forgot too."

We were so caught up in the moment.

Story of every surprise pregnancy.

Neither of us speaks as he guides me back up and down his cock, as if entranced by his cum inside me.

He bites into his lower lip and groans, "That's so fucking hot."

I moan, rotating my hips to where I'm nearly fucking him again.

"What a fucking sight," he grunts. "Your waxed pussy leaking with my cum. It's the sexiest thing I've ever seen, baby."

I moan, staring down, just as obsessed.

This man. His filthy mouth. It's all perfection.

Not using a condom was stupid.

But at this moment, I love that he's the first man to come inside me.

The first man I've had sex with, with no barrier between us.

It's beautiful.

Now, if I miss my period in a few weeks, I probably won't agree with this statement. I'll more likely have a panic attack.

But for now, I'm relishing this moment.

I'm lost in my thoughts and gasp when he cups me beneath my armpits and pulls me off his dick and lap. Before I can catch my next breath, he tosses me on the bed, climbs over me, and shoves his face between my legs.

He's relentless as he eats and finger-fucks me.

He doesn't slow down once until I'm squirming beneath him, my hands clawing at the sheets and my head thrashing from side to side.

He builds me up, up, up until I come crashing down.

And when I'm done, he pulls back and wipes his mouth. "Now, I'm strong."

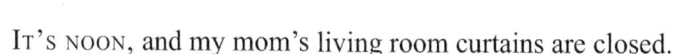

---

IT'S NOON, and my mom's living room curtains are closed.

I've never seen them shut during the day. Opening them is usually the first thing she does in the morning.

"You have to get natural light in to start your day," she always told us. "Sunny, stormy, overcast—it doesn't matter. You need to see the sky."

I could hardly look Monique in the eye when Damien and I

returned downstairs after what he referred to as *breakfast*. He stood to the side, allowing me to help Monique make the menu for this week.

*What is my life?*

Last week, I was eating ramen and almost-expired cereal, and now, I have a private chef? Well, Damien does, but he did it for me.

Julian, who's apparently on Pippa-sitting duty, came over, and Damien left. He made sure to tell me to be good before kissing me goodbye.

I peer over at Julian in the driver's seat of his Mercedes, taking in the similarities and differences between him and his brother. Julian is younger—my guess, around four or five years. Their hair is the same shade, but Damien's is messier and thicker. Both have a slight tilt on their noses, thick brows, and tall, lean bodies.

They are also men of few words.

Julian hardly spoke to me on the drive to my mom's. That might have to do with the fact that he hadn't wanted to bring me here. Damien and I had a five-minute-long argument. He'd wanted me to stay at his place, but I refused, insisting I needed to check on my mom.

I unfasten my seat belt. "Do you wait out here?"

He glowers. "Would you like me to come in and have girl talk with you?"

*Okay, rude.*

I offer him a sarcastic smile. "It might make you less tense."

He cuts the engine and pushes his black Ray-Bans up his sleek nose. "Hard pass. Soft isn't my strong suit. Don't stay long."

"Okey dokey."

He doesn't say a word as I leave the car.

The sun beats down on me as I walk to the front door and

*Sinful Sacrifice*

knock. Since Damien had the locks changed, I don't have a key yet.

*Mental reminder to get one.*

"How is she?" I ask Lanie when she answers the door, and I walk inside.

She releases her brown hair from its ponytail and redoes it. "Not good."

"No word from Dad?"

"No, I think he's finally gone for good this time." Understandable relief is in her tone.

Lanie turned eighteen this year and spent most of her childhood witnessing my parents argue nonstop. I at least got a few good years before my father fell into his gambling addiction.

We stop our conversation when my mom walks into the living room. Her hair is wet and ratty, and she's dressed in a polka-dot robe. She doesn't greet us while she settles on the couch and clicks the TV on.

It's a sad story. My mom, once a beautiful and gifted ballerina, wrecked by an undeserving man. Well, *men*, if you count the ones she grew up with.

They all ruined her.

That's something I'll never allow any of them to do to me.

We wait for my mom's next move. All morning, she dodged my calls and texts. Lanie said she wouldn't open her bedroom door for her.

In what seems like slow motion, she raises her eyes and locks them on mine. "No boyfriend this time?"

I flinch at the sneer in her tone.

There's a clear look of disgust on her face, as if Damien wronged her yesterday instead of helping.

My mom used to be kind and loving.

Known for always having a smile on her face, a jokester, but that isn't who she is anymore.

I fidget with my purse strap. "Damien is at work."

139

"Work?" she huffs. "What's his line of *work*, Pippa?"

"He works at a casino." I wrinkle my nose.

Lanie inhales a long breath.

Fire lights up in my mom's eyes.

"Are you kidding me?" She fists her hand and pounds it on the table. "Casinos have devastated our lives, Pippa!" She points at me, wiggling her finger. "Don't you think I don't know he's more than a man who *works at a casino*? I know a made man when I see one. Have you forgotten that I grew up surrounded by them?"

"Mom," I say around a sigh, "Damien is a good man."

I want to add that he helped us, got rid of Dad's debt, and rescued me when Dad's loan sharks came to me for payment.

But I don't because she'd find a way to blame him for that too.

"He's just like Cernach." She snatches the pack of cigarettes on the table and lights one. She recently picked up a new smoking habit.

My pulse thrums through my body as I try to calm the defensiveness rising inside me. "He's nothing like Cernach." I can't stop myself from gritting out the last word.

She frowns, deep wrinkles appearing on her forehead.

"All men want you to believe they're not who they truly are," she says with the least bit of interest. "But in the end, all the things hidden in the dark come to light." She continues puffing on her cigarette, looking at me with a snarl. "And that's when you'll realize I was right. He's exactly who I think he is."

"Heads-up, we're on Amara duty tonight," Damien says over the phone. "We're watching her at my place for a while."

I'm in Julian's car, waiting for him to return. He's in my

apartment, grabbing my dance bag. I forgot to put it on my list for Damien.

When I asked Julian if my apartment was now a crime scene, he rolled his eyes, shook his head, and stepped out of the car.

"Totally fine," I reply. "She's the sweetest."

"We'll probably make it back around the same time."

I only stayed at my mom's for a few hours. She spent half the time screaming and cursing like my father was standing in front of her. She spent the other half calling his phone relentlessly, but it always went to voicemail.

When she said she was going back to bed, Lanie retreated to her bedroom, wearing her headphones, and I left.

My family is completely broken.

To be honest, I think it's been that way for a long time.

Damien: I'm home now.

Me: Almost there.

As we pull up to Damien's brownstone, I admire the historic building that overlooks the Hudson River. The brick is a dark red, and the front door is the same black as Damien's hair.

Anyone would love to call this place their home.

Though with its location and size, it's out of most people's budgets.

I collect my bag from the back seat and sling it over my shoulder, and Julian follows me inside. Amara's giggles greet us. The smell of fresh garlic and tomato drifts through the air.

It's such a drastic change to where I just was.

This sounds, smells, *feels* like a happier home.

I pass the kitchen, noticing Monique and Clara, and shoot

them a quick hello. As I move deeper toward the living room, I stop and watch Damien with Amara. He's relaxed on the leather sectional while Amara animatedly tells him a story. She throws her arms up with every other word.

I love how attentive he is with her.

How his rough demeanor softens, layer by layer.

He does the same with me.

We're the few granted the gentle side of him.

He wrinkles his forehead and throws his head back, laughing when she makes a funny face. When he lowers his head, his gaze angles in my direction.

I cheekily smile at him, and it's like my nervous system settles as our eyes meet.

Amara's attention follows his. "Hi, Pippa!" She skips toward me, UGG slippers sweeping the wood floor and ponytail flying.

I grin at her. "Hi, Amara!"

She comes to a sliding stop and points at my bag. "What are those?"

I peer down to find my ballet slippers halfway hanging from my bag.

"Oh." I run my fingers over a sole. "My dance shoes."

"So cool!" Her face brightens up. "Can I see them on you?"

"Of course."

She follows me to the living room. I sit on the floor next to Damien's feet, and Amara kneels beside me.

"First, I put on my toe pads." I unzip my bag and pull them out. "Then, you have to make sure your foot is flat on the floor like this and your knees bent."

I demonstrate the proper form as she crawls closer, staring at my feet.

"Next, we tie them." I explain every move I make while wrapping the ribbon around my foot and ankle. "This is to make sure your ankles have great stability. That's important."

She nods repeatedly, hanging on to every detail.

*Sinful Sacrifice*

I love teaching dance at all levels, but introducing it to children is my favorite. Nothing is more genuine than innocent excitement. When someone isn't worried about expectations. They're there to simply learn and have fun.

When I'm finished tying it around my ankle, I loop the ribbons into a knot. Amara creeps so close that she's nearly sitting on my other foot.

I extend my leg when I'm finished. "And that's how you put on a ballet slipper."

"I want to do that!" She grins from ear to ear. "How'd you learn?"

"My mother taught me, and then I started teaching classes."

"Really?" Amara peeks up at Damien, pouting her lower lip. "Do you think Daddy will let me go to her dance classes?"

Damien scratches his head. "You'll have to ask him that."

I'm sure Antonio won't jump for joy to have his daughter attend my classes. My shoulders slump at the reality check that I don't have a studio to teach her in anyway.

"Will you show me how you dance while wearing them?" she asks.

I put the other shoe on and stand, and Amara giggles, making herself comfortable on the couch beside Damien. Her brown eyes are bright and wide while she waits for my next move. Damien rests his elbows on the armrests, giving me his undivided attention.

If I've learned one thing about Damien, the man loves watching me. It's like his new favorite hobby.

I spend the next twenty minutes giving them a crash course on ballet basics. Each time I peer at Damien, he mouths different words to me:

*Beautiful.*
*Gorgeous.*
*Perfection.*
*All mine.*

143

"Uncle Damien! Can I hold Ace?" Amara asks when dinner is over.

Monique's tofu spaghetti was one of the best dinners I'd had in a long time. It might even put L'ultima Cena to shame. Not that I'd ever tell the murder-eatery that. No one even complained that it was a meatless meal.

Damien is seated in a corner chair, working on his laptop, and I just finished helping Clara and Monique clean the kitchen.

"Ace?" I ask Damien.

"Ace, the snake!" Amara shouts, jumping off the couch.

*Ace the huh?*

I scan the room as if a snake is about to slither out from somewhere.

Damien drops his laptop to the floor and stands. "Only if you sit on the couch." His tone is strict yet also gentle. "Be right back." As he passes me, he drops a kiss to my cheek and retreats upstairs.

Clara joins Amara on the couch, and I steal Damien's seat. I rub my arms as Damien comes back into the living room with a snake around his arms.

*Since when does this man have a snake?*

He's never mentioned it once.

No heads-up that we have a reptile roommate.

"Ace!" Amara shouts, squirming in excitement. "I've missed you!"

Damien walks over to her and carefully hands her the snake. She cradles it in her arms as if she were holding a baby. Neither Clara nor Damien shows an ounce of anxiety at this child holding this scary-as-hell snake. Damien does stand at her side, watching them.

Ace isn't a huge snake, but his size doesn't lessen his

creepiness. His brown-and-gray scales are almost in a zigzag design, and his body is nothing but muscle.

"Ace is a saw-scaled viper," Amara explains, petting his head. "Do you want to hold him?"

"I'm okay," I reply. "You and Ace can spend some quality time together."

Ace's head turns toward me, and I swear, his dark black pupils stare straight into mine. He's probably plotting to bite me in my sleep since I declined to hold him.

Damien backs away from her as I lean in toward him.

"You should've given me a heads-up that we have a snake as a roomie," I comment.

He slips his hands into his pockets. "Ace isn't dangerous."

"He's *a snake*. Snakes can tighten their bodies around yours and strangle you—aka dangerous."

"Ace isn't dangerous! He's sweet," Amara squeals before giving him a kiss on the head next.

"He doesn't have venom," Damien explains. "It was removed."

I blink up at him. "You can do that?"

I figured they do it at zoos, sure, but for a civilian to do it?

He nods.

"Is that considered cruel?"

"It was better than the situation Ace was in before."

"And by *situation*, you mean?"

"Antonio bought him from some POS who'd purchased him overseas because he was poisonous. The asshole didn't take care of him. One day, we went to his house to collect a loan. Antonio saw how Ace was treated—in a small tank with hardly any room and looked nearly on the brink of starvation—and made him sell it to him. When we called the local animal rescue, they wouldn't take him. Antonio had his venom removed and took him home." He jerks his head toward Amara. "That's where he stayed until this one here tried to sneak him out of his tank and into her bedroom to snuggle with him at night. He asked me to take Ace. So, he either stays here or if I'm crashing at Antonio's for a long period, I take him with me."

Damien allows Amara to hold Ace for another twenty minutes, and she whines when he takes her from him.

Amara rattles on about how much she loves and misses Ace and follows Damien upstairs to return the snake to his bedroom … cage … wherever he lives. I should've done a better tour of the brownstone instead of riding Damien's cock earlier.

"He likes you," Clara comments when they're out of earshot. "Damien never watches Amara here, but he didn't want to leave you alone. Surprisingly, Antonio agreed to it."

"Does he …" I run my hands up my arms while peeking over at the staircase. "Has he brought other women around Amara before?"

"Never," she says with absolute certainty. "Only you, Pippa."

DURING THE CAR ride to Antonio's, Amara rambles about wanting to take dance classes, how much she wishes Ace would move back in with her, and how she wants earrings that match mine.

When we arrive, I wait in the car while Damien walks Amara and Clara inside. They invited me inside, but that was a big fat immediate no. The less untrusting stare downs from Antonio Lombardi, the better.

While I sit in the car, my mind wanders to how attentive Damien is with Amara. I've seen fathers act less interested in their *own* children—aka mine.

Damien told me Amara was his goddaughter, and he's definitely living up to the godfather role.

I tap my foot and mutter, "Don't ask. Don't ask. Don't ask,"

*Sinful Sacrifice*

to myself until the door opens and Damien slips behind the steering wheel.

"Do you want children?"

*And I asked. FML.*

Damien stops mid-start of the Range Rover, and there's a brief silence before he replies, "My mother is the only other person who's asked me that question."

"What did you tell her?" I croak out.

"That before I ever thought about kids, I'd need to make a woman happy as my wife first. And I wasn't sure if that'd ever happen."

My throat feels almost sore. "Why weren't you sure?"

"My job, this life—it hurts families. It's not for the faint of heart. Not only for me, but for whoever I marry as well. I need a woman who fully accepts me and the darkness inside my soul." He turns to me, the light limited, and I make out his furrowed brows. "I want the woman I have children with to want a family —*truly want* one, not by force."

He inhales a deep breath and continues, "Arranged marriages, like Cernach wants, can create hostile lives for children. Luckily, my parents loved each other. But Antonio's? They're miserable. Which is why I'd never agree or sign a marriage contract with Cernach unless you one hundred percent wanted it. Like I told you, I'd marry you in a minute, but I'd never force you." His voice lowers. "Are you asking me this because children with me is something you'd consider?"

A lump forms in my throat, and my heart races. "I always pictured myself having children after marriage."

"*Any* marriage?"

"A marriage that isn't arranged," I say with a sigh. "A marriage that started with dating and falling in love, built up over time. I'll only try marriage once, so I want to be damn sure it's the right one I take that chance with. I won't settle for less."

"Marriage once *with me*. I'll take it." He cups my face. "You,

147

my sweet dancer, would make an amazing baby mama for me." He smacks a gentle kiss to my forehead.

I laugh. "I think we have *a loooot* of steps before marriage and children."

"Ah, yes, your pain-in-the-ass steps."

I'm afraid steps won't be our problem.

No, it'll come straight from a monster in Boston.

If Cernach wants a marriage with me and Damien, I'll never do it.

Damien and I could always run off and marry without his knowledge, like my mother did, but look how that turned out. I need to have a long-term relationship work out before making as big of a step as marriage.

I refuse to marry before I'm ready.

Refuse to be Cernach's pawn.

Even if it means breaking my heart in the process.

## 22

# PIPPA

**One Month Later**

Satan, aka Antonio Lombardi, must've taken a break from hell today because he—okay, most likely Amara—invited me to her birthday party.

Antonio's parents are hosting the party in their massive estate's backyard. The colonial brick home could easily house ten families, and that's not counting the pool house built near the infinity pool.

The yard is like an oasis with brightly colored flowers, fountains that dump into the pool, and comfy furniture.

Now, I'm no accountant by any means, but unless the Lombardis have a shit ton of casinos—which, from my research, they don't—no way can a single location bring in an income to support a home like this. There's no way any of the homes I've been to, including Damien's, is supported by one casino.

I drop my gift bag on the table next to the others, and Damien does the same with his card. I had him take me to three different stores to find the perfect gift for Amara. Thoughtful gift-giving is important to me. I try to pay attention to people, to soak in the tidbits about themselves, so I can gift them something meaningful.

From those three stores, I found a stuffed snake that resembles Ace and a dance bag, where I put pointe shoes, a ballet beginner's book, and a dance outfit inside.

On the drive here, I asked Damien what his gift was.

He said, "Two thousand dollars," like that's normal for a five-year-old.

My life has changed drastically in the last month. I stay at Damien's every night now. I learned Ace sleeps in a tank in one of the five guest rooms. His sleeping setup is better than most people's.

I've also gotten to know some of the men Damien works with. On the days that I work, either Damien or one of them drives me.

Damien and I have found comfort with each other.

I've introduced him to my favorite shows and meals.

He's shared memories of his family. For hours at a time, I sit cross-legged on the couch or cuddled in bed next to him, listening to them. Hearing those stories and spending time with him have become some of my favorite things to do. I love seeing Damien's face as he recites them, reliving them in his head.

I learned his mother won the city's best chili four years in a row. That his father once participated in a hot dog eating contest and puked everywhere. Damien shuddered and said he'd never eat a hot dog again in his life. I also learned his sister was only months away from being named valedictorian of her college class.

This man, closed off to the world, is slowly opening himself up to me.

All day, every day, Damien displays the dark side of him. No one, other than Amara and me, are allowed to see any warmth through the cracks. All I want is to provide him a sense of comfort, like he has for me.

Clara swears I have.

Amara claims he smiles more when around me.

My dad is still MIA, and my mom is slowly starting to love herself again. She opens her blinds now and answers my calls. I even convinced her to attend an open studio night with me.

Her biggest problem, now that she's accepted my father is gone, is that she has nothing coming in without the studio income. I've helped as much as I can, but it's not easy with my Brew Bliss paychecks. She suggested I ask Damien for help, but I refused. He's done enough for me already.

As we walk closer to the party, Damien leans in to whisper in my ear. "Antonio's mother, Marsha, insisted on having the party. If Antonio is cranky today, that's why."

"A cranky Antonio?" I gasp, faking shock as my sandals flop against the warm concrete. "No way."

He chuckles, shaking his head.

When we reach the backyard, I take in the party decor. It's like a unicorn mom vomited all her unicorn babies here. They're *everywhere*.

In the pool, on the cutlery, the gift wrap, the bounce house.

I recognize most of the people from the funeral. Damien said it's close family only—another reason I was shocked I was invited. I frown, noticing there are only two other children. One of them looks a few years older than Amara, and another one is a toddler.

Poor Amara.

As I've spent more time with her, I've learned she doesn't have many friends. Clara homeschools her, and she doesn't do any outside extracurriculars. I understand Antonio is protective, but he also needs to let her have a life.

Not that I'll suggest that to him.

I'm not about to get drowned in that unicorn-infested pool.

"Happy birthday!" I squeal when we reach Amara and Clara.

Amara jumps up and down, barefoot, in her unicorn

swimsuit. "Uncle Damien!" She reaches out for his hand. "Let me show you my bounce house!"

Damien smirks at me before allowing her to drag him toward the bounce house.

*No way in hell is he getting in that thing.*

I will literally dash over there and record it if he does.

Clara follows them.

Since it's nine thousand degrees out here, a bounce house is a no-go for me.

"You're on my shit list."

My attention leaves them, and I whip around at the harsh voice to find Antonio approaching me, a drink in his hand and a glare on his rough face.

We've crossed paths a few times now, and this is the first time I haven't seen him wearing a suit. Considering the weather, I don't blame him for swapping it out for black pants and a short-sleeved shirt.

I flinch, crossing my arms. "Excuse me?"

He stops directly in front of me. "Amara won't stop asking me to take dance classes."

"Sorry." I rub my forehead. "She saw my pointe shoes and asked me to show her."

"You couldn't say no?" He quirks a brow and takes a sip of his drink. "Maybe shown her something simpler, like how to learn a new language or puzzle?"

"Dancing would be good for Amara." I offer a small, *please don't kill me* smile. "She'd love it."

"I see." He tips his glass in my direction. "Congrats. You're hired as her new teacher."

I fan myself with a napkin I stole from a table on the walk into the yard. "I don't teach anymore."

"You do now."

I open my mouth, prepared to dispute his job offer.

*No, thank you* on working for a made man.

They desire too much of their people. Too many of them also go missing.

"I pay well," he continues, as if reading my mind. "And knowing Damien, he'll probably make me pay you double since he's obsessed with you."

Butterflies swarm in my belly at his comment.

"You start tomorrow." He turns and walks away without waiting for me to accept the job.

Wait until I tell him my pay is five hundred an hour.

He might let me get out of the job then.

As much as I'd love to teach Amara—hell, I'd teach her for free—I don't want any employment tied to a Mafia-run family. It's too risky.

I slide my attention away from him to the inflatable bounce house across the yard. Damien stands outside it, the guard of the castle, and I make out Clara and Amara jumping inside.

I head in their direction, ready to kick both out in fear of a heatstroke. Just as I reach them, Amara rolls out of the house and Clara exits behind her.

She fans her face and catches her breath. "No more bounce houses unless they start installing ACs in them."

"Let's get you some water," I say, waving them toward the drink table.

We trek across the yard, and Amara tells me all the colors of her cake until we reach the table. I'm handing out waters when Antonio joins us.

Only this time, he's not alone.

Detective Kinney is standing next to him.

## 23

# PIPPA

IF THE HEAT has any positives, it's that if I pass out, I'll blame it on the damn sun. Because right now, I'm certain a panic attack will come in the next few minutes.

Damien tips his head toward Detective Kinney. "How's it going, Brock?"

"It's hot as hell out here," Brock, the traitorous detective, says. He tugs at his shirt collar as sweat builds along his hairline.

I'd be nervous, too, if I were an undercover agent working against *alleged* Mafia murderers.

Antonio's gaze is heavy on me. "Brock, this is Pippa."

Brock's jaw tenses as his attention swings to me. "Hi, Pippa. It's nice to meet you." A knowing, forced smile spreads across his face—a silent plea not to rat him out.

I nod, unscrew my water, and chug half of it.

This is further proof why I'll never go undercover. I don't care if it's going against killers or finding out who killed Bambi's mom; I'd give myself away in seconds. I wouldn't be sweating bullets like Brock. I'd be sweating beach balls.

They make small talk, but I hardly digest their conversation. All I'm listening for is the word *rat* or *cop*. Neither is said.

"Where's Vincent?" Brock asks. "I have a great story to tell him." He clasps Antonio's shoulder, who then immediately steps away and delivers a death stare.

Brock winces, and it takes him a moment to realize his accident. He holds up his hands in an *I'm innocent, man* signal.

Liar.

Antonio will have much bigger problems than a pat on the back if Brock slips deep enough inside their organization to take them down.

I rub my palm against my shorts as Brock and Antonio walk toward the crowded table, where Vincent sits with a group of men.

If I tell Damien about Brock, he'll know I spoke to a detective and kept that information from him for a month.

*Will he trust me after that?*

I could keep it to myself, but I'd feel worse.

That'd put him, Amara, Clara, all of them in harm's way.

I won't take Amara's father away from her. She already lost her mother.

I swallow and grab Damien's arm. "Can we talk privately?"

## 24

# DAMIEN

PIPPA LOOKS like she's seen a ghost when we enter the pool house.

Her breathing is a ragged mess.

If I pressed my hand to her chest, I'm positive her heart would be a wild animal inside.

"Pippa?" I ask, my voice turning gravelly. "What's wrong?"

She raises her hands in a similar gesture to how Brock did when he touched Antonio. "I need to tell you something, but you have to swear you won't hurt me."

If there's ever been a sentence that provokes madness inside me, it's that.

I'd never violently hurt Pippa.

I might fuck her hard.

Play a few mind games with her.

But hurt her in a way we'd never come back from?

Never.

She could charge at me with a knife and bludgeon me through the goddamn heart, and I wouldn't hurt her. I'd take the pain because I'd rather endure it than her.

It's easy for me to detach myself from the people I hurt.

From those whose final breaths I take.

But it'll never be that way with Pippa.

I'd take my own before hers.

"Pippa," I grit out, my patience running thin. "Start talking now."

I won't hurt her, but that doesn't mean I won't get angry.

While I'm considered calm in our line of business, you'll get no patience from me in situations like this.

I don't like secrets kept from me.

If I find out something is kept from me, I'll rip it out, root by root, until I have every single detail.

"First," she starts, "I want to clarify that I didn't say anything."

I hate how her voice shakes.

Like it's a struggle for her to rattle out what she wants to tell me.

"Spit it out," I snap.

Her stare turns pained, as if she really is prepared to jab a knife through my chest. "Brock—that guy out there—he came to the coffee shop to talk to me."

Fury burns through me, though not as a result from what Pippa expects.

From something completely different.

She retreats away, her back colliding with the wall. "He's a detective who asked me to gather intel against you and the Lombardi family." Her body slumps forward like it took all her energy to get that one sentence out. "I swear to you, I told him no. I wouldn't even take his business card."

I bolt toward her, and she braces herself against the wall.

"Damien—"

I stop her from continuing by pressing my finger to her lips. "Pippa, I'm not mad at you." I kiss her, lingering there to prove my words. "But right now, I have to go."

157

She grabs my arm as I step away from her. "Please don't kill him."

I tug out of her hold. "He's not who you need to worry about."

## 25

# DAMIEN

I WANT to rip the sun out of the fucking sky and throw it as I storm toward Antonio. The heat only adds to my frustration.

Who throws a birthday party in this weather?

Has no one heard of Chuck E. fucking Cheese?

Hell, I'd have thrown it at my place if it meant I didn't have to hang out in a goddamn kiln.

With each step I take, I will myself to calm down. As pissed as I am, I can't let my anger get the best of me. I have to wait to confront him in private.

Antonio is third in line for the boss role in the family, right behind Vinny. If I disrespect him in public, it'd make him look weak to the other men.

People need to fear him.

To know if you say the wrong word, he'll rip your head off.

Driving that fear is what keeps all of us alive.

Lucky for me, the only people at his table are Clara and Amara. Most of the people here are family members, whether blood or business-related. While I'm always involved in every Lombardi-related move, I keep my distance from some of the others. Antonio does as well.

"We need to talk," I say when I reach him.

Antonio pushes his sunglasses from the top of his head to his eyes, grabs his drink, and follows me toward the pool house. From the satisfied expression on his face, he already knows what this is about.

My strides are long, and as we pass a group of men, I notice Brock's attention glued to us.

*Fucking asshole.*

I'll deal with him later.

I swing the door open, and Pippa springs to her feet off the couch when we enter. Her eyes dart from me to Antonio and widen.

She has no idea what's happening yet.

She'll most likely be pissed when she learns, though.

"You sent Brock to her?" I ask Antonio as soon as he shuts the door behind us.

"You have her around my daughter, Damien," Antonio stresses. "I had to make sure I could trust her."

I curl my hands into fists.

Us sending Brock to speak with people isn't anything new. We do it to test their loyalty, to see if they're trustworthy. If they even entertain the idea of speaking to *Detective Kinney*, we get rid of them.

I didn't test Pippa because I was worried. In my gut, I knew I could trust her, but there was still that layer of concern. She despises Cernach, and we're in the same line of work. She could resent me for that.

But what I've hoped is that she knows there's more to me than the violence. My hatred toward those who wrong me is untamed, but my loyalty and compassion for those I care about are also untamed. It's a happy medium, in my opinion. I'd rip my heart out of my chest and give it to her if she needed one.

Antonio shrugs. "She didn't talk and hardly gave Brock the

time of day," he explains as Pippa stares at him, bug-eyed. "Do I feel a little better? Yes. Do I trust her completely?" He looks straight at Pippa. "You know I can't say that about anyone."

"You crossed a line, not giving me a heads-up," I sneer.

"Better I test her than my father." He motions between Pippa and me. "As soon as you two arrived today, he asked me if I'd sent Brock to her yet. He'd asked me to do it after the funeral. With all the time you're spending together and how involved you seem to be, she was on his radar."

Antonio and I have always been straightforward with each other. Neither of us has ever sent Brock to someone without the other knowing.

I point my finger at him. "That's the last test for her. Do you hear me?"

"You work for us, Damien. It's been this way for years, and it will always be this way. You get plenty of leniency, given who we are and what you are to me, but that doesn't mean complete freedom. I don't even have full freedom. Consider this a favor so she's more welcome."

Pippa stands to the sidelines, catching on to every word of our conversation.

Shaking my head, I curse under my breath. "Who was watching her?"

Pippa always has eyes on her—whether it be me, Julian, Emilio, or Luis. One of them saw her talking to Brock and didn't say anything to me. I might not be able to punch Antonio in the face, but you can bet your ass I'd punch any of them.

"Emilio," Antonio replies. "I made certain it wasn't Julian."

*Because he knew Julian would tell me.*

"I'm kicking Emilio's ass," I spit out, digging my thumb into the space between my brows.

"I ordered him not to tell you."

I'm pissed, but at the end of the day, Antonio is right. There's satisfaction in knowing she blew him off *and* told me who he was today. She could've hidden it all from me. But I'm still pissed at being left in the dark about it with Antonio.

"Wait," Pippa starts, stepping closer to us. "Are you telling me—"

"I'm not telling you anything," Antonio says impatiently and storms out of the pool house.

"Let me wrap my head around this," Pippa says, fully focused on the situation while rubbing her temples. "At first, I thought you left to go kill Brock or whatever it is you guys do." Her voice teeters toward rambling. "Kill, hack up, poison—"

I hold up my hand. "Pippa, please don't start listing off ways people can murder others."

"Do *you* murder others?"

"I think you know the answer to that." I flick my hand through the air. "Moving on."

"Don't speak to me like that."

"Don't ask me stupid questions, and I won't."

Her face burns, and I know I'm pissing her off.

But sometimes, I love a pissed-off Pippa.

It's hot as hell.

She storms toward me, hands on hips, attitude on one hundred.

*So hot.*

*So sexy.*

She slaps my chest. The pain matches that of a mere pinch.

But it stung her hand. I know from the way she suddenly jerked it back.

"Is Brock even a detective?" she bites out, returning the hand she slapped me with to her waist.

"Yes. We just pay him more than the state does to be a crooked one."

The Marchettis have most law enforcement on their payroll,

but we managed to snag a few with our checkbooks. At first, we had to blackmail Brock. Well, we used his father to blackmail him. A former governor screams scandal. It took us ten minutes to find *one* subject to blackmail him. An hour later, we had ten.

Since his father was no longer of good use to us, we extorted Brock instead. I'm beginning to think Brock enjoys the perks though.

*As long as he doesn't get too comfortable.*

"How very cliché of you," she mutters, rolling her eyes.

I snatch her elbow, and she releases a huff as I snap her around and pull her toward me. Her back collides with my chest, and I stretch my arm along her collarbone to prevent her from moving.

She trembles as I raise my hand and curl it around her throat. She swallows beneath my palm—once, twice, three times—each one heavier than the last. I give it a gentle squeeze, testing her, before lowering my hand down her body.

"Watch that smart mouth of yours," I hiss in her ear.

"Or what?"

"Or I'll drag Brock in here, so you can show him how well you suck my dick."

She attempts to wiggle out of my hold, but I don't loosen my grip. "You'd never."

I dip my head and nuzzle my nose against her neck. Her hair is in a ponytail, so it's easy for me to suck on her sensitive skin there.

"You're right," I say against it. "If he ever saw how beautiful you look with my cock in your mouth, I'd have to sever his goddamn head off." I lick up her neck and hold her still as her knees weaken. "That sight is for me and me only." I slide my hand down her shorts over her panties and play with her clit.

She throws her head back, resting it on my shoulder, her gaze finding mine. "Did you ever doubt my trust?"

"You have to doubt everyone's in this world."

"Did I pass your trust test, then?"

"You passed." I slip her panties to the side and finger her until she comes on my fingers.

*That's my good, trustworthy girl.*

## 26

# PIPPA

IF HE MAKES dinner for you, green flag, ladies.

Green freaking flag.

Don't side-eye me for ignoring the red ones, though.

Monique has the night off, so Damien offered to cook dinner. When I asked if he knew how to cook, he shared with me that his mother had made it a weekly ritual for him and Julian to spend an hour in the kitchen with her, much to their father's dismay. She knew the lifestyle was hard for women, and with their lack of interest in an arranged marriage, she didn't want them to starve to death if they stayed single.

Cooking has never been my strong suit. So much of my time was dedicated to dance that I never learned my way around a kitchen. My go-to meals are ramen, grilled cheese, and simple salads. Since my mother spent so much time at the studio and my father was gone gambling, those are also what I grew up eating.

I rarely get early nights with Damien. Unless we have plans or he's watching Amara, he works late. It's usually past three in the morning when he finally crawls into bed with me. Even with him gone so much, I don't feel alone.

No matter how busy he is, he always makes a point of

staying in contact. If he misses breakfast with me, he stops by Brew Bliss to order a coffee and wish me good morning. He texts and calls throughout the day. Despite being the busiest man I know, he always stays in touch.

Words of advice: if my Mafia boyfriend can text me amid his crimes, then so can yours.

It's so sexy watching Damien in the luxury all-black kitchen. The brownstone, clearly renovated from its original state, makes perfect use of the available open space. The natural lighting illuminating the room prevents it from appearing too dark, and the black marble adds to the polished touch. The state-of-the-art appliances are comparable to ones found in high-end restaurants.

"You know, I feel like I practically moved in with you," I comment, filling two glasses with wine and sitting on the island stool.

For the past thirty minutes, I've watched Damien navigate the kitchen. When I offered to help, he told me to sit there, have a drink, and relax.

"You look pretty comfortable here." His eyes are on me as he warms oil in a wok. "Might as well move in. I like coming home to you at night."

"I don't know if I'd be a good roommate candidate," I reply, attempting to sound like I'm joking but failing. I reach for my glass and take a satisfying sip. "I'm a terrible cook, I had a near-death experience when I cleaned my bathroom with too many chemicals at once, and I have a history of paying rent late."

That pretty much sums me up as a whole.

Don't blame me. Blame my hyperactive brain.

It's why I love ballet so much.

The constant flow of thoughts in my mind finds solace when I dance.

When I tie my pointe shoes and dance, my outside world fades away, and I'm in the moment.

Damien rests the wok on the burner and stretches across the

island to cup my face. "Pippa, those reasons mean absolutely nothing to me. I have a cleaner and a chef, and I'd never take a penny from you." He runs his thumb along my bottom lip. "There's nothing I want more than for you to live with me."

"Steps, remember?" I squeak out against his thumb, causing him to drop his hand from my face. "I'm already breaking so many of them."

"I'm ready to burn those steps to the ground," he grumbles.

I sigh.

"If you're not ready to move in with me officially, I understand, but you're getting a new apartment with a goddamn doorman." He presses his finger to my lips when I open them to argue. "And let's not discuss being able to afford it. I'm covering the cost, and that's nonnegotiable." He replaces his finger with his lips, smacking a kiss to them, and pulls back to return to cooking.

"I'm not comfortable with you spending so much money on me."

"If anyone deserves to be spoiled, it's you. That's how I want to spend my money. Give me that, baby."

"I just ..." My shoulders droop.

He adjusts the stove's heat to circle the island, spins me around in the stool, and perches himself on the edge of the marble.

His gaze penetrates mine. "Pippa, I know this feels rushed, but give me a chance. Forget about the steps, about what anyone else thinks. Block all of that out. Let our relationship unravel on our timing." He smooths his hand over my cheek, his signature move.

One night, I told him I loved when he did that.

"I do it for selfish reasons," is what he replied. "I do it to remind us both that you're mine, and you'll always be mine. Your face fits so well in my palm that I want to mold it there for the rest of our lives."

"I'm good with where we're at," he says, slipping me back into our conversation. "Are you?"

My heart skips as I gulp and whisper, "I'm good with where we're at too."

"Then, that's all that matters." He smirks. "Just me and you."

I blow out a long breath. "I'm scared, Damien."

"There's nothing to fear with us, Pippa. I'd sacrifice my heart before I hurt yours. If I'm not making you feel safe enough, let me know what else I need to do."

Tears prick my eyes. "You make me feel safer than anyone."

He opens his mouth to reply, but we both stare at my stomach when it rumbles.

He smirks before kissing me once, twice, three times. "Let's get you fed."

I slide off my stool as he releases me. "What can I help with?"

He raises his chin. "Alexa, play classical music." His eyes drink me in for a moment. "You can dance in the kitchen while I cook. Entertain me, my sweet dancer, and I'll give you a round of applause with my tongue later."

## 27

# DAMIEN

**Two Months Later**

My head throbs as I enter Antonio's office. We're post a four-hour meeting, where we discussed the record-breaking casino earnings and potential expansion to a second location. To which I voted in opposition. So did Antonio.

Laundering money through one location is risky as it is. I'll sacrifice money for a lesser headache. I'm already pushing my luck and in jeopardy of prison time for everything I do.

Antonio's jackass uncle, Sonny, kept pushing the matter, like it'd make his dick grow bigger, making the meeting drag *on and on*. Eventually and thankfully, Vincent kicked everyone out and said we'd revote in two weeks. My vote won't change.

Lucky Kings is more than a front for illicit financial activities. We also manage it as a legitimate company. Our income has increased fourfold in the past five years. We have a fleet of employees who focus on advertising, basic running of the casino, and even an HR department.

Rumors follow the casino, but many of our employees are law-abiding citizens who receive legal paychecks. They don't know what happens behind closed doors—how we wash five-dollar bills to convert them to hundreds or transfer money across so many overseas accounts that our accountants even have trouble keeping track.

"Are you still pissed at me?" Antonio asks, kicking his feet up on his desk.

Relaxing in the chair opposite his desk, I casually trace my finger around the edge of my whiskey glass. "I'm not pissed. I'm frustrated you hid it from me."

"Stop being frustrated. I did you a favor," he says in a dry tone. "Pippa can come around more." He steeples his fingers together. "There's another issue we need to discuss."

Just hearing the words *another issue* makes my head throb.

I'd like one day where there's no *another issue*.

Where it's sunshine and I can spend the day with Pippa without a million problems crawling around my brain like a virus.

I raise a brow. "What's that?"

He drops his feet off the desk and sits up straight. "Vinny is out of control. He's acting too reckless."

"Is there ever a time when he's not being reckless?"

Everyone knows the family's downfall will begin when Vincent steps down or dies and Vinny takes control of the family. I've overheard men discussing exit strategies to leave the country when that day comes.

Vinny is good at what he does, but he's also too impulsive.

He has bigger plans beyond running the Lombardi family.

He aspires to be the king of New York.

To dethrone Cristian Marchetti.

He runs his mouth too much about it.

Anyone with a functioning brain understands Cristian is the worst person to go to war with.

"If we're talking reckless, can I speak freely?" I ask him.

He provides a *you have the floor* gesture, and I gulp down my whiskey.

"You need to end things with Giana Marchetti."

Antonio has a secret.

A secret that'll take us to war if Vinny doesn't.

One that'll piss off Cristian Marchetti far more than Vinny singing his own rendition of Simba's "I Just Can't Wait to Be King."

"Cristian will kill you," I remind him for what feels like the thousandth time.

Any threat to his daughter is something Cristian will never tolerate. Not that I believe Antonio would ever intentionally hurt Gigi. From what I've heard, he has killed *for her*. But not many people, possibly including her, knows that.

I learned about his affair with Gigi when he dragged me to Italy with him, Amara, and Clara. We had a good trip, but there was no relaxing for me when I found out why we were there. He chased down Gigi at her aunt's in Tuscany. He'd hang out with Amara during the day and then wander off to fuck Gigi at night.

Antonio rises to his feet, strolls to the drink cart, and pours himself another. I shake my head, declining his refill offer.

"Keep an eye on my brother," he instructs me. "Rumor has it, Cristian is fucking his ex."

I flex my hand around my glass. "We might be fucked."

He nods. "I'm positive we're fucked."

---

REVENGE IS SO FUCKING SWEET.

It's my favorite goddamn flavor.

"You did a great job at hiding," I tell Herman, clicking my tongue against the roof of my mouth and circling him. "But you should've known it was only a matter of time before we found you."

"I didn't know who you were!" he cries out, drool falling from his mouth. He wiggles in his chair, struggling to break free from the tape restraining him in it. His movements become more frantic with each second. Even if he breaks the tape, he can't run with zip-tied ankles.

Or with the leg I shot a bullet through five minutes ago.

Herman Jackson. Forty-four. Piece-of-shit cyber hacker.

The man who helped the Popovs hack into my family's security system.

He's the last man on my list, and I can't wait to cross his name off.

After I watch him take his last breath, we'll have killed every man responsible for my family's murder.

I slide black leather gloves over my hands. Julian does the same before handing me a vial and keeping one for himself.

He's trying to keep his emotions in check, but I know my little brother.

I see the emotional storm in his eyes.

We agreed to do this together.

I play with the vial in my hand. Herman has finally shut his loud ass up, most likely trying to add up in his idiot head what we're doing.

While I was honest when I told Pippa we had Ace's venom removed, I withheld the information of what we had done with it. Antonio had it stored in vials and refrigerated them. We save the venom for the right moments. It's one of our methods of killing.

Julian and I decided we didn't want the men to go to prison.

We didn't want to recite some sob story to a courtroom about how our family's deaths destroyed us and we missed them so fucking much.

No, we wanted to kill those responsible ourselves.

*Sinful Sacrifice*

To take the final breaths from their bodies.
Julian glances at me in question, and I nod.
Herman thrashes his body from side to side.
Screaming.
Begging.
Apologizing.
Every word he says makes me sick.
The idea of him believing we'd spare his life is laughable.

We dip the syringes in the venom, and I watch in fascination as it fills with the transparent liquid. Each of us, using one hand, holds Herman's head back, restraining him. We use the other to puncture the needles into his neck.

He screams.
Wails.
Kicks his feet.

We sit in chairs opposite him. We've never given someone a double dose before. Due to our limited supply, we avoid wasting the venom. One always does the trick. Given the situation, Antonio gave us permission to use as much as we wanted.

I check my watch, waiting patiently.
*Ticktock.*
*Ticktock.*
The effects of the venom kick in fast.

With a satisfied smile, I watch Herman's death as if it's the performance of a lifetime. He opens his mouth and unleashes a gut-wrenching scream of pain.

Over and over.
Like how you'd replay a favorite song.
*I fucking love it.*

When Herman's neck starts swelling, Julian bursts into laughter.

More pained screams.
More satisfaction oozes from my bones.
Soon, Herman will hemorrhage.

His blood will clot, causing internal bleeding.

Then, his useless kidneys will fail him.

I whistle to the beat of his cries, and heat radiates through my chest.

It doesn't take long for the venom to work.

Fifteen minutes later, Herman is as dead as AOL's dial-up internet.

We share a moment of silence when he shuts his annoying ass up and his body collapses forward like a sack of rotten potatoes.

On the drive here, Julian and I discussed how long we wanted Herman to suffer. In the end, we settled on fast and painful.

Every week, when I visit my family's tombstones, I vow to kill every man who played a part in their deaths. Now, I can tell them we succeeded.

We spend the next half hour silently staring at Herman's dead body.

The foam that trickled out of his mouth has dried, crusting along his lips. The color of his skin is already starting to change.

"Let's get him to the morgue," I tell Julian, standing. "We'll pick him up later and scatter his ashes at the city dump, where he belongs."

We reverse a stolen SUV into the warehouse and roll Herman's body inside before tossing a tarp over it, along with gas cans and other shit to avoid suspicion if we're pulled over.

I slip the mortician two hundred dollars and leave.

I have a surprise for my dancer tonight.

## 28

# PIPPA

I reread my *Sexy but Stress-Free Date Night* checklist on my phone.

Damien is coming home early, and I've planned the perfect date night for us.

His *jobs* have become more demanding, and each day that passes, the tension on his face deepens.

On numerous occasions, I've asked if he wants to talk about it. He shakes his head and changes the subject. Since he ruled out therapy sessions from Dr. Yours Truly, I discovered other ways to boost his mood—sex; introducing him to my favorite shows, which usually put him to sleep; and dancing for him.

His favorite is the third.

"I understand now," he once told me. "When you said dancing calms you."

"What do you mean?"

"Watching you dance calms me. You pull me into your world and take my breath away with each delicate movement you make. The way your body flows with the harmony of the music is beautiful. It erases my worries, my troubles fading away as if they never existed at all."

When he walks through the door tonight, I want him to forget his troubles and pain, for him to relax.

My master plan started this morning. Much to Emilio's dismay, he chaperoned me on a shopping trip with Darcy and Genesis. We gathered the date-night necessities—lingerie, bubble bath, champagne, and chocolate. Now, I'm just waiting for my man to come home.

Emilio is seated at the island, drinking coffee and texting. Out of all the men Damien has appointed on Pippa duty, Emilio is my least favorite. Not that I disclosed that to him. He might be boring, but he's still a man who murders people for a living.

When I asked Damien what Emilio's deal was, he explained that Emilio struggles with his role within the Lombardi family. Unlike Damien and Julian, who adjusted well with the fact that they had no other life choices, Emilio didn't. I guess his dad is a real asshole, too, and he and Emilio constantly butt heads.

My thoughts slip from my phone to the door when it opens. Damien walks in, holding a black garment bag.

Emilio stands and tucks his phone inside his pocket. "Am I good to go?"

"You're good," Damien replies, his eyes fastened on me.

Emilio leaves, and my mouth waters as Damien comes closer. His suit jacket is unbuttoned, his cuff links undone. I see him every day, and not one has passed where I didn't find him fucking sexy.

I stand from the couch, meeting him halfway.

"Go change into this." He hands me the garment bag. "We leave in thirty minutes."

"To go where?" I tug at the hem of my tee.

I saved the lingerie for later. Damien would've flipped his shit if he had walked in to see me lounging in a lace nightie in front of Emilio.

"It's a surprise." He lowers his head, brushing a kiss against my lips. "Now, go get dressed, baby."

He swats at my ass as I dash toward the stairs and follows me.

I haven't *officially* moved in with Damien, but he cleared out half his closet for me. Since then, nearly my entire wardrobe has moved residences from my cubbyhole-sized apartment closet to here.

When we started dating, I had no issue fitting all my belongings in my apartment closet. But after all Damien's spoiling, not even half would fit now.

I stroll through the bedroom and French doors that lead into the closet. Kicking out of my slippers, I hang the garment bag over my robe hook. I unzip the bag, my smile building with each inch.

The bag falls open, revealing a blush-pink gown.

It's simple yet elegant with a V-neck and a length that sweeps the floor. I feather my fingers along the satin and notice Damien standing in the doorway, watching me. He rests against the length of the doorframe, his gaze sweeping down my body as I strip out of my clothes.

He inches into the closet yet keeps his distance as I glide the gown off its hanger. The dress is heaven, brushing my skin as I slip it on. Damien retreats to his side of the closet, swapping his black suit for a tux. He opens his watch drawer, selects a gold Rolex, and fastens it around his wrist.

I shudder when his gaze returns to me, and he licks his lips. His eyes lower down my body, drinking me in, and he whistles.

Raising his hand, he gestures for me to turn, facing the mirror. While staring at our reflections, I watch his gaze drift from my face, down my collarbone, to my cleavage, then down my waist. It lingers there as he cups his hands on my hips.

He bites his bottom lip before whispering, "Let me." Crowding closer, he toys with my dress zipper that extends down my back to the base of my ass.

I breathe out a moan as he raises the zipper in slow motion, his free hand now stroking my shoulder.

"This color," he mutters, burrowing his face against my neck, his voice as silky as the dress. "It's the color of your cheeks when you blush after I've made you come." He plays with the thin strap, slipping it down my shoulder, and slides his lips along my collarbone to place a gentle kiss there. "I can't wait to see this color on your skin later tonight when my mouth is between your legs."

My cheeks warm, blooming with the pink he loves.

"Time for your surprise, my sweet dancer," he says against my skin.

---

I DON'T HAVE patience for surprises.

Maybe because the only *surprises* I had growing up were shut-off utilities and whatever scam of the week my father was working on.

"Will you give me a hint?" I plead with Damien in the back seat before adding flirtation to my tone. "*Just a little one.*"

"You're lucky you're sexy as hell," he replies with a chuckle.

I hate how poorly lit our space is, making it difficult to see more of his face. I love when he chuckles. There's always a sliver of a smile on his handsome face when he does.

He withdraws two tickets from his blazer pocket, passes them to me, and turns on the overhead light. I gasp as I read them.

Two front-row tickets to New York City Ballet's *Swan Lake*.

Once, he asked what my dream ballet to attend was. I casually mentioned the show being on my bucket list but didn't expect him to take me. I've replied to that question with the same answer since I was a child.

It was on my Santa wish list four years in a row before I eventually quit asking. My father once told me Santa didn't have a budget for things like that.

This is yet another quality I admire in Damien.

He listens. Truly listens.

When we talk, he absorbs my words like they hold a secret puzzle within them.

My heart thumps in my chest when we arrive at the theater. Augusto parks and opens the back door.

Just like every time he has a driver, Damien doesn't allow him to assist me out of the SUV. He cups my hand, holding me as I step out.

Augusto tells us to have fun, and Damien guides me into the building. The lobby is quiet as we head straight to the theater. Peering up, I admire the gold-leaf ceiling and crystal chandelier. The room itself is a masterpiece.

I've been to this theater two other times. Once during a third-grade field trip and the other when I brought my mother for a matinee show on Mother's Day. Each visit increased my love of ballet more. Growing up, this was where I dreamed of dancing. Unfortunately, life got in the way of that.

As I stand here, bliss spreads through my body.

I'm in absolute heaven.

If heaven had a population of two.

No other soul is in the theater.

No people making random chatter or filing in, searching for their seats before the show starts.

I slip my hand up Damien's wrist to check the time on his watch. "How is no one here yet? The show starts in ten minutes."

Here I was, stressed we were on time.

"No one else is coming," Damien says with absolute certainty.

I inch closer, our bodies brushing, as if we were in on a secret. "What?"

His lips curl into a smirk. "It's a private show for us, baby."

I gape at him, shivers spreading over every inch of my skin. "Are you serious?"

He slowly nods.

My mouth falls open, and it takes me a moment to recollect myself from the rush of happiness flowing through me. "You spoil me too much."

Damien releases my hand to rest his on my waist, drawing me in closer. The smell of his intoxicating cologne swallows the air around us. With the way he's hungrily staring at me, even if the theater were flooded with people, he'd still absorb all my attention.

He brushes his bruised knuckles across my cheek, and I shiver.

Bruises. Cuts. Blood.

They've become frequent accessories on Damien.

My body softens at his touch as I appreciate the roughness of his skin brushing mine. I love how they collide, like two different worlds merging into one.

Once, after drinking too much wine, I referred to us as a strawberry couple. He stared at me as if I'd lost my mind.

"Rough on the outside, aka you—" I said.

"Please refrain from comparing me to a fruit again," he interrupted me. "While I don't fit into the comparison of a fruit, I'd have to say you taste as sweet as one."

The next day, I bought strawberry-printed pajamas.

That night, he came home with chocolate-dipped strawberries. He squeezed the juices between my legs and licked it up while fingering me.

Damien saying my name breaks me away from my thoughts. With his hand still on my waist, he stares down at me in awe, a tenderness in them I've never witnessed before.

"You've completely changed my life," he says, his tone matching the warmth in his eyes. "Because of you, I don't come home alone to a cold bed. No matter what condition I'm in—broken, battered, bloody—you're my strength. You see the best in me even though I don't deserve it. You giving me that is something priceless. The least I can do is spoil the shit out of you and make every dream of yours come true."

I stare at him, speechless.

Good thing he's holding me, or his heavy words would've dropped me to my knees.

He presses his soft lips to mine. The kiss lingers, both of us wanting more, but neither pushing it. *No, thank you* on being arrested for indecent exposure.

I'm absolutely, no doubt in my mind, falling in love with this man.

*He's the one for me.*

I gulp in thick breaths when he separates from me, trying my hardest to come up with a response.

*He's all of that for me.*

*My home. My strength. My heart.*

I blink, attempting to conjure a prose as perfect as his in my mind.

I have a way with dancing. It seems Damien has a way with words.

"Let me escort you to our seats," he says, interrupting my brainstorming. "The show is about to start." He falls back a few steps and crooks his elbow.

I lace my arm through his, feeling on top of the world. "Where exactly are our seats?"

"Wherever you want them to be." He motions toward the room. "Your pick, baby."

I test three different seats in two different rows before finding one with the perfect view. Damien is a patient man each time we move and try another.

Just as I'm making myself comfortable in my final selection, the orchestra files out, taking their chairs in the pit. Damien squeezes his hand over mine, interlacing our fingers as the gold-fringed bottom curtain opens and the show starts.

Tears prick at my eyes, eventually slipping down my cheeks. My makeup will be a wild mess by the time this is over.

I cry as the dancers unfold their beautiful love story.

I cry for the love and devotion this man is showing me.

Neither of us was looking for love. If we're being honest, Damien was looking to possibly murder my father. But here we are, falling in love with each other.

Now, I just hope the fate I wished for stays on my side.

"OH, no, I'm not finished with you yet." Damien pulls me against his wall of a body to stop me from walking toward the theater's exit.

My eyes are glossy. And just as I suspected, my cheeks are mascara-stained.

The ballet is over. The dancers took their bows and left the stage ten minutes ago. I stayed in my seat for another five minutes, collecting myself.

Tonight wasn't only a show.

It was an experience.

One I'll never forget.

Damien shifts our still-connected bodies to face the stage. I hear low chatter as a man carrying a circular table appears onstage. Two others follow him, a chair in each one's hand.

He interlaces our fingers, and the lighting is hazy as he escorts me along the perimeter of the stage. This feels so off-limits.

A gray-haired man, wearing white gloves and a black tux, stands at the base of the stairs leading onto the stage.

He stands up straighter when we reach him. "Good evening, Pippa and Damien. Did you enjoy the show?"

"I'd be bouncing on my toes if I wasn't in heels." "It was amazing." With the amount of adrenaline pouring through me, I'll be up for hours. It's like someone fed fifteen espresso shots through my veins via IV.

When the man offers me his hand to assist me up the stairs, Damien stops him to do it himself.

Geesh, he needs to put out a bulletin that he's the official Pippa helper. I'm starting to feel rude, ignoring men's help.

My heels clack against the stage as we walk across it. An entire table setup is now in the middle, complete with a white tablecloth draped over the table and two chairs across from each other. A candle, smelling of fresh-cut roses, flickers in the middle.

Damien helps me into my chair, waiting for me to adjust my dress and get comfortable before taking his. As he sits across from me, he runs his hand along his tight jaw. He's doing his best at hiding his stress to make the night perfect for me. *For us.*

As I smooth my napkin along my lap, I find my mother's warning about him so wrong.

Yes, Damien is dangerous. A murderer. A man on the FBI's watch list. *Yes, I googled that.* But his name doesn't belong on the list with the other cliché assholes who serve the mob.

Men who chose their own self-preservation over others' lives.

Men with egos so large that they kill anyone who threatens it.

He's nothing like Cernach. Corruption might flood his veins, but those veins still flow into a noble heart.

"I can't believe you did this," I say, choking up again.

I don't even want to know how much of a hot mess I look like.

"Baby"—Damien's tender tone resurfaces—"if it makes you happy, believe me, I'm doing it."

Two servers approach our table. One holds two salad plates and squeezes forward to drop them between us. The other pours champagne inside our glasses while reciting tonight's menu. Every item—from the appetizer all the way to the dessert—is one of my favorites.

Get you a man who's spent their entire life committing crime while evading prison time. They pay attention to every small detail.

The men tell us to enjoy and leave the stage.

"How did you do this?" I ask, picking up my fork and stabbing a piece of romaine lettuce with it.

"I made some calls." Damien shrugs, as if it was no biggie.

"Oh, yes," I say around a heavy laugh. "I forgot how easy it is to *make some calls* and reserve a private showing of the New York City Ballet company."

I hope those *calls* involved monetary promises, not threats.

He meets my stare and smirks. "Did you enjoy the show?"

"I very much did." I drop my fork, the lettuce still attached to the side of my plate. "What did *you* think?"

"I enjoyed it." He shrugs, scooping up the champagne glass.

"You were bored."

"I was not."

"Your eyes were more on me than the stage."

"That's because I enjoy watching you more. No need for a stage."

"You watch me when I'm onstage." So far, he's attended three of my shows. At this point, I might feel more anxiety *if* he doesn't come.

"Exactly—because it's *you* onstage. The world could be ending around me, and if you're onstage, I'm fucked because nothing could drag my attention away from you."

"This is seriously the best night of my life," I slur as we walk into the townhome.

Okay, Damien is walking us both while I use him as a personal cane. I might've celebrated with too much champagne.

We ate. We drank.

We talked. We laughed.

We fell in love even more.

After our three-course dinner, the show's director, Margaret, came out and introduced herself. I nearly face-planted from my chair. I've followed Margaret's journey for a while and always wanted to meet her.

I spent the next thirty minutes talking with her. Damien sat there, listening, never acting bored or pressuring me to leave. Before she left, he took our picture. Well, *pictures* since he's proving himself to be even more perfect after taking ten photos to make sure I had a good one.

Damien grips me tight, as if worried I'll topple over, and helps me up the stairs.

So much for giving him a stress-free night.

Drunk-sitting me definitely wasn't on my list.

It's not really a great stress reliever either.

Admittingly, I'm an annoying drunk.

But I'd rather be an annoying drunk than an angry one.

A win is a win.

He flips on the light when we reach the bedroom. I wobble in my one heel—pretty sure the other one is somewhere in the back seat—and Damien stabilizes me on our walk to the closet.

I grip his shoulder as he unzips and helps me out of my dress. It falls at my feet, hitting the top of his loafers, and I step out of it.

"Don't let it stay on the floor," I whisper, still holding him. "It's too pretty."

I hang on to his blazer sleeve as he leans down to scoop the dress in his arms and drape it over the island. His gaze flicks from the dress to me, and his stare burns down my body so hot that it's like he's never witnessed me so naked.

He inches closer, the toes of his loafers hitting my bare ones, and skims the pads of his fingers along my cheekbones.

"I love you, Pippa."

If he wasn't holding me up, I'd have fallen on my ass.

Not from being tipsy, but from the reality that he's falling as hard as I am.

## 29

# DAMIEN

I DIDN'T MEAN to say those words

Like the bullet of an enemy, they came out of nowhere.

Speaking of bullets, I'm on the edge of sweating more than when I've had the cold barrel of a gun shoved against my skull.

Death doesn't scare me.

But feelings? Honesty? Goddamn love?

Those are the fucking boogeymen in my life.

*I. Love. You.*

And while I hadn't expected to say them, no truer words have ever left my mouth.

Our breathing—hers short, mine long—is the only noise in the closet.

Pippa stares at me in shock, and her fingers slip from my blazer sleeve in what seems like slow motion.

The room is hot, like I suddenly replaced the closet with a sauna.

I sweep a hand over my face to collect myself before tearing my blazer off and dropping it on the floor.

*No going back now.*

Might as well continue showing her a side of myself no one sees.

No more hiding from her by slipping on my mask. I do it with enough people.

I cock my head to the side, taking in every inch of her face.

Her high cheekbones, how she sucks in her cheeks when breathing, the way her plump lips pucker as she thinks.

When I'm with her, it's like I'm losing my sanity.

I'm wrapped up in her, forgetting where I am, who I am, how the fucking world works.

But in a good way.

Maybe it's the opposite.

Maybe she's leading the way for me, helping me *find* a speckle of sanity within myself.

I clear my throat, more words coming. "I've never said those words to a woman not in my family. But something I've learned these past few months is how fast you can lose someone." I ball my hand into a tight fist and press it against my heart. "I bleed for you, Pippa. You've danced your way into this cold heart of mine, somehow slipping yourself through the shattered cracks."

Her hand shakes as she reaches out and places it over my fist.

The warmth of her touch spills through my hand, my chest, straight to this organ I once referred to as useless.

Pippa accepts my past, my darkness, my work.

*All of me.*

I've never felt so cut the fuck open before, bleeding for someone.

"I love you, Damien," she whispers, slipping her hand from my fist up to my neck, smoothing her nails over the skin.

I clasp my hand around her wrist and force her to dig her nails deeper into my skin. I want her to mark and sink her entire being inside me.

And she does.

"You're my protector." She stands on my feet to give herself better height and hovers her lips across from mine. "The only man in this dark world I trust and ever want to touch me is you."

I bite into my lip, miserably suppressing a groan, when she plunges her nails into my neck.

"Say it again," I demand. The tenderness that occupied my voice earlier is now long gone.

Madness swirls inside me as I need her to say those words like a broken record.

"I love you, Damien," she says, her lips brushing mine with each word. "I'm yours."

"That's right. All mine." I nip at her lip before biting into it, tugging it back as if I want to rip it apart and consume her. "Prepare for me to fuck what's mine, baby."

That beautiful blush appears on her cheeks.

"That pink," I say in wonder. "Let's see how it compares to your pussy lips."

She gasps when I hoist her on the island, spread her toned thighs as wide as possible, and settle between them. Her body trembles as I smooth my hands over her legs. The softness of her skin is a luxury against my callous palms. Resting one hand on her knee, I slip off her panties and open my mouth, allowing spit to drop from my lips onto her waxed pussy.

"I'm going to dominate this body," I say, slapping her pussy and smearing my spit all over it. "And you're going to let me, aren't you?"

"Yes," she moans, throwing her head back.

I'm going to prove exactly what she said.

*That she's goddamn mine.*

That includes every inch of her sexy-as-hell body.

I might've said those cherished three words gently.

But that gentleness is gone.

The chandelier above the island provides enough light to fit the requirements of a surgical room. I've never seen Pippa's pretty pussy as on display as this. It's glistening, pink, and so ready for my mouth.

I crack my neck and flex my fingers like a man ready to start a hard day's work.

"The color of your pussy and your blushing are my favorite pinks," I say, teasingly running a finger along her slit. "So beautiful, baby."

Cupping each ass cheek in my hand, I lift her pussy to my mouth. She moans as I lick from right above her asshole to her pussy. Her body shudders, and she squirms in my hold as I shove three fingers inside her.

I lower my face and devour her sweet pussy.

I suck on her clit.

As I eat her, I mutter, "I love you," against her folds.

I tongue it from side to side, moaning, "You're mine."

I wasn't lying when I told her the world could be ending around us and she'd still have all my attention.

*My sweet ballerina, falling in love with the cold-blooded killer.*

I slide half her body off the edge, giving myself a better angle, and in a matter of seconds, she comes all over my face.

I step back as she moans my name and hurriedly unbuckle my pants and shove them down to my knees. I don't bother kicking them off or removing my shoes. I raise my button-up, holding it with one hand, while gripping my cock with the other.

All that's coming from Pippa are moans and begs for me to fuck her.

"Condom," she pants.

I open her panty drawer to collect one. I keep rubbers stashed all over this place now. I speedily rip it open with my teeth, toss the wrapper on the floor, and roll it onto my throbbing cock.

I'll die if I'm not inside her soon.

"Damien, hurry." She tightens her legs around my waist to

jerk me closer, giving Ace a run for his money on grip action. "I need you inside me before I fuck myself with my own fingers."

*Oh, she has threats, huh?*

I anchor one hand on her waist, the other on my cock, and thrust inside her. Her body drives up, sliding along the island, but I don't let up.

I fuck my sweet dancer, the woman I love, how she deserves to be fucked.

She moans, her back arching. My hips will be bruised after impaling the island repeatedly. She whips her head from side to side, throwing her arm out and knocking shit off the island. My dick throbs, swelling inside her and needing more.

"You said you're mine," I say, sliding my hand up her stomach, over her bra, and to her throat. I stretch it around her neck, my eyes boring into hers. Her eyes widen as I circle my grip to behind her neck and raise her head. Bowing mine, I meet her in the middle. "No goddamn take-backs."

All my life, I've told people we don't give refunds at Lucky Kings.

I'm not about to change that now in my own home.

Her muscles contract around my cock, her pussy growing wetter, the juices slapping against my thighs. She tenses her muscles, her face scrunching, and I keep her face up as she comes apart beneath me.

Mine is building, building, building.

My dick throbs with the need to release, and when I do, I feel my cum pumping out of me. I throw my head back, ramming my hips forward, and plant myself inside her.

We're catching our breaths.

Coming down from our high.

But just like I told her in the theater, I'm not done with her yet.

I'll never be.

I slowly pull out, toss the condom in the trash, put on another, and then fuck her on the vanity. It's hard and rough.

Then, I move her to our bed, where I make love to her, nice and slow, putting her back together.

And when I collapse on top of her and spread my hand over her damp hair, I smile. "You're all mine, sweet dancer."

She returns the smile. "And you're all mine."

"No fucking take-backs."

## 30

# PIPPA

I'M LEAVING Brew Bliss after my shift when my mom calls me.

"Pippa, honey," she says as I climb into the passenger seat of Julian's Mercedes. "Are you busy?"

"Nope," I reply. "Just getting off work."

"Come meet me. I have a surprise."

"Where?" I adjust the air vents in front of me because even though New York is in a heat wave, Julian keeps it like a freezer in here. Even a snowman would freeze to death.

She squeals out an address, her voice radiating with a happiness I haven't heard from her in years. I recite it out loud to Julian.

Instead of pulling onto the street, he snatches his phone from the cupholder. "Let me okay this with Damien."

I drop my purse on the floor. "Damien isn't my boss, nor am I on house arrest." I smack the center console. "Now, let's go."

He shoots me a *yeah, sure* expression and holds the phone to his ear.

I bend down to collect my phone from my bag while Julian waits for Damien to answer.

"Hey, Damien, Pippa—"

Just as Julian starts talking, I hit Damien's name on my screen.

Julian pauses, snapping his attention to me. "Are you seriously calling him right now?"

He pulls the phone from his ear. My guess is, Damien just ended their call because seconds later, Damien answers mine.

"My mom wants me to meet her somewhere," I explain through the speaker.

"Where?" he snaps.

Julian pulls up the address on the car's GPS, and I repeat it to Damien.

"It's only a fifteen-minute drive," I add to further get my way.

"Fine," Damien says with plenty of annoyance. "But you call me when you leave, Julian stays with you at all times, and if it's anything shady, you leave right away."

"Yes, Dad." I blow out a dramatic breath. "Geesh."

Julian shakes his head.

"I'll punish you for that attitude later," Damien says. "Be good."

He ends the call, and I toss my phone back into my bag while staring at Julian in satisfaction. "See, that's how it's done."

Julian shifts the car into drive and pulls away from the curb. "What you did earns no bragging rights. My brother is obsessed with you. You could ask him to buy you a goddamn goat, and he'd ask you to choose your favorite color. And probably make me take it on fucking walks."

"A goat walker." I make myself comfortable in the seat. "That's a job I'd sign up for."

"If only we could sign up for jobs." He clicks the turn signal. "I definitely wouldn't have chosen *this one*."

From his tone and the glance he sends in my direction, I'm positive he isn't referring to working at the casino ... or his criminal employer.

He's referring to the job of watching me.

In Julian's eyes, chauffeuring me around is a bigger inconvenience than actual murder.

"I'd consider this"—I pause to motion between us—"the easiest part of your job. All you have to do is drive me around and provide snacks."

"Like some goddamn soccer mom."

"You want me to sign you up for the bake sale as well?"

"At this point, I'd rather make cupcakes than tote you around."

I gasp, faking deep offense. "I like to believe I'm a good time. Your brother surely thinks I am."

He flips me off.

"Look at all the things I've introduced you to—"

"Headaches," he interrupts.

"I was thinking more along the lines of *Game of Thrones*, foods, hanging out with me and the girls."

"Thank you for reminding me that I need to have a discussion with Damien and make it clear I'm not a babysitter for you and *your girls*."

"Oh, come on. We both know you love watching Genesis."

He flinches at her name. "Mute yourself, or I'm kicking you out on the curb. You can walk to your destination." He glances at the GPS. "It's only a five-minute walk. It'll give you some fresh air."

"I think it's cute."

He slams his foot on the brakes, and I throw my hands in front of me so my head doesn't collide with the glove compartment.

From what I've learned, Julian doesn't have many triggers.

His family is one.

And it seems Genesis is on that list.

"It's not cute," he grits out, working his jaw and turning up the air. "She's my deceased sister's best friend. I watch over her and Darcy because it's what my sister would've wanted. But that's it. Now, change the subject, or you're going home. You can pout there."

"Someone sure woke up on the wrong side of the bed," I grumble, massaging my wrist.

"I haven't slept in thirty hours."

"Ah, so someone is *sleep-deprived*. That makes me cranky too."

"I'm killing my fucking brother."

The GPS informs us we've arrived at our destination. I spot my mom and Lanie standing in front of a building as Julian parks. The storefront they're looking at has a *Space Available* sign in the window.

There's a sudden urge to put the air-conditioning on me again when I see Cernach approaching them. My body burns in hatred as I step out of the car and slam the door.

I briefly hear Julian say, "Oh shit," while he joins me outside.

We cross the street, and my mother's face brightens under the sun when she notices me.

"Look, Pippa!" She points toward the window they've been staring at. "This is where we're opening my new studio."

I want to vomit.

A trickle of guilt drips inside me for my lack of enthusiasm. Unfortunately, I can't fake joy over something that'll ruin her in the end.

It's so easy to put the pieces together.

Cernach's presence.

My mom needing money and a new dance studio.

There are only two sources she can get money—a bank or Cernach.

Considering my father ruined her credit and put her upside down in debt, the first is out of the question. Which brings us to my calculated uncle who'd kill the entire human species if it meant getting what he wanted.

"No." I violently shake my head as Cernach stands next to her, looking smug. "Don't do this. Don't you fall into his trap."

If Julian wasn't next to me, I'd be more careful with my words.

But thankfully, his protection allows me to speak more freely.

My mom backs up a step at my lack of excitement. "Are you not happy for me? This is life-changing."

"Unless he gives you the business, no strings attached, the only way it'll change your life is, he'll control you again," I argue.

"We need the income." She whips her arm toward the building. "This is it."

It's like her ears are broken.

Like my words are flying straight over her head into traffic.

"No, this is a leash he's attaching to you."

I peer at Lanie, standing there in a summer dress and Chucks, looking not only confused but scared shitless too. I'm uncertain if the fear is of Cernach hurting me or that she fears him. She hasn't been around my uncle much.

"Leash?" Cernach huffs out. "I'm helping my dear sister. What kind of brother would I be if I didn't?"

I'm almost expecting him to pat her on the head like a good little dog.

I've never wanted to punch a righteous smirk off someone's face so bad.

If my mom believes him, she doesn't need to open a new studio. She needs to walk her ass straight to the hospital and have them check her for *has lost her mind* syndrome.

Cernach scoots closer to her, mirroring Julian with me.

*Oh, give me a break.*

My mother straightens her back, composing herself. "Now that your father is gone, I need money to support us."

"There are plenty of jobs in the city," I bite out.

197

For years, she's told me horror stories of Cernach.

I didn't get princess bedtime stories. I got tales of my mother's trauma.

Warnings of how women are treated in that life.

I experienced my mother's emotional wounds because she had no one else to pour them out to. And now, she's suddenly okay with his behavior?

"This also helps you," she quickly adds. "You don't have to work at the coffee shop anymore. You can teach here."

Cernach rolls his eyes, growing impatient with me. "I took care of her problem. Show some gratitude."

"No, you gave me more problems," I fire back, noticing people are staring.

She can't run the studio alone, even if Cernach funds it. I'll have to help her. Her arthritis makes it difficult to teach classes. It's not that I mind doing it since I've been by her side for years, but I refuse to do it with Cernach as a partner.

Cernach scrubs his hands together. "The contracts have already been signed. The studio is your mother's." He levels his eyes on me. "Now, I think we should plan your wedding."

"Wedding?" Lanie gasps, green eyes widening. "You're getting married?"

I ball my hands into fists, and Julian steps closer to me. "I'm not marrying anyone."

"Oh, come on," Cernach draws out mockingly. "What's the big deal? You're already living with Damien. Why not marry him and help your family out in the process?"

I love Damien, and under any other circumstances, I'd love to marry him, but never with Cernach involved. Cernach tarnishes everything he touches, and I'll be damned if I let him in any way.

"You stay the hell away from me." I don't wait for him to reply or for my mother to say another word before spinning on my heel and storming toward the car.

As I settle myself in the passenger seat, a hard truth hits me. There's only one way I can get Cernach to leave me alone. It's ending what he wants.

---

I CALL Damien as soon as Julian swerves onto the road and hits the first red light. My hands are too shaky to hold the phone or search my purse for my AirPods, so I put the call on speaker.

"What's wrong?" he immediately asks when he hears the shakiness in my voice.

"Cernach—he's getting my mother right where he wants her," I reply. "Getting *me* right where he wants me."

Make no mistake, he'll use my mother as a tool of manipulation.

At this point, I'm about to ask if *he* wants to marry a Lombardi if he's so desperate for an arrangement between them.

"Fuck," Damien hisses. "Have Julian bring you to the casino."

Julian makes a U-turn, causing a car to blare its horn, and drives in the opposite direction.

Damien is waiting for us when Julian reaches the casino's back entrance. A few men are standing guard, sipping water and talking among each other. I jump out of the car and run straight into his arms.

"We'll get this figured out," he says, soothingly running his hand over my back and veering me inside the casino.

We head straight toward his office and don't say a word until he shuts the door behind him. Somewhere along our walk, Julian cut a right into another room.

I collapse on the sofa as Damien kneels on the floor at my feet. He listens intently as I replay what happened with Cernach and my mother. I add some expletives and rub my forehead, and a few tears slip down my cheeks.

Damien is quiet for a moment before saying, "I'll open a studio for you then. That'll fix our Cernach problem."

I go completely still. "You'll what?"

"Open a studio for you."

A mild whoosh of vertigo strikes me. Damien rises to his feet and strolls toward his desk. In his eyes, the problem is solved.

In mine, it isn't.

I flick at the hair tie around my wrist. "As much as I appreciate your offer, it'd put me in the same position as her. I wouldn't own the studio, and you could easily take it away from me." I shoot him a *no offense* stare.

It's not that I don't trust Damien. I can't see him pulling a Cernach power move, but anything can happen. I've seen people turn on each other for less.

He sits in his chair, snatches a pen, and clicks it open and closed while reclining in his chair. "I'll put it in your name. The studio will be all yours."

I sniffle. "You'd really do that for me?"

"I'll do anything for you."

## 31

# DAMIEN

I'VE SPENT all morning on the phone with my attorney and real estate agent, setting things in motion to find Pippa studio space.

When she came to my office yesterday, upset about Cernach playing master manipulator, I found an easy solution. She's always dreamed of opening her own studio, and I take pleasure in making her dreams come true.

Pippa-pleasing is my favorite hobby.

I'm mid-text to Pippa when someone knocks on my door.

"Come in," I shout, hitting Send and dropping the phone to my desk.

Julian appears in the doorway. "Cernach Koglin is here to speak with you."

"Send him in," I tell him.

Cernach did me a favor by coming here. It saves me the trouble of hunting him down to inform him his studio plan didn't work out in his favor. He needs to drop the devoted-brother charade and take his ass back to Boston. Enya can work at Pippa's studio. Problem solved.

Julian leaves the office and returns with a pompous Cernach and one of his men. I don't bother standing to greet them. He came to me. I have no obligation to show him respect. He isn't *my* boss.

That doesn't mean I minimize his power, though. He didn't become the sole standing Irish mob boss in Boston for his ethical practices.

Unlike New York, where several Mafia families cohabitate—the O'Connors, also the Irish mob—Cernach won't allow others in his city. You either take it from him by force or die. Anyone who's tried is dead. Along with their families.

Since Cernach wants to have friends in this meeting, Julian stays as well.

I spin a pen between my fingers while waiting for Cernach's next move. The only option of sitting—other than on my lap, desk, or the floor—is the small sofa. I don't like visitors, and what better way is there to deter them from hanging out than having limited seating?

He casts a glance at the sofa, decides against it, and stands tall in front of my desk. "I have some things I'd like to discuss with you."

I've always been surprised at how heavy his Irish accent is. He's a son of immigrants, but he was born here in the States.

"You have the floor." I do a sweeping motion of the room. "*For five minutes.*" I raise my hand to check my watch, tapping its face.

"Pippa's father is creating problems," he says, cutting straight to the chase. That's a quality I like in a man.

I aim my pen at him. "Maybe for you. He's not creating any for me."

"He owes a lot of people a lot of money."

"What happened to Cernach, the helpful big brother? Be as good as you act and pay his debts *for your baby sister.*"

"I'm not paying no deadbeat's debts," he spits.

I shrug, dropping the pen on my desk. "Not my problem. He doesn't owe me money."

"He did until he sent Pippa in here to pay up."

I stare at him, unaffected. He wanted a reaction from me. I won't give him that.

I shrug and tap my watch.

"He's attempting to blackmail me for money, saying he'll embarrass Enya for who knows what." He smooths his hand over his round belly, covered by his suit jacket. "He'll come for Pippa next."

"Again, Paul isn't my problem."

"Are you not involved with my niece?" He raises a furry brow. "I'd say that is your problem."

"Pippa is none of your concern."

"You don't want to protect her?"

I have no interest in entertaining his mind-fuck games. "I'm not killing Pippa's father," I say with an annoyed sigh. "While, personally, I couldn't give two fucks if Paul lives or dies, Pippa does."

"Paul's a piece of shit," he hisses.

"Don't care. The only reason I'd kill Paul is if he hurts Pippa or she requests it. She hasn't. He might be scum, but Pippa still loves her father."

He glowers, unhappy I failed to take his bait. "When do you plan to make an honest woman out of my niece?"

I crack my neck to each side, wishing I were doing it to his turkey neck instead. "I'd never force her hand."

"You don't want to marry her?"

I go quiet, working my jaw. Just like I told her, I'd marry her in a damn second. But I'm not a man who forces devotion on a woman. I'd rather lie in bed alone at night than next to someone who wishes they weren't there.

He runs a hand over his jaw, as if thinking. "Maybe I'll kill Paul, making her fall right into my hands, and I'll find her a new husband. A *useful* one to me."

I stare at him in indifference.

My blood boils inside, ready to explode and scorch the fucker's skin off, but I won't prove his words affect me.

I don't show my emotions. He could stab me and pull out a fucking kidney, and I'd stare at him coldly without muttering a word.

Eh, I might laugh in his face.

"If we merge our families, we could do great things," he says, bouncing back to idea number one. He rubs the skin around his mouth. "I'm sure you're aware, I have outstanding weapon connections. Men would fear us as allies, which is exactly what all of us want in this world."

No, I'd rather have his niece than power.

But to each their own.

Cernach has been trying to strike a deal with the Lombardis for years.

Four families run New York—the Marchettis, Cavallaros, O'Connors, and Lombardis. Rumor is, Cernach wants to expand out of Boston and add himself to that list.

I rest my palm on my desk and stand. "Your five minutes have passed, Cernach. I have a meeting." I button my suit jacket. "Go play a round of blackjack on me."

## 32

# PIPPA

"I HAVE GREAT NEWS," I squeal to my mother over speakerphone. I sound so similar to the other day when she called me and had me meet her at the studio space. I called her four times this morning, ready to tell her we don't have to be under Cernach's thumb. "You don't need to open a dance studio with Cernach. Damien is helping me open one for us."

I take a bite of my peanut butter toast and wash it down with a sip of OJ before smiling in satisfaction. Cernach will be out of our lives.

Good freaking riddance.

"Your boyfriend of only a few months?" she asks around a scoff.

My smile collapses.

"Going with Cernach is a better idea," she adds with too much confidence for a woman in her position.

"Damien said he'll put the studio in my name." I shift on the island stool, dragging my knees to my chest.

"Who's to say he'll actually do that? That he won't take it when you break up?"

*When* you break up.

Not *if*.

My mother has an ugly outlook on love, yes.

But not every man is like my father and Cernach.

After what they put her through, I don't know if anyone will ever be able to convince her otherwise.

"He said he'd put it in my name," I repeat, shoving my plate up the island, my appetite now gone.

"Like a man would do that with no strings attached."

"You think Cernach's deal doesn't have strings attached?" It has more than strings. It has a metal chain, a block tied to her ankle, and he'll be at the top, playing puppeteer.

"Cernach is family."

"He's a manipulator. You've told me that yourself all my life."

"We've already signed the documents. The space is mine, and we start moving in next week. We need to sit down and draw up a class schedule for you since you'll teach most of them. My arthritis acts up too much for me to do more than two a week."

It's like nothing I said registered.

"I'm not working anywhere Cernach-related," I say. "Damien is opening a studio for me. That's my plan."

"Are you kidding me?" she screams. "I'm telling you right now, if you open a dance studio even remotely near here, I'll never forgive you. I am your family, your mother. Are you really going to take something like this away from me?"

Tears form in my eyes, and my voice cracks. "Mom—"

"I thought you'd be happy for me getting a new studio. I'm trusting my brother will do right by me. He's apologized for hurting me in the past, and we've moved past our issues. We can trust him, Pippa. Tell your boyfriend we don't need his help. If you open your own studio, I'll have no choice but to see it as a betrayal. We'll talk later. Bye." She hangs up without letting me get a word in.

*Wow.*

She sounds so much like the Koglins.

My mother is reverting to her roots, forgetting they're full of decay.

I roughly slide my phone along the island and drag my hand through my wet hair.

"Fuck that," I hear from behind me.

I spin around in the stool to find Emilio staring in my direction. He hardly talks to me. Sometimes, I forget he's even here.

"Fuck what?" I ask.

He lowers his phone, his dark brows furrowing. "Your mom and that guilt-trip shit. She's wrong. If shit doesn't work out with you and Damien, he'd never take anything from you. That's not the type of man he is."

This is probably the most personal conversation we've ever shared. As annoyed as I am that he eavesdropped on my call—well, not exactly eavesdropped since I did have it on speaker—it's nice to hear someone confirm my feelings are valid.

She's guilt-tripping me.

I gulp, a tear sliding down my cheek.

The problem is, it'll work.

There's this sense of loyalty that will never allow me to leave my family behind—even if it means surrendering my dreams and my happiness.

I'M STILL in my pajamas when Damien gets home.

I called off work and have been sitting in self-pity all day. My phone sits on the counter with ten missed calls and four texts from my mom. Even though I don't want to ignore them, eventually, I'll read and reply.

It's what I always do.

I must've looked super pathetic after my call with her because Emilio ordered us lunch and even watched a movie with me.

"Good news," Damien says, dropping a manila folder, papers stacked inside, next to me on the island.

"What are those?"

"Possible locations for your studio."

I stare at the folder like it's toxic, like it's what poisoned my dreams. Not my family.

Damien turns me in the chair, nudges my legs apart with his body, and steps between them. "What do you say I take you to dinner and then we look at them, see which you like best?"

I peer away from him, feeling my heartbeat drumming in my throat. "I can't open a studio, Damien." Each word stings as it leaves my mouth.

He grips my knee in his hand. "What do you mean?"

Emilio stands from his chair and walks toward the door. He makes a quick pit stop to squeeze my shoulder. Damien raises a brow at the sudden change in our relationship.

"Call if you need anything," Emilio tells him, as if he anticipates Damien needing him after we're finished talking.

"My mom signed the paperwork with Cernach," I say, my voice raspy. "The deal is done. She's opening the studio."

His nostrils flare, and he draws back a few inches. "He'll screw her over. He'll screw *you* over."

"I explained that to her, but she wouldn't listen."

"Did you tell her you're opening one?"

"I did. She said that if I do, she'll never forgive me." I lower my gaze, refusing to meet his eyes, scared he'll view me as weak. "Because I'll be her competition and turn my back on my family."

He shakes his head in frustration. "Don't let them take away your dream. Don't let Cernach win."

My shoulders slump. "I'm afraid he already has."

## 33

# DAMIEN

I want to drive to Boston, rip Cernach's head off, and throw it into the Charles River.

When he visited my office, I should've pulled out my pistol and shot the bastard dead.

I falsely believed I'd solved the dance-studio dilemma. Cernach was worried about Paul's broke ass, so I assumed most of his attention was there. I stupidly failed to remember how cunning he is. Like me, he's able to focus on numerous problems simultaneously.

That's my mistake.

That shit is on me.

"We need to talk," Antonio says as I sit in his passenger seat, post disposal of a man's body who'd attempted to sexually assault a Lucky Kings employee in the parking lot.

It felt good, killing him, the release and satisfaction I needed.

As I bashed the man's skull in, I imagined he was Cernach.

When I dug the grave, I pictured rolling his body into it.

I flick my Zippo open, watch the flame dance, and blow it out. "Yeah?"

"Vinny is uncontrollable." He massages the back of his neck. "More than he's ever been."

I nod in agreement. His brother's recklessness is growing. He's failing to realize that being boss—or next in line currently—doesn't bestow immortality. Truth be told, it's the contrary. People want to kill kings so they can become one.

That very reason is why Vinny is running his mouth about taking Cristian Marchetti down. He wants the throne of New York. Vinny is also too bullheaded to comprehend that his mistakes also become our mistakes to handle.

We've raised the issue during the family meetings Vinny has been absent for. Vincent is too blinded, too stubborn, to admit his eldest son isn't fit for the job.

"I'm not even don, and I'm carrying the weight of this goddamn family," he clips, stress lining his face.

Everyone knows Antonio will eventually become don.

Vincent will die, either by suffering another stroke or from pissing off the wrong person. Vinny won't make it past forty. One of our enemies will murder his ass. Or one of us, honestly.

"In the next six months, we'll be at war with the Marchettis," he says, stating a fact and grinding his teeth.

I slip the Zippo inside my pocket. "You know I have your back." My loyalty will always lie with Antonio, even above his father.

Damn sure over Vinny's, boss or not.

Growing up, I used to beat the shit out of Vinny. Our fathers would make us fight in the backyard and place bets on who'd win. I always did. I should've bashed his skull in on the concrete and watched him bleed out while I had the chance.

"How's the Cernach-Pippa situation going?" he asks.

"I'd enjoy digging a hole for Cernach in these woods, if that answers your question."

"She seemed down last night."

Pippa teaches Amara dance at his house three times a week

now. He had the basement renovated into a dance studio. Allowing Pippa inside his home shows the truth about her character. He trusts very few.

"I've lost count of the number of times I've been tempted to drive to Boston and stab a knife through that ugly fucker's heart."

"I don't want a war with the goddamn Irish, Damien."

"No one said you have to fight it."

"If you're in a war, I'm in a war." He blows out a long breath. "Have a sit-down with Cernach. Figure out a solution."

"The only solution he wants is for me to marry Pippa and create a business relationship between the families."

"Have you discussed the possibility with my father?"

"No."

"Why not?"

"Pippa doesn't want to marry me."

He whistles. "Damn." It doesn't take him but a few seconds for the truth to dawn on him. "She won't marry you because it's what Cernach wants."

"Pippa might love me, but her hate for Cernach is stronger."

"That's a *you* problem then. Fix it. Make her love for you greater than her disdain for her bastard uncle."

THE TOPIC of a dance studio hasn't come up again. The folder of the real estate options sits on the island, unopened, like a grave for her dreams.

Instead of celebrating that night, we ordered takeout and hardly spoke. She went to bed early while I stayed up late, working.

Miscommunication leads to the death of relationships. I

won't risk losing the best thing that's ever happened to me over unsaid words.

Pippa is working behind the counter when I enter Brew Bliss. I stand in line, tapping my foot, and order a black coffee. She whips around at my voice, nearly overfilling the cup she's holding.

Emilio was supposed to take her home today.

*Change of plans, sweetheart.*

After she makes my coffee, I take a seat at the corner table, where I always sit. I once had to pay a man two hundred dollars to switch tables with me. If I hadn't been in Pippa's workplace, I'd have knocked him the fuck out.

I drop my coffee in the trash when her shift ends and walk her to the car. The fresh air, combined with her perfume and smell of espresso, makes my cock jerk. It's been days since I've been deep inside her tight pussy, and fuck, I miss it.

Pippa snaps her seat belt in when we're inside the Range Rover. "I didn't expect you today."

Turning in the driver's seat, I cup the back of her head, drawing her to me. She licks her lips right before I devour her sweet mouth.

"I missed you," I say. "I didn't get any work done because I couldn't stop thinking about you."

She smiles against my lips. "You saw me last night."

"Even a single moment from you is too long."

Her face lights up. "I missed you too."

I plant a kiss on the tip of her nose and pull out onto the street.

"Where are we going?" she asks when we turn in the opposite direction of home.

"It's a surprise." I drum my fingers along the steering wheel.

"Damien, the king of surprises," she says with a giggle.

When we reach our destination, I park in front of the brick building. Pippa might get angry with me for doing this behind her back, but I don't care. It's better than her being at Cernach's mercy.

"What's this?" she asks when I help her outside and lead us toward the sidewalk.

I pluck a key from my pocket and hand it to her. "Your dance studio."

It's a small space but enough for what she needs. The front is a wall of streak-free windows, allowing a sneak peek inside. It's a loft layout, one large room, and I've already scheduled setup to install all dance studio necessities.

"Let's go see your new space." I clasp her hand, leading her to the door.

She tries to hide it, but I don't miss the way her hand shakes as she unlocks it. The smell of fresh paint wafts through the air when we walk inside.

"You don't have to do anything," I explain, closing the door behind us. "The space is in your name, and the rent is paid for the next ten years. The Lombardi family controls this block, so you're safe."

She's quiet as her gaze slowly creeps around the room, taking in the space. I stand there, shoving my hands into my pockets, waiting in anticipation.

"Thank you," she finally says, her voice as wistful as I know she'll move around this space. Her eyes are teary when she finally turns to peer at me. "This ..." She stops to swipe at her eyes. "I've never had someone do something so special for me. I love it, but—"

"You can do whatever you want with it," I interrupt, knowing she's ready to reject my offer. Not only is she under Cernach's thumb but she's also under Enya's. "Open a studio, or let it sit here and do nothing. It's here if you ever need it."

While I've offered to fully support her, she wants her own financial security. I want to give her that. My hope is she'll convince Enya this is the right avenue to take.

I tenderly cup her face in my hands, using the pad of my thumb to clean her tears. I stare at her, transfixed and obsessed, fully aware I'm completely done for when it comes to her.

She gathers herself, inhaling deep breaths, and I grunt when she launches herself toward me. As I catch her, she wraps her legs around my waist, and I cup her ass cheeks to hold her in place.

"Thank you, Damien." She loops her arms around my neck. "I love you." She smacks a kiss to my lips. "I love you." *Another kiss.* "I love you so damn much." More tears fall down her face, smearing along my skin.

I lower her to her feet and give her a tour of the space. It's simple, just how I wanted it. Pippa doesn't need to worry about maintenance. I want her to have it easy here, to do what she loves without stress.

"You're too good to me," she whispers.

"I think you have it the other way around," I say. "You're too good for any man in this world, but somehow, you've lost your mind and settled for me."

This woman is my everything.

I need to do all that I can not to lose her.

WE STOP at a local pizza joint for dinner.

Pippa takes a giant bite of pizza, and the cheese stretches from her mouth. She laughs, slicing through it with her finger, and swallows her bite.

"Cernach visited my office," I tell her, leaning forward to wipe the corner of her mouth with my napkin.

"Is he still on his bullshit regarding marriage contracts?" she asks.

I nod as the server returns with water refills.

"You told him no, right?"

"I told him that's your decision to make. Like you, I'm not a fan of arranged marriages."

"Yet you were okay with having an arranged marriage with me?"

"Yes, because I'd marry you, contract or not, in a heartbeat."

"Do the Lombardis have marriage contracts?"

"Arranged marriages are part of this life. My parents'. Antonio's. All of ours."

"Antonio's? What happened to Amara's mom?"

"Sienna overdosed."

Pippa winces. "Wow. Poor Amara. Poor Sienna."

Antonio wasn't a bad husband to Sienna, but he was an absent one. He wasn't cruel, but it was clear to everyone he didn't want the marriage. Neither did she.

"Sometimes, when women aren't happy in their marriages, they turn to things they shouldn't," I say. I was there during the aftermath of her death. I'm also around when Amara asks why she doesn't have a mommy like other girls. "They find something to replace the love they don't get from their husbands."

It's why I've always been against an arranged marriage. Vincent knows I'm loyal to the Lombardi family, but if there's anything that'll make me walk away, it's them forcing me to commit to a woman I don't want.

"Thank you for understanding me," she says in a hushed voice, extending her arm across the table and taking my hand.

One thing Cernach's dumbass doesn't understand is that marrying Pippa wouldn't guarantee a contract with the Lombardis. I'm not the don of the family. Hell, Lombardi blood doesn't even flow through my veins.

The only way he'd score a guaranteed deal is with Vinny or Antonio.

I won't tell him that, though, and I'll do everything in my power to keep him from finding out.

---

LIKE A RODENT that won't go away, Cernach pays me another visit at the casino. It's like I'm his goddamn caretaker at this point.

"Paul has been taken care of," he says with pride, like I hired him to do the job.

I recline in my chair, crossing my arms behind my head. "What does that mean?" As soon as the question leaves my mouth, I regret asking it.

In a situation like this, I'd like to remain in the dark. That way, if Pippa mentions Paul, I won't have to hide this from her.

He lifts his chin. "Consider this me doing you a favor."

I jerk up in my chair and cock my head to the side. "Please tell me how Pippa's father being *taken care of* is doing me a favor? I made it clear to you I didn't give two fucks if the scumbag was dead or alive. He was your problem. Not mine."

"He would've come to Pippa next, making her pay his debts. Did you want her in that situation?"

"And I told you, if that time came, I'd handle it then."

Cernach snarls his lip at my lack of appreciation.

The fucker can suck my dick if he thinks I'd ever be grateful to him for shit.

He wiggles his finger in my direction. "Enya told me about your studio plan with Pippa," he spits, his mood now the opposite of what it was when he entered my office. "Nice try, but no dice, Bellini."

He leans back on his heels, and I mentally cross my fingers that he falls and cracks his head open.

Unfortunately, he doesn't.

"As a man in the business of knowing your odds of winning, you should know you'll lose this game."

I smack my palms on my desk and rise to my feet. "Watch how you're speaking to me, Cernach."

"Pippa will always choose her mother. They've been through too much together. Keep playing games with me, and I'll get Enya so far in my grips that Pippa will end up marrying any bastard I want. Might as well use the whore for something."

I circle my desk and charge toward him. Before he can make a move to grab for a weapon, I snatch him by the collar and shove him against the wall.

He laughs when I get in his face. "I'm a *boss*, boy. You're a *worker*." He grunts out a laugh. "Vincent Lombardi will raise hell if you harm me because he knows it'd start a war. I'll ask him for your head, or I'll kill half the Lombardi men and everyone in this shithole casino."

I grind my teeth, hating the accuracy of his words.

"Leave Pippa alone." I slam my hand against the wall, only inches from his face. "Boss or not, I'll destroy you." I swiftly pull back, the blood in my veins on fire. If I don't get away from him, I'm bound to do something that'll cause a shit ton of problems.

Cernach straightens his suit. "You're disrespecting the wrong man, Damien."

"And you're underestimating the wrong man, Cernach."

## 34

# PIPPA

THREE.

That's how many times I've been to the studio this week.

It's empty, and I've yet to select a name.

Damien came home yesterday with a new *name brainstorming notebook*, as he called it.

Ten.

That's how many times I've begged my mother to see the studio, but she refuses. She won't even let Lanie come.

My back is against the mirrored wall, my knees pulled to my chest, and tears fall down my cheeks as I stare ahead at the blurred moving traffic.

Fucking broken.

That's been my state nearly every day.

This should be the happiest time of my life, but instead, I'm falling apart.

My gaze slips to the door when it opens. Damien's loafers squeak against the hardwood as he moves across the room toward me. His perfect face falls slack when his eyes meet my sorrow-filled ones. I peer down, an attempt to hide my pain from him.

He places my dance bag on the floor before sitting across from me.

"Baby," he whispers, his voice hoarse, "look at me."

I shake my head, glaring at the floor as if it were my worst enemy.

"I can't," I sob. "I want this. I want it *so, so bad*, but I can't have it."

He scoots closer, our knees brushing.

I shudder when he slides his hand between my thighs to capture my face in his hand. My chin shakes as he lifts it with two fingers.

He waits until I meet his eyes before brushing his knuckle against my cheek. "Yes, you can. You deserve this, Pippa."

I shake my head violently.

"Do it for you. I'll be by your side every step of the way."

"My mom and Lanie—they're all I have," I cry out. "My dad left. Her family disowned her. We're all alone, and now, I'm turning my back on them. *Hurting them.*"

A slight wince crosses his face at what I said. "That's where you're wrong, baby. You also have me." Another brush of his knuckle. "Amara, Antonio, Emilio, Julian, all the dancers who will come in here. You'll change their lives and give them the same dream as you—to dance. Good things will come from this."

"They're your family." I sniffle and use my arm to wipe away the snot under my nose. It's gross, but Damien doesn't even cringe at it.

"If they didn't care for you, they'd refuse to be around you. Emilio wouldn't have texted me, worried, telling me to get here to you. They might not show emotion, but they care. *I care.*"

"My mom—"

He presses a finger to my lips. "She'll be hurt at first, but eventually, she'll realize you did what's best for you. When Cernach screws her over, you'll have this for her to fall back on."

His hand runs over my face once more before lowering to my trembling hand. "Come on. Let's see your dance. Break your new studio in, baby."

My breathing hitches when he rises to his knees, unzips the bag, and then helps me lace up my pointe shoes. I timidly smile at him while he helps me to my feet, doing the same. He makes sure I'm stable before setting me free.

Crossing his arms, he gives me a head nod and rests his back against the wall, waiting.

I inhale.

Exhale.

Inhale. Exhale.

A grin breaks out across his face as I start to dance.

I shut my eyes, swaying into my own world.

A world of peace and passion and love.

A world I wish I could stay in forever.

## 35

# DAMIEN

Vincent called me into his office.

A phone call from a don out of nowhere can go one of two ways—a promotion or a death sentence. Even if you think you haven't done anything against code, it's still alarming. Bosses can become paranoid. Vincent could have even just a twinge of distrust regarding your loyalty and decide you no longer deserved to breathe.

While my family's loyalty to them has never been questioned, in this life, there's always that chance.

When I knock on the door, he yells for me to enter. He sits behind his desk, smoke swirling from a lit cigar in an ashtray, and motions for me to shut the door.

Vincent's office resembles all the other geriatric Lombardi offices. They're always packed with memorabilia and photos covering the walls.

My gaze slips toward one of him with the former New York governor.

Another of his grandfather standing in front of the casino at its grand opening.

Him with a young Vinny and Antonio.

*So many damn photos.*

Even some with men he's killed for dishonor.

He pops open a cigar box, offering me one, and I nod.

I don't want it, but it'd be disrespectful to decline. He cuts the tip of a cigar and passes it to me. I take it, along with a lighter, and watch the tip burn red when the flame hits it. He slides me a spare ashtray, and I take a seat near the corner of his antique desk.

"Cernach Koglin called me," he says between deep tokes.

I remain unreadable. "What did he want?"

"To discuss Paul Elsher and his daughter." He gurgles out a laugh through the cigar. "The name didn't even ring a bell until he sent me pictures of Paul—before and after his death. Like a makeover, only homicide-style." He smirks, loving what Cernach did.

Vincent is one of the most ruthless men I know. Cernach doesn't even give him a run for his money.

That confirms that Cernach killed Paul.

I nod and puff the cigar.

"He wants you to marry his niece."

"I'm aware." Two more puffs.

"He laid out a worthy argument for us to join an alliance with the Koglins."

"If we set up an alliance with them, the O'Connors would see that as crossing them. That would be risky."

We made a pact with the other families to never cross each other, or it's war. The other three families against the one who threw the first punch.

"The O'Connors can fuck themselves. They're beginning to bore me, and they have nothing to offer."

I lean forward to tap ashes into the tray. "Pippa doesn't want to marry me."

"Why's that a problem?"

"I also don't want to marry her," I lie.

It's the first time I've lied to his face.

He stares, long and hard, questioning my honesty. I've known Vincent my entire life, trained with him, killed with him, and sat in hour-long meetings together. He knows I'm lying through my teeth, and I'm taking a risk by doing it.

"Ah," he says, drawing that word out, smoke circling him. "Then, I'll tell Cernach no deal."

"I appreciate it, boss." I'd like to get the hell out of this office, but my cigar isn't finished. I take as many long inhales as I can, wishing I could eat the fucking thing and be done with it.

We smoke in silence for a good ten minutes until Vincent picks up conversation again. He talks about Amara and how much he appreciates how well I watch over her. He invites me to one of their weekly family dinners.

I nod, pretending I won't make up an excuse when that night comes.

When my cigar is nothing but a stub, I snuff it out in the ashtray and raise my brow in question. A silent ask for permission to go.

He holds up a finger. "You're like a second son to me, Damien, so I want to ask you this one question."

I nod again.

"If you don't want to marry his niece, then you're okay with me marrying her off to one of our other men?"

"No," I clip without hesitation.

Vincent rubs at his long chin. "That's all I needed to know."

I stand and head toward the door.

"I'm giving you this favor for the sacrifice your family has made for mine," he says to my back. "This is your only one, and don't you lie to me again."

I peer back at him and tip my head forward. "Thank you, Vincent."

## 36

# PIPPA

I PRIDE myself on good customer service. As the old saying goes, I leave my problems at the door when I come into work.

Right now, though, I'm ready to poison a customer's coffee.

Cernach's hateful eyes are glued on me while he orders his coffee at the front counter. He asks for it black, plain.

I dump five sugar packets inside his cup.

After he collects his coffee, he takes a seat at the table Damien normally sits at. I narrow my eyes at him, and a hint of satisfaction rumbles through me when he takes his first sip of coffee.

His face twists in disgust as he swallows it down. He whips his head toward me and glares.

I check my watch.

Fifteen minutes until my shift ends.

The asshole timed it perfectly.

He came in before Julian arrives for pickup, so he wouldn't see him. But late enough where he wouldn't have to wait long.

I'm shaky for the next fifteen minutes.

I spill two coffees and have to throw one out after realizing I used creamer instead of soy milk.

When my shift ends, I move to him with hesitation.

He's here for me—that much is obvious. Knowing him, he won't let up until I speak with him. Might as well get it over with in public.

"Pippa," he greets when I approach him. "Fancy seeing you here."

I plop down on the chair across from him and cross my arms. "What do you want, Cernach?"

"I thought I'd pay you a visit." He forces an exaggerated smirk. "Check on my favorite niece."

I scoff.

"You no longer live in your shithole apartment."

"Stalking is illegal, you know."

"It's funny you believe I mull over what's legal or not." The gold rings on his fingers slide against each other as he levels his elbows on the table. Seconds later, he raises them at the realization that it's sticky. "Your mother said you're living with Damien now."

I glare at him, choosing not to answer.

"I found your father." He says this with too much smugness.

"Did you do something to him?" I hiss, leaning in closer.

He studies one of his gaudy rings. "Ask your little roommate, Damien."

"Excuse me? I don't appreciate mind games."

"Damien knows what happened to him," he tells me, boredom in his tone.

I flinch.

"Paul has a weak pain tolerance. I don't know if you knew that." He stretches out in the chair, pulling at the sticky syrup residue on his shirt. "He bled for a day before I eventually put him out of his misery."

"Why?" I dig my nails into the bottom of the table. "He did nothing to you."

"Untrue." He clucks his tongue. "He tried to blackmail me and your mother. I did it for her. *For you.* Be appreciative."

I rear back. "You want a *thank-you* for murdering my father?"

"A thank-you. A box of chocolates. Your submission. All will do."

"What will it take for you to get out of our lives?"

"Pippa, I'll never be out of your life." He scrubs the top of his lip. "Now, I got in contact with Vincent Lombardi, your little boyfriend's boss. I wanted to discuss a contract between our families."

I open my mouth, but he holds his hand up and continues speaking. "Vincent will only sign a contract with me if Damien agrees to marry you, which he declined. I want that alliance, and I won't let you ruin it for me. Make yourself useful, spread your legs like a slut, and convince him to sign those papers."

My hand burns to smack him across the face.

"Let's make this simple, shall we?"

I give him the deepest death stare I've ever given anyone.

"We both know I have a tremendous amount of power over you, your mother, *Lanie.* If I want something, I get it, and I want you to convince Damien to marry you." He taps the table three times. "Don't make me force you. I'm never gentle."

I jump up from my chair, my lungs feeling like they're collapsing.

"You're half a Koglin," he rushes out. "Remember that. Women do what they're told in this family."

I hold my purse against my chest and dash out of Brew Bliss. Behind me, I hear Jane calling out, asking me if I'm okay.

*I'm dying.*

*Hyperventilating.*
*Can't breathe.*

"Pippa? What the hell?" Julian asks when I swing open the door and jump inside his car.

"Go!" I scream at the top of my lungs before shoving his shoulder. "Go now!"

"What happened?" His attention darts to Brew Bliss, his hand moving to his gun in his waistband, as if he's waiting to murder the next person who exits.

I loosen my shoulders, knowing I need to calm myself. "Nothing ..." I swat at my shirt. "I started my period and need to get home."

The tension in his face eases. "Should I stop and get you something?"

If I wasn't in panic mode, I'd laugh. This Mafia killer is asking if we need to make a tampon pit stop. Maybe Damien is right about them caring about me and seeing me as their family.

*Does he also know Cernach murdered my father?*

"No," I say quietly. "We don't need to stop."

I'm quiet as he drives me home. He collects his phone from the cupholder and texts—my guess is, he's telling Damien something is wrong with me.

My phone vibrates in my purse, confirming my suspicion is correct when I read the text.

> Damien: Julian said you're upset?

I reply to him.

> Me: Just started my period. Not feeling well.

> Damien: Want me to come home?

> Me: No. I'll be okay. Probably take a nap.

227

When we're home, I head straight to the bedroom. Luckily, my period story checked out because Julian didn't ask any more questions.

As much as I want to collect my belongings, throw them in a bag, and leave, I can't. With Julian downstairs, there's no way I'm walking out the front door. Unless I jump out of a two-story window and dodge the perimeter cameras, I'm stuck here.

It doesn't take long for Damien to step into the bedroom and softly shut the door behind him. He's not wearing his blazer, and he loosens his cuff links as he strolls toward the bed.

"Did you know Cernach killed my father?" I ask coldly.

His expression remains unreadable as he comes closer.

"Did you know?" I bite out.

"Yes."

My heart drops in my chest. "You didn't think to tell me?"

He scrubs a hand over his jaw. "I didn't want to hurt you."

"Oh, you didn't want to hurt me?" I repeat around a long swallow. "You, out of all people, should know how bad it hurts for a parent to die, let alone have someone hide it from you."

He jerks back, my words hitting him like a punch in the gut. "If there was a way for me to erase the hurt of losing my parents from my fucked-up brain, absolutely, I'd want that. No questions asked. It's a never-ending pain."

"You shouldn't get to make that choice for me."

"You're right," he says, his voice mellow. "I'm sorry."

My heart shatters with sadness.

It's also searing with anger.

Flip-flopping with which emotion is the strongest.

"I can't do this anymore," I whisper.

*This isn't what I want.*

*But it's what needs to be done.*

"Don't say something you'll regret," he bites out, sitting on the edge of the bed next to me.

I choke back tears. "We need to end this."

Turning, he snatches my pillow and tosses it back into the same spot. "Go to bed. We'll talk about this in the morning when our emotions aren't so high."

He's being calm with me, something not of his usual nature.

"I'm serious," I say, holding my ground.

"Go to bed," he finally roars, his patience dwindling. "We'll talk in the morning." He sprawls out his legs, hanging his head between them, and lowers his voice. "Everything I do is to shield you from pain. *Everything*. You said it yourself. You thought your father was gone for good."

"Gone for good but still alive."

He shakes his head.

"Do you love me, Damien?"

He raises his head. "You know I do."

"Break up with me, then." Tears flood my eyes.

He jerks back. "Absolutely fucking not."

"Please," I plead, grabbing at his sleeve. "Cernach won't stop until he gets his way. Until he gets a contract and *you*."

"I took care of that. Vincent declined his request."

"He knows Vincent only declined because of you. Cernach needs to know I can't marry you because you don't want me."

He pulls away and stands. His nostrils flare. "I do fucking want you!"

I stare up at him in anguish. "Let me go. Don't make me run."

"I'll kill Cernach, then. If you need him dead to make you happy, then that's what I'll do." Spit flies from his mouth.

"You kill him, you start a war with the Koglins. I won't let you do that. If you love me, do this for me. Don't make me flee New York."

"You're giving us up, just like that?" He snaps his fingers with the last word.

I stand, inches from him, and place my hand over his cheek. His breathing is so hard that I'm waiting for his lungs to fly from his chest. I stare at him with the most heartache I've ever experienced in my soul.

"In another life, we'd be perfect together," I whisper. "He killed my father. I'll do nothing for him. Tell him you don't want me, that you got tired of me and decided I wasn't worth it."

He violently shakes his head.

"I'm sorry, Damien."

"You're not sorry," he grits out. "You're being selfish."

"If you're not with someone when Cernach dies, maybe things will change."

"I don't want anyone else!" he screams.

"I'll move my things back into my apartment," I sob.

He walks away from me, moving away from the bed and snatching a bag from the closet. When he returns, he's tossing his shit into it. "You'll stay here."

"I can't—"

His intense stare narrows on me. "I'll crash at Antonio's, and you'll stay here until I get you a new apartment. You might be leaving me, but that doesn't mean I'll stop protecting you." His eyes are glossy as he throws the bag over his shoulder and kisses my forehead. "You're making a mistake, but it's your mistake to make."

He leaves the bedroom, and I collapse to my knees, falling apart.

Removing Cernach's control from my life means breaking my heart in the process. But I'll sacrifice that happiness to make sure my father's murderer doesn't get what he wants from me.

## 37

# DAMIEN

"What the hell happened to you?" Antonio asks, sliding into the Range Rover's passenger seat.

I've been parked in his driveway for the past hour.

I'm sure I look as sleep-deprived as I feel.

"I hope you don't plan on driving," he adds, eyeing the whiskey bottle nestled in the cupholder. It's there, just in case, but I haven't touched it yet.

I won't because in the back of my mind, there's hope Pippa will call, asking me to come home, and we'll work shit out. I spent last night sitting outside the townhouse, making sure she didn't flee to her apartment. Not that she could get inside it. I had all the locks changed.

"Pippa ended things," I say.

He blows out a long breath. "Why?"

"Cernach." I grit out his name in distaste. "This life. All of it."

He nods. "This life is hard on women."

Understanding flashes on his face. He didn't love Sienna, but she was the mother of his child. Her death left his daughter motherless, and he blames this life for that.

"I won't force her to be with me." I grind my teeth.

"I wouldn't judge you if you did force her."

"Pippa wouldn't go for that, and I respect her too much." I could easily go to Cernach, and we could force her hand, lock her into a marriage with me until she came to terms that she was mine.

Antonio clasps me on the back. "You're a good man, Damien."

"I understand why she's doing it. I'm just pissed."

"Don't go killing an Irish boss on me, okay? I already have enough headaches." He opens the door and steps out, leaving me alone in my agony, my anger, my fucking madness.

# PART II

# The sacrifice

## 38

# PIPPA

**Eleven Months Later**

He still watches me.

Deep down, if I'm being honest, I like it.

As I leave my apartment, I catch sight of the familiar black SUV parked on the street. With every step I take toward The Ballet Studio—*my* dance studio—I sense his attention locked on me.

Two days after my breakup with Damien, I told my mother I'd never work anywhere Cernach-affiliated. I'd rather stay at Brew Bliss forever and never have my dream of a studio before I fell into his trap. She refused my job offer to work at The Ballet Studio, and our relationship has suffered.

Her not being angry with Cernach is a mystery to me.

Cernach murdered her husband.

Treated her as a bargaining chip when she grew up.

He also ruined her daughter's relationship.

The other day, when I glanced at the time, and it read 11:11, I wished someone would murder his ass.

My apartment is located a short walk from the studio. When I tried to move back into my old apartment, Damien refused it. Not only did he lease me a new apartment but he takes care of the rent too. When I told the landlord to start charging me, he refused, telling me he wasn't risking Damien murdering him.

I stroll down the sidewalk, feeling the warmth of the sun on my skin. When I enter the studio, I fall back a step.

*Happy Birthday* balloons fill the room.

A wrapped present sits on a table next to a stack of class schedule flyers.

I move toward the table but stop and turn when the door opens. Damien appears in the doorway.

The air suddenly feels heavy and suffocating.

Like he's stealing my breaths, a reminder I'm only halfway living without him. Shutting my eyes for a moment, I exhale a deep breath.

He turns the lock. "Happy birthday, my sweet dancer."

"Did you do this?" I gesture toward the balloons, already knowing the answer.

He tucks his hands into his pockets, coming closer. "I wanted you to have a nice birthday."

*He remembered.*

Damien always remembers.

Gulping, I take in every inch of him.

My same Damien, only different.

Tension seems to radiate through every inch of his body.

The year has taken a toll on him, and I hate that.

Hate that it takes so much away from all of us.

I keep up with the rumors around the Mafia world, and I know they're having issues with nearly everyone in New York City. I also learn of these things when Antonio refuses to allow Amara to attend classes at the studio for security reasons.

Damien slides his tongue along the front of his teeth.

*I've missed him so damn much.*

I don't budge as he draws closer. Taking my trembling hand, he guides me to the small office in the back. My back meets the wall, his body inches from mine, and he audibly sucks in a breath.

He buries his face in the hollow of my neck, both of us falling silent. As he places gentle kisses on my collarbone, he mutters, "I've missed you," against my skin.

I open my mouth to say something, but no words come.

It's ecstasy when his mouth moves to meet mine.

He kisses me as if he wants to shove all our memories back through them.

He tastes the same.

His mouth feels the same.

All of it *perfection*.

My breath catches when he slides his hand up my shorts. Our tongues tangle, creating their own dance, and he shoves my panties to the side. He groans, gliding his fingers through my wetness. When he pushes them inside me, I brace myself against the wall.

He isn't gentle as he finger-fucks me, his thumb teasing my clit. He locks eyes with me, staring deeply. I can't resist touching his cheek and running my fingers across his skin. He sighs, a trace of rigidness fading from his face.

A rush of warmth travels through my body. It's as if fire were coursing through my veins.

"That's it. Drench my fingers with your cum, baby," he says against my mouth. "I want to jack off later and still feel your juices on my hand. I want to smear it all over my cock, remembering how wet your pussy gets, like a fucking lake, baby."

His words set me off, and I fuck his hand, slamming my hips against him.

*I'm closer and closer and closer and closer.*

As my release breaks free, he continues caressing me as I moan out his name. He supports me as my knees wobble, and I come down from my high.

"Happy birthday, baby," he says, kissing me on the lips.

I bend forward when he steps back and leaves.

# 39

# DAMIEN

### Two Months Later

The Lombardi family is at war.

Correction: *wars*.

War with the Marchettis.

A civil war with Antonio's uncle, Sonny.

So much has happened within the past year.

The pro of violence is, it offers a momentary escape from the unhappiness of losing Pippa.

The downside is, people I care about are at risk of dying.

Cristian murdered Vinny after he kidnapped Natalia, Cristian's fiancée, who also happened to be Vinny's ex and Cristian's daughter, Gigi's, best friend.

Seeking revenge, Vincent attempted to kill Cristian's son, Benny. Instead of the bullet hitting Benny, it struck his wife, Neomi. She survived, thank fuck.

Vincent's act not only created more problems with the Marchettis but also with Severino Cavallaro, Neomi's father and our largest weapons supplier. As expected, we lost that relationship. Shortly after, Vincent passed away from a stroke before Cristian or Severino could kill him.

After his passing, Antonio assumed leadership as boss of the Lombardi family. Sonny is now making a claim for the title, causing a split within the family. Half of the traitorous men have aligned with Sonny, and the other half remain loyal to us.

If we want to stay alive and get rid of Sonny and his men, we're in desperate need of weapons. Cernach Koglin is our final hope.

I know the bastard won't make this easy and will want more than a simple cash deal. This time, he knows we're at his mercy.

As we step inside the dank warehouse, Cernach is waiting with a smug grin. Three men stand behind him, like soldiers, staring at us in distrust.

"I'm only doing this because I detest your son-of-a-bitch uncle," Cernach bites out.

Rumor has it, Sonny fucked one of Cernach's mistresses during a trip to Boston. Even after Sonny mailed him a thousand-dollar check with a note saying, *Payment for your whore for the night*, Cernach still holds a grudge against him.

Antonio cuts straight to the chase, opening the duffel bag of guns on the table Cernach brought us.

"And before I give you these, I want to make a deal," Cernach adds with a huff as Antonio unloads three AK-47s.

"What kind of deal are you looking for?" he asks Cernach, inspecting the guns.

"After you kill Sonny and his men, you marry my daughter, Riona."

Antonio raises his hand, showing off his wedding band. "I can't do that. I'm already married."

"To who?" Cernach grunts.

"Giana Marchetti."

"Giana Marchetti." Cernach pauses, as if waiting for Antonio to tell him he's fucking with him. His eyes widen when Antonio doesn't. "As in Cristian Marchetti's daughter?"

"The one and only."

Cernach barks out a laugh. "You're married to the daughter of the man who wants to murder you?" He runs a hand through his beard. "You hold a gun to her head?"

"I'd never do anything like that." Antonio smirks.

That's precisely what he did.

He took Gigi captive, held a gun to her and a priest's head, and forced her to say her vows to him. That made reason nine fucking hundred thousand to have Antonio on Cristian's kill list. Adding to the problem, Antonio hasn't returned Gigi. He's not keeping her out of spite. He loves Gigi and fears Sonny will hurt her.

Cernach snorts and then directs his focus past Antonio. He shifts his gaze from Julian to Emilio and then rests it on me.

"If you can't marry my daughter, then I want one of them." He drums his fingers along his chin. "I want a capo ... someone high in rank. Not some schmuck."

When he realizes no one is eager to volunteer, he points at each of us, one by one. I'm last, and I glare at him.

I already know who he's choosing.

As soon as Antonio said he was unavailable, I knew it.

"Damien," he says, shocking the others, but not me. "You're the type of man I desire my Riona to marry."

I work my jaw, not saying a word.

"No contract, no guns," he adds.

Sonny made it clear anyone who supports Antonio will die. While I stopped fearing death at the age of twelve, I still need to protect the ones I love. Knowing Sonny's brutality, I'm unsure if he'd spare Clara's and Amara's lives. He's determined to get rid of anyone bearing the Lombardi name.

Right before I killed one of Sonny's men, he mentioned

Pippa, knowing she's one of my weaknesses. Broken up or not, it's still my responsibility to keep her safe.

Pippa left me, threw away our future.

There's no chance for us to marry.

I've accepted a lonely life. After losing Pippa, I knew it was a bad idea to ever bring an innocent woman into my world—especially after all the violence we've had lately.

Antonio shakes his head. "Sorry, Cernach—"

I step to his side and interrupt him, "I'll do it."

This is a sacrifice I must make.

I hate it, but I hate losing people I love more.

Antonio holds up his hand. "Damien—"

"I'll do it," I grind out. Each of those words pains my throat as I say them.

"Excellent." Cernach snaps his fingers in the air.

One of his men produces a document, dropping it beside the guns.

Cernach draws a pen from his coat and taps it against the papers. "I need both of your signatures here, and the deal is done. You can take your weapons and leave."

"You'll also continue providing us with firearms." I jerk my head toward the paper. "I want that in writing."

"And going forward, you only charge us half," Antonio adds. "Damien is a capo. He's worth it."

My hand sweats as I scribble my name on the dotted line and pass the pen to Antonio.

"You sure?" he asks from under his breath while taking the pen from me.

I lower my voice so he's the only one to hear me. "If this is what it takes to get rid of Sonny, then that's what I have to do."

His tone matches mine. "You know who Riona is, right?"

I straighten my collar. "I know exactly who Riona is."

This is what I must do to end the war.

But I don't know if Pippa will ever forgive me for agreeing to marry her cousin.

## 40

# DAMIEN

**One Month Later**

"Sacrifices are inevitable in every life."

Those are the words my father would tell my mother when he returned home, battered and bloody, asking for her to stitch him up. She'd repeat them when people questioned why she looked the other way when he committed his crimes.

Those sacrifices cost their lives and forever changed mine.

And now, it's my turn to sacrifice.

I crumple the marriage contract into a ball, strike a match, and watch flames devour it. The words that determine my future bleed into each other. As I toss it in the trash, the paper shrivels up and turns into nothing but a pile of ashes.

The most fucked-up part?

I can set it on fire a thousand times, but the outcome will never change. Cernach saw our desperation when he offered the deal, and now, I have to honor my word and lose everything.

The trash can falls on its side when I kick it. I sit back in my chair, my spine as stiff as a rod.

All hell will break loose today.

The wedding invitations are being sent out, and I know Pippa will come. She'll pour her anger out on me, and I'll consume it because it's what I deserve.

My attention shifts to the door at the sound of a knock.

"Yeah?" I shout, sitting upright.

Julian takes that as permission to enter my office. "We found another one."

I stand, snag my blazer from the back of the chair, and shrug it on. "Where?"

His lips ease into a smirk. "The stupid motherfucker came into the casino, thinking we wouldn't notice him."

"Our prey walked straight to its predator."

Julian chuckles. "Good day for us."

At least that's one positive since it'll turn into hell later.

For the past few weeks, we've been focused on killing Sonny's henchmen. Sonny is dead, and now, we're picking off his men one by fucking one. It's a shame I'm running out of them, though.

In my eyes, it's Sonny's fault I signed the contract.

So, every motherfucker who helped him needs to die.

Julian follows me out of Lucky Kings to my new Mercedes GL 550, and we drive to the warehouse.

As I enter the building, slipping on black leather gloves, Emilio greets me while standing in front of a man bound to a chair. My footsteps echo through the large space as I stalk straight to them. Monty, who once pledged his loyalty to Antonio's father, pitifully stares at me with swollen eyes and a mouth covered in blood, his shoulders hunched in defeat.

When they said may the best man win, he chose the wrong fucking man.

Since I have a business meeting in thirty minutes, I can't take my time with him. Monty shrinks back in the chair as I raise my Glock, and I catch the sound of a plea before I shoot him in the face.

His head droops, blood dripping on his lap, and I kick the chair. Satisfaction ripples through me when his body collapses to the ground with a heavy thump.

"Take care of the body," I instruct them before removing gloves and tucking my Glock into my waistband.

Emilio salutes me, and Julian nods.

As I exit the warehouse, I wonder what time she'll come to me.

***

EIGHT HOURS LATER, she does.

I'm aware she's coming before she arrives at Antonio's. As I sit back and stare at my phone, I watch the pin tracing her path on the screen—compliments of the GPS tracker I planted in her car.

She takes a left.

A right.

*Getting closer and closer.*

Vito, the gate guard, calls and interrupts my tracking.

"I have one pissed-off dance teacher here," he says around an annoying-ass chuckle. "Do you want me to allow her through?"

"Yes." I hang up, push out of my chair, and slip my phone into my pocket while walking toward the door.

*Welcome to the shit show.*

Her silver Audi's headlights beam through the darkness as she races down the driveway and abruptly brakes. In a matter of seconds, she's out of the car.

Leaving the door open, I step backward and wait for her. We have snipers stationed all over the property, and they're nosy. We're not having this conversation in the open. It'll also be easier to trap her inside and prevent her from leaving until she hears me out.

She enters the house like a storm of beauty and madness.

Her face is red and charged with betrayal.

"Pippa—" I raise my palm as she stampedes toward me.

If I wasn't so pissed and it wasn't *her*, I'd find such a petite woman coming for my blood comical. I'd also applaud her for having balls bigger than most men in this city.

"Fuck you, Damien," she screams, her ponytail swinging with the force of her pace as she comes closer. "I wish I'd never met you, let alone allowed you to touch me."

People have beaten the shit out of me.

Teased me.

Shot me once.

But the strike of her words hit harder than any of them.

"I'm warning you, Pippa," I grit out.

"And I'm warning you to never speak to me again." She slices her hand through the air as if it'll rip apart all our history. "That's the last words you'll ever hear me say."

I scoff when she turns to leave.

*Don't think so, sweetheart.*

I clutch her forearm, yanking her backward, and her back falls against my chest.

"What the hell—"

I spin her around, pinning her against the wall, and rest my hands against them. She doesn't jump, and there's no fear in her eyes.

She huffs, glaring at me as if I'm her worst enemy, not a man she once gave herself to.

Our breathing matches exhale by exhale as I stare down at the most beautiful woman in this world. That belief hasn't changed since the first time I saw her and chased her down.

I've murdered for her.

Spilled my secrets.

Fucked.

*Loved.*

Now, I've killed that with the flick of my signature.

Since her height is nowhere near mine, I dip my head so our faces are level.

"Warning me? *Or what?*" She rises on her tiptoes to better square off with me.

"Let me explain." I work my jaw, clenching my teeth so hard that I'm surprised my face doesn't fracture.

"Fuck you," she spits. "And I want the GPS you planted, *without my permission*, removed from my car right fucking now."

Instead of answering her, I fixate on her lips.

Wanting to attack them with my mouth.

Suck on the corner like she used to love.

Her smacking my shoulder snaps me back into reality.

"Not happening." I'd allow someone to skin me alive before I stopped watching her every move.

She attempts to shove my chest, but I don't flinch.

"Fine. I'll sell my car or gift it to my cousin for your nuptial gift."

I inch my hand back and slam it against the wall. "Watch your mouth."

This demented heart of mine corrodes more when I think about the engagement.

"Why?" she taunts. "Does the truth hurt?"

I glare down at her.

"Who should I bring as my date to your wedding?" She taps the edge of her mouth with her purple nails. "You know what they say? Weddings are the best places to find one-night stands."

*My sweet dancer must've forgotten who I am if she thinks that'll happen.*

"Stop while you're ahead, Pippa," I bite out.

"Maybe he'll fuck me better than you did."

I've let her talk her shit, but now, that's over.

It's time I set her straight.

"He had no choice, Pippa," someone says behind me instead.

I separate from her to find Antonio entering the living room —a reminder that we created this scene in his home.

Pippa moves around me, staring at Antonio, wide-eyed. "Everyone has choices." A long breath leaves her. "You men love to convince us otherwise. I didn't leave this life because I was stupid. I left it because of *this*, because I'm smart."

Pippa doesn't carry the same level of attitude with Antonio as she does me.

He'd never hurt her. He knows if anyone ever laid a hand on her—boss or not—I'd become his worst enemy.

Her response reminds me why we're in this situation, to begin with.

*Because she fucking left.*

I stop behind her, the urge to tug her ponytail and make her drop to her knees in front of me strong. "Maybe if you didn't, I'd be marrying you instead."

She waves her hand in the air. "Good riddance I did then."

I'm so close, and she shudders when I lower my lips to her ear.

My dancer might believe she hates me. Her body says otherwise.

"You left because you're a fucking coward," I sneer.

"That's enough," Antonio barks. "Pippa, go home."

Pippa pushes herself away from me while steadying her gaze on Antonio. "Fine. I don't want one of your men following me."

"It'll be them or me," I say coldly.

Keeping her back to me, she lifts her hand and extends her middle finger over her shoulder.

I snatch her wrist, give it a twist, and turn her to face me. "Flip me off again, and I'll hold you against the wall and shove that finger inside your pussy until you stop with your fucking attitude."

She jerks from my hold. "I hate you."

When she heads for the door and I attempt to follow, Antonio blocks me.

"Leo will trail her," he says. "We need to talk in my office."

Leo is Antonio's cousin and is just as involved in this life as him.

I might be Antonio's underboss, but he's still the boss. So, while I have plenty of freedom, if he says we need to talk, then we need to talk. As long as someone trails her, I'm okay.

Pippa gets into her car, and I call Leo.

"Make sure you watch Pippa until I tell you otherwise," I instruct while following Antonio into his office.

"On it," he replies.

*Did Pippa actually believe I'd remove her trackers?*

I'll keep one on her until the day I take my last breath.

Hell, I've arranged for someone to do it even after my death.

"Do you want me to break off your engagement?" Antonio asks.

I massage my temples. "We can't. Koglin isn't a man you breach contracts with. We're trying to get back on our feet. If we break this contract, we'll have even more enemies."

Antonio strolls to the bar cart, grabs two tumblers, and pours double shots of whiskey. When he passes one to me, I drink it in a single gulp. Rather than pouring me a refill, he hands me the entire bottle of Johnnie Walker.

"You're off for the rest of the night," he says. "Stay here. Leave. Do whatever you want. If you leave, wait to finish that until you return."

I've been sleeping here lately, watching Amara when he's working. Now that Pippa no longer lives in the brownstone, it's lonely as hell, and I have a deep-seated hatred for silence.

I lift a chin in his direction, hold up the bottle in thanks, and stalk outside toward my SUV.

As soon as I start the engine, I call Leo, Antonio's cousin. "Where are you?"

"Sitting outside Pippa's apartment building."

"Stay there. I'm on my way."

It takes me twelve minutes to drive to the outskirts of suburbia and another fifteen to the city. Antonio's home is distanced from the city, hidden behind a high fence and trees. It once belonged to some old asshole president.

The traffic becomes busier the closer I get to Pippa's, and I parallel park behind Leo's black BMW.

I call him back. "You're free to leave."

Making myself comfortable, I watch Pippa through the window as she moves around her fourth-floor apartment. When she reaches her bedroom an hour later, she closes the curtains, but I keep my eyes on her silhouette behind them.

I don't care if she broke up with me.

If she hates me.

If I have a marriage contract.

I'm not letting her go.

# 41

# PIPPA

He's getting married.

Those three words have become a constant in my head the past week.

I'll never forget when my phone beeped with an Evite notification. I had a strawberry milkshake in one hand and was watching a rerun of *Girls*. My hand shook when I opened the email, and I dropped the milkshake onto my blanket.

*Join us to celebrate the nuptials of Damien Bellini and Riona Koglin.*

They didn't include a cutesy engagement photo or registry.

I stared at the screen in a daze, like someone was playing a cruel prank on me.

For so long, I'd trusted fate to determine my love life.

Turns out, fate played a cruel game with my heart.

"Today will be a better day," I sing to myself while throwing my hair in a messy bun. "We're already starting out better than the last two, considering I brushed my hair."

As I'm finishing off my hair with a pink ribbon, my phone vibrates.

My mom's name flashes across the screen.

A warning. A bad freaking omen.

She never calls or texts.

"Pippa." She rushes out my name in one breath when I answer the call. "Can you come over, please?"

I stiffen at the alarm in her voice. "What's wrong?"

"Lanie needs your help."

All it takes is hearing my sister's name, and I race out the door, driving to my mom's. A blacked-out Bentley is parked in the driveway when I arrive.

Shoving my keys inside my bag, I run into the house. The door is unlocked, and Cernach is the first person I see.

"I'll call you back," he says into his phone before ending the call and shoving it into his pocket while staring me down.

A warning from my mother that Satan was here would've been nice.

The Fedora man who was with Cernach when he came to my apartment stands to his side. My mom and Lanie are squeezed beside each other on the old couch.

Lanie's cheeks are red and blotchy, and my mother stares at me with a cold bitterness. It's sad but funny in a way. She's looking at me how she should be looking at her brother.

"It took you long enough to get here," Cernach says, sneering at me.

I offer him a sarcastic smile. "Had I known you were here, I'd have taken longer."

He waggles his fat finger at me. "One of these days, that smart mouth of yours will get you killed."

I scoff. "What do you want, Cernach?"

"I'd like to discuss Lanie's marriage." He pushes his glasses up his nose, as if ready to make a business deal.

Lanie scoots closer to my mother, who hasn't looked away from Cernach and me since I walked in.

"Excuse me?" I grimace. "You're not marrying her off."

"Yes, I am," Cernach argues while the man next to him nods.

"We don't live by Koglin rules here."

His face is stolid. "She does when she signed a contract."

My attention whips to Lanie. "You did what?"

Lanie violently shakes her head as tears fall down her cheeks.

"You see"—Cernach's voice makes my skin crawl, and he strolls toward the couch, as if preparing to auction Lanie off—"Lanie got herself into some trouble for shoplifting. Your mother called me for help."

"What?" I blink at her. "Why didn't you call me?"

"Why would she call you?" Cernach says as Lanie looks away from me, suddenly very interested in studying her chipped nails. "Do you have connections with the prosecutor or the money to pay an attorney?"

I want to bitch-slap that smug expression off his face.

He'd probably shoot me in mine for it, though.

"I got your sister out of trouble. You're welcome," Cernach continues when I don't answer his question. His beady eyes level on me. "But as you should know, a Koglin doesn't hand out favors for free. I explained to Lanie I'd only pay the attorney if she became a true Koglin, and true Koglins do what's expected of them. She signed my contract, I paid her fees, and your dear sister isn't sitting in a jail cell."

Clenching my fists, I dig my nails inside my palms.

"Now, if you don't want me to marry her off, I have an offer for you," he adds as if doing me the favor of a lifetime.

I cross my arms. "Spoiler alert: I'm not doing anything for you."

"Maybe not for me." He pauses to dramatically rest his hand on his heart, as if my words wounded him. "But what about for your baby sister?"

I peer at a terrified Lanie and attempt to soften my tone. "Why didn't you call me?"

"I didn't know what that meant," she stutters out. "All I wanted was out of trouble."

"Your sister is dumb—that's why," Cernach says, shrugging at Lanie. "No offense, twit, but I'm retracting my offer to pay your college tuition. You'll fail out, and it'll be a giant waste of my money."

Lanie glares at him but drops it when my mother taps her knee.

"What will you do if she refuses?" I ask. "Take her to court for breach of contract? I'd love to see the judge's face when they reads your terms."

"If she refuses to be a good little wife to someone, then I'll sell her to a brutal man who will rape her anytime he wants."

Lanie whimpers.

My poor sister.

She might be old enough to join the military, but she's just as much of an adult as I am a starfish. My mother sheltered her too much. The poor thing didn't even think to question Cernach's motives.

My mother's entire body stiffens, and she stares at him, wide-eyed, but doesn't say a word.

*What the living fuck?*

While I want to go off on her, I need to focus on Cernach first.

"Now, back to my offer." Cernach rubs his hands together. "I had a husband picked out for her. The grandson of a man I'd like to do business with. Unfortunately, the grandson finds Lanie too young to marry."

"Smart man," I comment.

"I showed him a picture of you. He has no problem with your age."

"I have a problem with his."

"You don't even know how old he is," my mom says, finally inputting her voice.

It's pro-Cernach, of course.

Lord forbid she sticks up for her daughters.

"I don't care how old he is," I argue, my head throbbing. "The answer is no."

Cernach snaps his fingers and motions toward Fedora Man, who passes him a folded paper. He opens it, holding a photo up on display.

"You'll marry the grandson." He stops to tap the photo of a man who's nearly half in the grave. "Or your sister will marry the grandfather. One of you cunts will marry into that family. Now, which one is it?" His lips turn into a crooked smile. "Look at me, being kind and allowing you to make your own choices." He holds up his fist mockingly. "Women's rights."

My heart batters in my chest, like a wild animal begging for freedom.

I step closer to him. "You want me to marry someone for the sake of a contract? I'll marry Damien, like you've wanted all these years. Riona can marry the grandson."

Cernach chuckles. "That offer no longer stands. You should've taken it when I gave you the opportunity." He smacks the photo. "Now, whose wedding are we planning next?"

I stand there, glaring at him.

"This is your best bet at a tolerable marriage. He's a decent man who travels frequently and is gone for long periods of time. He won't require much of you. You're lucky I'm not forcing you to marry the grandfather just to spite you for all the trouble you've given me."

Lanie cries in my mom's arms.

My mom stares at me in expectation.

Cernach leans back on his heels and starts counting down on his fingers.

"Fine," I snap, narrowing my eyes at him. "I'll do it."

Cernach is running out of women to use as bargaining chips

to fuel his power. We're nothing but a means to an end with him. Pawns to be moved at his will.

"That's my good niece," Cernach says, clapping his hands a single time.

Damien was desperate when he agreed to marry Riona.

And now, I'm just as desperate.

---

I SHOULD'VE MARRIED DAMIEN.

I tried to play a hard bargain with Cernach and stupidly forgot who I was dealing with.

Regret has haunted me all day.

I canceled two dance classes and completely messed up every dance routine during another.

I throw my pointe shoe across the studio and curse it as I clean up after class.

Two more to go, and I can go home and sit in my sorrows. If Cernach didn't have Lanie in his grips, I'd fled New York. You can't marry off a woman you can't find.

The chime above the door rings, and I whip around to find Damien in the doorway.

"You need to leave," I say, scooping up the thrown shoe. "I have class in five minutes."

He locks the door behind him, so similar to how he did it on my birthday. "Your next class starts in fifteen minutes."

I glower at him. "Stop stalking me."

"No."

"How about you tell me your schedule then?" A hint of mockery is in my tone. "Tell me your honeymoon schedule, the times you plan to fuck my cousin."

He recoils at my words like he ate something rotten.

"I wish I could shove those words back down your throat."

He stalks toward me. "The only woman we should ever speak about me fucking is you."

The closer he comes, the more I feel like I need him to wrap his arms around my body and comfort me.

My body, my heart, my everything will never forget our history.

I should force him out and push him away, but I don't. I stand there, frozen in place.

He reaches out and cups my cheek with his cold hand. "I don't want Riona."

There's so much silent apology in his tone—like it's seeping off his hand and through my skin.

"Yet ..." It takes me a moment to finish my sentence. "You're marrying her."

Unlike his voice, mine has more spitefulness than softness.

He scowls, his brows bunching. "I had no choice."

"You could've said no."

"If I'd said no, people would've died. I—or even *you*—would've died. We needed a weapons deal, and no one in the city would sell to us. Cernach was our only option, and that was his stipulation."

"How convenient that it had to be *you*."

"It was me or no deal."

I straighten my shoulders and shuffle back a step, hating the loss of his touch, but knowing it's for the best. "I'm attending your wedding. Per Cernach's orders."

A hint of a smirk plays at his mouth. "Good. I love seeing you every chance I get. Wear something sexy and easy for me to take off."

*The nerve of this man.*

Swear to God.

"Over my dead body." I swat at his hand, creating more distance between us. "If you ever think I'll allow a married man to touch me, you're highly mistaken."

"I'm not married, my sweet dancer."

"Do I really need to make the correction that you're engaged? You know I'd never get involved with a married man—history or not. I have morals, unlike you, it seems."

"Since that first day you danced for me in your apartment, you're the only woman I've touched." A sly expression crosses his face. "Let's not act like you haven't let me touch you since we've broken up either. Who do you call when you're lonely at night, Pippa?"

I hate that I shudder.

That he's using my body against me.

*Ugh.*

"That stops now." I point toward the floor and gasp when he presses my back against the wall. There's not even a second to push him away before he crowds me, rubbing me between my legs.

*Goddd.*

Why does he do this to me?

"I haven't touched your cousin once," he says, making small circles against my clit. "No woman will ever make me crazy like you."

I give him another second of touching me.

Of making me feel good.

Which is stupid, considering the longer he touches me, the more worked up I become.

A moan leaving my lips snaps me back into reality.

I shove him away. "Don't act like you won't fuck her after you marry." I swipe the sliver of space between us. "This is over, Damien. We're done."

"I hate it when lies leave your pretty little mouth." He traces my lips with his finger. "Speaking of mouths, remember all the ways I made you come with mine?" He grins when chills run over my body.

It's time to strike.

To ruin this mood.

And if there's anything I know that'll piss Damien off, it's what I'm about to tell him.

"This might be the time I tell you I'm also getting married."

*And, yes, I was right.*

He winces, as if I delivered the hardest slap he'd ever felt and jerks back. "What the fuck are you talking about?"

"Oh, Cernach didn't tell you? He also put me on the market." I tap his chest condescendingly. "To our future nuptials. Maybe we can honeymoon together."

His entire demeanor changes.

He's now all business.

"Marrying who?" he bites out.

"Some guy. I don't know." I shrug.

"I'll get you out of it."

"Maybe I want a husband."

He steps forward, causing me to hit my back against the wall again. "You ever let another man touch you, I'll gut him from the inside out and make you watch me. This is one thing you should know not to test me on."

"We're no longer together. It's time we both move on."

He wipes the side of his mouth. "I love it when you're wrong —because I get to punish your mouth for it."

He stares back at the door when a group appears.

One person attempts to tug at the door handle to come in.

The dancers for my next class.

"I'll handle Cernach. We'll talk soon."

"We're done, Damien," I say to his back. "Have a nice marriage."

He shakes his head while looking at me deeply. "We'll never be done."

## 42

# DAMIEN

Per my GPS, the drive time from New York to Boston is a little under five hours.

I make it there in less than three.

No one manipulates what's mine and gets away with it.

Cernach might've used my weakness to play games with me, but I'll be damned if he does with Pippa.

I turn down the dark street that leads to the estate's steel gates. There's a risk that he or one of his men will shoot me. Men like Cernach, like me, don't like surprise visitors.

It's a risk I'm willing to take if it stops him from marrying Pippa off to some rat bastard of his choosing.

As expected, a guard stops me at the gate and radios Cernach, who instructs him to allow me clearance. Arm guards line the length of the drive, and I resist the urge to give them the finger as I pass. Or shoot them.

Given how flashy Cernach is, his home is what I'd imagined. His estate spans at least ten acres, and trees conceal his home from any main roads. When I reach the front, a fleet of expensive cars line the circular drive.

A tall man who looks like he hasn't seen the sun in ages is

waiting for me in the open doorway. I'm surprised he doesn't search me for weapons before waving me inside. Without saying a word, he leads me straight into an office where Cernach sits behind his desk, surrounded by a thin cloud of smoke.

There are many ways I've imagined killing this man.

Antonio told me I couldn't carry out any of them.

I've moved up as the underboss of the Lombardi family and his partner at the casino. But at the end of the day, he makes the rules. Every action we take creates a ripple effect throughout our organization.

Even if I killed him, it wouldn't void the contract. His underboss could insist it remain in effect. No matter what, I'm in debt with the Koglins.

"Damien," he greets as if we're old friends. He signals for the man to leave, settles his cigar on an ashtray, and offers me one as the door shuts.

I shake my head.

He stands, strolls to the bar in the corner, and offers me a drink next.

I decline again.

He could offer me an extra heart, and I'd also decline that.

"Surely someone taught you declining cigars and drinks from your future father-in-law is considered disrespectful." He pours himself a glass of Bushmills whiskey.

"I'm not here for you to school me on manners." I don't care to rub elbows with the fucker. Personally, I'd love to watch him die.

"I'm glad you came. Saved me a trip to New York." He gestures for me to sit, and I do. "I wanted to make sure you received a copy of the contract I mailed."

"Yes. I burned it."

"Don't you worry." He chuckles, returning to his chair and settling his drink on the desk. "I have plenty of copies."

I shift in my chair, not saying a word.

"Do you remember everything in it?"

"Word for word."

"Clause number two?" He swipes his cigar from the ashtray.

"I will marry your daughter."

"Clause three?"

"You go fuck yourself."

"Clause three is you keep your hands to yourself when it comes to other women, at least until after your wedding." He straightens his back, and ashes fall on his belly. "I won't have my Riona embarrassed by your infidelity, especially with a woman in our family."

I smirk. "Don't worry, Cernach. I won't fuck your wife, if that's your concern."

He points his cigar in my direction. "Remember who helped you when no one else would."

"You helping us is why I signed your contract."

"You can't blame me for using someone's moment of weakness against them. You would've done the same."

He's right.

I don't know a man who wouldn't have.

"I'm here to discuss something with you."

He raises a brow.

"You won't marry Pippa off."

"Ah, I figured you'd be upset about that. If she told you, you're already breaking clause three." He levels his eyes on me. "You can't have her, do you hear me? You'll marry Riona and never touch Pippa again."

I work my jaw.

He moves in closer. "Since I love making deals with you, here's another."

I lean back in my chair, crossing my legs, already knowing this deal will piss me the fuck off.

"I won't draft a marriage contract with Pippa's name on it

until six months after your marriage if you get Riona pregnant. You do that, and I let Pippa off the hook."

There's an urge to snub that cigar out on his face.

"Do we have a deal?"

"Yeah, we have a deal," I snarl before standing and leaving his office without another word.

On my way toward the front door, I run into Riona.

We've never met in person.

I only know what she looks like because Julian Googled her to see what my future wife looked like.

Riona isn't bad to look at.

She just isn't Pippa.

That's the ultimate turn off.

There are similarities between them.

If we marry, all I'll think about is Pippa.

"Hi, Damien," she says. "My father never formally introduced us."

I run a hand through my hair. "Yeah."

"Do you want to stay for dinner?"

"I have a tight schedule." I walk away and yell, "Maybe another time," over my back.

We do need to have a chat.

Get her pregnant within six months.

Yet another sacrifice I have to make.

## 43

# PIPPA

I swear, it's Mafia wedding season.

And I'm ready for the damn finale.

Today is Antonio and Gigi's special day.

While they're already married, Gigi wanted a real wedding. The first time she and Antonio said their vows was when he was holding her hostage and she had no choice.

For a while, there was uncertainty if there'd ever be a formal wedding since Gigi said she wouldn't have one unless Cristian walked her down the aisle. Somehow, Antonio convinced Cristian to agree. From what I heard, it wasn't with violence but with guilt-tripping.

Only a few months ago, Cristian Marchetti wanted to kill Antonio for taking Gigi hostage. One would've expected nothing but bloodshed if the Lombardis and Marchettis were within the same space. But here we are, commemorating love.

I'm sure Cristian still wants to kill Antonio, but he's refraining for the sake of his daughter.

I've met Gigi a few times during Amara's dance classes. Her curly and dark hair, beauty, and olive complexion bring the image of a Mafia *princess* to life. Antonio met his match with her, but I can tell he enjoys it.

Genesis is my plus-one. I tried to RSVP *no*, but telling Antonio no doesn't mean no.

"Amara wants you there to see her flower-girl walk, so you'll be there," he said.

I'm almost positive Damien also had a hand in my *mandatory* attendance.

Since his visit to the studio, he's called and texted relentlessly.

I've ignored him.

So, he keeps calling and texting.

People might find that stalkerish, but in Damien's head, that's his version of giving me space.

Not giving me space would be breaking into my apartment and taking me hostage.

The wedding is in the prettiest courtyard I've ever seen. I've stepped straight into a fairy tale, ready to witness the Mafia king and queen recite their vows.

When Julian sees us, he stops mid-conversation with Emilio. He briefly looks at me before fixating on Genesis. His gaze wanders down her body as he licks his bottom lip.

Genesis smiles at him.

He tilts his chin in our direction.

"I have a question," I say when we take our seats near the back.

"Yeah?" she asks, her eyes back on Julian.

"Have you and Julian ever …"

She turns to face me. "Ever what?"

"You know …"

Her red lips curl into a smirk as she waits for me to say it.

"Hook up?"

"He fingered me in the back of a club once." She shrugs.

I slap her shoulder. "I knew it!"

"Relax. It's not a big deal."

"Does anyone else know?" I scan the crowd, as if ready for her to single out someone.

She drops her voice. "Emilio."

"Emilio?"

"He was sitting in the booth."

"Julian finger-fucked you in front of Emilio?"

"God, can you say it any freaking louder?" She swats at me. "No more secrets for you, big mouth."

I grin. "I bet it was hot as hell. I've seen Julian's hands."

"Ugh, we're not friends anymore."

"Too late for that. The day you took me to Serenebelle is the day you got stuck with me for life."

She blows an upward breath. "The price I pay for a free spa day."

I laugh, throwing my head back. As I slowly lower it, my gaze meets Damien's. Dressed in a black tux, he stands as Antonio's best man at the altar. He stares at me, his face brooding and eyes burning, as if I'm an object he can never let out of his sight.

Everyone hushes, and all attention—minus Damien's because it doesn't leave me—turns toward Cristian escorting Gigi down the aisle. I watch the beautiful bride in awe. Not in as much awe as Antonio, who looks hopelessly in love. This man risked death to be with her.

As they recite their vows, I struggle to hold back tears.

This is how a wedding should be.

How a bride and groom should feel.

You should be able to see the love and devotion in their eyes like you do Gigi's and Antonio's.

They defied people to marry each other.

Nearly caused a war for their love.

Gigi refused to back down and demanded nothing but true love.

"Gigi is stunning, obvi," Genesis comments. "But Cristian Marchetti? I'd call him Daddy any-damn-time. His wife is lucky."

"I'm pretty sure he's also lucky to have his wife."

"True, Natalia is hot as hell. If a woman marries an older man, it should be someone like Cristian. Rich, hot AF, and willing to murder your ex."

I nudge her with my elbow. "That dead ex is the groom's brother."

She flicks her hand through the air. "Oh, please. No one liked Vinny, including Antonio."

"Oh my God, I can't with you."

My gaze slips back to Damien.

He's still watching me.

I shut my eyes, my mistake haunting me.

I should've said yes a long time ago.

My stubbornness cost me love.

Cost me *everything*.

---

THE SUN SETS around the courtyard, adding to its beauty.

After the wedding, we retreated inside the ballroom to watch the first dance. Cristian and Gigi shared their father-daughter dance, and then Genesis and I went outside again. We need fresh air, and the many open bars throughout the castle-like building and courtyard are nice too. Cristian spared no expense on Gigi's wedding.

"We're in Mafia heaven," Genesis sings out. "Or if we're being technical, hell. No way is God granting any of them a ticket to heaven."

"I should've brought Darcy as my plus-one," I grumble, shaking my head.

"Darcy wouldn't have been as much fun." She wiggles her shoulders. "I'm the fun-time one of our group."

"Genesis, what a surprise to see you here," a man says, approaching us. He holds out his hand toward me. "Luca. I don't believe we've *formally* met."

Luca is hot as hell with dark hair and a seductive smile.

I also recognize him from the blog post I read forever ago when researching Damien.

"Luca is a Marchetti," Genesis explains, as if giving a report. "Marchettis are nothing but trouble. I wouldn't speak to him if I were you."

Luca smirks at her, and I can't believe she's speaking to *him* like that. "Oh, baby Genesis, do I need to shut your smart mouth by making you come on my fingers again?"

I pull back in disbelief. "Wait ... you and him?"

Genesis rolls her eyes. "I was, like, sixteen when I let him finger me with his inexperienced hand. I hope your trigger finger has improved since the last time you played with my clit."

Good thing I haven't taken a sip of the champagne yet.

I'd have spit it out.

"Genesis," I tease, "you little finger whore."

She doesn't look one bit embarrassed. "Getting fingered doesn't add to my body count, *and* I get off. Win-win for me."

*That is a good point.*

"How about I pull up that dress of yours and show you how much I've improved?" Luca asks, stepping closer. "We both know you *love* an audience."

"I'll pass." She smiles at him with no shame.

If someone was publicly talking about fingers in my vagina, my entire body would turn the blush pink Damien loves so much.

That's something I admire about Genesis.

She doesn't care what anyone thinks of her.

Genesis gestures to me. "This is Pippa. She's Amara's dance teacher and strictly off-limits."

"Wrong," a stern voice says from behind me.

I whip around to find Benny, Cristian's son, approaching us.

*All these men just sneak up out of nowhere.*

Do they learn that in Mafia school or something?

Benny's hand is clasped around his wife, Neomi's. While I've never met her, everyone knows who she is. She's also the woman who was accidentally shot in the crosshairs of Antonio's father calling a hit against Benny.

She's petite and around the same height as me, and like all the other Marchetti Mafia wives, she's stunning.

"Don't let Luca convince you he doesn't know who she is," Benny adds, joining our group. "The asshole just enjoys playing games with people."

I'm quiet for a moment, taking in Benny while also not wanting to appear rude for doing it in front of his wife. He's the younger version of Cristian. People claim he'll be as ruthless as his father when he takes over.

Luca points at me with his glass. "You're the dancer Damien is obsessed with and also his fiancée's cousin."

"You're such a jerk," Neomi says while Genesis mutters, "Asshole."

"What?" Luca throws out his arms and shrugs. "We watched the Lombardis for months"—his eyes dart straight to me—"*and you*. You're quite the dancer. Care to share a dance with me?"

"I don't think Antonio would appreciate me murdering someone at his wedding."

I nearly drop my glass at the sound of Damien's voice.

It terrifies me yet is my favorite tune.

It was once my comfort song, and now, it's my heartbreak one.

He squeezes between Genesis and me, glowering at Luca.

"I was afraid you'd ruin the fun," Luca says, unfazed. He knows Damien won't ruin the wedding. "Genesis, we're back to you, then."

"She's good," Julian says, joining us.

Luca places his hand over his heart. "The Bellini brothers wound me, taking all the gorgeous women here."

"How about you go dance with Isabella then?" Neomi comments.

Luca shakes his head. "Nah, I stay far away from you Cavallaro sisters. If your father even catches a whiff of me with Isabella, he'll immediately attempt to draft a marriage contract."

It's wild. Not too long ago, most of these men wanted to kill each other.

Insert Gigi, a woman, to tame them.

To end the war.

The power of a damn woman.

Damien snatches my glass, settles it on the table, and captures my hand. "Come on. You owe me a dance."

*Owe him?*

I hear Genesis mutter something along the lines of, "Bad idea," as Damien hauls me away.

"Are you nuts?" I ask while he pulls me into the building and through the crowd. "People will tell Cernach."

The orchestra plays a rendition of a song I recognize but can't put a name to. Right before we reach the dance floor, Damien cuts a right to the stone staircase. If it wasn't for him leading the way, I'd lose my balance from the lack of light. He doesn't stop until we're outside on a balcony overlooking the courtyard.

Releasing my hand, he spins me around to face the now-empty altar. "That could've been us," he says in what sounds like agony.

I tremble when he shoves the weight of his chest against my back and holds me in place.

His mouth lowers to my ear. "We could've had this a year ago. The ceremony. The vows. The fucking first dance. I had it in my calendar, remember?" A sneer joins his tone, an attempt to hide the pain in his voice. "The day I ask Pippa to marry me."

I shut my eyes, a tear falling down my cheek, remembering that morning.

How I'd declared I needed a year, and he made a show of scheduling it on his phone.

"You gave it up. Gave *us* up." He raises his hand to my neck, giving it a squeeze before stroking the skin. "You walked away out of stubbornness." He scoffs. "You think you didn't let Cernach win by leaving me? He didn't win just that fight with you, Pippa. He won the goddamn war."

More tears slip down my cheeks.

Heartbreak rises through my entire body as I gulp down sobs.

Regret pours through me like it's somehow joined my blood.

*I did this.*

*I ruined us.*

And now, there's no way to fix it.

I grip his arm on my chest. "I made a mistake, Damien."

"A mistake that can't be changed," he spits.

"I asked Cernach to change the contract and let us marry instead, but he said no."

"Why would he? You wronged him, and he'll make us pay for it."

Staring ahead, I take in the beauty of the lit-up courtyard and people celebrating this moment of love. I'll never have this with the man I love.

"Had you not destroyed us, there'd be a ring on your finger," he continues, his voice thick with emotion. "Our life might've been chaotic at times, but we'd be happy." He lifts his hand to my chin, holding it firmly. "Look at it. Look at what we could've had."

"I'm sorry," I say around swallows.

Around sobs.

Around goddamn agony.

My heart is shattering.

The person who put me together before can't anymore.

I blink through the tears.

"Imagine what we'd have," he says, as if wanting to continue to make me suffer. "You'd wear a pink gown to our wedding, your hair down in curls, and I wouldn't be able to take my eyes off you as you walked down the aisle. The woman I cherish more than anything in this messed-up world of mine would have my name, would be *mine* forever. But you took that away from me."

He's taking his pain out on me.

I don't blame him.

I caused it.

He always said he never wanted an arranged marriage.

Never wanted to marry a woman who didn't love him.

That's exactly what he has to do with Riona.

It's also what I'll have to do when Cernach marries me off.

He retreats a step when the music changes, and I rotate to face him.

The pain that was in his voice matches the hurt on his face.

That same pain scorches through me as we stare each other down.

"I'm sorry," I sob, unable to stop myself from walking straight into his arms and shoving my face into his chest.

My chest caves in when he pulls away from me.

I wait for him to leave me like I did him.

To make me suffer.

He backs up and spreads his arm along the railing.

I stare at him, my breathing heavy, as he drops one arm to hold out his hand.

"Can I have one last dance?"

He doesn't give me a second to answer before pulling me back into his arms. I relax against his hard chest, against the warmth of him, and the song changes.

I know I shouldn't be here with him like this.

He's engaged to my cousin, for Christ's sake.

But *one last dance.*

*This last one.*

He brushes his nose against mine and drags his hands down my spine, resting them on my lower back. We aren't as much dancing as I'm just allowing him to hold me.

"I got you out of your marriage contract with Cernach," he says, kissing my forehead.

"What?" When I attempt to draw back, he squeezes me tighter in his hold. "How?"

"That doesn't matter."

This time, it's not me trying to pull away.

It's him.

"What did you have to do for Cernach?" I cry out, my arms falling slack at my sides.

"It doesn't matter."

"Yes, it does. There's always a price with him."

"I told you before that I'll pay any price for you." He kisses my forehead again and walks away.

Leaving me alone on the balcony to feel the pain I caused us both.

Leaving me alone, staring at an altar, at what could've been our future.

***

THERE'S PRACTICALLY a syllabus for Riona's wedding events.

*Engagement announcement party.* I missed that one, thank God.

*Engagement party.* Where I currently am. FML.

*Bachelor and bachelorette parties.* No, freaking thank you. If Cernach forces me, I'm faking my death.

*Rehearsal dinner.*

*Wedding.*

My aunt Fedelma, Cernach's wife, is behind the packed schedule. That woman calls herself the Irish Martha Stewart. She likes to keep herself busy and away from her husband. Not that I can blame her.

Cernach insisted we attend tonight's dinner. I've yet to mention Damien saying he got me out of the marriage agreement. If I do, Cernach will know we've been in contact.

The invitation said the *social* starts at seven and dinner begins at eight.

We're here at 7:59. I'll blame it on too much traffic during our drive from New York to Boston.

"I'm really sorry," Lanie whispers as I hand The Ritz-Carlton valet my keys.

I offer her a timid smile. "It's okay, I promise."

Her shoulders slump.

I can't blame my naive sister for believing she could trust Cernach. She didn't hear the stories I did. She saw him open the studio and help our mom.

My mom lingers behind us. I hardly spoke to her on the drive here. I'd have preferred we rode separately, but she doesn't have a car.

Sometimes, I war with myself on whether to hate or pity her.

Then, I think about how I'd act in the same situation. If a man treated my daughters how Cernach treats us, I'd either kill him or run. I wouldn't care what it cost me. I'd put them above everything.

She had the guts to stick up for herself many years ago when it was her freedom on the line. Yet she won't do it for us. I'll never forgive her for that.

I hate that I search the ballroom for Damien as soon as we enter.

He's not here yet.

I accept a champagne glass from a server and pretend to listen while my mom introduces me to family members I don't care to meet. My attention stays on the entrance as I wait for him.

My breath stops when I see him.

He repeats the action I did, his gaze coasting across the room. I know this because his search stops when his eyes land on me.

It's been two weeks since I saw him at Gigi and Antonio's wedding.

Since he cruelly reminded me that our heartbreak is my fault.

His eyes are frozen on me, overflowing with hurt, and sadness rushes through me. Our eye contact is quickly broken when Cernach steps in front of me.

"Tardiness is disrespectful," he says, glaring at my mom, Lanie, and me. "I told you I wanted you here at seven."

"Traffic was bad." I shrug. "Sorry."

I took the longest route I could and went five under the speed limit.

"Lose the attitude, bitch," he snaps. "Your future husband is here, so I need you to behave." He snatches my elbow and starts nearly dragging me to a group of men across the ballroom.

My heart twists in my chest.

I feel Damien's eyes burning into me with each step I take.

"Sorry to interrupt, gentlemen," Cernach says, his tone much more civil than it was with me. "I thought it was time I introduced you to my beautiful niece Pippa."

*Oh, gag me.*

I scan the three men.

A tall man with a broad jawline and dark hair steps closer. "Hello, Pippa." His accent is thick Russian. "I'm Igor. Your uncle has told me great things about you, but I have to say, he minimized your beauty."

Cernach releases me, and I allow Igor to take my hand.

"Thank you," I say softly.

Igor's hand is smooth as it holds mine. He places a kiss to the top and holds my palm over his heart. Good thing my back is to Damien because I'm sure there's fire in his eyes. Igor isn't terrible-looking, and so far, he doesn't seem like a complete sociopath.

Like Cernach said, he could stick me with the grandfather, who currently has drool dripping from his bottom lip. That man should be in a nursing home, completing his will, not searching for a new wife.

Igor slips his hand up my arm, settling my elbow through his. "Let's have dinner, so I can get to know you better."

I continue avoiding eye contact with Damien as we make our way to the table. While plenty of Riona's friends and family are here, Damien doesn't have one person. No Antonio, Julian, or Emilio.

Just him.

I'm sure that'll piss Cernach off since I notice place cards with their names on them. They'd have come if Damien had asked, so he did it to spite Cernach. To show him he'll do the bare minimum in his marriage.

Igor's seated next to me, and Lanie sits to my other side. My mom is beside her. My back straightens when Riona and Damien take the chairs across from us.

One person I pity is Riona.

As she sits, she offers me a withdrawn smile.

While I haven't spoken with her, I know she's in for a hard marriage.

Her husband doesn't love her.

He wants someone else.

Cernach is stealing her chance of finding true love.

We start dinner with a toast to the newlyweds. As the first course is served, Cernach gloats over some business deal he recently closed. I tune him out. He could tell me he learned the secret as to why Edward from *Twilight* sparkled, and I still wouldn't pay attention.

I stare at Damien. He's hardly spoken a word to anyone.

Neither has Riona.

"Cernach tells me you're a dancer," Igor comments.

I skim my gaze to him and smile. "I am."

"What kind of dance?" He wipes the corners of his mouth with his napkin.

"Ballet. I teach now actually."

He stares at me with more interest. "Wow, what studio?"

"Mine. The Ballet Studio."

"Having your own studio? That's quite impressive."

My cheeks warm, and I hate it.

They're only supposed to do that for the engaged man across from me.

"Maybe someday, I can come watch you dance," Igor says, snapping my attention back to him.

"Yeah." I shyly nod a few times while hoping Damien doesn't lose his shit over that comment.

Igor seems nice so far, but nice guys don't mingle with Cernach. Damien and Antonio included. I do respect Igor refusing to marry Lanie because of her age. Most guys would've jumped at the chance to marry her.

While she's young, she's also gorgeous in an innocent way. She's a skinnier and taller version of me with lighter hair. Plenty of boys knocked on our door, growing up, asking her out, but she's too consumed with school and dancing than dating.

"Cernach said you're available tomorrow?" Igor continues.

"Maybe we can have lunch. They have the Boston Ballet here. I could get us tickets."

Damien slams his knife down on the table before picking it back up. He clenches his hold on the handle—so tight that his knuckles turn white.

"I appreciate the invite, but I drove my mom and sister here. I can't stay," I reply.

"Too late," Cernach says like he's been listening to the entire conversation. "I already arranged for Enya to drive your car home with Lanie. Igor will drive you home tomorrow after you spend the afternoon together."

"Oh, you live in New York?" I ask Igor.

He nods. "I have a home there, yes. I have one in all of my favorite cities—New York, Miami, Dubai, and London. New York is my favorite, though." A smile builds along his lips. "Although it might become more of my favorite if you're there."

I can't even look at Damien this time.

"Aw," my mom chimes in. "What a sweet thing to say." She snatches her wine glass. "Now, that's good husband material."

I nearly gag at the word *husband*.

She's the last person I want to determine whether someone is *husband material*.

"I actually asked Pippa to help me tomorrow," Damien says, knocking back the remainder of his drink. "She's helping me look for a house for Riona and me here in Boston."

This time, I'm the one snatching my knife, gripping it tight.

*House in Boston?*

I hold up my hand. "I think you made plans with a different Pippa. That isn't in my agenda." I smile smugly at him.

"I don't think there's another Pippa Charlotte Elsher around here," Damien says, fake looking around the room and cocking his head to the side. "You must've forgotten. We discussed it at Antonio Lombardi's wedding when we ran into each other."

Everyone's eyes are on us.

Cernach clasps his hands, the noise loud. "I'm sure my Riona wants to select her own house. She and Pippa don't know each other well enough for her to decide such a thing. Pippa, you'll spend the day with Igor. Riona and Damien will go house-hunting." His cold glare whips to Damien. "It'll give the future newlyweds time to get to know each other." He leans back in his chair, offering the table a self-satisfied smile. "*Both sets of newlyweds.*"

## 44

# DAMIEN

"I don't appreciate the games you're playing," Cernach spits, seated behind his desk. "Pippa isn't yours. Riona is. I expect you to keep your hands to yourself."

After dinner, he requested I come to his house and speak to him in his office about my behavior tonight. The imbecile played right into my hands.

"We made a deal." I flick open my Zippo. "You said you'd keep Pippa's name out of marriage contracts, yet you introduced her to a possible husband tonight and called them *newlyweds*. I don't appreciate the games *you're* playing."

He throws out his arms. "Have I married her off yet?"

"You paraded her around and called her a newlywed. Stop, or I'll slit the throat of every man you introduce her to."

"You don't want to cross me."

He waggles his finger toward me in warning. I want to rip it off his wrinkled hand and feed it through the paper shredder in the corner.

"No one is crossing you," I say with a bored sigh. "We made a verbal agreement. No husbands for Pippa. I want that in writing now that you can't be trusted."

"On the terms of you giving me a grandchild. I want my Riona pregnant."

I resist the urge to recoil at the thought of knocking Riona up. I'll come up with a plan to get out of that. Possibly hire a sperm donor.

"I agreed to that end of the deal."

"I'm very protective of my daughter. You remember that."

I raise a brow. "So protective that you're marrying her off to a man she hardly knows? A man you sold illegal weapons to, knowing his intention for them was to murder men?"

Cernach might care for his daughter, but he doesn't love her.

A loving father would never do that.

"I chose you as her husband because I love her," he fires back. "I witnessed how protective you were with Pippa. I expect Riona to receive the same treatment. She's a good girl. You can learn to like her. She'll be your wife and main priority."

I slip my hands into my pockets. "Is your wife your main priority?"

He slams his mouth shut, at a loss for words.

I snap my fingers, scoffing.

I might not be a married man yet, but a husband who loves his wife would never hesitate when asked that question.

"You think on that." I tap my knuckles against his desk. "You can answer it next time I see you."

I turn to leave, but he speaks to my back.

"Riona will hate Pippa if she lets you touch her," he states, full of himself. "Now, I'm not a fan of my niece, but I know she won't let a married man touch her. This is the one time I appreciate her having morals."

Not replying, I leave his office.

Odhrán, his underboss, stands in the doorway.

"Bathroom?" I ask.

He points toward the opposite end of the foyer.

"Thanks. Cernach asked me to tell you he'd like to speak with you."

It's a lie, but I don't want eyes on me.

Odhrán is no younger than sixty, and every time I see him, he's wearing a fedora over his bald head. A Celtic tattoo runs up his neck, matching the one on Cernach's hand.

Odhrán nods, and I pretend to walk in the direction he indicated.

As soon as he disappears inside Cernach's office, I turn in the opposite direction. It's time to see the woman I'm not supposed to touch.

## 45

# PIPPA

I GET the luxury of staying at Cernach's prison of a mansion tonight.

After the engagement dinner, my mom left *in my car* with Lanie, and I rode here with my aunt and grandmother. During the drive, my grandmother, who I've only met twice, asked me if I was going to lose weight when it was time for my wedding.

I can't wait to get the fuck out of Boston.

Cernach has stained it for me indefinitely.

I tried to tell them I'd stay in a hotel, but Cernach refused. Probably thought I'd make a run for it.

So, now, I'm here, a princess trapped in the dark castle, waiting for Prince Charming to save me. Only first, he needs to stop by Cernach's office and sign a contract.

I'm flipping through possible Netflix movies to watch when my phone vibrates with a text.

**Damien: Let me in.**

My pulse charges in my throat.

I flick my attention from the two-story window to the door.

*Let him in from where?*

Is he being metaphorical, like let him back into my life?

*Sinful Sacrifice*

Or literal, like open something?

I jump out of bed at the light knock on the door.

My head buzzes as I tiptoe toward the door and crack it open. As soon as it's ajar an inch, Damien forces it open and walks inside. I stare at him warily while he shuts the door with his heel and locks it.

"What are you doing?" I hiss. "Cernach has cameras all over this place."

I lost count of how many I noticed while walking upstairs.

Damien breezily walks toward the closet like no big deal and opens it.

"How did you even get up here?"

"Cernach invited me." He jerks clothing Cernach provided for me off the hangers and tosses them on the bed.

"Cernach invited you?" I repeat slowly.

Cool as a cucumber, he draws out a bottle of his signature cologne from his blazer pocket. I lose track of my train of thought when he starts spraying the clothing and bed.

And by spray, I mean, absolutely dousing them.

I cough as the scent inundates the room.

"What the hell are you doing?" I question around another cough.

I eye him in suspicion as he stalks toward me. He stares down at me, his eyes intense, and without saying a word, he moves his spray-a-thon to me.

He sprays my hair first, then my neck, and then down my body until hitting my bare feet.

While it's potent as hell, I breathe in the smell.

It reminds me of waking up next to him.

That smell accompanied every shared hug, kiss, lovemaking.

*It smells like home.*

"There," he says, smoothing his hand over my hair as if I'm a finished product. "That should do."

"That should do what?" I raise my shoulder and smell myself.

His dark eyes coast down my body, as if making certain he didn't miss a spot.

He doesn't speak until he's finished his inspection. "If you're around any other man in Boston, you'll smell like me." He smirks in satisfaction. "I'm a man who likes to mark his territory." He inches closer, lowers his head, and runs his lips along my jawline. "And you, Pippa, are my goddamn territory." Stepping back, he buttons his blazer. "I'll pick you up tomorrow to take you back to New York."

"I'm not riding home with you," I correct, crossing my arms as he eases around me. "Igor is taking me back."

"If I say I'm taking you home tomorrow, I'm taking you home." He knocks his knuckles against the door. "Lock this behind me. Have dreams of how good I eat your pussy. Good night, my sweet dancer."

WHILE I'LL PUBLICLY TAKE it to my grave I didn't say this, I slept pretty damn well last night.

Cernach might be a grade-A asshole, but he didn't skimp on providing comfortable sleeping arrangements for his visitors.

I woke up this morning in a cloud of Damien's scent. It was just as strong as when I'd gone to bed. I took a thirty-minute shower, but his scent still lingers on my skin and hair. Just like he wanted it.

He accomplished his goal of *marking his territory*.

When I walked into the foyer, every house employee I passed turned up their noses, sniffing the air.

The housekeeper knocked on my door early this morning and told me to report to the sunroom for breakfast.

While I expected a room full of people, Riona is alone at the table, eating. An entire breakfast spread is situated across the table. My stomach rumbles as I take in all my options.

Riona peers up at me and smiles. "Good morning, Pippa."

After dinner, she went out with her bridesmaids, so we didn't have a chance to talk. She'd invited me to go with them, but I politely declined. She continued to stay quiet during dinner, sat straight in her chair with the perfect posture, and anytime she did speak, it was spoken with elegant grace.

"Good morning," I say, moving into the room, uncertain how to start this conversation. It'd be nice to know how much she knows about my history with Damien—or even if she knows anything.

"I suppose now's a good time for us to chat." She takes a bite of her omelet and sets her fork to the side of her plate.

A breeze floats through the open double doors that show off a gorgeous flower garden. The sound of fountains flow through the air. Awkwardness follows me as I take the chair across from her.

"Pippa, you know how my father is," she says, jumping straight to the point. "Even if I told him I didn't want to marry Damien, it wouldn't matter."

"Did you tell him you didn't want to marry Damien?" I reach across the table, grab the orange juice carafe, and pour myself a glass.

"No, I didn't."

"Do you *want* to marry him?"

"Not necessarily." Sighing, she adjusts her dress strap. "I know you and Damien were involved before, though I'm unsure how serious. Men in my family don't love their wives, so I'm not expecting that from him. My father could've chosen a worse man." She offers me a soothing smile. "Igor is nice too. He'd make a decent husband."

My shoulders slump as I take a sip of orange juice. "Isn't that sad, though?" I ask over the rim. "That you don't expect your husband to love you?"

A brief silence passes as she peers down at the table, scraping her French-manicured nail over the cloth. "You know, when I heard stories of your mom and you growing up, I was jealous."

Unsure of how to reply, I wait for her to continue.

"You were able to escape this world," she says with sadness. "But now, I've learned none of us ever *escape* it. This world waits until it's ready for us and then sucks us in. Your shackles were loosened until they had a use for you."

She smooths out her napkin on her lap before bunching it in her hand and placing it on the table. "Can I ask you a favor?"

"What's that?" I ask as she stands.

"Please don't fuck my husband."

She doesn't say another word while leaving the room.

I'M STILL in the sunroom when Cernach storms inside. His footsteps are so heavy that the floor rattles. The man who follows him around, who I learned last night is Odhrán, is behind him.

"Igor can no longer take you out for the day," he snaps, his face red as he grips his phone tight. "*Someone* blew up his goddamn car last night. Be thankful he's not dead."

I try to hold it back, but there's no stopping my lips from curling into a smile.

"Don't gloating, you little bitch." He points his phone toward me. "We know exactly who did this." An evil smirk spreads across his grim face. "I know just the news that'll wipe that smile off your cunt face."

I don't ask him what the news is.

I only stare straight ahead.

The news won't be good.

I'd rather walk home on foot than hear whatever this *news* is.

The cords in his neck move. "You won't be smirking long when you learn Riona is pregnant with Damien's baby."

I recoil in the chair, a wave of dizziness hitting me.

My stomach churns, the threat of my pancakes coming back up strong.

"Oh, it seems Damien forgot to tell you about that *other* contract he signed." He snorts dismissively. "Not too confident anymore, are you, whore?"

I stare down at the knife on the table.

God, how good it'd feel to stab it into that neck of his.

Into his mouth so he'll shut the hell up.

His eyes narrow, and he stands there, unmoving, like a man who feeds from other's pain.

"Since your date is no longer able to take you out, you can call for a ride or walk for all I care," he says before charging out of the room.

I gag, vomit threatening to make its way up, and push my plate away.

It takes me a moment to catch my breath before I slam my napkin on the table and stand. "Fuck this."

Fleeing the room, I dash up the stairs. I collect my phone as soon as I'm in the guest room, rip off the clothes from the hangers, and throw them across the room. I'm not wearing anything this evil-ass family provides me.

"I need to get out of here," I say between panicked pants.

*"You won't be smirking long when you learn Riona is pregnant with Damien's baby."*

Nausea swirls in my stomach each time I repeat those words to myself.

She can't be pregnant yet.

Cernach would lose his shit if they consummated their marriage without saying their vows first.

*The other contract he signed.*

Just like he agreed to marry Riona, he's also agreed to knock her up.

My phone vibrates on the bed.

I snatch it to find a text on the screen.

> Damien: I heard you need a ride to NY. You can ride with me now. I'll be there in 45.

*Forty-five minutes.*

That's how much time I have to get out of here.

I'm not riding back to New York with him.

I wince while putting on my heels from last night. It'll be a bitch, walking in these, but it's an uncomfortableness I'll deal with. I hurriedly open the Uber app on my phone and book a ride.

Cernach isn't in sight as I rush out of the house. As I walk outside and down the drive, I feel guns and eyes on me. No one attempts to stop me, but I'm sure I look like a hot mess, doing the walk of shame.

It takes me ten minutes to reach the gate. A guard approaches me, giving my body a once-over in approval.

"Where are you going?" he asks in a thick Irish accent, hitching his gun over his shoulder. "Bad news for ya. The closest Starbucks is a forty-minute walk."

*Don't flip him off.*

*Don't give him attitude.*

I tuck my hands in front of me and sweeten my tone. "Can you give me a ride?" I practically stole my tone from Riona from breakfast.

"Fuck no," he automatically says, tugging on his hoop earring. "I take orders from Cernach, and last I checked, you're not him."

Another man approaches us. "You suck my dick, I'll take

you." He thrusts his hips forward and gives me a crooked-tooth smile.

I swat my hand through the air. "Just open the gate, please."

"Are you allowed to leave?" Hoop Earrings asks before pulling a radio from his pocket. "No one comes and goes without his permission." He hits a button on his radio and speaks into it. "Dark-haired woman, wearing a sexy pink dress, is asking to leave."

"She's good," a staticky voice says on the other end.

Hoop Earrings peers at me. "Have a nice walk. Your feet will hurt in those shoes."

As soon as I'm outside the gates, I sit on the ground. Hoop Earrings was right. No way am I walking miles in these heels. I'll have my driver pick me up here. I just couldn't stay inside Cernach's walls any longer.

My Uber driver, Fred, moved the air vent in his face when I slid into his car. He's hardly said a word since picking me up at Cernach's gates.

I am grateful he arrived in twenty minutes, giving me plenty of time to flee before Damien arrives at Cernach's.

Damien even going to Cernach's is risky. It's obvious he blew up Igor's car, and as a man who grew up in the mob, he knows how dangerous pissing off a mob boss is.

Cernach is a brutal leader.

I pluck my AirPods into my ears and select my favorite Halsey song. Shutting my eyes, I relax my head back and brainstorm on ways to elude all these crazy men in my life.

I need to get out of New York.

That much is clear.

My decision is made, and I start plotting in my head.

My body slams forward at the impact of Fred slamming on his brakes.

I remove an AirPod as Fred yells, "Whoa! Whoa!"

I scramble forward and look out the windshield. A black SUV is parked in the middle of the road with its driver's side door open, blocking all traffic.

My body freezes when the back door opens.

"You know you can't run from me," the masculine voice says.

## 46

# DAMIEN

A$\text{LTHOUGH IRRITATING}$, it's fun when Pippa disobeys me.

I get to punish her for it.

Most of the time, she gets the patient version of me, but she loses that when she doesn't listen. I told her I was driving her back to New York, so that meant I'm goddamn driving her back.

The Uber driver mutters something about calling the cops while I fix my stare on Pippa in the back seat.

*Did she think I wouldn't find her?*

Everything she owns is tracked by me.

If possible, I'd put a damn device in her skull.

"Let's go." I snap my fingers and jerk my chin toward my Mercedes in the road.

She stubbornly crosses her arms. "I'm not going anywhere with you."

I stick my head inside the car. "Shall I kill your driver, then?"

"What?!" Fred yelps, a tremble in his tone.

Since I hacked into her phone, I knew who Fred was and his background information before she even got into his car. I also disabled his phone and car camera without him knowing it.

My parents might have invested in expensive schooling for

me, but they made sure I was skilled at hacking into shit. That's priceless.

Pippa is precious cargo, and I won't allow anyone else to drive her. I also want to spend time with her. What better way than when she's trapped in a vehicle with me?

Pippa leans in closer. "You really need to stop threatening violence to get what you want."

"Why?" I raise a brow. "It gets me what I want. Now, get your ass out of this car."

"Sorry, Fred." She shoots him an apologetic look, but that look turns ice cold when it shifts to me. "I'm only doing this so you don't kill an innocent man."

I place my hand on my chest. "Me? Never."

I step back a few steps, allowing her space to exit the car, and she snubs my attempt to help her out.

As soon as she's out of the car, Fred hits the gas, makes a U-turn, and speeds off.

Pippa stands in the road, scanning her surroundings. My sweet dancer knows she's at my mercy. If she tries to make a run for it, she has nowhere to go. The closest town is a forty-minute walk, and this road has little traffic.

Since she still loves to test me, I make sure she doesn't try by grabbing hold of her ponytail on my way back to the Mercedes. She winces, slapping at my arm while I pull her toward the SUV, as if having her on a leash.

"I told you I'm taking you back to New York," I say, not releasing her until we're at the passenger door, and I shove her inside. "And that's what I'm doing."

"I hate you," she snaps while I shut the door in her face. Her glare follows me through the windshield as I circle the front of the car.

"Now, what the fuck's your problem?" I ask after sliding behind the wheel and driving off.

"Why'd you bomb Igor's car?"

"I didn't bomb anyone's car."

She sucks in an irritated breath. "You're impossible."

"Don't act like you give two fucks about Igor."

"Maybe I do." She unclasps her heels and tosses them on the floorboard.

I cast her a glance. "I'll bomb his house with him in it next time, then."

"I was looking forward to spending the day with him, and then you had to ruin it."

"You were looking forward to spending the day with him?" I repeat, the words slowly falling from my mouth, as if wanting her to comprehend the bullshit she just said.

She juts her chin out. "Yes, he seemed like a nice guy."

"He isn't a nice guy."

"And *you* are?"

"Fuck no, but that doesn't mean you're not mine." I flash her a smile. "Fortunately for me, my sweet dancer, you enjoy how crazed I am for you. You accepted my insanity, so that makes you mine."

She curls her upper lip. "Do you expect me to still be yours when you get my cousin pregnant?"

Gritting my teeth, I tighten my knuckles around the steering wheel.

So, that's what brought out this attitude.

Someone—a fucker named Cernach, I assume—disclosed my other contract.

"That's how you're getting me out of Cernach marrying me off, isn't it? Having a baby with Riona?" She grimaces. "So much for you not touching her."

I rub my nose. "I did it for you."

"You're going to fuck my cousin for me?" She claps before making a *bravo* motion. "That's definitely what's best for me."

"Don't press me on the issue."

Lowering my speed, I attempt to relax my rampant heart.

Pippa doesn't help with that problem when she flings open the door. I slam on the brakes and swerve over to the side of the road as she jumps from the SUV.

*Is she fucking nuts?*

As I shift into park, she scrambles away, barefoot, from the road toward the middle of fucking nowhere, surrounded by trees. She peers over her shoulder, watching me follow, and doesn't increase her speed.

This woman loves to fuck with my goddamn head.

We walk deeper into the wooded area, the SUV or road no longer in view.

My dancer isn't doing this to escape me.

She doesn't want to be rescued.

She's doing this to push my buttons.

To make me feel the pain she's feeling.

If only she knew I'm feeling it tenfold.

I lengthen my strides, easily catching up to her, and snatch her ponytail again.

"God, I hate you—"

She gasps, not finishing her sentence, when I swing her around and slam her back against a tree. I've spent the past twenty-four hours watching another man flirt with her, dealing with Cernach, and being in Boston. This isn't the time or place for her to test me.

I'm about to show her that.

Her chest heaves in and out as she glowers at me.

I wait until she stops glaring.

Until her eyes soften.

Until she can give me a goddamn minute.

She loses a breath when I place my hand on her heart, feeling her heart beat as wildly as mine.

Biting into my lower lip, I lower one hand to bunch up her dress. When she tries to stop me, I press my palm tighter into her chest, pinning her against the tree.

My sweet dancer needs to learn something.

I might be obsessed with her, but that doesn't mean I relinquish my power. I'm a man who thrives under control. I might give her a minute to run her sweet mouth, but I'll be sure to fuck it until it's sore after. No smart mouth goes unpunished.

I hurriedly unbuckle my belt.

She doesn't attempt to fight me as I lower my pants and free my cock. It's hard and throbbing and in need of her tight pussy.

"Maybe I should put a baby in you first," I snarl, stroking myself. "That way, you'll be stuck with me forever."

My cock jerks just at the thought of Pippa pregnant with my baby.

*Fuck. I'm going to come before taking a dip in her pussy.*

"Maybe I should ask Igor to put a baby inside me," she fires back. "He might fuck better than you do."

My blood boils. That fucking mouth of hers.

My veins jump beneath my skin.

Keeping one hand on her chest, I furiously undo my tie, force her mouth open, and shove my tie inside it. "I'll take that out when you stop spewing out bullshit lies or when I'm ready to stick my big dick inside." To further show she pushed my buttons too far, I use my finger to ram it deeper inside her mouth.

She doesn't attempt to fight me as I push my entire hand inside her panties. I cup her pussy, roughly rubbing my palm against her clit. She's soaked for me, nearly dripping down my fingers.

Her chin trembles as I wrap her thigh around my waist, rip her panties, and thrust my cock inside her.

"You are mine," I grunt, thrusting harder with each word.

Her skull smacks against the tree, but I don't slow my strokes.

"Don't you ever talk about another man putting a baby inside you." I plunge my cock inside her wet pussy, keeping my hand on her chest before raising it to wrap around her throat.

There's an urge to feel the pulse.

To see if her heart is as wild as mine.

I grin in satisfaction when it is.

"You talk about another man inside you again," I say, the words breathed out between our heavy pants, "I'll make you watch me rip his goddamn heart out and then fuck you next to his bleeding body."

Hurriedly pulling out of her, I twist her body around and push her toward the tree. She catches herself with her hands. Circling my hands around her waist, I push her ass in the air, smack it hard, and shove my cock inside her from behind.

"Do I make myself clear?" I ask through clenched teeth.

She spits out the tie and peers at me over her shoulder. "Fuck me harder, and I'll let you know."

I smack her ass so hard that I swear it vibrates off the trees. "Be careful, or I'll shove his heart down your fucking throat, where my tie just was." Another smack to her ass.

Her head hits the tree, and I grab her ponytail again to pull her back against my chest. Her head falls against the crook of my shoulder, and I use my free hand to wrap around her throat, holding her in place.

I fuck her like we're wild animals here.

Fuck her so good so she knows she'll never belong to anyone else.

"Do you think I'd ever want to fuck anyone other than you, baby?" More thrusts, more moans, another neck squeeze so tight that I nearly have her in a choke hold as we fuck. "We've been broken up for how long? Yet you're still the only woman I've touched." I reach around to play with her clit. "You call me when you need my dick, and I come running *every single time*. And I'll always come running because I'm goddamn yours."

She falls forward onto the ground, and I do the same.

We're on the ground, and I'm fucking her from behind.

We've never fucked so dirty.

So un-prim and proper.

So wild before.

When she comes, it lights every nerve ending inside me on fire.

It takes me only a few strokes to do the same. I jerk her ponytail back and kiss her throat as I groan into her neck. I keep pumping my hips, shoving my cum deep inside her.

If she wants to talk about having babies, I'll make sure it's my cum that fills her.

As we come down from our high, I help her to her feet and swipe what dirt I can from her dress. She looks like a hot mess—barefoot, dirty, and wild, freshly fucked hair.

I straighten my clothes, and she acts somewhat sane on our walk back to the SUV.

"I'm still pissed at you," she says as I start driving again.

"Your pussy isn't pissed at me." I smirk. "And I'm not having a baby with Riona."

"What will you do, then? Have a stork deliver Cernach a grandchild?"

"I'll figure it out."

"Riona won't have sex with another man, if that's what you're thinking. She knows what even a rumor of adultery would do to her reputation."

"I gave you an orgasm. That means we don't mutter the word *Cernach* or *Riona* for the rest of the ride."

"Fine. I get to control the music."

"Have at it."

She grabs the cord and plugs her phone to sync it.

We listen to her *music* for a good thirty minutes before she puts on an audiobook with decent fucking scenes. I mentally take notes on one scene, knowing I'll be fucking her like that later.

It's dark when we make it back to New York.

She's yawning as I pull up to her apartment building.

"Thanks for the last fuck." She steps out of the SUV and rushes across the sidewalk.

If she thinks I'm letting her off the hook for her comment, my tree fucking must've given her a concussion.

I jump out of the car, grab the back of her neck, and haul her into my chest. "You must mean last fuck of the day, but you'll never be my last fuck, sweet dancer. You're my best and only fuck for the rest of my life."

"IF YOU'RE PLOTTING against Cernach, I need to be in the know," Antonio says, his voice low.

We're in the casino bar. Sometimes, we have a drink here to make sure things are running smoothly. It's good for employees to know we're involved. It's also good for the patrons to know we keep an eye on things.

We're in a separate area of the bar, away from people, and we have plenty of privacy, where others won't overhear our conversation.

I raise my pinkie and signal for a refill to the bartender. "Would I ever plot anything without your support?"

"Past Damien wouldn't, but this shit with Pippa is messing with your head." He downs the remainder of his drink and taps his head with the empty glass.

I nod in appreciation when the bartender delivers another round and lean back in my stool. "So, you'd be okay if Gigi was set to marry another man?"

"Gigi was set to marry another man." He scoops the new glass in his hand. "You know what I did."

"Ah, I forgot about that game you played with Elijah."

"It wasn't a game. Gigi needed to know that a woman should never marry a man who wouldn't die for her." He puts the glass to his lips and smirks against it. "In fact, I think every bride should have their partner pass that test before marrying them."

When our families were at war, Gigi agreed to find a husband to gain better connections for the Marchettis. Antonio found out, lost his shit, and shoved her fiancé, Elijah, in his trunk. After taking them to a cabin in the middle of nowhere, he shoved a gun to her head and another to Elijah's. He told Elijah he had the choice to either save himself or Gigi.

Elijah chose himself. Antonio shot him in the head.

"War with Cernach would be quite a headache, given his weapons connections, but as your friend, if Pippa is that important to you, I'll do it. You've lost a lot for my family, risked your life, and always protected us with no questions asked. You treat my daughter as if she were your own and protected Gigi, though you were never her biggest fan—"

"The girl never stops running her mouth and watches the worst movies," I input.

He laughs. "What I'm saying is that you deserve the same loyalty from me. If we do this, Pippa needs to understand she can't play games. Her life will be on the line just as much as ours, and she can't turn her back on us."

"We can't go to war with Cernach." I chug my whiskey in one gulp. "I need to go. Riona is in New York. We have a dinner date."

---

I MEET RIONA IN A HIGH-END, overpriced diner where Cernach arranged. This isn't our first meetup. None of them have been fun or eventful. It's always boring small talk.

The server delivers a chocolate milkshake for her and water for me. She thanks the server and removes the wrapper from the straw.

"I know you're in love with my cousin," she says, sliding the straw inside the shake. "I asked her not to fuck you after we marry."

With each meetup, I'm at least getting to know a different side of Riona. It's wild how much character comes out of women when they're allowed to speak freely and have personalities.

Riona fits the innocent wife-in-waiting role. She's polite, gorgeous, and well put together. Her Irish traits are much stronger than Pippa's, but Pippa also isn't full Irish. Paul was half-Italian, which is where Pippa inherited her darker hair from.

I scratch the back of my neck, not bothering to comment on what she said.

"When was the last time you touched her?" she pushes.

I snatch her wrapper and ball it up. "Don't ask for answers you won't like."

"But I want to know whether I'll like it or not."

"I don't kiss and tell."

"Do you fuck and tell?" She pulls her straw from the cup and licks the shake from the side.

I lean back and stretch my arm along the back of the booth, studying her. "Speaking of fucking, has anyone touched your pussy before? Have you saved yourself for me?"

She looks away from me and focuses on her shake.

"Don't worry. I'm not one of those weirdos who insists on having virgin wives. In fact, I hope to God you're not one."

"I'm a virgin," she whispers.

"Are you sure about that?" I'm great at reading people and knowing when they're lying to my face. "Secrets don't stay secrets long, Riona. They always come to light."

"Then, you'd better make sure yours don't come out either." She raises her head to lock eyes with me. "You'll be my husband, and we'll have a baby. Otherwise, your precious Pippa will fuck another man chosen by my father."

## 47

# PIPPA

*I should've done this a long time ago.*

I'm running.

Call me a coward. I don't care.

For the past two days, I've done nothing but make lists.

Pros and cons.

For my love life.

For my career.

For my family.

I finally decided to do what was best for me after finding out Igor's last name and googling him. Igor isn't only a wealthy friend of Cernach's. He's a Russian crime lord and the son of an oligarch.

I already got myself wrapped up in the Irish mob and the Mafia. I'm not about to throw in an entirely different organization. I'd be a damn mob slut at that point.

My nerves rattle through my body as I dump all my electronics on my bed before double-checking I haven't missed anything. I can't have one item Damien can trace me with. I throw on a jacket and walk to the studio. Damien most likely has eyes on me, so I unlock the front door, as if everything is normal.

I snatch the duffel bag in the back room. Spare clothes and cash are shoved inside. A blue BMW is parked in the back alley with its headlights off.

Pulling a hoodie over my head, I duck into the BMW.

"Hi, Pippa," Levi says.

Levi is the father of one of my dancer students, who's asked me out on several occasions. Multiple times, he's offered to use the company jet to take me on vacation. I've always declined the invites, but when he brought in his daughter for class two days ago, an idea hit me.

Levi was my ticket out of New York.

If I book a flight, Damien will know.

If I drive somewhere, Damien will know.

Cernach most likely as well.

Sure, Damien could hunt me down sooner or later, but hopefully, he'll give up. He'll marry Riona, and they'll have a baby and live their lives.

Levi drives to a private airplane lot and parks. I throw my duffel bag over my shoulder, and he helps me out of the car.

"This is your plane?" I ask as he leads me toward a jet.

"My company's," he replies, rubbing underneath his nose and picking up his pace. "I can use it whenever."

The sky is growing dark as we enter the jet. The fact that I've never flown shows how sheltered I've been. Levi is close behind me, and I swear I feel a slight touch of his hand on my waist.

I brush it off.

*He's probably making sure I don't fall down the steps, right?*

I stop in the aisle and take in the plane in awe.

*So, this is how the other half lives.*

*Hmm. Not too bad.*

According to Google, Igor jet sets around in one of these on the regular.

The door shuts, and I turn around to find Levi plopping down on the sofa.

"I knew you were in a rush to get out of town, so the pilot is already in the pit and ready to go." He smiles. "I figured I'd tag along to keep you company. Maybe we can spend a few days together before I fly back."

My stomach clenches, and I nod, trying not to show my disappointment.

I was so wrapped up in getting my escape plan together that I didn't think of what I'd do with Levi. My dumbass thought he'd just lend his jet to a poor girl in need. No questions or favors asked.

"Oh, good," I say with a smile, knowing damn well after this flight, I'll never see him again.

A bit of shame creeps through me, like I'm using him.

But it's not like I held a gun to his head and forced him to do this.

Since Damien covered my rent for a year, I have a healthy savings. I decided to put that money to good use and book a long-term rental in Hawaii. While I'd have preferred somewhere out of the country, I didn't have time to wait for a passport.

I refuse to attend another Riona-Damien wedding event.

Refuse to hear their names and baby in the same sentence.

I don't want to be under any of their thumbs any longer.

To stay under the radar, I booked everything with Lanie's computer and a prepaid card. No matter how many anti-hacking software I install on my devices, Damien always breaks through them.

Levi collapses on the sofa and taps the spot next to him. I sit on the opposite edge, as far from him as possible.

From what I've learned about Levi, he's a divorcée who works for some big-shot investment firm. While I haven't asked his age, my age-dar is giving off mid-fifties range.

"Why are you sitting so far over there?" he asks, scooting closer.

"I just like my space." Another forced smile.

"Would you like me to make you something to drink?" He points toward the bar.

"Water is fine."

"Oh, water is no fun." He runs two fingers over his mustache. "Come on. Have a drink with me, Pippa. We have a long flight to Hawaii."

I clasp my hands in my lap. "Water is fine. I'm not a big drinker."

Disappointment floods his face, and he whips around to make a mixed drink for himself. With a grunt of disapproval, he hands me a bottle of water.

All the kindness he had in the car during our small talk has dissolved.

Levi openly stares at me while returning with his drink. I clutch my bag to my chest when he plops down so close that he's nearly sitting on my lap. When I start to stand, he slaps his hand on my thigh.

"I helped you out. Now, you help me," he says, his voice a sad attempt to sound sensual.

*Leave it to me.*

*Always choosing the worst men to do literally anything with.*

"Levi," I grit out, slapping his hand away from me. "Go back to your side of the couch."

He rubs himself between his legs before attempting to grab my wrist.

I try to wrangle out of his hold while unzipping my bag with my free hand. I might've left my phone, but I brought other necessities. One of them being pepper spray. Damien told me to never leave my apartment without it.

My body tightens when I hear a gunshot and then a short, sudden crack. Levi grunts and collapses face down against my shoulder. Blood splatters from his face onto me and pours from his head.

I scream at the top of my lungs, attempting to push Levi's dead body off me, when the shooter comes into view.

*You've got to be kidding me.*

"What the hell?" I scream. "What are you doing here?"

Damien smirks, standing tall, and slips his gun inside his waistband. "Oh, you didn't know I got my pilot's license?"

## 48

# DAMIEN

*You can run, but you can't hide.*

If the day comes that I marry Pippa, that'll be in my vows.

I'd track her to the edge of the earth if I had to.

To damn Mars.

She'll never escape me.

My sweet dancer underestimated me, assuming I only tracked her through vehicles and electronics. I have access to her studio cameras and overheard her conversation with that degenerate Levi the other day. I hacked into his phone and read through his texts, listened in on his calls, and knew he wasn't flying Pippa to Hawaii as a gentleman.

My sweet dancer should've known that.

Now, she's covered in some asshole's blood, looking at me like *I'm* the one who lost their mind.

Before anyone arrived at the airport, I made myself comfortable in the cockpit. As soon as the pilot stepped inside, I held a gun to his head.

I could either kill Levi on the ground or in the air. It would've been boring, going to his house and putting a bullet through his brain. Shooting him in front of Pippa also taught her a lesson.

Plus, I can add *killing an asshole on a private jet* to my list.

Not that anyone will know it's me. I already set up the perfect reason for Levi's death. I learned he was stealing from clients and poaching from his partners. He was about to lose everyone, and not able to take it, he booked a trip on the jet—which his partners had told him not to—and shot himself in the head.

How tragic. The poor guy hadn't sought out help first.

I pull Levi's leg, tugging him away from Pippa, and watch him slump to the floor, a blood trail following. I've killed enough men to set up a suicide scene. As soon as the jet lands, Julian and Emilio will make sure it's right, and the pilot will be briefed on the statement he'll give the police.

I doubt his partners or ex-wife will care about his death. His daughter is better off without him anyway.

Pippa jumps off the sofa, careful not to hit Levi's body, and scrambles as far away from him as she can. "What did you do, install a tracking device in my veins?"

I pop my neck. "Trust me, if I could, I most definitely would." I slide my hands into my pants pockets. "When will you learn that I know everything you do?"

"I told you to stop that."

"I told you I never would."

"What about the pilot?"

"I didn't kill him."

"He knows I came on this plane with Levi."

"He doesn't give two fucks about Levi's life."

"You can't just kill people who get in your way, Damien."

I jerk my chin toward Levi's body. "I can't?" Smirking, I crowd closer to her, leaning in, and she falls back before collapsing in a seat. "I will kill anyone who gets in the way of your safety, my ownership of you, or really, who just pisses me off." I kneel at her feet and rest my hands on her knees. "It's a waste of your breath to preach it's wrong to kill those deserving of death. It will never change my mind or convince me to be a better man."

Violence is in my DNA.

It's who I am.

So is protecting what and who I love.

"What happens when there comes a time I cross or piss you off? Will you hurt me then?" She gestures toward Levi's corpse, where his blood is beginning to stain the flooring. "Will you hurt me like that?"

Anger is in her voice, not fear.

Deep down, Pippa knows I'd never hurt her.

"Baby, you've pissed me off aplenty." I nudge myself between her legs and collect her soft face in my palm. "Even if I tried forcing myself, I physically can never hurt you. My body won't allow me to hurt someone who's embedded themselves inside me. You're inside my heart, and if I hurt you, it'd destroy me at the same time."

I have limits in my violence.

I kill men who deserve it.

Never children. Never women.

She shudders, her body craving me, but she fights against it.

I brush my thumb over her cheek. "We're going back to New York. You try to run from me again, I'll chain you to my bed and lock you in my bedroom." I pluck her bottom lip with my thumb. "Do I make myself clear?"

She glares at me. "Why don't you focus less on me and more on your wedding?"

"I'll focus on my wedding the day I marry you."

49

# PIPPA

**Two Weeks Later**

My emotions have been a wild mess the past few weeks.

Well, months, honestly.

Some days, I mourn my relationship with Damien.

Others, I'm so angry.

At him. At my family. At myself for ruining our future.

He's marrying Riona, and then what am I supposed to do? Stay single forever? He wants to kill any man interested in me. Yes, Levi was a scumbag, but he didn't deserve to die. Maybe a good ass-kicking or castration.

After the jet incident, Damien drove me home, lecturing me like I was a teenager caught sneaking out. I told him he wasn't staying the night, so he sat outside my building all night. He also has eyes on me all the time now. Unless I become a ghost, I'm stuck in New York forever.

"Why are you going to this wedding again?" Genesis asks while making herself comfortable on the hotel bed. "You know what'd be super cute? If when they ask if anyone objects to the marriage, you stand up and recite a love speech for Damien." She slips a gummy worm in her mouth.

I sit on the edge of the bed and slip on my heels. "My uncle would shoot me. So, no, not super cute."

Darcy scoffs. "Damien would murder his ass."

Genesis nods repeatedly. "If someone so much as pinched you wrong, they'd get Damien's wrath."

"Ugh." I throw my head back. "Let's not talk about the groom."

"I'm so pissed at him for following through with this marriage," Genesis adds.

I stand and inspect my reflection in the mirror. "He didn't have a choice."

My dress is the blush pink that drives Damien crazy. If I'm going to attend my ex's rehearsal dinner and wedding, might as well look hot.

Darcy and Genesis came to Boston with me, and we booked a suite in the nicest hotel. While they aren't invited to the wedding—Damien chose not to provide a guest list for himself —they're here for moral support.

I've come—okay, I'm *trying*—to come to terms with everything.

Damien didn't fall in love with Riona and propose.

He doesn't love her. That at least makes me feel better.

A few days ago, Cernach came to the dance studio to make it clear I would attend the rehearsal dinner and wedding. Why the rehearsal dinner is beyond me since I'm not involved in the wedding.

All I need to rehearse for the nuptials from hell is not getting too drunk on champagne, where I say something stupid.

Cernach invited Igor to the dinner and wedding, which most likely prompted my invite.

At least I'll see it with my own eyes.

Watching Damien exchange vows with my cousin will be the

reality check I need. It'll be the kick in the ass that any hope for us is gone.

A reality bitch slap, if you will.

While I've let an engaged Damien touch me aplenty, that'll stop when he's married.

When he's made a commitment to Riona.

Our dark love story will come to its ultimate end.

---

LANIE and my mother meet me at The Ritz for the rehearsal dinner.

Confusion rattles through me on why they were invited. Neither is involved in the wedding either.

My mother claimed it was Cernach wanting *all* his family there. It's like someone unscrewed her head and implanted a new brain inside it. My father really did a number on her for her to run back to the family that'd done nothing but shit on her.

Fewer people are here than at the engagement dinner. As we walk into the room, Lanie stays at my side like a security blanket. She still fears Cernach will marry her off. Before I marry anyone, I'm demanding a clause in the contract where he can't do that."

Though I'm unsure if it'll happen.

We don't get much say in business decisions.

A long table is set up at the front of the room with circular tables surrounding it. I stand to the side, running my hands down my arms, and gulp when my gaze lands on Damien and Riona.

They're talking with a group of people. Like with my mother's change of character, it seems to have also rubbed off on them. Damien isn't acting distant toward Riona. His arm is wrapped around her waist, and she's leaning into him. While they don't look madly in love, they don't resemble an unhappy couple.

*What the actual fuck?*

He doesn't look miserable.

They look comfortable, as if this isn't the first time they've touched.

Fire sets through my veins.

My grandmother, Laosie, joins them, wrapping Riona in a tight hug. A twinge of jealousy hits me. I never had grandparents who cared. But from the stories my mother told me, she isn't a caring grandmother. She turned her back on my mother as fast as the others did.

God, what is this, *feel sorry for myself* day?

I knew this would happen and thought I was prepared.

Cernach approaches the happy couple's group. I cross my arms and glare at them. If there was one superpower I'd choose at the moment, it'd be to light people on fire with my eyes.

Or to be able to Stephen King's *Carrie* them.

Yeah, that'd be better.

Cernach announces everyone should take their seats and prepare for a wonderful dinner. Like last time, there's assigned seating. Unlike last time, I'm not across from the soon-to-be-married couple.

They're seated at the front table, joined by Cernach and my aunt, along with the wedding party. Damien's side looks empty with it just being him.

Cernach stands and raises his glass. "I'd like to make a toast to the happy couple."

I can't stop myself from rolling my eyes and already gulping down my champagne. Just as a server passes, I stand and swipe a glass off their tray.

I won't toast to them.

I'll toast to getting wasted and forgetting this night though.

"To Riona and Damien," Cernach says, his voice loud and gruff.

I raise my glass, and the words are barely audible as they leave my mouth.

Okay, I don't say, *To Riona and Damien.*

I say, "To Cernach going to hell."

And it's as if the gods like me for once because after everyone gulps down, Cernach loses his balance and staggers backward. The chair behind him crashes to its side, and Cernach falls.

"Cernach!" Aunt Fedelma screams, rising from her chair.

Gasps and chatter flow through the room.

Riona and Damien jump up from their chairs. Damien, as if a concerned son-in-law, helps Cernach to his feet. But without Damien's help, Cernach slumps forward. The room turns into an uproar. Some race over to Cernach as he starts to seize while others, like me, are frozen in place, staring at each other, wide-eyed.

I sit back and sip my champagne, enjoying the show, as Cernach starts frothing at the mouth. He gasps for air, attempting to yell someone's name, but can't get the words out.

My mom starts crying next to me, but I only smirk in pleasure.

I might not have been able to *Carrie* him, but it appears someone did *something*.

*Please, let this be the end of him.*

## 50

# DAMIEN

**Three Weeks Ago**

The back booth of the old pub smells like feet and stale air.

Yesterday, I got a call from Riona, asking me to meet her. She also requested I come alone and not tell Cernach.

Poor thing didn't know I loathe speaking to her father. The less information I can give the bastard, the better.

The smell of a light perfume mixes with the air, and a figure wearing a dark-hooded poncho slides across from me. Riona lowers the hood and stares at me, wide-eyed.

I interlace my fingers, rest my hands on the table, and wait for her to start. I'm not one to begin meetings if I didn't call for them.

"Do you want to kill my father, Damien?"

I love when people get straight to the point.

I also love when they shock the shit out of me.

She looks me dead in the eye, completely poker-faced.

"Who's that?" I jerk my chin toward a man at the bar.

He's turned, his body facing the wall but angled enough to keep an eye on us. Riona entered with him, but they separated near the entrance. One thing she needs to learn is that I see everything.

Sometimes, I call it out. Sometimes, I don't.

She remains stone-faced. "My cousin Kian."

"Why is Kian here?"

"He's my ride."

"You could've called an Uber."

"He's also here to have my back."

"I don't like liars, Riona."

She blows out an upward breath. "He's my cousin and my ride, and he wants to make a deal with you as much as I do."

"What kind of *deal* are you trying to make?" I grab the watered-down Jack and Coke that I've yet to take a sip of.

"We have a few things in common, Damien." She clears her throat and straightens her poncho. "You don't want to marry me, and I don't want to marry you."

I nod, silently waiting for her to go on.

"You want my father to die, and I also want him to die."

I tap my fingers on the table.

She releases a long exhale. "My father killed the man I love. He brutally murdered him because he wasn't acceptable as a husband and didn't bring him an incentive. He killed him and then contracted me to marry you. For that, I need him to suffer."

"Sorry, but I don't do work with people I'm worried can't finish the job." I start to get up, but she catches my arm to stop me.

"Oh, I'll finish the job, and when we're finished, I'll figure out a way to get you out of marrying me."

"You don't think that'll look suspicious?"

"Not if we do it right."

"Start talking."

"I have three strategies." She pulls a notebook from her bag and opens it.

I slam my hand on it. "First things first. You don't *note* your plans to kill someone."

She jerks the notepad out from under my hold. "I didn't *note* my plans to kill anyone." She rolls her eyes. "In here is a suspense novel I'm writing."

I tug the notepad away from her hold, slide it to myself, and open the flashlight on my phone to read it better. She has plans written in fictional format with a character named Billy dying in different ways.

"I'll obviously throw that away once we agree on the cause of death," she inputs.

My eyes shift to her cousin. "Does he know of your plan?"

"He's helping us."

I huff out. "I've seen him with your father. He can't be trusted."

"We're the two people you can trust. Nobody hates my father more than we do."

"Text Kian and tell him to come over here."

She roughly pulls her phone from her bag, unlocks it, and types. I keep my eyes on Kian as he quickly pulls his from his pocket, checks the text, and then shoves it back in while standing.

Riona scoots over in the booth as Kian sits next to her.

I down my drink. "So, Riona wants Cernach to die because he killed her lover. What's your story?"

Kian is a redheaded, pale-skinned man, and my guess is, he's around the same age as Pippa. I'm also assuming he's Pippa's cousin as well. Like I told Riona, I've seen him around Cernach a few times, but he's never stood out or said anything.

He relaxes in the booth and waves his hand in the air, stopping the server. He orders a round for him and Riona, and I decline another drink.

After the server delivers their drinks, they make themselves comfortable and provide me a tell-all of how much their generation really hates Cernach's guts. They give me a rundown that could be an entire Netflix series of all the fucked-up shit he's done.

Odhrán is Kian's father, who beat his mother, Sheila—Cernach's youngest sister—until she could no longer handle it anymore and committed suicide. Sheila had begged Cernach to let her divorce Odhrán, but Cernach refused since he was his underboss.

As each word of his story leaves Kian's mouth with disdain, his face gets redder and his tone sharper. He wipes his hand across his jaw and continues with more reasons, driving the point home that he's goddamn serious. He's ready for Cernach *and* his father to die.

His best friend was Riona's lover, who his father and Cernach murdered. They made Riona sit back and watch as they beat him to a bloody pulp and then cut off his head. Cernach did a good job of hiding what he'd done because he knew if anyone found out Riona had been with another man, no one would marry her. By the time he finishes that story, I understand why they want Cernach to suffer.

Kian raises his glass in a cheers gesture. "What do you say, Damien? Do you hate Cernach enough to help us kill him?"

Even though I've been game to kill Cernach for as long as I can remember, I allow a few seconds to pass before answering them.

"We'll come up with a plan," I say. "When the time comes, I'll decide if it's strong enough that we can get away with it. If we make even one mistake, we die. And no offense, but I'll let you go down with the ship."

Kian rubs his forehead.

I see Riona visibly gulp.

I know I won't fuck up.

If anything happens, it'll be from their carelessness.

"If we do this, we do it smart." I rip a page from Riona's

notebook. "You burn this shit and act like the dutiful daughter. I don't want to see you slip *once*." I ball up the sheet in my hand and point toward Kian with it. "And you become closer to Cernach. Kiss his fucking ass. Make him think you have more loyalty to him than your own goddamn dick. Do you hear me?"

Kian nods. "I got you."

"We're prepared to do whatever is necessary," Riona hurries out.

I scrub my hands together. "Let's get started, then."

## 51

# DAMIEN

A DEAD CERNACH was a lovely sight.

If it hadn't drawn suspicion, I'd have taken a picture of him lying there, lifeless-looking, like the corpse I always imagined him as.

It felt more satisfying than I'd thought it would.

I hate that I have to fake concern for his death.

To pretend I give two fucks about the piece of shit.

I wish he'd faced a more violent death since the motherfucker cost me a year of not having Pippa. Unfortunately, that wasn't a smart plan. We needed something discreet, something we could easily pin on Odhrán.

People expect violence from me. After slaughtering the men responsible for my father's death, I'm known for executing savage death sentences. I prefer to see blood when I'm killing a man—or at least administer a little venom into their veins. It's so fun when they find out it's inside them.

Plus, Ace gets offended when we don't use his venom enough.

What kind of snake uncle would I be if I neglected him like that?

While I'd have loved to poison Cernach via Ace's venom, Cernach wouldn't have died from ingesting the venom. It would have had to be injected into his veins. Me standing behind him with a needle would have looked too obvious.

We needed Cernach's death to be a show so people would demand his killer be punished. There was also the need to be sure that pinning it on Odhrán would be believable. Odhrán is known for his appreciation of poisoning his victims, so we used that to our advantage.

Riona did a great job with her acting skills.

She fell to her knees, sobbing, yelling for someone to help her father. She hugged him, screaming, "Why?"

I questioned her ability when I discovered she had written a damn nonfiction breakdown of how she wanted him to die, but she's carrying through with her promise of not fucking up.

Odhrán immediately went into boss mode, throwing out demands. He told those not considered *close family* to leave and then directed all the men who had stayed behind to meet them at their place.

Their place was code for a back warehouse of their sanitation business property. Like a good almost husband, I stepped in when Odhrán tried stopping Riona from attending the meeting.

I stand to the side, toothpick in my mouth, as men make themselves comfortable at a long wood table with a Celtic cross carved in the middle.

Odhrán stands at the front of the room. "Cernach is gone." He glances up at the ceiling and says, "Rest in peace, boss," before positioning his stare on the group. "As his underboss, I'll step up as boss."

"Step up?" Riona questions, moving toward him. "As the only child in the Koglin bloodline, I succeed him, not you."

Odhrán's eyes flare. "The family ran by some young bitch?" he asks around a raspy huff.

"Call her a bitch one more time, and I'll gut you," I comment in a bored tone.

Odhrán's cold gaze swings to me. "Oh, *now*, you want to play the dutiful husband? Cernach dying doesn't mean you get out of the marriage contract. In fact, I suspect you have something to do with this since you don't want this marriage with Riona."

I peer at Riona. "Have I mentioned ending my contract with your family?"

Riona shakes her head. "Damien knows you don't break contracts with Koglins without consequences, *period*." She crosses her arms and steps side by side with Odhrán. "In fact, Damien swore he'd help me find my father's killer." She dramatically swipes away a tear from her cheek.

Kian bursts into the room, just as planned, and interrupts. A man dressed in a kitchen uniform is behind him. We paid Wayne five thousand dollars to lie for us.

"Let me guess," Kian starts, working his jaw. "He's trying to step up as boss." He stares angrily at his father while shaking his head. "I didn't want to believe it, Dad. I never thought *you*, out of all people, would turn on the family. That you'd be so disgusting and disloyal."

The twelve other men in the room watch Odhrán with guarded eyes as Kian starts his speech. A few square their shoulders, as if ready for battle to protect their fallen king.

I fucking love it.

Kian pushes Wayne forward. "Tell them what you told me."

Wayne's attention pings to each dangerous man in the room. We prepared him for this, telling him no one would touch him so long as he recited what he was paid to.

"While I was filling the champagne trays"—Wayne pauses to point at Odhrán—"he told me he needed the glass for the father of the bride because he was his taste tester." He clears his throat. "He said he was the only one who handled the man's drinks."

"You're a goddamn liar," Odhrán screams.

"I figured you'd say that." Kian collects his phone from his pocket, hits the screen, and holds it up for everyone to see. "Here's surveillance footage of you speaking to him." A few moments pass, and the video shows Odhrán speaking with Wayne. "Unfortunately, they don't have audio with their cameras, but it's pretty clear you're speaking with him and take a glass."

We set that up. Wayne stopped Odhrán to check if anyone had any allergies. He then told Odhrán to take a glass to make sure it was up to par. Kian makes sure to close the video as soon as Odhrán takes the glass on-screen.

"Taste tester?" Riona gasps. "You're not my father's taste tester."

"That conversation is a lie," Odhrán screams while the other men start standing.

"You ..." Riona chokes back fake tears. "You murdered my father all because you wanted to be boss. After everything he did for you."

It could be that emotions are high, but the Koglin men are buying their story. I do have to give Riona and Kian credit for selling it well. Personally? I'd always do more research before believing hearsay.

That's what happens when a boss is dead, though.

The lack of leadership means stupid decision-making by members.

Stepping forward, I draw my Glock from my waistband. "Do you want to do the honors?"

Riona takes the Glock from me while two men snatch each of Odhrán's arms and shove him into an abandoned chair. Riona stands behind him, snatches his fedora off, presses the gun barrel to the back of Odhrán's head, and pulls the trigger.

## 52

# PIPPA

The cold air-conditioning of Damien's brownstone hits my skin.

While it appeared none of Damien's friends or family attended the rehearsal dinner, they were just lingering in the shadows.

As soon as Cernach's death madness happened, Julian discreetly slipped to my table and said, "Let's go."

I grabbed my mom and Lanie, and we hightailed it out of there. Julian picked up Genesis and Darcy from the hotel and drove us straight back to New York.

Hardly anyone spoke during the ride. My mom and Lanie cried. Darcy and Genesis stayed on their phones. And I sat in the back seat with endless questions. Julian took Darcy and Genesis to Genesis's house and then dropped off my mom and Lanie at home before driving me to Damien's.

"What happened?" I ask Julian as I walk toward the couch and sit, ready to get these heels off my feet. "Where's Damien?"

"It wasn't safe for you to stay there." He drags his phone from his blazer pocket.

"Because Cernach is dead?"

Even though no one has confirmed it, I know it's true.

Riona cried that he wasn't breathing.

My aunt said he didn't have a pulse.

I should feel on top of the world with his death, but I don't.

Cernach's death doesn't end our troubles.

He isn't just one man. He's an entire organization.

One man dies, and another man steps up.

With Cernach not having any sons or brothers, my guess is, the next boss will be Odhrán. They'd never allow a woman to be in charge. My mom told me so on numerous occasions.

"Do you think they'll suspect Damien?" I ask. "He's the obvious one, right? The outsider?" I cross my arms, glaring at Julian. "If Damien *was* responsible, why didn't anyone tell me?"

"Those are questions you'll need to ask him." Julian's eyes are on his phone as he types.

"Why? I'm sure you know the answers."

"That doesn't mean I answer." He holds up his phone. "I'm going to make some phone calls." He walks toward Damien's office and shuts the door behind him.

I remove my heels and wiggle my toes at their freedom. My feet are sore, and there are red lines where the straps circled my ankles. Had I known Cernach would bite the bullet and we wouldn't get through dinner, I'd have worn leggings and a tank.

I guess I can look at the bright side.

I dressed up for the celebration of Cernach's death.

*But* should I be celebrating?

*Is Damien okay?*

*What is going on?*

*Will he have to step up?*

Ugh, too many questions.

Holding my heels by their straps in one hand, I walk upstairs to change from my dress and steal something more comfortable of Damien's.

"Hi, Ace," I say with a salute while passing his bedroom. "I hate to say it, but I missed you, pal."

I flick on the light and walk into the bedroom. Everything looks the same as when I left that day. The same comforter, decor, everything. Even the book I was reading back then is still on the nightstand.

When I reach the closet, I fall back a step.

Damien's clothes aren't the only ones in the closet. I meander around the island and inspect the women's clothes.

*My clothes.*

I pull at a dress that was in my closet before I left for Boston because I contemplated wearing it. My shoes line the shelf where they were when I lived with him. Half of my closet has been moved into here.

I start opening drawers, finding the same. My panties and bras are all in their old place. So are my leggings and tanks. I peer over at the chaise running alongside the end of the island to find my dance bag.

*Great. Now, I have even more questions.*

After changing, I drape the dress over the island and enter the bathroom to clean my face. My toiletries and makeup bag are there, in the same space where I kept them before.

I wander toward the vanity, ready to wash my face and hunt down Julian to ask him how and *why* they moved me in. Considering their line of work, you'd think they'd know Damien and Riona's marriage contract doesn't just poof and disappear into thin air.

As I move closer to the vanity, I discover an envelope with my name scribbled in Damien's handwriting. Opening it, I find a letter. I unfold it and gasp.

## 53

# DAMIEN

Odhrán's dead body is slumped in the chair.

His blood decorates the wall in splashes.

Some men have sat back down in their seats while others stand in front of Riona, waiting for what she'll say next.

I stand to the side, arms crossed, and allow her to do her thing. She and Kian have rehearsed this several times. We've gone through different scenarios of questions the men might ask her and ways to argue concerns they might have.

Not one woman works on the crime side of the Koglin family. Most are homemakers and wives who are left in the dark about inside matters. I told Riona she could step aside and allow Kian to take the boss role, and for a second, I thought she'd try to shoot me.

She stared at me, ready to put my ass in its place, when I held up my hand and said, "You're proving yourself. But the real test isn't until it's time to kill Odhrán. You can't have hesitation. No one will respect you if you don't murder him in front of them. Don't flinch when the bullet collides with his skull. Ignore any splattered blood. Remain confident and unemotional in your killing."

That was exactly what she did.

The Riona I'd met—the timid, innocent Mafia daughter—was nothing but a front.

In reality, Riona was a scorned woman, ready to seek vengeance for her love. I'm proud to have helped her achieve that.

I'm also glad I helped Kian get his revenge for the violence his mother suffered at the hands of his father *and* for the loss of his friend. Everyone got their revenge, and now, Cernach is dead. I couldn't have asked for a better ending.

Now, it's time to create the perfect one.

With Pippa as my wife.

I raise my leg, rest my foot on the concrete wall, and drum my fingers along my knee. We have one more task to complete, the final box in our plan that needs to be checked off.

I was nervous about Riona executing our plan. So far, she's done well. I need her to keep the momentum because she's holding my future in her hands.

Riona kicks the chair, causing it to topple, and Odhrán's body falls to the ground. Kian grabs him by the shirt collar and pulls him away from the front of the room. The floor streaks with his blood in its path.

She clears her throat. "As I said before, I'm my father's only child, and I take over. Behind the scenes, my father made sure I was ready for this day when it came."

I can't help but chuckle at her lie.

"Odhrán knew that my father wanted me to take over, and he was jealous of that. He told my father on numerous occasions. Some of you might be worried about a woman taking the lead, so that's why Kian will be at my side. He's been in this world as much as me, and he's proven his loyalty." She scans the room. "As for the elders, the ones who've been in this family for decades, best believe I will call on all of you for your help and advice. We are a family, and we will work together as one."

Her eyes lock on me for a moment, and she offers me a flicker of a smile. "I'm promising to you today that I will be the boss you expect." She grabs the pin from her hair, letting her red curls loose. "With that being said, that role will be incredibly time-consuming. I'm not in a position to put time into being someone's wife, especially a wife for a man in a different family—"

"He signed a contract—" a balding man in the corner interrupts, violently shaking his head.

Riona speaks over him. "I'm aware, and as my father always said, no one breaks a contract with the Koglins. It doesn't matter who's in charge. While I told Damien we can't marry, he still has to honor the deal he made with this family. I have contracted him to marry my cousin Pippa. My father was in the works to find her a husband, for her to finally pay her dues in this family, and I believe this is the best way. He'll marry Pippa, and when the day comes that I decide to marry, I'll make sure it's approved by all of you." She scrubs her hands together and doesn't even wince at the blood on them. "Now, who wants to help me get rid of this asshole's body?"

*Damn, she just made me proud.*

Never underestimate the power of a woman to get shit done.

Also, never underestimate her to mind-fuck men who've done just that.

## 54

# PIPPA

I TAKE the letter and sit on the edge of the bed.

> PIPPA,
> I'LL NEVER FORGET THE DAY WE SAT IN YOUR LIVING ROOM, TALKING ABOUT MARRIAGE, AND YOU HAD STIPULATIONS. ONE WAS A HUNDRED-WORD ESSAY ON WHAT KIND OF HUSBAND I'D BE. HERE YOU GO, MY SWEET DANCER.
> I'M BEYOND WANTING YOU. I NEED YOU, AND I WON'T BE COMPLETE UNTIL I HAVE YOU. IF YOU ACCEPT ME AS YOUR HUSBAND, I'LL BE LOYAL, ALWAYS PROTECT YOU, AND WATCH EVERY DANCE ROUTINE. WHILE I MIGHT NOT BE THE FUNNIEST, I'LL DO EVERYTHING I CAN TO ALWAYS MAKE YOU SMILE. I WANT TO BE YOUR FIRST KISS IN THE MORNING AND YOUR LAST ONE GOOD NIGHT. AND IF THERE'S EVER A TIME I'M FAILING AT BEING THE PERFECT MAN FOR YOU, TELL ME. I'LL CORRECT EVERY MISTAKE I'M MAKING BECAUSE I LOVE YOU SO DAMN MUCH.

*I WENT OVER MY WORD COUNT, BUT I'LL ALWAYS GO THE EXTRA MILE FOR YOU.*

I place the letter on my heart.

Who knew a murderous criminal could say so many sweet things?

I break down in tears.

I cry for the time we lost and the uncertainty of our future.

We can't get back time, but if there's another chance for us, I'll never make that mistake again.

Being left in the dark sucks. If Damien was involved in Cernach's death, it would've saved me plenty of stress if he'd told me. I wouldn't have tried to run off and witness a murder on a private jet had I known Cernach would soon be dead.

Letter in hand, I trek downstairs. Julian is still in the office, but I can hear him talking on the other side of the door as I pour myself a glass of water.

Taking my water, I sprawl out on the couch and try to call Damien.

No answer.

I text next.

> Me: Please call or text. I need to know you're okay.

I sit there, not turning the TV on or scrolling through social media, with only Damien on my mind. *I need to know he's okay.* I attempt to put all the clues I missed together. Nothing adds up.

"At least tell me he's okay," I say in desperation when Julian finally leaves the office and steps into the living room.

Julian's face softens. "Yeah, he's okay. He'll be home soon."

*Okay* doesn't mean our problem is solved. Unless Damien kills the entire Koglin family, not marrying Riona would still be a breach of contract.

Julian's phone rings, and he leaves for another call.

I wait and wait until eventually, I fall asleep.

---

THE DOOR CLICKING open wakes me. I stir on the couch, realizing at some point, Julian must've draped a blanket over me. The smell of Damien flows through the room like a calmative.

He's the fragrance of comfort, of devotion, of home.

My body instantly relaxes when he's around.

Damien scoops me up in his strong arms, and I put mine around his shoulders while he walks us upstairs.

He flicks the bedroom light on, drags the comforter back, and settles me in bed. No matter what, he always wants to take care of me. I prop myself against the pillow and watch him while he moves around the room. His tux is wrinkled, his bow tie unknotted, and his hair disheveled. He's the picture of a man who's had a night from hell.

He silently walks into the bathroom and shuts the door behind him. I slip out of bed when the shower starts. As I slowly open the door, he peers up at me.

Again, it's so familiar of the night in the guest room bathroom at Antonio's, when I kissed his bruises.

This time, there are some differences.

There are no bloody knuckles, bruises, or blood.

Just pure exhaustion on his face.

"Go back to bed, baby," he says, his voice hoarse.

As much as I want to start asking questions, I hold back.

He needs rest, sleep, a sense of calm, like he always provides me.

I shuffle toward him, stand on my tiptoes, and kiss him. "I'll be out there waiting for you."

He lowers his forehead, resting it against mine, and releases a deep sigh. "Thank you."

My body feels lighter when he presses a kiss to my forehead. I turn, starting to leave, but then come to a halt and swing around. "But first, I need to brush my teeth."

A flicker of a smile hits his lips. "Go right ahead."

He undresses and slips into the shower while I brush. Joining him crosses my mind, but just like grilling him with questions, I refrain. Our shared showers are never simple. Damien always commits to pleasuring me into multiple orgasms and sometimes thinks I'm a damn gymnast in the different positions he manages to put us in. He needs a mental and physical break.

He isn't one of those men who can relax and let me pleasure him. He wants to do ninety percent of the pleasuring and saves only ten percent for himself.

After brushing my teeth, I climb into bed but am wide awake. Not too long after, a shirtless Damien crawls into bed and wraps me tight in his arms.

For so long, I wasn't sure if this would ever happen again.

Now, it's perfect, and I won't ever let us go.

---

I MISSED the comfort of being in bed next to Damien. As I turn on my side, Damien is propped up, back against the headboard, and on his phone.

"Good morning," I say around a long yawn.

He lowers his phone. "Good morning, baby."

I scoot closer to him, the soft sheets sliding against my skin. Damien raises his arm, nestling me close as I cuddle closer.

"Is this allowed?" I gesture back and forth between us.

He runs his fingers through my tangled hair. "You in my arms is always allowed."

"But what about Riona ... you and she ..." My voice trails off, my mouth dry.

"We're done." He abruptly holds up his finger. "Not that we were anything before."

I hate that I'm about to ruin the start of a good morning. "Cernach might be dead, but there's still a contract, Damien."

*How does he not realize this?*

He works out a tangle in my hair. "Riona demanded you and I marry to fulfill the Koglin-Lombardi agreement."

I blink up at him. "Wait, what?"

"Riona is the boss of the Koglin family, and she needs to focus on that, not marriage," he says matter-of-factly, as if he were Riona's PR person. "She knew she couldn't let me out of the deal without making herself look weak, so she told them she was forcing you to marry me instead."

*Ah, so the only way the Koglin men would agree is if some woman was forced into marriage.*

I crawl out from under his hold to settle on my knees in front of him. My butt hits the back of my thighs as I stare at him in shock. "Are you serious?"

Circling his arm around my waist, he draws me onto his lap until I'm straddling him. "You're officially mine."

A fusion of emotions coils inside me.

This is everything I've wanted.

Yet it's been arranged how I didn't want—a contract.

But even so, the contract won't benefit Cernach's dead ass now.

I run my palms up his bare chest. "I know I said I never wanted to be contracted into a marriage, but I'll make this exception for you."

He grabs one of my wrists, raises it from his chest, and smacks a soft kiss to my palm. "Good, because I'm fucking you right now, and then we're going to the courthouse to make you my wife."

"What?" I stutter.

"I'm not waiting one more day to make you mine." He brushes his hand along my face, sliding hair from my eyes. "I'll give you the perfect wedding later, whatever you want, but I'm done waiting. Today, I'll call you my wife." He lowers my hand on his chest down to his hard cock. "Now, ride your soon-to-be husband's dick, my sweet dancer."

He curls his free hand around the back of my neck and pulls me forward. Our lips meet, the kiss heavy, and he immediately slips his tongue inside my mouth.

We make out, my hips grinding against his cock, before he raises me to push down his pants. His throbbing dick springs free.

"Condom?" he asks. Unless we forget, which we have a few times, he usually always asks first.

"No condom." I grip his shoulders. "I want to feel all of you inside me."

He rips my panties and slams me down on his cock with no warning.

We moan as I grind against him, finding my pace. Waves of pleasure swoosh through me as he eases his hand up my stomach to cup my breast. It feels like he's leaving a path of fire everywhere he touches me.

He turns my skin warm.

I thaw out his heart.

We balance each other.

"It's always so perfect with you," I pant. "Your big cock feels so good."

"Fuuuuck," he says around a long groan. "I love feeling your pussy clench around my dick." He lowers his head to my chest and sucks my nipple.

The room is the epitome of sex-starved.

The loud, desperate moans.

*Sinful Sacrifice*

The sound of our bodies slapping against each other's.

The begging for more.

I slip my fingers through his hair, holding him against my chest as he sucks my other nipple.

I ride him harder, starving for more and needing to feel every inch of him. He always makes me feel like I'm on top of the world.

"I'm almost there ... almost there," I say, sounding like I'm babbling.

He takes a deep breath, separating from my chest, and locks his hands on my waist. As if on cue, knowing I'm about to fall apart, he holds me in place and fucks me hard.

"Oh God, right there," I groan. "Please don't fucking stop." I rest my head on his shoulder and bite into the skin as he pounds into me, hitting my G-spot as if it's the only direction he knows to take.

He fucks me hard.

So fucking hard.

I bite into his skin again as a burst of pleasure courses through me. I lose all power of my body, and I cry out his name. He continues relentlessly fucking me so hard that my head hits the headboard a few times.

I lower my head and kiss him.

His muscles clench, tightening, and I know he's close.

"Come inside me. Fill me up," I say into his mouth. "You said you were going to put a baby inside me when we were in the woods? Do it." I'm not sure how I manage to put a hint of warning in my voice, considering he's fucked nearly every ounce of energy out of me.

But it does the job.

He jabs his hips forward and holds us still, connected, as if wanting to make sure he fills me with every drop of his cum.

He groans as my sweaty body falls on his.

"That was so amazing," I say against his skin.

He smacks my ass once. Twice. Three times.

"You deserve more than that," he says. "You knew you were going to make me come so fucking hard when you told me to fill you with my cum."

I hoist myself on my elbow. "Why do you think I did it? *To not* make you come? My body needed a break because you were about to fuck the life out of me."

He kisses up my jaw. "Can't have that, can I, baby?"

I carefully pull off him, and his eyes are pinned to the view of his cum dripping out of me. His cock is coated with our juices. He lowers his hand and strokes me a few times before shoving his fingers inside, as if not wanting to waste anything.

I groan, almost ready for another round at his touch, and sigh in disappointment when it doesn't stay there long. He rolls to his side and opens the nightstand drawer, collecting something from it.

"Put your left hand on my cock, baby," he says. "Cover it with our cum."

I do what he said, his cock hardening again as I do. Once it's covered, he gestures for me to come closer. He grips my wrist and opens his other hand to reveal a diamond ring.

He doesn't give me time to see the ring before jerking me closer. My body trembles when he licks down my ring finger and then slides the ring down it. It fits perfectly.

He drags me back onto his lap, careful to adjust me around his cock, and holds my hand up. My jaw drops as I admire the beauty of it. Typical Damien, always loving to spoil me, chose a ring that does just that.

The band is gold and lined with the same diamond pattern as the necklace he gave me before our first date. I smile at the memory. The large pink diamond sparkles with every angle I turn it.

*I didn't even know you could find pink diamonds like this.*

"I bought that the same month I met you," he tells me. "I knew eventually, somehow, you'd become my wife."

"Are ... are you serious?" I stutter.

"You were made for me, Pippa." His abs clench when he drags himself up so we sit more upright. He waits until our eyes are pinned on each other before going on. "And at this point, I'm not asking you to marry me. I'm telling you, after this, you're getting your ass dressed, and we're getting married."

---

THE SUN SHINES with no interruption from clouds, and traffic is surprisingly tolerable, as if it doesn't want to give us any problems on our way to commit to each other. All signs for a great day to get married.

Not that the weather or traffic would influence my decision.

I've never been one for wedding superstitions.

What's in the sky, the temperature, or how gorgeous your dress is—those don't matter. In my eyes, the only indication that you'll have a good marriage is having a good partner.

Someone you trust.

Who wants the same future as you.

Who'd do absolutely everything in their power to never hurt you.

Because in the end, your looks will alter, the weather will change, and life will throw you hard balls. True love is the only factor in your marriage that can't change, and our love is too strong to falter. We've been through so much together.

On the drive to the city hall, I mentioned his note and told him I loved it.

"You mean my *essay*," he replied. "I meant every single word, baby. Every single damn word."

Tears are in my eyes as I stare at Damien and say, "I do," when it's time.

He stands across from me, so handsome in his suit, and repeats, "I do," so definite and precise.

Two words.

So damn powerful.

As we seal our marriage with a kiss, butterflies swarm my stomach.

No one can take this away from us now.

No one can throw our names into a marriage contract.

We're one now.

I had no problem with Damien wanting to rush to get married. I'd wasted over a year because of my stubbornness. I couldn't do it for another day.

Damien inches back some, his arm wrapped around my waist, and says, "My wife, Mrs. Bellini," before placing another kiss to my lips.

I chose the blush-pink dress I wore to *Swan Lake*, which I've now deemed as my good-luck dress. I wore it the first time Damien told me he loved me and now, when we've devoted ourselves to each other for the rest of our lives.

We hear congrats and clapping from people as we pass them in the halls. The sun heats us, warming our faces as we step outside.

"Congrats," Julian says, hugging Damien and then me.

"Thanks, brother-in-law," I say, hugging him back.

He's our only witness.

There's no guilt about not inviting others. I love the idea of a small ceremony. Damien told me he'd give me the perfect wedding later, but I'm in no rush.

Just like with the weather, a perfect wedding doesn't mean a perfect marriage either.

Sure, we're not being traditional, but I don't care.

Nothing in our lives has ever been traditional.

We both avoided marriage contracts and fought against the rules.

As we reach the bottom steps, Damien takes my hand and brings it to his mouth. "Finally, you're all mine."

"And you're mine," I whisper, a bright grin spreading across my face.

"Always have been and always will be."

## 55

# DAMIEN

"Your plan worked out," Antonio says, squeezing a stress ball from behind his desk in his home office.

I relax in the chair across from him. "You doubted me, didn't you?"

"No, I doubted your coconspirators. You know I don't trust people." He tosses the ball on the desk. "What's the plan with Riona and the Koglins?"

"Surprisingly, the bastards didn't contest her becoming boss."

"Shocking, knowing how Cernach treated women."

"I'm positive a large part of their acceptance has to do with her killing Odhrán and Kian being at her side. Had it been her alone, they'd never have gone for it."

He arches a brow. "Our weapons deal?"

"Still in order. Same as with Cernach." I smirk. "Better rates, though."

He snaps his fingers and points at me. "Good job. Now, the dance studio. When are you telling Pippa's mom that hers is getting shut down?"

One thing about Antonio is, he is going to ask all the

goddamn headache-inducing questions. The man always needs to not only have his ducks in a row but also others' ducks.

After looking through the books, Riona shared that Enya's dance studio had been in the red every single month. She wasn't booking enough classes and was hardly able to keep the limited hours they had. It's surprising Cernach's cheap ass hates losing money. He did it to keep control of Enya.

Riona also said she's selling the building the studio is in. No matter what, Enya's studio is getting shut down.

I rub at my temples. "We're going to her house later today to rip off the Band-Aid. Hopefully, she'll agree to work at Pippa's studio."

"I'm sure that'll be fun," he deadpans.

"Personally, I always thought Enya having a studio was a bad idea. It's Pippa's feelings I'm worried about. Her mother seems to be … unstable at times."

"You mean, she treats her daughter like shit?"

I nod.

He snaps forward in his chair. "That's one thing you need to make clear when you're married. Do not let *anyone treat* your wife like shit. I don't care if it's a parent, a friend, the king of the motherfucking planet. I will correct every person who doesn't treat Gigi like the princess she is. I'm not telling you to hurt Enya, but what I'm saying is, you have to set her straight. Her problems are not Pippa's, and Pippa should not suffer for them."

Antonio isn't bullshitting. When Cristian was playing hardball with Gigi, he risked his life, going there and telling him he was fucking up. He even handed him pictures of what he was missing. Just as his speech said, he doesn't play when it comes to Gigi's feelings.

I stand from my chair. "I'll see you at work next week?"

He rears back. "Next week?"

"Yes, I'm taking my wife on our honeymoon." I smirk. "I have to make sure she's treated like the princess she is, right?"

He scowls at me. "Go before I change my mind and find some random asshole for you to murder because I don't like my words being used against me."

As soon as I leave his office, Gigi calls out my name.

I rub my temples harder this time, knowing she's about to be a pain in my ass. She's in the kitchen, eating a bowl of M&M's and glaring as if I were here to deliver her divorce papers.

"I hear a congrats are in order." She glares and tosses an M&M toward me. "Why didn't you invite me to your wedding? Me? I'm, like, one of your favorite people."

"You're my least favorite here," I say, cracking my neck. "There wasn't a wedding either. I'm sure Antonio also told you that." Although, I can't be too mad at her since she's the one who moved all of Pippa's belongings back to the brownstone while we were at the rehearsal dinner.

"He did." She raises a shoulder and smirks. "I'm just bored, and I wanted to give you a headache. *But* I'd better get an invite and a front-row seat if you have a wedding." She snatches another M&M and points at me with it. "Tell Pippa I'm throwing her a bachelorette party. Strip club, here we come." She waves her hands in the air at the same time Antonio comes up behind her, snatches her wrist, and eats the M&M from her hand.

"You're not going anywhere with half-naked men," he tells her.

"Nor are you taking Pippa," I add.

"Oh, yes, I am," she argues.

Antonio flicks his hand through the air. "Don't listen to her bullshit. She's fully aware that if any other man has his junk near her, he will absolutely lose it. I'll hold the knife in her goddamn hand and force her to cut it off to teach her a lesson."

That's Antonio's way of romancing Gigi. Somehow, she fell for his psychotic ass. He's worse than I am.

Gigi crosses her arms. "True, with people knowing you and my father, they probably won't even look at me."

"That's just how I like it, baby." He steals another M&M as she glares at him.

---

For as long as I can remember, I scoffed at marriage.

I witnessed men marry for the sake of a contract and business deal.

I saw women miserable in those marriages.

A happy marriage was a rarity, and I thought it was something I'd never find, but everything changed when I met Pippa. Suddenly, I believed in marriage. I imagined my life with her as my bride. But imagining and getting it are too different obstacles.

She walked away from me.

But now, I have her back, and I'm never letting her go.

The satisfaction of calling her my wife is a high I don't think I'll ever come down from.

After leaving Antonio's, I drive to Pippa's dance studio and park in front of the building. I stay in my SUV and watch her through the windows. It's one of my favorite things to do. Except now, I don't have to do it like a goddamn creeper.

Now, she's mine.

I swallow, fully entranced by her as she finishes her last class of the day.

Leaning back, I make myself comfortable.

Her body. The way she moves. How gentle she is with her students.

She's so damn gorgeous.

*And all mine.*

## 56

# DAMIEN

**Four Months Later**

Life has been chaotic yet calm at the same time.

The casino is busier than ever, and even though most problems with my job outside the casino have settled, we always have situations to handle.

Enya agreed to work at Pippa's studio. Not that she had much choice. Riona evicted her and sold the building in under a month.

Married life can't get any better. While no marriage is perfect, ours is pretty damn close.

"You make a beautiful groom," Julian sarcastically says.

I adjust my cuff links. "Pippa will kick my ass if I kick yours on our wedding day, so I'll let that slide."

He chuckles. "I'd like to add that your elopement was much less stressful."

Even with my hectic schedule, I helped Pippa with every aspect of wedding planning. At first, I hadn't been sure if she wanted my help, but she asked for my opinion on every step. I agreed with her choices most of the time since my wife has impeccable fucking taste. The times I didn't, I didn't voice it.

Today isn't about me. It's about her.

I'm damn excited to see her walk down the aisle and to say our vows again.

Sometimes, I even dream of how she looked the last time she said, "I do," before I slipped the ring on her finger.

Two nights ago, I made her give me hints about her dress while fucking her.

"His wedding is much calmer than mine," Antonio comments from a corner chair, sipping on his drink. "Imagine having a wedding with a full guest list with Lombardis, Marchettis, and Cavallaros. I don't know how many times Gigi prayed for no murders during our ceremony."

"Nah." I shake my head. "If there's anyone who knows people won't fuck with them, it's Gigi Marchetti—"

"Lombardi," Antonio sternly corrects.

I crack at smile at how possessive he is of his wife and then check my watch. Thirty minutes before I'm scheduled to make my way to the end of the altar.

I haven't seen Pippa since last night because her little troublesome friend group—Genesis, Darcy, Gigi, Natalia, Neomi, and the Cavallaro sisters—decided to throw her a bachelorette party.

There were no strippers involved.

They stayed at Neomi and Benny's home on the Marchetti property. No one comes and goes from there without being tracked.

Our attention turns to the door at the sound of a knock. Julian, who's closest to the door, takes a few strides and swings it open.

Genesis stands in front of him, and her attention lands straight on me. "Pippa said she's not walking down the aisle."

## 57

# PIPPA

"It won't zip," I sob, clumsily stepping out of my dress and nearly face-planting on the floor, wearing only a bra and panties.

Genesis catches me just in time.

We've tried everything possible and then some to fit me into my wedding dress. I had it tailored months ago, not thinking I'd have that much weight fluctuation.

"I've sucked in all I can suck in," I cry. My breaths are wheezy since I haven't taken a full once since we started the exhausting project of *how can we make Pippa skinnier*. "The only way I'm fitting in that dress is one of you squeezing me so tight until my eyes pop out."

Darcy scrunches her nose. "Ew, Ms. Morbid."

"That's it. I can't walk down the aisle." Like the dramatic bride I swore not to be, I collapse on the floor, settling my back against the wall, and bow my head as tears stream down my face. "You can all go. Grab a gift bag on your way out."

"Honey," my mom softly says, sitting next to me and stroking my arm. "We'll figure something out."

From the corner of my eye, I see Genesis leave the room.

"You can use my wedding dress," Gigi offers before adding, "That isn't a bad-luck thing, is it?"

"Hmm, I don't know," Neomi says. "Let me google it."

Neomi reaches for her phone, and I tune out their bad-luck conversation. Even if it isn't considered bad luck, no way can I fit into Gigi's dress. I won't risk trying either because I'd feel terrible if I busted a button.

My shoulders slump in shame for not trying on the dress again days ago. It was even on my wedding checklist to do that last week. But I got too busy. Really, I forgot to check things off that list two weeks ago because I stupidly thought I had everything finished.

"Do you want me to go to your house and get you another dress?" Lanie asks, squatting next to me. "It's only a thirty-minute drive."

I blink away tears.

*No, because I don't know what will fit me in my closet.*

Lately, my wardrobe has consisted of leggings and sweats.

There's a reason I can't fit in my dress.

Too much unprotected sex with my husband.

The door opens, and I hear loud footsteps.

"Baby, what's wrong?" Damien asks as I slowly lift my head.

He stands in front of me, clad in his tux, looking like the perfect husband he is. Lanie slides away from me as Damien takes her place. My heart stops as our eyes meet, and I see the panic in his.

My lower lip trembles as he uses his thumb to collect tears from my cheek. My makeup is ruined, and my hair slipped from its updo on my almost fall. I look far from a bride ready for her big day.

"I can't fit into my dress," I cry out. "I should've tried it on before."

His chest relaxes. "That's not a big deal."

*Says the guy who isn't expected to walk down the aisle in a beautiful gown.*

"It's not fine." I throw my arm out toward the dress puddled on the floor. "I have nothing to wear down the aisle."

My mom stands. "Let's give them a minute," she tells the room.

Damien's worried gaze stays on me as my bridesmaids shuffle out of the bridal suite. He holds out his hand, helping me off the floor, and walks me to the couch. As I make myself comfortable, he swipes a water bottle, unscrews the cap, and hands it to me.

"Is there a backup dress or something else you can wear?" He drags his hand through his hair.

I shake my head. "I ruined our wedding day." As I take a sip of water, some drips from the corner of my mouth.

He takes the seat next to me. "You haven't ruined anything, and don't forget—we're already married. If you don't want to walk down that aisle, you don't have to. I can tell everyone to leave, or if you want, you can wear sweats for all I care."

I scoot up the couch, snuggling next to him, and drag my knees to my chest.

He rests his hand on my knee. "I'm sorry your dress doesn't fit."

"I gained weight," I croak out.

He starts stroking my hair.

"'I'm ... also pregnant."

His hand stops.

There's a moment of silence.

I wish I'd stayed where I was so I could see the expression on his face.

"I guess all those times I said I was putting a baby in you finally worked, huh?" He turns me in his arms, situating me to straddle him.

As I flick my gaze to his, there's nothing but elation on his face.

It's not that I was nervous he'd be mad about it. He's stated multiple times, not only during sex, that he can't wait to have a baby with me.

He cradles my chin in his hand and caresses my cheek. "Are you not happy?"

"No," I choke out.

His eyes widen.

"No—shoot, I didn't mean no to that," I rush out, scrambling for words. "I mean, *no*, that's not why I'm upset. I'm just emotional, and now, I don't have a wedding dress, and I don't know what I'm going to do. I can't go out there in my panties." My words are nothing but rambles that come out all in one breath.

"First, no way in hell are you walking down the aisle in your panties." He lowers his hand to rest on my belly and smiles.

I cup my hand over his. I already like the warmth of it there, and I know it'll become a regular place for his hand as our baby grows.

"What do you want to do?" he asks. "You decide, and I'm with you."

I gesture toward what I wore here—sweats and a zip-up jacket. "Those are my only options of walk-down-the-aisle attire."

"Wear them, then."

"Sweats?" I sputter out. "The bride wore sweats—so romantic."

"It does have a nice ring to it."

I play with his bow tie. "Let me paint this picture for you. There you are, standing at the altar, looking all handsome in your tux, waiting for your perfect bride. She comes out wearing a gym outfit."

"I'd still think you're the most beautiful woman I've ever seen."

"No, you in a tux and me dressed like that won't fit."

"I'll wear my sweats too, then."

I jerk back. "What?"

"I have sweats in my bag. I'll go change. That way, we match."

I stare at him, slack-jawed.

"This is your wedding. No one else's. If you feel more comfortable in sweats right now, then wear sweats, baby. In fact, I think you might be onto something. Sweats sound better than this lame-ass tux too."

I hold back a laugh. "You wear a suit nearly every single day."

Only a few people have seen the man walk around in sweats. Which is fine with me because him in gray sweats is mouthwatering. I nearly jump his bones every single time.

I narrow my eyes. "They'd better not be gray sweatpants."

He shakes his head, a wide smile building. "Baby, you told me those are meant for your eyes only. They're black, basic as fuck." His hand returns to my stomach, and he massages it in small circles with his thumb, causing goose bumps to form. "What do you say, baby?" He nods, as if the baby is talking. "Oh, you think Mommy should definitely wear her sweats? Okay then." His gaze travels back to mine. "Baby Bellini suggests her mom wear whatever she feels comfortable in."

"You're crazy," I say around a laugh.

He clamps his hand around my waist and slowly assists me to my feet before standing. "I'll go change and be right back, baby. Do you want me to send the girls in to help you?"

I bite into the corner of my lip. "Yes, please."

He smacks a kiss to my lips. "I'll meet you at the altar."

"Will you walk me down it?" I mutter. "Be there with me?"

"I'll see you *at the front of the aisle*," he corrects.

This man … God, he's perfection.

He leaves the room, and the girls return.

They touch up my makeup and hair.

I change into black sweats and The Ballet Studio zip-up jacket.

"So, I just thought of a great idea," Genesis says as I sit to tie my sneakers. "Why don't we all put on the clothes we wore here? Screw being formal."

I nearly squeal in delight and wrap my arms around her.

This is what true friends are—ones who always figure out a way to make you comfortable.

"Oh my God," I groan. "Please do."

They change, and fifteen minutes later, we leave the suite.

As promised, Damien waits for me at the front of the aisle.

His best men have also changed out of their tuxes.

Not fitting into my dress isn't a bad omen.

It's just proving another reason Damien is the perfect man for me.

He will change anything, go against everything, to make me happy.

"My beautiful bride," he says, turning to kiss me. "God, you look amazing."

While we won't have that moment where the groom watches me walk down the aisle, we'll have the one where the groom made his wife comfortable while making that walk with her.

We'll take those steps together, just like we have every single other one.

*Love:* ✓
*Marriage:* ✓
*Baby:* ✓

Maybe, just maybe, fate doesn't hate me.

I said I wanted all the steps to true love, and while it wasn't the easiest on my heart, it's what he gave me.

Tears fall down my face as we start walking down the aisle. We don't do it arm in arm. Damien won't allow it. He takes my hand, clasping it tight in his, and stares at me the entire walk down the aisle.

He is getting his walk-down-the-aisle moment, just a different version. The closer we get to the altar, the more I notice his eyes growing glossy.

It's us.

Our moment.

Our wedding, like he said.

We separate when we make it to the altar. Damien swipes at his eyes and casts me a reassuring smile.

The ceremony starts.

It's similar to what we had at the courthouse, but this time, we have our vows and all our loved ones joining us. I asked him to save his until our official ceremony.

Damien says his first. He doesn't take out a paper to read from. At first, it might look like an unorganized groom, but I know better. Everything Damien says comes straight from the heart. He's probably had them memorized since the first time he told me he'd marry me, contract or not.

He doesn't say them loud.

Just an octave above whispering.

*"Pippa, shortly after I met you, I lost everything. My world crumbled, and you were there to pick me up, piece by piece, when I thought I was forever shattered. I came to your door, a broken man you hardly knew, and you comforted me. I think that's the moment I realized I was in love with you. Even if it was early or that I'd skipped enough steps to build a skyscraper, I knew you were the only piece that could truly put me back together."*

A sob comes from his chest, and his eyes haven't left mine once as he continues.

*"You once told me your happily ever after would never come with terms and conditions, but, my sweet dancer, I owe you the terms and conditions of being your husband. I promise, in our marriage, I will treat you with all the respect and love you deserve. Every day, I will strive to be a better husband than the day before. You have my every promise that I'll never break the contract of love you've given me and the faith of allowing me to have your heart. It's safe with me. You're safe with me."* Then, he leans in and mouths, *"So is our baby,"* to me before saying, *"I love you."*

I don't know *how* he expects me to say vows after those.

He literally just gave me vows that'd win a Grammy, an Emmy, and even a Super Bowl at this point. I'm sobbing, and the more emotion that grows in his eyes, the more worked up I become.

He takes my hand, squeezes it, and doesn't release me.

I already feel like I've somewhat failed by pulling out my paper. Damien has always said he's not good with words, but the man sure knows how to show the hell up. My hand shakes in his, resulting in another squeeze, as I start speaking in the same volume as he did.

*"To my lover, my protector, my everything. The day I walked into Lucky Kings, I was terrified for my life. Little did I know, I'd end up meeting the person I'd want to spend the rest of my life with. You didn't take my life. You gave me a life. You taught me not to fear the unexpected, even if it didn't fit my step-by-step plan. Sometimes, life gives us detours. Thank you for giving me the grace of your patience and never turning your back on me, even when I allowed my stubbornness to not only get the best of me,*

but us. I love you and will love you until the end of my days." I pause to smile at him. "And I promise to always dance for you when you're down."

I stare down at our connected hands, seeing our matching tattoos.

*Live Once*—the O being a heart.

We got them during our honeymoon in Hawaii.

After I broke down at dinner and apologized that I hadn't realized that sometimes, we didn't get second chances at love or life. I could've lost him because of my stubbornness. We only live once, and it's too short not to tell the person you love that you love them, not to say screw all your rules and do what makes you happy.

Tears are streaming down my face.

He blinks away his own tears.

With this being our second wedding, I didn't expect it to be so damn emotional. I should've known better and had us say our vows where there wasn't a crowd of sixty people.

But honestly, at this moment, it's only the two of us.

And soon, three.

# EPILOGUE

# DAMIEN

**Seven Months Later**

They say good things in life can change bad men.

I was raised in a world of violence and destruction.

My career was the same.

I believed I'd never have a real relationship and my life would always be wrapped around my job.

Then, I met Pippa.

With our baby girl on the way soon, I vowed to be a better man.

But sometimes, it's pretty fucking hard.

And sorry, baby girl, but sometimes, Dad has to kill idiots.

I pistol-whip the man tied up in the chair before me. Blood drops from his lip and onto the floor. His eye is swollen, and he already has a gunshot wound—compliments of my Glock—on his shoulder.

"You shattered the window of *my wife's* dance studio and stole from her," I grind out.

He cries out in pain when I slam the handle of the gun to the top of his head. "I'm sorry, man! I didn't know it was your wife's!"

This asshole threw a brick through The Ballet Studio's window, ran inside, and stole what he could. He didn't get much since the alarm spooked him, and no one was inside. Still though, you don't get away with hurting my wife, and that hurt my goddamn wife.

"I'm sorry," Jack—yeah, I think his name is Jack—continues to ramble like I give a shit.

He could tell me he's sorry a hundred times and tattoo that on his skin, and I wouldn't give two shits. I've been good since Pippa doesn't exactly like when I come home bloody and bruised, but technically, Jack will be the only one bloody.

"I just thought it was some random place," Jack wails, and I hit him upside the head again because his voice grates on my nerves.

Just as I'm about to ram the gun into his skull again, my phone rings. I roll my eyes at Jack's cries while fishing my phone from my pocket.

Pippa.

"Hey, babe," I answer. "I'm kind—"

"The baby is coming!" she screams. "Get your ass home!"

"On my way." I end the call, shoot Jack in the head, and tell Julian to clean up the mess because his niece is about to be born.

---

"And this is your nursery that Mama decorated for you," I coo while cradling my daughter in my arms, showing her the nursery for her first time.

Pippa was in labor for ten hours. I lost count of the number of times she said she was kicking my ass for knocking her up. I laughed it off, which only pissed her off more. I held her hand, assuring her everything would be okay, as she gave birth to our beautiful baby girl, Alessia Lake Bellini.

Now, three days later, we're home.

Lanie is covering all of Pippa's classes at the studio. For the next four weeks, we'll be adjusting to life with a newborn.

I take Alessia on a tour of the ballerina-themed nursery. The furniture is pink, the wallpaper a ballet-slipper print, and stuffed ballerina dolls are set up around the room. Pippa oversaw the decor, and I was in charge of building everything. I'll never forget the memories of the hours we spent in this room, getting everything perfect for Alessia's arrival.

After the wedding, we decided to keep the news of the pregnancy between us. Pippa wanted time to process it and us to enjoy knowing it was our secret. We went on a second honeymoon to Paris for two weeks and then shared the surprise with everyone when we got home.

Since then, Alessia became spoiled.

Not only by us but also by our friends and family.

"I love you," Pippa whispers before softly kissing Alessia's head.

"So does your daddy," I say, holding her tiny hand in mine.

I finish my tour, showing her the closet and her tutu onesie that says, *My First Tutu*. When we're finished, we spend another thirty minutes picking apart which feature Alessia got from us.

She has Pippa's nose.

My eyes.

Pippa's cuteness.

I can't wait to meet more of my daughter every day.

To be a father.

I gulp, shutting my eyes, wishing my family were here to meet her. But I know they're looking down, smiling, and loving the new baby Bellini. I'll make sure to share stories of them with Alessia as she grows up.

By the end of the day, we're yawning and exhausted. Pippa

carefully lays Alessia down to sleep, and we make ourselves comfortable in bed.

"I think I could sleep for a hundred nights," Pippa says, blowing out a breath.

I turn to her, wrapping her in my arms, and hold her.

"Pippa," I whisper.

She peers up at me with sleepy eyes. "Yes?"

I run my hand along her arm. "Thank you for making the sacrifice of loving me."

## the end

# ALSO BY CHARITY FERRELL

## MARCHETTI MAFIA SERIES

Gorgeous Monster

Gorgeous Prince

Gorgeous Villain

## BLUE BEECH SERIES

(each book can be read as a standalone)

Just A Fling

Just One Night

Just Exes

Just Neighbors

Just Roommates

Just Friends

## TWISTED FOX SERIES

(each book can be read as a standalone)

Stirred

Shaken

Straight Up

Chaser

Last Round

## ONLY YOU SERIES: A BLUE BEECH SECOND GENERATION

(each book can be read as a standalone)

Only Rivals

**STANDALONES**

Bad For You

Beneath Our Faults

Beneath Our Loss

Pretty and Reckless

Thorns and Roses

Wild Thoughts

**RISKY DUET**

Risky

Worth The Risk

# ABOUT THE AUTHOR

Charity Ferrell is a USA Today and Wall Street Journal bestselling author of the Twisted Fox and Blue Beech series. She resides in Indianapolis, Indiana. She loves writing about broken people finding love while adding humor and heartbreak along with it. Angst is her happy place.

When she's not writing, she's making a Starbucks run, shopping online, or spending time with her family.

Printed in Great Britain
by Amazon

47074328R00209